NO ROMANCING THE PASSENGERS

OBSESSED INTENTIONS

BOOK ONE

LEE WIMMER

ACKNOWLEDGMENTS

I am blessed by the support, love, and prayers of my amazing wife, Kathy, and the many professionals who have shaped this novel in one way or another. From rejection letters to the completed manuscript, this has been a God-inspired, God-timed journey. When God called me to start writing in December 2018, I was not qualified to put the pen to the page, but under His guidance, I began anyway. Then He led me to the talented people He wanted on this project.

With the help of an outstanding editor, Deirdre Lockhart at Brilliant Cut Editing, and Emilie Haney, a truly talented cover and book designer, along with Hightower Publications, I'm happy to share His inspiration, the series, OBSESSED INTENTIONS, with you.

PROLOGUE

I t's late evening, mid-October, the day after the southwest monsoon withdrew from the entire nation of India, ending monsoon season. The vast greenish-blue water surrounding the port of Kochi slaps against the *Disillusioned Illusion*'s hull. DR—Dr. Ray to his colleagues—lounges alone on the stern's lower deck.

The sun clings to the darkening horizon as voices and the scent of food from a nearby restaurant fill the air. The ocean's soothing rhythm pulses through his senses like a heartbeat—one with an expectation. Another magical night begins to set in while the sun relinquishes its hold on the horizon's end, nature's big show and his refuge vanquished as a crescent moon winks of the night's possibilities.

With his hopes for a romantic adventure, possibly a woman to love now in question, DR exhales, grabs the back of his head with both hands, eyes closed, and roughs up his hair. Only weeks earlier, he'd thought it too soon for romance, but now, it's all he can think about.

Has he blown it?

"Why is romance so hard for me?" he asks aloud, knowing the answer. His is a life full of days where you can see the sun and moon at the same time, where promises dim or flicker out so trouble can shine through. And evenings like this give him too much time to contemplate the past, supposing the inevitable is going to happen —again.

During their first conversation ten days earlier, after the others left to go on a tour, she'd stayed. While they discussed the ship's security, her eyes took delight in searching him, but he barely noticed, only knowing she pleased his.

"I'm here to get on with my life. It's time for a new adventure, and who knows... maybe love." Debbie had returned her focus to the sea and then back to studying him. She'd sipped her coffee while leaning toward the railing, the early morning sun reflecting in her eyes. "It's been five years. I'm ready—No, no, I *need* to live again."

Somehow, even lacking the finer romantic skills, he'd known she was trying to convince herself as well as him. She'd held her pert chin so high, the sunlight caressing her simple beauty, the breeze blowing her perfume.

Shifting now, he swallows hard. Oh, how he remembers her perfume, its magical lasso drawing him that morning, and now too.

That stupid rule. Why now?

Laughter and voices drift from the marina and his pool up front, travelers and his passengers enjoying an evening filled with sangrias and fun, getting to know one another while he lingers, stuck in an all-too-familiar place. His thoughts and hopes of a new love rising and falling faster than the ocean's tide. Even in this exotic setting with hopes of romance, he shivers as that place fixed in time draws him like an eddy in the current.

Why me? Am I a bad person? Was it my fault? Or did God forsake me?

Some people say God takes a bad thing and uses it to make things better, all things working together for good. He snorts. "Try telling that to someone who has experienced a lot of 'all things.' They don't always see it that way."

He didn't. Once he loved God—but things change, people change.

CHAPTER
ONE

Eleven years earlier...

At Dukes School of Archaeology in Madrid, DR had his first run-in with Gail Kelly. The school, located in the heart of downtown and offering many other sciences, boasted a pulse so quick and electric it drew thousands of young adventurous students every year. So she should've blended in. She did not, and again, he found himself approaching her as they received their scores for the latest test.

"You're so used to getting your way, always being first. Are you an only child?" He cocked his hip against the desk beside her and pushed his sandy hair back from his eyes.

"So? What's it to you?" She huffed, then returned to her desk, and slunk down beside her best friend.

"It's nothing to me." But he spoke just loudly enough to make sure she heard it. Yeah, crybaby.

As coincidence or fate would have it, they shared the same major, archeology. Already, they were sharing classes. Their studies pushed them together, and their competitive natures clashed. Didn't matter how much the girl impressed him—no way was he willing to settle for second place, which apparently further fueled her dislike of him.

"See how smug he is? He's a know it all. That's what he is." Her lip curled under, and her scowl deepened while she glared at the second-place marks on her test score. "We'll just have to study harder—that's all. Great. More nights and weekends in the library. Probably not far from Mr. America." She shuddered.

"You mean *you'll* have to study harder. I'm not in your *friendly* little competition." Her roommate's snicker carried to DR. "I've got a life."

When Suzette picked up her books and strode away, leaving the steaming Gail behind, DR headed over to the feisty redhead.

"Why are you so hateful toward me? I haven't done anything to you. I can't help my test grades are better than yours." Or that, even though she was Miss Cold as Ice, he found her attractive. Who could help but love her long curly red hair and porcelain skin sprinkled with just enough freckles to make her look real and alive? It must be one of those fatal-attraction things. "Besides, I didn't travel to Spain to get bogged down by a disappointed local." He flopped down at a desk closer to the professor's than hers, and the chair slid noisily on the tile floor before he picked up and inspected a stapler, lost in thought.

"Ohh. You make me so mad." She reached out, snatched the stapler, and slammed it on the desk, then stormed out.

"So mature," he called after her. "Why don't you go home to Daddy? He'll fix everything." Oops. The words escaped unchecked, unintended. Hopefully, she didn't hear them.

Her dad, her deadbeat dad, though Irish, lived in America and wouldn't fix anything. Rumor was he'd run out on her mom when he learned she was pregnant, leaving his father's house in Dublin for his mother's house in Boston. Not a word in twenty years. Which explained why Americans were on her do-not-resuscitate list.

DR stayed in the class, waiting for the smoke to clear. Around six feet tall with a slight muscular build, he'd become the mark of flirty lovestruck European girls. "Handsome and Michigan strong," his mom often said.

"DR, you sure have quite the way with the ladies." The professor reentered the class, passing a fuming Gail on the way in.

"I know." DR spread out his hands. "It's my gift."

One of many. He ducked his head down. He only came to Spain to study because he thought, if he could get away from all the local do-gooders, then he could find that elusive state of mind—peace—once-and-for-all. Of course, the fact that it would take three years or less, instead of the six it normally took in the States to get his doctorate didn't hurt.

"If it's peace you wanted, I don't think that's the way to find it." The professor often laughed about their competitiveness. "But your competition just might help you two become my best and brightest students."

Starting with summer school three years later, before Gail's second-to-last year and DR's final year at the Dukes, Gail began meeting him in the afternoons to discuss the classes they shared. Their competitiveness had eased into a sort of friend-helping-friend situation. Or so she let him believe.

"Are you going to study this afternoon? I'll save you a spot at the window if you want." Kicking at a weed growing through the sidewalk under a huge elm tree near the language laboratory, DR flashed a smile.

She snagged his Italian thesaurus for her next class and winked. "I'll be there."

She shook her head as DR sauntered off. Where'd the guy think she'd be? They'd been meeting every afternoon, after all. At first, it was just studying and classwork. But...

Her roommate walking alongside her nudged her shoulder. "I thought you didn't like him. What's changed?"

"I don't know. I mean I know I *didn't* like him. But there's something different about him. It's kind of like I sense a destiny." After straightening her half tee around her shoulders, she hugged his thesaurus to her side. Too bad, it wasn't him. "I feel different around him. I like who I am with him. Is that crazy?"

"Maybe." Suzette shrugged. "But I gotta admit he's easy on the eyes."

Gail laughed. "I know, right? I love his dimples and... Well, I'm very attracted to him."

"The other girls know he's off-limits." Suzette's dark eyes flashed with suppressed laughter. "*They* can read your body language—even if he can't. All those languages you guys are learning, and you can't seem to communicate."

"I've been putting out little feelers, but he's not adept at the girl thing. So all my attempts have been unsuccessful." She'd have to talk to her mom this weekend about the introverted, handsome American who shared her same loves. Like DR, she loved the sea, having lived just a short walk from the Mediterranean.

In Madrid, festivities abounded right on the streets, especially in August, yet when afternoon came, here she remained—stuck in the library. She tapped her pen against her textbook, the dusty drapes failing to block the vivid August sun from casting a glare across her pages. She sprang up and moved them aside. Funny how hard it was to be indoors in the sunshine, so easy to remember playing on the shore with her mother and Kayleigh.... She swallowed hard, hurting over losing Kayleigh when she was eight. They'd never even learned what killed her, blood clots or a brain aneurysm or something.

"Mom said to give him a push. Well, here goes." Drapes aside, she spun around.

DR closed his textbook. A shock of blond hair fell over his brow as he tilted his head at her. Michigan Strong his mom called him. A good description. "You okay?"

"Yep." She plopped back into her seat and resumed clicking the back of her pen.

"You know that's annoying, right?"

"I do." She didn't stop. If that's what she had to do to get his attention, she'd do it.

"Gail?" Anderson, a classmate, approached and jammed his hands in his chino pockets. "I was wondering if you'd like to go to the festival Friday?"

"Would I ever!" *Just not with you.* Wow, what impeccable timing. Since she began studying with DR, she hadn't dated, finally admitting to herself she didn't want to go out with anyone but him. She just never told him so. Watching DR out of the corner of her eye, she gushed. "I'd love to go."

Never wavering, he kept reading his book. Seriously? Didn't he care at all?

"Great." Anderson rocked back on his heels, bouncing a bit as he beamed. "Man, I've wanted to ask you out for a long time, but I wasn't sure, you know? You're always with DR, but you guys aren't dating, right?"

"Nope, we're not dating." She kept her tone even, her gaze on DR. Did his ears redden? Was he embarrassed people thought they were a couple, or was he upset by something?

"We'll have a blast." Anderson pulled his hands from his pockets and rubbed them together in a let's-get-at-this gesture. "Pick you up at four?"

"I can't wait. I didn't think you would ever ask. See you Friday at four." She smiled, even stooping to bat her baby blues—anything to get a reaction from DR. Nothing. Maybe "Michigan Strong" meant he was like stone. Had she really agreed to go to that festival, Virgen de La Paloma? Yuck. With him, double yuck.

Anderson sauntered away, whistling before a librarian shushed him.

Gail flipped her red hair over her shoulder and clicked her pen again. Okay, fine. If that's how it had to be, that's how it had to be. She gave herself a firm nod. She was ready for romance, ready for love, and if DR wasn't going to be the one, then she'd better get to it. Her mother had almost missed her chance at love. It had taken Gail's prodding to push her into the arms of the man who became her stepfather. If she could do it for her mother, she'd better be just as good at doing it for herself.

"I hope the weather will be good Friday." She tossed the pen on the desk. "What are you going to be doing?"

"I don't know," he mumbled, his American twang stronger than usual, the way it got when he thought he was going to flub a question in class. "I guess I'll be here, studying like usual. Besides, I came to Madrid to get away from religion. The last thing I want to do is go celebrate a virgin saint."

"Well, suit yourself. We study every day. Sometimes, I want to let my hair down." She shook said hair around her shoulders, holding her head up, biting on her upper lip. What was wrong with him, anyway? Didn't he care about her? Why couldn't he have sprung to his feet and told Anderson, "No. No, she won't, not Friday or any other day—she's my girl!"

No. Not gonna happen. Mr. Michigan Strong just sat there, miserable, as if their little world wasn't changing one tiny bit.

Friday afternoon, Gail's big date came as DR sat studying, alone, in the library. Well, almost alone. Everyone in town seemed to be enjoying the festival, especially the nonreligious, except him and Sierra, the girl stuck working the evening shift. She leaned against the desk, staring off into space, a thousand miles away. Probably wishing he'd stop being a stick-in-the-mud and leave, so she could go to the fair and meet her boyfriend.

Hands behind his head, he clawed his fingers through his hair and tousled it as if trying to wake up, an unbroken boyhood habit. He closed his eyes and whispered to himself. "Why can't I tell Gail I'm falling in love with her? Why is love and all the things that go with it so tough for me? I love everything about her, how she holds her head back and just laughs and how she winks at me. Why?"

He pulled at his hair, tugging at its roots. "Our entire family is outgoing, confident. My little brother's going to be a DJ, and here I am, for crying aloud. I can't even share my feelings with my dream girl." His voice became louder. "Yes... yes, Gail *is* my dream girl."

Jamming back his chair, he sprang to his feet. "What am I doing in this library all alone? I've got to go get my girl!"

Sierra snapped her head up and flashed a smile. "Leaving, DR?"

The phone rang as he nodded and strolled past.

"I'm sorry, honey." Sierra's giddy voice followed him while she answered. "He's left. No one's here except me, and I'm closing up. I'm so ready to be at the festival."

Over at the festival, he couldn't find Gail. After what seemed like hours, he spotted Anderson with his friends around a table one of the pubs brought out onto the street. They were playing a game archaeology students called Bones.

"Anderson." DR waved his hands above his head from a narrow roadway leading to the main celebration. Streamers stretched across the road while guitar music and disc jockeys vied for attention as raucous partiers and reverent worshippers alike packed the streets, ready to celebrate well into the hot August night.

Folks in traditional chulapo costumes lined the way, laughing and dancing. In the center of the square, a stage had been built atop a fountain where a band was playing the authentic Spanish flamenco.

Ducking in and out, past the traditional procession of firemen and well-dressed maidens and gentlemen, he ran. He veered past a float toting the festival's main purpose, a nearly life-sized gold-framed painting of the virgin saint, said to have healed the son of King Charles IV, at least according to the king's wife, Maria Luisa de Parma. Then after nearly tripping in the street before the float, he cut behind the bar to avoid fighting through the lines of colorfully dressed partygoers.

"Anderson. Anderson, where's Gail?" Hands on knees, he sucked in air. At least, he finally had Anderson's attention.

"She called this morning." Anderson cracked the top of his Coke, fizz bubbling free before he gulped it. "She said she was going to her parents' home tomorrow and had to make an early night of it."

DR straightened up. She hadn't gone out with him after all. His core shivered. The festival now took on a different meaning. Christians were blending in, no preachers in sight. Of course, wasn't that always the way?

Anderson's face contorted as he readied for his turn in their game of Bones. "I wish she'd just said no like I expected. Then I could've gotten a date with that pretty little blonde, Martha Ralese. And I wouldn't be stuck here with a couple of guys."

"Hey!" They shook their fists.

"Sorry."

Dice bounced across the table.

"Great." DR slapped his classmate's back, then winced. "Um, I mean... I'm sorry to hear that. Hope you still have some fun tonight. Looks like you rolled a winner, though. See you guys later."

Anderson might've said something, but in his haste, his heart beating so fast, DR didn't hear. All he could hear was the pulsing in his head, each whoosh saying, "Call her, call her, call her."

He was in love and knew it now. It wouldn't—no, *couldn't*—wait until Monday.

He reached into his pocket for his phone while jogging toward Gail's room. Ah, there was Martha with her parents, or at least he thought they were her parents. "Martha," he shouted. "Anderson's over by the bar near the main stage and wants to talk to you."

He stopped just long enough to call Gail's room. One ring... two... Whew, she answered. She hadn't left yet. "Gail—"

"Bzzt." Someone made a buzzer noise. "Wrong answer, jerk." Suzette, her roommate, spoke up. "Gail left for Malaga around four o'clock. She was pretty upset and ugly crying—probably shouldn't have been driving. You two have another fight?"

"No, not a fight. I was just blind. That's all. Thanks, Suz. I'll see you."

He hung up and headed to his room. It was too late for the five-hour drive to the coast tonight. "Why, why, why—why hadn't I seen it? How could I be so blind?"

The next day, he reached her hometown around noon. His grip tight on the steering wheel, he craned his neck toward the marina on the way to her family's bungalow. The Mekenzie-Gail, MG, was still docked. They hadn't taken it out for a jaunt like most weekends. Whew. His shoulders relaxed. He drove to their home, heart pounding and palms sweating.

Parked out front, he sat there and took slow breaths. What kind of coward was he? Surely, he wouldn't wimp out after driving five hours. He shoved himself from the driver's seat and strode up the redbrick sidewalk he'd help Nicolas lay. His hand shook as he knocked and waited.

The door opened, and blue eyes peeped up at him from the face he loved. She stood frozen in the doorway, then half ran, half jumped into his waiting arms, and wrapped her legs around his waist.

"I can't believe it." She spoke between the kisses she planted on his face. "You came all the way here... for me?"

It was now or never. He drew in a deep breath and pushed out equally deep words. "I'm... I'm in love with you. After last night, I couldn't wait to tell you. I'm so glad you didn't go out with Anderson."

He held his breath now. Would he hear the same?

"I love you too!" she shrieked. "I just wanted to give you a shove."

Her mom, Mekie, now standing in the front room, began clapping. Gail's stepfather joined her. "Well, it's about time." Hands on her cheeks, she teared up, then put her arm around Nicolas.

Even with her parents watching, DR couldn't help stealing another kiss, and they held each other so tight. It was the best weekend ever and a day he'd *never* forget. After that, their confessed love grew to consume their world. Once Gail graduated the following year, they married in October and began their travel and life's work.

As newlyweds, they joined a team of four fellow archaeology graduates from the Dukes School. Their exploration began on the coast of India, where no matter how close they were, it wasn't enough. Desires and need burning wildly.

Their growing knowledge of local languages and customs began helping them discover larger, more valuable sites and develop friendships with local leaders. One friendship, made over a year into their exploration, had a profound impact on their exploration.

"There, see the broken windows and gates? Hired vandals from a nearby village did that. I'm sure of it." Chief Mnortarmillc pointed at several houses on the village outskirts. "As village leader, I'm supposed to fix all this and stop the violence, but without funds, it's not possible." He shook his head and extended his hand to continue the tour. "I'll help you any way I can, but I have to be careful to observe tradition and law."

"Chief, thank you." Gail's face lit up. She wrapped her arms around herself and held her shoulders as her words gushed free. "We can't express how happy this makes us."

"Why would another village do this?" DR kicked at a broken bolt.

"They want our land for a factory or something." His eyes downcast and his body slumped, Chief Mnortarmillc leaned against a stone entranceway.

"Thank you, Chief. Gail and I are well versed in India's antiquities law passed in 1978. We assure you everything will comply with the law and your village will get its rightful share if we find anything." DR slid his arm around Gail, and they walked back to the village's main street and checked into their rented room.

"Did you see how sad the chief was? They are desperate." Gail pulled off her tan canvas work vest and hat, shook her hair out, then flopped back on the bed, stretching. "Bed's a little hard."

Smacking the mattress to feel the firmness, he laughed. "Maybe we should just sleep on the floor. I guess it's all in what you get used to." He stretched out beside her, leaned on his right elbow, and slid his left arm across her belly. "Tomorrow, let's search around the village's south side. Then we'll move clockwise until we cover the perimeter."

"Okay." She touched his face, and her finger traced a path along his jaw to his mouth. "But we can only stay a month, so we don't want to waste any time."

After several weeks, their friendship and grace were rewarded. Chief Mnortarmillc, the elected Pradhan, whom this village simply called chief, embraced their exploration, even sharing his village's historical documents and landmarks.

"You just don't get these types of intricate skills… not without a wealthy past," Gail insisted as she watched the local women making pottery, weaving baskets, and piecing together clothing for sale. "The richness of their crafts scarcely suits a people living in abject poverty."

So, they kept at it.

Today, DR paused to stretch his back, his fond gaze lingering on his wife. What had Mom always said to him and his brothers? "When you find that special girl, remember to leave her special. Don't try to change her." He'd lived by that, and as they most often explored Gail's ideas, his radiant bride shone even more brilliantly. Her confidence grew, and so did her love for him.

"Tired?" She nudged his shoulder.

He raked a hand through his sweaty hair. "Maybe a bit—hungrier, though."

No longer running from the do-gooders, not looking over his shoulder, he'd relaxed in this country so far from his own culture and focused on their future, wherever that would take them. And the hardness of their plight made their passions burn even more.

"Funny, we're all hungry here, you and I and the locals. But there's something more than the hunger in my belly." Her blue eyes shimmered. "I *feel* it, DR. It's here. The discovery, just out of reach, and I'm so hungry for it I might faint."

That was his Gail, such passion. He looped an arm around her waist and drew her closer. "You believe it's here. No one but us believes in it."

"It was the hunger that drove the rest of the team away long before we reached this village, not just the personality conflicts. I do wish Clyde McMillen stayed. He lasted the longest, a year over the others."

"Living on mainly fruits, vegetables, and the occasional treat of meat, with tremendous money pressures, hasn't been easy." He shrugged. "I don't blame them for giving up."

She tucked her head against his shoulder. In their time exploring India, they'd learned to do more with less from the locals they visited. Their appreciation deepened for the less fortunate who often shared their skimpy meals.

DR loosened his grip on her. In the sunlight beyond a warehouse, a young boy was playing with something shiny. From this vantage point, it looked like a silver fish. He let go of Gail and ran toward the boy. "Hey, boy. What's that you have in your hand?"

The startled child dropped the medallion on the ground, then bent, and picked it up, about to run. But seeming to realize he couldn't escape, he ducked and covered his head.

"I'm not going to hurt you. I promise." Exhaling to calm himself, DR lowered his voice, crouched over the muddy street, and rested a gentle hand on the boy's shoulder. "Can I see what you have?"

When he took the item from the boy's halfway extended hand, the boy kept cowering.

DR lifted it to the light—a small silver medallion hammered into the shape of a fish. "Don't be afraid. I won't hurt you. Where did you get this?" He pushed his vest open and took out a handkerchief to wipe his brow. "Can you show me?"

At the boy's nod, DR laughed aloud over what he'd discovered and waved his wife over. "Gail, come quickly."

By the time she reached them, he'd talked the boy into taking them on a hike up the valley to where he found the medallion. Gail chattered in excited bursts as they walked through a gorge cut by monsoon rains. Flooding had pulled down trees and left boulders strewn about like pieces of a board game. The vegetation was matted down and mired in mud where he'd found the piece, leaving only a stone here or there visible. Watermarks circled the trees still standing upward of fifteen to twenty feet off the ground.

Gail leaned in close to DR. "He found it on village lands, and what a stroke of luck! The floods removed the silt, overgrowth, and debris but spared the tombs. These burial grounds must be at least a thousand years old." She pointed at the exposed stone parts of different burial chambers.

Sweat and dirt streaked her face after they scraped mud and debris off one of the exposed stones. She pushed a handful of hair out of her face, laughing. DR handed the boy his cell phone and asked him to take their picture.

"You were right, baby. You were right." He hugged her and spun her around and around until her legs stuck straight out. Then he kissed her, dirty face, and all, as they celebrated.

The chief celebrated. The village celebrated.

The monsoon rains had caused major damage further down the valley. But the burial chambers were deep enough that the floods only unearthed the grounds with minimal damage. Although several smaller tombs were washed open—probably where the silver fish medallion came from.

Their friendship being such, the chief allowed them to begin their work on the ancient burial grounds after contacting state and national authorities.

They promised to respect and care for the dead buried there. It took them and their Indian counterparts a month of digging to enter the first chamber, one of six former chief entombments. The first chief uncovered had taken a vast part of the wealth the village once enjoyed with him—at least he tried. His extravagant entombment claimed a prominent position on the grounds, so they started with it.

They brought in reliable teams recommended by the Dukes School and Itasham, their former professor, to work with Indian authorities. Then they also taught several tribe members how to preserve treasures found in the tombs of a few other elders and sent teams to dig with the tribe in those tombs too. The grateful chief allowed them to remove most of the artifacts, as the tribe was well compensated and needed the money, but removing the artifacts also protected the find from rival villages and thieves.

As the archaeology world hailed them as heroes, offers of grants and support from major corporations and universities poured in. Everyone wanted a piece of the action, including a now-desperate Clyde McMillen.

They set up a laboratory not far from where DR had grown up in Michigan. Mainly because of grants from a major supporter of ancient history. With that, they promised to give the village near Kolkata a large sum up front and help build a museum to house the pieces covered by the Indian government's antiquities law.

Soon, they were buying their house on Wall Lake near their lab in Delton and taking advantage of the nearby university to catalog the enormous find.

Along with the crates of artifacts from nearly eight thousand miles away came winter. Malaga's balmy temperatures in the forties made it a tropical paradise in comparison. Gail had made it clear she'd prefer to go back to Malaga as she moved to Wall Lake. But as the lows hit minus seven in February those first two winters, DR's heart warmed when she took up snowboarding and loved it.

"Baby." She nudged his shoulder now, her cheeks still atingle from the cold. "You've got to try it. It's such a rush, feeling the cold air on your face as you come down the slope."

"I'll give it a try." He tugged at her knit cap. "But I won't look nearly as good in the bibs."

She planted her cold hands on either side of his face, smirking when he winced. "As long as we're on the slopes together. No reason I should be the only one freezing in this land of yours."

She looped her arm through his, then jammed a cozy hat on his head. "C'mon, baby. Enough work for one day." She dragged him from their lab into the bright sunshine and hauled him to Marcie's Place, where they brewed her favorite coffee.

"Hey, Pauline." She released him and patted the older lady's arm as he kicked the snow from his shoes and rubbed his hands together. "Ignore DR. Sometimes he thinks he's an artifact that can stay under glass in that lab. One of these days, I'm going to catalog him and put him on some old shelf. You girls got a story for me today?"

"Don't let her sit down, ladies." DR puffed warm air into his cupped hands, then winked at the well-groomed ladies, their thinning hair tinted silvery blues or henna reds. "She'll be here for hours, picking your brains on local history, and we're headed to the slopes, apparently."

Gail gave the girls a wave. "Say hi to Willie for me when she pops in."

Like him, Gail loved their work, spending hours documenting every item at their home and lab. Their house on the east side of Wall Lake was ideal for outdoor living and boating, but the open sea had begun calling their names.

"What do you say we try a different area next time?" DR asked, sipping his wine later that evening. "I'm getting worn out on the Indian Ocean thing." He savored the sweet red's sensation on his tongue. Nicolas, his father-in-law, sent them a case of his favorite the other day.

"I know you are." She pouted, sharing her huge blue puppy-dog eyes. "But I just love our friends. I want to see some different places too. Maybe we can take one more trip to Kolkata? Afterward, we can sail up the coast of Portugal and around to Bilbao. Nicolas loves it there and said we'd have a fun trip. Then we can go further, maybe France?" Leaning over, she kissed his lips, then winked.

"Why do you do that to me?" He took her hand, closed his eyes, and shook his head as if to shudder. "You know I can't resist your kisses or your winks."

"Why do you think I do it?" She giggled and kissed him again.

They sat on their deck for hours planning their next big trip to India, a dream they loved undertaking. Soon, they began telling everyone they'd be returning to the sea. "You can only hold back the desires of the heart for so long."

"The Dream Maker Express is calling. 'Adventure is out there.' " DR smiled as he stole a line from Ellie, a character in a movie, and pointed toward the lake, making Gail laugh.

Gail was his confidant and he hers. They shared the same thoughts, the same heart. There was only one thing he didn't share with her, not knowing she also didn't share one with him. Soon, it would raise its ugly head. Among the things they had shared most was how much they abhorred Christian fanatics. Gail would say, and he agreed, "They are nonintellectuals searching for something that's just a fantasy, a way to justify their failures."

But Gail had a secret. She'd started to change a year earlier, and she'd never discussed it with him. On several trips back to Malaga, she began questioning faith or rather her lack of it. She'd seen so many pass into the "afterlife," what she called death, having rummaged around in burial grounds digging people up for science. She saw a peace at Christian funerals she couldn't describe or explain, but not so much for nonbelievers. There was no hope of anything for a nonbeliever, just the end. Hope was something she wanted and something she needed. Then she began wondering.

Today, she hunted through her purse for her keys, her friend bracing a shoulder against the front doorway as she waited. "Willie, I should be the happiest woman alive. I love my life. But something is missing. When I went to Malaga, I saw how horrible one of my mom's friends' funeral was. Then at another, there seemed to be a peace. I don't even know how to explain it, but I felt different at the believer's funeral."

"Believers have a future. The others do too, just not one to look forward to, so sometimes you can see their regret as they die." Willie scooped Gail's keys from the dish in the hall and dangled them before her until Gail groaned and held her hand out for them. As a DJ, Willie shared the Morning Drive show with DR's brother, Mike, at WREAL

Christian radio station in Delton. "Funerals are a bad place, no matter, but when there's no hope, the spirit gets heavy. Maybe that's what you feel."

"I've heard all about that, about becoming like a child and all. But how would I begin to tell DR, even if I want it, and I... Well, I still don't know." Gail pulled on her flats to go over to the Hammer Throw. Hopefully, they still had those gray pillows for the bedroom.

"The important thing is that you understand, not just the precepts of Christianity, but the gospel of Jesus Christ, what it means for you—no matter what DR thinks. You have to decide, you alone. No one else will answer for your decision, not me, not DR, and if that's what's making you feel empty, mind you, it won't just go away." Willie slung her sweater off the entryway hook and pulled it on, then took Gail's arm. "Okay, we're ready."

Gail shut the door and started down the steps. "If he finds out I'm talking about God, he'll go plumb off. He ran halfway around the world to get away from all that. If he thinks, I'm a believer...." She shook her head and unlocked her Jeep by remote. "Let's talk about this later. I'm ready to spend some money. DR's going to laugh when he sees more pillows." For sure, but nothing a glass of sweet red wouldn't smooth away. Well, sweet red and maybe a kiss.

Willie shared Gail's love for the outdoors and the lake. They'd been spending hours and hours together, and with those new pillows in place, they soon migrated to Gail's back deck. They discussed faith and things they both enjoyed.

They'd met at Marcie's. Willie didn't talk about the laws of the Bible. Rather, she shared the gospel and her love with simplicity, and as they whiled away the days, DR buried himself in the artifacts they'd unearthed.

He usually came home tired, seldom asking how Gail spent her time away from the lab. Today was no different. She and Willie halted their conversation as the back door swung open and DR stepped out onto the deck, waving his phone to display a picture and alight with an endearing boyish excitement. "Sweetheart, you've got to see what was in today's work. There are pieces I would have never suspected. You were right. Those people had some serious skills. Oh." He lowered the phone. "Hi, Willie."

"I'd better be going." Willie slid to her feet, and DR dropped into the seat she'd occupied.

Then the seasons of life changed again. After only three blissful years in Delton, Gail died, struck down by a pulmonary embolism. Her passing was much like Kayleigh's, so sudden and too soon. It left DR shaken to the core and Mekie and Nicolas crushed.

Without her, he stopped cataloging their find. He stopped almost everything, including living. He was simply breathing in and out, existing. Their beautiful home on the lake had become its own tomb of memories.

After the memorial, DR stayed in Malaga for six months, living with Nicolas and Mekie. They adored him and he them. He stayed busy reading and studying, still having his books from the Dukes School.

Then he spent another six months at the school brushing up on his language skills, while his home, along with the crates from India, sat untouched. Money wasn't an issue any longer. But he still had a lot of work to finish their Indian dig, and crates kept arriving weekly. His Indian friends were counting on him, so he took Clyde McMillen on to wrap it up. McMillen had asked to work on the artifacts with the local university, helping document and assess each piece some four years earlier. He was happy to share in it now, and he needed the income and lab practice, being an archaeologist.

"Make sure we treat Chief Mnortarmillc right," DR instructed McMillen before going to Madrid. "I don't want to lose his confidence. He's been gracious to us. He also has connections we might need one day."

CHAPTER
TWO

D R was beginning their dream without her, without the love of his life. Life wasn't going to wait any longer, and soon, he'd be on his way. A new journey, a new life waiting. They'd spent so many summer evenings enjoying a glass of red wine on the deck, just sitting, talking, and listening to the lake. He could still feel her presence in their home and on the deck. She'd grown even more beautiful in her last days, taking on a glow. Her red hair a shade darker, her eyes sparkling like sapphires. He almost asked if she was pregnant. She seemed so free, so happy. She rolled her head and laughed so hard when he held her at times. She was amazing, and she was his. Every moment he had with her was like being... well, in heaven. Memories that cut both ways.

He was left to box up their memories, their possessions.

One final evening before the new adventure, he left home and went to the coffeehouse to meet his brother and Willie. He arrived a little early. Rubbing cold hands together, he slid into the corner table overlooking the backyard and kept his head down so Pauline and her coffee cronies wouldn't try to talk to him.

Finally, the bell dinged over the door, and Mike, six feet tall like DR, ducked inside and shoved his coworker forward. Mike reached to hug him. "You know Willie, don't you?"

"Sure, we've met a few times." Remembering her from his deck with Gail, DR outstretched his hand and shook hers. "Willie, how have you been?"

"It's good to see you." She flashed an uneasy smile and slid in beside Mike.

"So, DR, are you ready for the big trip? Have you made all your plans for your new adventure?" Mike surveyed the crowd, then apparently not seeing anyone familiar, sat down.

"I have appointments to inspect a few yachts. I'm interested in one, but I'll see. Depends on the price." DR sipped his coffee and glanced out the window. "Plus, the interviews for my crew. I have good prospects for my first mate. The first week or so will be hectic, but I'm up to it." He offered Mike the creamer.

Willie planted an elbow on the table and propped her chin on her upraised palm. She tapped the table with her other index finger. "Mike said you were going back to where you and Gail made your discovery. You must be looking forward to seeing some of your old friends again."

"Yes and no." He let out a heavy breath but couldn't release the memories holding his chest. "I cherish my memories, but I'm not looking forward to confronting them. Anyway, we're stopping in other cities first. So that'll be fun."

"So..." Mike spread out his hands, then glanced at Willie for a go-ahead nod. "We were wondering how you might feel about sharing your adventure with our listeners on the Morning Drive show. We can keep it at about twenty minutes, and our listeners would love to hear about it."

"Hmm." DR blew the heat off his coffee before sipping. "That sounds interesting. What do you have in mind?"

"What do you think?" Mike nudged Willie. "Maybe a question-and-answer session?"

"Yeah, of course. We could come up with the questions ahead of time to keep the flow smooth and friendly." She extended her arms toward DR. "Are you game?"

"Sure. Why not?" He flattened both palms on the table. "Let's give it a shot. We can talk about it after I get everything smoothed out in Marsala."

Willie swirled her coffee around in her cup. Her long delicate fingers glided over the cup in a steady rhythm. As if feeling his gaze, she raised hers. Large brown eyes, luminescent now, blinked at him before she ducked her head and refocused on her coffee. Curly black hair tumbled across her cheeks, falling just above her breasts as it framed her oval face.

He winced. He shouldn't be noticing things like that, should he?

He sank back against his booth and braced an arm across the leather seat. "This is nice, guys. Thanks for getting me out."

"Yeah." Mike swigged the last of his coffee. "Sharing a meal or a drink helps encourage friendly discussions—you and I, seems we get at each other's throats too often."

Right. Christianity. DR's shoulders stiffened. Still, even here, an uneasiness always hung over them. They didn't have much to talk about. Something had stolen their common ground while he was young.

Blenders whirred. Someone laughed. Pauline's group hadn't tried to hound him or even cast pitying looks his way. DR stretched out his legs. He could do this. He could even *like* it.

"Well." Mike drummed his hands on the table. "I've got to get home to Alyssa and the kids, but we gotta do this again, bro. Your stories—man, you sure know a way to spin a tale and whisk a guy off to faraway places. Wish I'd had half of your adventures. It'll be exciting doing the show with you."

As Mike got up to leave, he patted Willie's shoulder. "I'll see you in the morning. Don't keep my brother out too late." Then he grinned at DR. "It's been fun. Let's get together again in a day or so?"

DR stood to man hug him. "Sure, we'll do something."

Mike edged around a family of five jostling to the only remaining table. Must be near on dinnertime with the way the place was filling up.

"Is everything okay?" The server, Rachael, stopped by their table. "Can I get you something?"

"Do you have any of those world-famous éclairs left, the ones with the custard-overloaded centers?" Willie slipped her hair back over her shoulders. "I missed dinner."

Sounded good actually. "I'll have one of those too."

Then Willie did the unthinkable. "I'm so sorry Gail passed. She was my best friend. We spent a lot of time together her last year. I can't imagine how terrible it must be for you."

"It's been a nightmare." He rubbed the sudden thrumming between his brows. "For her mom and dad too. I didn't realize you'd known Gail so well."

"Indeed." Willie waved a hand. "We often prayed Mekie would make up with her grandmother in Ireland before she passed on. Gail wanted to meet her family. It's so sad."

His head snapped up at the word *prayed*.

Rachael returned with the eclairs and the checks.

Clenching and unclenching his fists under the table, DR restrained himself. But really, who did Willie think she was? Gail never prayed one day in her life. Gail *laughed* at people who prayed.

"How do you know about Mekie?" Good. Somehow, he kept his tone calm. "Did Gail talk about her? She was a private person when it came to her family."

The chatter in the coffeehouse was getting louder—or perhaps his patience was growing thinner. Willie plucked the overloaded éclair from its delicate paper doily, closing her eyes in apparent delight as she bit into the creamy concoction, not paying attention to his changing attitude. She held up her hand as if to say, "One minute, please."

He shifted in his seat. The leather bench felt sticky, trying to hold him somewhere he didn't want to be. Sure, Gail and Willie spent time together, but this? Couldn't have been. Gail's conversations about believers were always snide and cutting. But that had been a while. Had things changed?

"I've been around enough people with your simplistic worldview to know they say God only hears from believers, except the sinner's prayer. So, God wouldn't hear her anyway." He crammed half the éclair in his mouth and mumbled around it, not caring if it was rude. "She hated everything about God, so let's change the subject."

Finished with her eclair, Willie fixed her gaze on him. She didn't seem to notice that he was getting mad. She whispered something as if talking to someone he couldn't see. But that didn't make sense. Unless she was praying?

Then she flicked her hair behind her shoulders again, squared those shoulders up, and met his gaze like a professor about to give a lecture. "I promised Gail I wouldn't say a word to anyone until she worked it out. We know that never happened, so here goes. Look in her journals. She wrote in them every day. We talked about it a lot. We talked about her feelings of emptiness. Even though she adored you and your life together, an emptiness kept coming back on her, like something was missing. She wanted to talk about faith. I never pushed her."

Tears welled up in her dewy brown eyes. "She became the friend I've always wanted. She was so full of life, you know. It wasn't children she missed, although she wanted them. It was much deeper."

Willie let out a deep breath. "The last time she visited her mom, she started wondering about her lack of faith. She knew her grandmother was a woman of strong Christian faith. Even though faith had let her mom down, Gail wondered if that was God or the human element in faith. You know how she liked to dig beneath the surface, never one to settle and believe what we could see, always searching to find out if there was more to it. So, we started talking about it." She stabbed a finger against the table twice. "Right here."

He held up his hand to stop her, but she pushed it to the side and down and threaded her cold fingers through his.

"Gail meant so much to me." She squeezed his hand, then released it, and got a tissue from her purse. "She planned to tell you at the right time. You know the rest. I want to leave it to Gail, to her journals, to her words—read them, DR. She found the peace she was missing, and when she died, she was the happiest woman on earth. She adored you, so don't get mad at me or her."

He stared out the window, unseeing. Heat pulsed through his veins, his insides churning faster than that blender smashing ice. He couldn't lose control right here in the coffee shop.

No way would Gail ever become one of those, those Bible thumpers—*no way*. Unless somebody stole into her confidence and brainwashed her. That's what they do. Did Gail have a weak moment? Did Willie brainwash her?

"I'll get this. It'll be my treat." She picked up the checks.

"Did you brainwash her?"

"Read her journals. It was her decision to make, not mine, yours, or anyone else's. Read her journals."

"Is that all you people know how to do—lie?"

Willie pushed up from the table, ready to speak.

But he grabbed her arm.

"You—keep your hands off me!" She shook herself loose. "Go home. Read Gail's own words. Everything's in her journals. Good night, DR."

He slumped back into his seat. This couldn't be happening. "Why would Gail become weak? Weak was never in her description," he grumbled to himself. "No way."

Head in his hands, elbows on the table, he sat there. This evening was just a terrible lie, and that was that.

He pushed from the booth, nearly plowing over Rachael as she sidestepped. He strode to his Jeep, then took the long way home to calm himself, driving recklessly on the narrow roads, ugly thoughts twisting through his mind. Good thing he didn't meet anyone. Dusk on the lake was peaceful, a time he enjoyed, but not tonight.

He wouldn't read her journals. They were her private thoughts. There'd be no second-guessing how she lived with him or within herself. He'd remember things the way they were, a dream come true.

He parked, headed straight to the kitchen Gail designed, and poured a tall glass of chardonnay. One of her favorites, other than Nicolas's sweet red. He took his drink to the deck, to the settee. She'd picked out the overstuffed cushions and what must've been every pillow the Hammer Throw had. He plunked one in his lap now and caressed the canvas material. He'd laughed so hard that day carrying them all in the house. She'd had great taste. A hint of a smile tugged at his lips.

The wine began calming him, but one was his limit. He always teased Gail that he was a cheap date. Alcohol put him to sleep. He twisted the glass in his hand, its smooth crystal soothing. His gaze slid toward the house, toward their bedroom, his mind opening the drawer he'd left shut. He had sworn he'd never look at her journals, and he didn't want anyone reading his.

The crisp breeze picked up as if eager to remind him this was Michigan in late September. Not that he'd forget. After all, he grew up just an hour away in Albion. Tonight seemed eerily familiar. Nights like this from his childhood haunted him. *The night* and all its evilness changed the course of his life, the dreamwalkers, what some evangelicals called God's spirits, beginning to affect hundreds, maybe thousands of lives through him.

He ground his teeth. He'd shielded his two younger brothers like a shepherd looking out for his flock—with a wolf nearby. To this day, no one except Mom and Dad knew why he was so mad at God, not even Gail.

He'd turned nine that summer. Mike was four and Timmy two. His God-fearing parents taught him and his brothers to love the Lord.

That summer, their church held a revival in the town's ballpark. Though their farmhouse was a good drive, they'd come to pray for new converts each night. And he loved playing with his friends behind the big tent during those long, languid nights.

Funny how everybody remembers those as "the good times," times of football and cookouts, revival, and transformation. Most for God, but some not. Still, a time many couldn't forget.

His life was transformed too. On the last night.

He sank back in the settee, sinking back into the past. A voice drawing him in...

"Stevie, how would you like to make a dollar? Help me load the chairs on my truck, and I'll give you one."

"Yes, sir. I'll stay, if Dad doesn't mind." In Albion back then, a dollar was a lot.

Fred, the evangelist, asked DR's dad if he could stay behind and help. Dad agreed as long as the preacher promised to bring Stevie up by the house when they were through.

DR closed his eyes, bringing the cool glass to the throbbing at one temple, still hearing those words like it was yesterday.... Had he ever been so happy again? All because he was going to earn a whole dollar.

He sipped the wine, tears dampening his collar. Only now, they were half for losing Gail and half for his boyhood.

CHAPTER
THREE

After they loaded the chairs on the truck, true to his word, the evangelist gave him the dollar. He took it out of his pocket and stretched it as if to pop it. "Here you go, Stevie, one United States dollar. Just like I promised."

He hoisted Stevie—a young DR—up into the truck's passenger seat, then walked over to the church's pastor, calling over his shoulder. "I'll be right back."

The men's voices drifted through the cab's open window while Stevie refolded the dollar bill lengthwise, pressing it crisp. "Well, Brian, we've had another great revival. You've got a good group of converts, maybe even a few tongue talkers. God willing, maybe we'll do this again next year."

"Bless you, Fred. Have a safe trip home. Thanks again for preaching."

Stevie tucked the dollar in his jeans pocket as the men of God hugged and said goodbye.

Then Fred started the flatbed truck and began to pull out of the gravel parking lot and head down Albion's narrow back roads. The CD player whirled to life, blaring the song "Spirit in the Sky" before Fred could turn it down.

"I love that song. You believe that, don't you, Stevie? You've got a friend, Jesus?" Smiling, Fred shook his head up and down to the beat.

"Yes, sir. Momma says Jesus loves us." Stevie looked straight ahead to watch the line on the road pass by.

"Yes, He does, and don't you ever forget it." Fred reached over and patted Stevie's shoulder. "I'm parched. What do you say we stop and get a bottle of pop?"

Pop? What a treat! Stevie grinned, working his tongue around a loose molar. "Sure, sir. Can I have a Moon Pie too?" They rarely had money for extras like Moon Pies and pops at home. "Pastor, what is a tongue talker?"

"You know... I'd like a Moon Pie too. Let's see. Hmm, how can I explain tongue talker? They speak God's language, and He hears them. Some can sense the spirits too, dreamwalkers the old-timers called the spirits. Those that are good, God shows them, down in here." He patted his stomach.

"You see, we live in a world at war. There are dreamwalkers, good guys, and then there's powers and principalities, demons, the bad guys. The good guys are God's helpers, who we know as the heavenly hosts or ministering spirits, along with the Holy Spirit, who is God too. We know the Holy Spirit wins, but the bad guys, the demons, and satanic forces, are trying to steal our souls to keep us from heaven."

Confused, Stevie pulled a face.

And the pastor laughed. "That's probably more than you can understand now, but I'm loving your enthusiasm for God, son. So you just keep learning and trusting God more, okay?"

"Yes, sir. I like hearing about the angels and God." And thinking about the Moon Pies and Pop.

Fred drove for another minute or so, smiling, coming to Mrs. Grilton's country store.

"Yep," DR whispered. "I can see it even now...."

The store's paint had almost faded into oblivion. There, on the back roads of Albion, that seemed to be the way then. The economy was slowing from its boom days. Factories shuttered, moved south or to China, away from the union labor in the north. Still, some parts of Albion were booming like the local college. Their enrollment increased every year. The downtown businesses thrived on the students. Still did...

Mrs. Grilton came out of the back when they entered her store. Apron pockets full of string beans, she slid her feet along the floor, and her gray-haired head bobbed with the motion. "I heard it's been a good week at the revival."

Fred nodded and reached for the pies.

"Somebody said over eighty-two people came up. That right, Pastor?"

After Fred had gotten them both a Moon Pie and an RC Cola, he put the money on the counter and winked at Stevie. "Yes, ma'am. It's been a good week. The Spirit was moving, choosing, and calling. Ninety-one souls. The church will do a great job helping them too. Pastor Brian, he's a real man of God."

"You've done a good job, Pastor." She scooped up the money. "I attended a few nights. I hadn't seen that many people saved in years."

"Thank you, but it was all the Holy Spirit. He put the fear in them. All I did was throw in the line where He showed me."

"I guess you're heading home now. Well... you be safe." She shuffled toward the back, stopping at the back-wall sink to get something.

They went over to a table by the checkerboard positioned near one of the two large potbelly stoves she kept burning. As they sat and enjoyed their snacks, they watched Butch and Bernie, the Griltons' cat, and dog in the nearby corner. Bernie, an old hound dog, stretched out on the sagging wood floor, wagging his tail. Each time his tail crashed to the floor, the noise seemed to gong for another of those hundred years the dog must've lived. Butch, their orange tabby kitten, slapped at that tail and now and then pounced on it. He put his head down, stuck his tail high into the air, and after shaking it sideways a few times, bounded straight up, trying to catch the dog's tail. Stevie and Fred laughed until their sides split.

The front door opened with a squeak, and as Bill stepped into the light where he could see well, he nodded to Stevie and Fred.

Looking back, DR could guess what Bill had been drinking at the Snuggery, a little hole-in-the-wall more like a shack. You could get bootleg whiskey if you were a regular and local. It was cheaper and got faster results. The Snuggery bought it by the barrelful, a gallon jug at a time, bringing it up from the foothills of Virginia. It was Franklin County 'shine, "finest in all the land."

"Well, hello. Fancy seeing you here with the preacher man. Where's your dad?" Standing a good distance from the preacher, Bill scuffled his feet like someone feeling guilty.

"Hi, Uncle Bill." Stevie waved with his RC. "They all went home. I helped Pastor load his truck. Guess what? He gave me a dollar—a *whole* dollar—and bought me a Moon Pie and a soda!"

"Well now, that is a treat." Bill eyed the preacher, and his voice dipped into a grumble, barely audible. "They normally don't give, do they? Only take, take, take."

"Okay, Stevie. That was a good snack, but I'd better get you home before your mom and dad start to worry."

"Yes, sir." Stevie hopped off his stool, looking back at Butch and Bernie as his uncle lumbered to the counter. "Thanks for the pop and snack. It was fun."

"You're very welcome. It was my good pleasure, especially for such a fine young helper." Fred clamped a hand on Stevie's shoulder. "I look at you, and I see such promise in your eyes. God's going to you use you mightily."

Bill paused at his words.

Saying goodbye, they descended the cracked and crumbling cement steps.

"Be careful, watch your step, and don't fall," Fred instructed, and Stevie took them one at a time.

"Mrs. Grilton says she's been putting off repairs. Her husband has the gout, and she don't know how long they'll stay open anyways." He skipped the last two, landing on his feet. "They're the only store this far back from town. And business isn't what it used to be, Dad said."

"True enough. A few years and maybe they'll be a thing of the past too."

Fred had parked over by the air pump because of the size of his truck, so he and Stevie had a good walk across the dirt and gravel parking lot.

As they walked, Bill exited the store, waved his arms, and shouted. "You know, Pastor, I'd be more than happy to take him up with me. I'm going to see his dad. Makes no sense in you driving it too. Besides, it's getting dark. If you don't know the roads up there, you could get lost."

Fred tipped his head to one side, looking Uncle Bill up and down, then stretched out a hand with a grin. "That's mighty thoughtful of you. Stevie, are you okay going with your uncle, or do you want me to ride you up there?"

He mustn't have been able to smell the booze on Bill.

"Aw, sure." Stevie slid his hand into his pocket, still tasting Moon Pie and cola. The dollar bill crinkled beneath his fingertips.

"Alrighty then. Thanks, Bill." Fred hugged Stevie, then tousled his hair. "I'll see you next time I come through, son."

With a nod at the evangelist, Stevie scrambled toward Bill's car. Once red, now the thing could only boast a shade of pink. He yanked the door open, quick to climb in before slowing his uncle down. He gave one last wave to Fred before the man of God went bouncing down the back roads.

Stevie settled into Bill's car, crinkling his nose at the reek of cigarettes and alcohol, losing the wonderful flavor of the night's excitement—Moon Pies and pop and kittens and hound-dog tails. The old Caprice's interior, worn and filthy, appeared like someone was living in it.

When Stevie held his nose, Bill chortled and slapped Stevie's back. "Now, it's not that bad, is it?"

"Uncle Bill." Stevie lowered his hand from his nose, craning his neck as Bill made the turn from the lot. "Why are we going back to the church?"

"I left my jacket. Someone might get it if I don't go back for it now."

The drive lasted forever. Stevie scooched as close to the door as he could, but his uncle began reaching for him, trying to love on him. Stevie was trapped with nowhere to go, so Bill would get his way.

The daydream always ended, still, many years later, with a flood of tears cascading down his cheeks. No one else knew about it. He'd never told anybody except his daddy, but his mom knew too.

Stevie told his dad the night of the first attack. But Dad never did anything about it. Stevie overheard him talking to Mom.

"I don't want people to hear about Bill or Stevie, especially at church," Dad had said, not knowing Stevie was listening outside their door. "What would they think about Stevie—or us?"

"Mike, he attacked our son. He molested my boy. You've got to call the police. You gotta do something. What's wrong with you? Don't you love your little boy?"

"You know I love Stevie, but I can't. No, I just can't. Now let it go, Tammy Rae. Leave Bill alone—you hear me? It's something I'll have to live with, so that's all I want to hear about it. Do you understand? And this will have to be our secret, you hear me?"

Nothing would be done. Not now, not ever.

Stevie leaned against the wall outside their bedroom, crying, afraid Bill would come back. Stevie would no longer be himself. He'd heard it all, and it seared into his memory. He'd never told Gail or anyone, just his dad. Mom wanted to call the police but had to act like she didn't know anything.

Bill came by their house again two years later when Steven was eleven. His mother was outside picking tomatoes and cucumbers from the garden, and Steven was alone watching his brothers. His dad had never gone to the police. Steven made sure no one touched his brothers, even hiding them to protect them. Each time, something inside told him when and where to take them.

"Better not tell your dad again, or it'll be your little brothers next time. Besides, your dad doesn't want to ruin his good Christian name," Bill threatened, laughing about the tongue talkers and dreamwalkers as he left....

The wine helped. Now, DR could sleep.

Early the next day, the movers carted away most of their furniture and possessions, leaving the lake house almost empty with just a few pieces of furniture to live on. The sale sign would go up, and the best chapters of his life would close. Soon, his new adventure halfway around the world would begin—just as he and Gail had planned, with a few tweaks.

CHAPTER
FOUR

After visiting with his family, DR needed a break. A break from Delton, family, and do-gooders. Malaga was getting closer by the minute. As he dropped off his Jeep at a dealership in Ann Arbor, a light rain began falling, an appropriate end for this sad chapter. He hired a driver to take him the remaining forty-five minutes to Detroit for his flight.

On the plane, he daydreamed about Marsala, about his adventure. Too bad, Nicolas and Mekie weren't coming along. He could be himself with them, but he felt like an outsider in Delton.

The skyway to the luggage area was open, and the salty scent of the Mediterranean awakened his senses. With the skies clear, things were looking up as he was met with the longest, tightest, and warmest hugs he could remember. Ever since he'd followed Gail to Malaga and confessed his love for her, her parents loved and supported him.

Monday morning came too fast, but with Nicolas's help, DR put the rest of his plans, once just a dream, on paper. Now he had to execute them. Should be easy enough.

"Do you really want to add that rule? I don't know." Nicolas shook his head, checking out the passengers' photos DR had copied to send to each of the passengers so they could familiarize themselves with the others. Along with contact information and the rules, which included the soon-to-be dreaded "no romancing the passengers," DR also sent a list of housekeeping duties they could select to volunteer to help with during the cruise.

"Yes. There has to be some order on board. Otherwise, male egos and tempers might get involved. When Gail and I joined the team after getting married, I watched the eyes and attitudes of the other men. Their jealousy helped separate the team." He shuffled the pictures and lists into manila envelopes, ready to mail.

The next day, they drove DR to the airport, and he was on his way. He loaded his luggage in the airport cart, and while the porter rolled it away, he reached for his in-laws with both arms. "I wish you guys were coming along."

"We will see you soon. We love you."

"I love you both too."

Boarding the plane, he found his seat beside a young lady with a baby. Great, there'd be no sleeping on this flight, but maybe the baby wouldn't be a crier. At least it was asleep now, but what were the odds a baby could sleep the entire way?

With the baby nestled on her shoulder, the mother introduced herself as Kim Ricci, an American who'd moved to Marsala five years earlier after marrying a local. She shifted the kid lower on her navy tank top, her shoulder-length curly brown hair bouncing over the baby's face. Her skin, tanned a deep bronze, made her brown eyes seem even darker. "It's nice to have this one sleeping more than twenty minutes at a time finally. The first six months, all you do is focus on them. Now, I can relax and enjoy some adult conversation."

Probably good that he and Gail never had a kid. DR eyed the boy's long lashes against pudgy cheeks. He'd never be able to take care of one of those little guys by himself.

"We're heading back home. My husband's been tied up at a conference the last four days, so I went over to see some of my girlfriends. It's the first time I've taken Corey. It's not quite as easy traveling with him, but the girls all loved making over him. How about you? Have you ever been to Marsala before?"

"No. It just happened to be the best place for me to start my next venture." He twisted halfway around in his seat to talk to her.

"What type of venture?"

"I'm putting together a cruise to India and other places I used to explore with my wife. We're starting out in Jeddah and then stopping in a few of India's port cities."

"Oh... So you're in travel and hospitality? Is your wife coming too?"

"Actually, I'm an archaeologist. I'm just switching gears, taking others with similar backgrounds and passion to see some of the wonders I've experienced." He peered out into space. "My wife won't be coming. She passed on over a year ago. We loved sailing and exploring, so I'm following some of our plans and striking out again. I may start exploring, digging, in the future, but for now... Well, I just want to travel, to sail the seas."

"I'm so sorry about your wife." She ducked her head and tucked her boy's arm back into the snuggly. "Well, it all sounds like fun. We love sailing too. If I can help in any way, I'll be glad to. My family knows a lot of people in and around the area. My Marco may be able to help—he has friends and connections in the major shipping companies around Marsala—and some of the society ladies in Marsala may want to help you. They seem to know just about everyone or everything that goes on in the city." She waved a finger at him and raised an eye suggestively. "But that can bring its own set of problems, especially for such a handsome widower."

"Thanks, Kim. In America, it helps to know someone, but in the European and Middle Eastern countries, it can be a lifesaver."

Their three-hour flight was already ending, and Kim was rising, shifting her now-waking son to her shoulder again as she slung her carry-on over her other shoulder.

"It's so nice to meet someone from home and be able to talk." She held out her hand. "I miss Houston. Life's so different here, but I love it. We'd enjoy having you come visit with us so we could hear more about your adventure. We're always looking for something different to try. Maybe Marco could help connect you with some of his friends."

"That would be sweet. I'd love to get together." Standing to the side, he moved his carry-on to make room as another passenger squeezed by.

"I'll check with him first. I never know when his schedule might change." She jostled her son as the boy started fussing. "Marco's days are straightforward unless they have luncheons or dinners."

"That sounds great. I'm already looking forward to meeting him. Here, let me carry that." He scooped the shoulder bag from her before it dropped, then balanced it while he scribbled on a business card. "Here's the number I'm staying at. I'll be in and out, but you can always reach me on my cell phone."

He helped her to the chauffeured car before returning her bag, then strolled a short distance to the taxi stand. On the ride to his hotel, he was able to stretch out his legs after the cramped airplane seating. Maybe this would all pan out. Kim seemed social, but maybe it was too good to be true—who knew if a word she said was factual anyway.

The taxi driver eyed him in the rearview mirror. "American, yes?" A grin stretched out his already wide mouth when DR nodded. "Welcome to Marsala—most beautiful beaches in the Mediterranean, yes? It lives up to the name the Moors gave it so many centuries ago— Port of God, Marsa Allah. Such a rich culture we have here, sir. A vibrant Arab influence woven into society, history, food, and architecture. Oh, yes, good sir, nowhere will you find a port like Port of God."

"Great." DR craned his neck to take in the city's busy seaport located to facilitate commercial and private traffic. "I'll be able to find the yacht I'm looking for here."

The words *Port of God* whispered around him.

As he twisted back around, his thoughts slid to his Tuesday-morning appointment to inspect an Italian vessel named the *SiCillian Summer Escape*, a 140-foot yacht. Would it be as promising as it looked online?

Even as DR organized his rendezvous of past discoveries with an adventure on the sea, in Hollywood, more deadly plans were being made to bring down the US president. He wouldn't be allowed to win another four years, no matter the cost. Worlds would collide soon as dangerous plots by some of the world's elite could set a new course, a new destiny. DR's hopes, dreams, and adventure, along with months of preparation, soon to be trashed.

When DR rang the bell on the front desk, Luigi Cancio, the marina's manager, and oldest salesman, came forward to shake his hand. Apparently, he'd been waiting for their appointment. "Welcome, welcome, senor!" Luigi flicked back a hunk of once black hair, now graying. His blue eyes had also faded after years of Mediterranean sun. "I hope your travels have been well, sì? We have wonderful yachts to show you today, including the *SiCillian Summer*. But first, let me show you the *Italian Retreat*. It's docked right here at the marina. This thirty-meter vessel has all the bells and whistles."

Though its size wasn't enough, DR let the man guide him through it, considering all the luxury items Luigi rambled off, before DR pointed out its shortcomings. "I'd rather have too much, than not enough."

"Yes, Mr. Ray." Luigi bowed, his obsequious manner making DR wonder. With the guy's long history at the port, surely not all of it was good. "I'm afraid I must agree. Let's take the golf cart for a short ride to see your prize."

"Please, call me DR." DR bent himself and tucked his long legs into the cart. "I hear Mr. Ray, and I'm looking around for my dad."

"Very well. As you wish... DR." Luigi pushed down on the cart's fuel pedal. It leapt forward, and after about five minutes of friendly conversation and enjoying the sights, they arrived where the *SS* was docked. Having permission to tour the yacht, they climbed aboard.

Heart racing, DR wanted to pinch himself. "She's incredible, well worth the golf-cart ride."

"She is, sir—DR. Her price is also, um, shall we say incredible? But she's worth every cent. When cruising through the Suez Canal, her size of forty meters and power will be an asset. Her four decks are all custom designed, and the antenna and satellite deck over the helm is ideal for a water cannon. As you know, special attention to security always pays off in the Indian Ocean and the canal. Even if you never, God forbid, come under attack, the peace of mind far outweighs saving a few dollars." Luigi stretched himself taller. "The *SiCillian Summer* is the only vessel in the area for sale that can deliver everything on your must-have list."

DR breathed in the salty Mediterranean air. The dock was much nicer here in the high-rent gated community. No small yachts or homes, only the wealthiest of the wealthy. So it would come with a price, which Luigi soon confirmed.

"The price... um, is twelve million euros. You had a different budget in mind, sì? Most do, but where you're planning to travel is particularly active now. Just last month, terrorists attacked a smaller vessel in the Red Sea." He patted the vessel's stainless steel Sub-Zero refrigerator. "Besides, look at her. She is one in a million."

Unfolding his arms, DR ran an admiring touch along the galley's cherrywood finish. The builders spared no expense, for sure, choosing only the best materials and top-of-the-line appliances. He followed Luigi along the plush passageway to the captain's quarters, turning in a circle to see it from all angles. The airy space offered a pleasing grandeur, and oversized port windows allowed for excellent views and natural light.

"Yes, I heard about that incident too." He tilted his head back to study the recessed lighting.

"We didn't use to see such things happen much. But the pirates are getting desperate—and bolder. The US-Iranian sanctions are cutting the pirates and terrorists off from money." Luigi rocked back on his heels, his portly belly jiggling. "So, they have to steal more to feed their plots."

"I'm hiring a security firm to equip my vessel, but I want to speak to Marco Ricci first. He may have inside information and connections with the best company."

"Ah, yes..." Luigi's Italian accent dragged the words out as they rounded the top step and entered the bridge. "You know Marco. Well, why didn't you say so? He is a friend of ours and helps us very much. Maybe I can do something extra for a friend of Marco's, yes? So how do you like the bridge? She has all of today's modern electronics."

"I don't know Marco. I mean... well, I've met his wife on the plane here. Kim invited me to meet Marco. She suggested he might be able to help me cut through some red tape. You know what it's like getting through the canal, how knowing the right people and procedures can get you through much quicker." DR slung himself into the plush leather captain's chair. "I love the bridge. The whole vessel's top shelf. A little more than I want to spend, but maybe you can help me?"

"Of course, we'll get their best price for you. It's what I do." But Luigi's sideways glance had DR wondering. "Yes, and I know Marco. He is a good man. If his wife likes you, he will like you too. Someone was looking over you when you sat beside Kim on that plane."

After a two-hour tour of the vessel, they trundled back in the golf cart to the marina. Luigi looked DR over, obviously still trying to sound out his thoughts.

DR shifted uneasily. Indeed, why was all this falling into place? Every time things started to go well, something knocked it off track. Still... As Luigi stopped at the marina, DR stayed in his seat rubbing his jaw. "I... I'll have you work on the price for me. I think she's the one."

"Excellent. I'll get that number for you, and remember, when you decide she's the one, you can have her immediately." Luigi tossed the cart key in its key slot, then reached to shake DR's hand. "So, I'll go get that price and let you know the exact amount. Check back this evening."

DR strode toward his one-o'clock appointment with another first-mate candidate. With the passengers all lined up, now all he needed was his crew. Dressed in jean shorts, he'd told Gabriele to come dressed casually too. Who needed formality in interviews? After all, they'd be on the *Disillusioned Illusion* for long periods of time, and he was all about building relationships. The sun shone over his shoulder as he strolled the ancient stone walkway.

In Delton, Willie ground her teeth as Mike leaned back in his chair and drummed his hands on his desk in rhythm with the rain pounding at his window. The chill was on—and not just outside.

"You know DR blamed me." Red mottled Mike's face. "He said I never should've left him alone with 'that woman.' He ranted for fifteen minutes about you."

Mike glared at her. "He told me you were *supposedly* a friend of Gail's, more likely a pushy liar that had better keep 'her goody-two-shoes attitude' away from him. Do you know how long it's been since DR and I had a good conversation like that?" He shoved away from the desk. "Now you've destroyed the whole evening. You never know when to quit."

The side door opened, and Giggles, the station's manager, stepped in between them—again. "Guys, tone it down a notch, okay?" She gave them each a look. "You're my A-team. As you're my hosts for the Early Morning Drive show, I need you to be a cohesive pair. Especially now that the broadcast institute's ratings are coming out. So come on, *puhleeese*. The station needs the highest ratings possible to maintain our advertising purposes."

Mike nodded as Giggles walked away.

Willie crossed her arms. She didn't need to be treated like a novice. They all knew every review was money and WREAL, although Christian, was a commercial station, not donor-driven. The ratings could make or break their year.

Giggles, the owner's daughter, had stepped in between them before. Willie... Well, sometimes she just didn't know when to stop. Didn't mean she'd apologize for it.

"I don't get it." Mike raked a hand through his hair and faced Willie, keeping his voice low. "I'm warning you—let it go. He doesn't want to hear it, and neither do I."

She jammed her hands on her hips, fighting the urge to, well, *fight*. Then her lips quirked. "You're pretty headstrong too." *Seriously, God, the jerk still thinks the success of the morning show is because of him.*

She winced as a twinge of conscience reminded her they both should know to give God the credit, being a Christian station. *Sorry, God. I guess arrogance can pop up anywhere—doesn't mean I'm ready to apologize yet.*

"Years ago..." Mike's shoulders deflated. The color drained from his face, and the heat seeped from his voice. He rubbed the pinched space between his brows. "I asked Dad what happened to DR, why he hated God so much. Dad only stiffened his jaw, and that was that. But it's not, Willie. There's something there. DR doesn't even like being called by his given name anymore. Somewhere, something turned him—and I warned you before we went in the coffeehouse not to push anything."

"I get it." She came around to the other side where Mike sat. She almost reached to touch his arm, a peace-offering gesture he probably wouldn't accept right now. "I do. But you gotta see my side too. I've seen your brother through Gail's eyes—a man who was faithful, supportive, and above all, capable of loving a woman the way she needs it... and the way I'd want it."

Pushing a pile of advertising brochures to the side, she leaned against his desk. *Did I really say that?*

"What in the world are you talking about?" He twirled around in his chair to get a better look at her. "Have you lost your mind?" His lips flattened as he leaned forward to grab his cup of cold coffee left over from breakfast.

"See? I do know him. Gail told me all about their courtship, how he wasn't chasing after the girls like all the other boys, how he was her friend long before becoming her lover." She slid her hip onto the desk. *Where am I going with this?* "A man like that, a man who can celebrate the woman he loves—he's just got to be..." But she shut up.

Mike eyed her, then looked down inside the coffee cup, and set it on the far side of the desk. He spread out his hands and motioned for her to continue.

Knowing where this was going, she slumped back off the desk and bit her lip. No way would she say more.

DR was even more handsome now at thirty-one, his sandy hair still so crazy thick, and his eyes deep enough to search your soul. *Face it, girl. You're attracted to him like no other man you've ever met.* Maybe it was because of his great physique and dark tan, his inner man, or did Gail plant a seed? Whatever it was, these feelings—these inconvenient desires... Well, she just had them. *Is it futile?*

"You can lay off, Mike. It's not like I'm gonna see him again or speak to him. I get it. I was too forceful in declaring my message, but it felt like God was pushing me too. I know I'm too headstrong." Would God let her find that true love she so wanted and needed? Had she saved herself in vain?

Mike softened, stood, and pulled her into his arms, slapping her back in an awkward man hug. "Sorry. No reason to let this squabble be the end of a successful friendship."

He smelled like DR. She scooted back as if burned. No, God was a rewarder of those who seek, who knock, and who ask. She wasn't going to start losing faith now... or its hope. But did God have another way for her, and she just missed it?

At twenty-seven, she'd never known a man. Her desires for DR were starting to drive her thoughts to places she'd rarely been. *God, You'd better give me the grace.*

The interviews Mike set up with DR would begin next Tuesday—if DR didn't change his mind. They'd set the calls for once a week. The planning had to begin now since DR would be on the high seas.

Without Willie—of course.

CHAPTER
FIVE

Now, going to meet Gabriele better be productive. DR strode toward Cannoli Café, a mom-and-pop pasta house and bar that Kim promised served "the best sangria in all of Italy."

He rounded the corner, the café just ahead on the right, then slowed his steps. The police had arrived too. Somebody, an older man, was lying on the ground while another man, much younger, was being handcuffed.

Great, probably Gabriele. Things had been going too smoothly.

Rolling his eyes, DR maneuvered past them and stepped inside. His eyes adjusted to the dim lighting as he gathered himself. Wow, the pizza smelled awesome. Ah, there it was—the handkerchief over the edge of a table, their sign to find each other.

He crossed the space, his fisherman's sandals slapping the hardwood flooring, then reached his hand out. "Hello... Gabriele? Hi, I'm Steven Ray, but please, call me DR."

Gabriele rose to shake his hand. "I'm pleased to meet you. Please, join me."

DR studied him. Gabriele pulled at his eyebrow and sometimes looked away when he spoke. Was he trying to hide something? He reminded DR of a wacky shrink on one of those Christmas shows about Santa Claus.

"So, your resume said you're from Spain. How long have you lived in Marsala?"

"Actually, I misspoke. I didn't understand at the time that you were looking for someone from this area." Gabriele lit a cigarette, not being polite, not asking DR if he'd mind.

He did. He detested cigarette smoke more than he detested Christians, but he didn't say anything.

Gabriele described his experience working on vessels sailing from Marsala. After about an hour, DR said he'd give the meeting serious thought. The cigarette thing was a sticking point. And the shiftiness, the eyebrow thing. He'd have to interview another candidate.

His next appointment wasn't until five thirty, leaving him time to get fresh air by the beach. Seemingly moments later, his phone alarm rang, and his stomach rumbled along with it. Dinner better be better than the pizza earlier. He clipped along the five-minute walk from his hotel to the café and stepped into a bustling atmosphere, the dinner crowd coming in and some happy-hour folks already happy.

Lorenzo promised to use the handkerchief trick. Without it, DR may have taken a while to locate the guy stuck in a nook near the back.

Hmm... Lorenzo could be a quarterback. Six foot four, maybe just under two twenty, he had dark-black hair trimmed like a sailor's should be and dark eyes alight, seemingly dancing with excitement—also like a sailor's should be.

"Lorenzo?" DR extended a hand.

"Hello, DR." Lorenzo stood to shake hands. "I hope this table is okay. It's all they had when I came in."

"Sure, this is great." DR slid into the loop-backed chair and slapped the red-and-white checkered tablecloth. "It's out of the way and comfortable. Now if the service is as good as everything smells, we'll be in cotton."

"It's been great so far. Here, try one of these olives. You won't find any fresher ones around." Lorenzo slid the bowl toward DR and gestured toward it as the waitress approached.

She began smiling and twisting as if she were going to dance. "Lorenzo," she sang out the guy's name in a musical tone, her fingers tucking wisps of long black hair back into her bun. "I see your date made it."

"Oh, and don't pay Cillia any thought either. She's my sister and always stirring things up." Rolling his eyes, Lorenzo shook his head.

Pretty, warm, and friendly, the girl exemplified everything DR expected in an Italian waitress, her loving attitude radiant in the aura surrounding her.

"My brother is excited to meet you. It's all he has talked about for days." She poked at Lorenzo with a sharp red fingernail. "Can I bring you a drink? Or maybe an appetizer before ordering?"

"I need a moment." Caught off guard, DR motioned to Lorenzo. "Are you ready to order? My treat."

"Thank you, but no, I have a long drive later. Sis here needs a ride after work. The men here get, well, how should we say? Um, carried away after having a couple glasses of booze."

"Isn't he so sweet?" Cillia cocked her hip against the table and rubbed her brother's back. "The world's best brother. Okay, I'll be back to get your order."

"Well, you weren't wrong." DR grinned at his companion. "Not only is the service great but we're also attended by lively conversation. Now, if the food's just as good—"

"Oh, it is. I recommended the cannoli."

"Have you and your sister always been this close?"

"No." Lorenzo drummed his hands on the tabletop. "Not until my sickness three years ago."

Sickness? DR bit back the question. "I didn't mean to pry. It's just you seem so close, and it's good to see."

"It's old news now, and I've learned so much since. Besides, if I get the job, you'll find out. I contracted a virus while at sea in the navy. It went into my liver somehow, and I almost died. The virus destroyed most of my liver before I even knew I was ill. I needed a new liver, or it was good night nurse. Sis, my beautiful sis, ended up being a match and gave me a portion of hers, risking her own life for mine."

"That is true love." DR leaned back in his seat, brows raised. "So, how is your liver now? Will sailing on long voyages cause you any concerns or health issues?"

Lorenzo traced a line along the checked tablecloth. "It took about a year, but I'm recovered now. But I do worry about Sis. She's still alone, and I ought to watch out for her too."

"We'll be out to sea for at least three, four, even five weeks at a time, maybe longer?" DR cocked his head, studying the guy. "Can you be gone that long without worrying too much?"

"No worries." Lorenzo waved. "I have to get used to being away. Besides, she'll like being rid of her smother brother."

Soon, Cillia sauntered back. "You boys come up with what you want?" When they both ordered a light sandwich, she laughed and wagged a finger between them. "Making it easy on me, are you?"

Watching her bound away, DR rolled his shoulders, shoulders still weighed down, even now. "I wish I still had her outlook on life. It's as if she doesn't have a care in the world." His weight constantly followed him, night, and day. No matter where he ran, the anchor never let go, an accuser stood by, especially since Gail died.

They laughed, then settled down to discuss the upcoming voyage.

"One of the main things I'm looking for is someone with skills to help with port authorities."

"I get that. Procedures can be daunting." Lorenzo leaned back in his chair, lifting the front legs off the wood floor, and crossed his arms over his chest. "From the itinerary you outlined, I also imagine you'd want someone who knows the canal and has contacts with the Felix agents?"

Man, this sounded too good to be true. DR let the makings of a smile show, sizing up his companion. He pushed his hair back. "I take it you have those contacts?"

"I do. As second-in-command of an Italian navy destroyer's

navigation team, you get to know the people you deal with. In case you don't remember my résumé, I also speak three languages besides Italian—kinda a must for international sailing, don't you think?"

"That would depend on what they are?"

"Spanish and Arabic, as well as English obviously. Which you can see I'm fluent in from our conversation."

Several hours later, DR left the café. If everything checked out, he'd found his first mate.

The next morning, he rolled out of bed with things looking good. Today, unless something went wrong, he'd get his *Disillusioned Illusion.*

Senator Carl Brummengarten leaned back in his plush leather chair in DC, not risking the speakerphone for this conversation.

"You have information about the whereabouts of the entertainers I ordered, for my club?"

"Yes, sir." Carl fumbled to shift his grip on the cell phone. The dang thing was so small. "They're in Aden, Yemen. I've sent my boat. Our friends will transport the entertainers to the club. I'm sorry, but—"

"Senator, don't give me any excuses. Now I know why this country is so screwed up. You can't even plan to transport twelve kids from Yemen on time. Make sure it happens—and soon. My guests are looking forward to some foreign entertainment."

"I'm on top of it."

The phone went dead.

Carl slumped back in his chair. The jerk was so arrogant. *I'm a US senator. I don't have to take his abuse.*

If only that were true.

Walking to the marina, DR enjoyed the early morning air as he sipped a piping hot cup of black coffee. Herring gulls fought for every crumb the early morning walkers unknowingly dropped outside a pastry shop. DR hugged the rail to avoid the shop now swamped with the pesky scavengers. After a few more steps, he turned into the marina's sales area and rang the bell. "Luigi, are you back there?"

Luigi emerged carrying a box of souvenir key chains and fanny packs to lure tourists. He crossed to the spinner rack, placed the box on his work cart, then started hanging the key chains. "Oh, DR, you're early."

DR approached and winced at Luigi's creased brow. "Something's changed?"

"Sì. I'm afraid I have news. Not good news either. The *SiCillian Summer*'s owner passed on a few days ago. His son, he still wants to sell her, yes."

Here we go again. DR brought his hands over his mouth, breathing deeply, exhaling loudly. *Fate always finds a way.* "So then what's the problem?"

"Well, first, the estate must be settled, yes? I've contacted the lawyers, but you know how slow they can be to return a man's call." Luigi put down the trinket. "The yacht may be held up in the courts now, without a little... lubrication."

"Really?" DR held out his hands, then turned in a circle of disgust.

"DR, I'm sorry." Luigi stepped closer and clapped a hand on DR's shoulder. "We must wait until we get a word before we can proceed. Can you give the *Italian Retreat* more thought?"

"I can't work with her size." DR put his hands behind his head and tousled his hair. Then he drew his elbows together in front of him and pulled his head downward while rubbing his cheeks. "When do you expect to hear back from the seller?"

"Let me give them another call." Luigi pushed up his jacket sleeve and tilted his watch face into view. "I don't know if he'll work with us any on the price, not like his dad would have." He hung the last key chain, then went to make the call.

As Luigi walked away, DR's cell phone rang. He slid it from his khaki shorts pocket and swiped the screen. Kim's contact flashed as he answered.

"Hi, DR. Remember me? Kim from the plane? I've spoken with Marco, and we'd love to have lunch—today, maybe?"

"That sounds great. I need something to perk me up."

"Bad day?"

"Just a disappointment." He massaged his temples, then pivoted to face the *SiCillian Summer*, now out of his reach and view, far beyond the marina. "When and where would you recommend?"

"I'll do more than recommend." Her bright laugh jittered through. "You see, I already made reservations. Eleven forty-five, Harbor House Café. Can you find it? It's a couple of blocks up from the marina."

"That's perfect. I'm at the marina now—oh, excuse me, Kim. The marina manager is headed my way. I'll see you soon."

"Sounds good, and bring your troubles. Who knows, maybe we can help."

Luigi extended both hands and clasped one of DR's. "I got through. Maybe we'll know something by the end of the day. They still want to sell her."

When they stepped out onto the pier, a seagull squawked as they impeded his meal, and the ocean brine intensified. The *Italian Retreat* came into full view, rocking to and fro, and DR's chest tightened. He had to have the *SS* and none other. "I'm meeting with the Riccis for lunch today. Marco might help me line something up. Having all the contacts I need will be a great start anyway."

With the sun rising toward its midpoint and a breeze rocking the boats, the shimmering water beckoning. Ahh... so close to a perfect day.

"What timing." Luigi slapped his hands together. "Maybe Marco can help. He knows the magistrate. May I go with you? I haven't seen him in some time."

"Let me call Kim just to make sure." DR fished his phone out again, turning sideways for privacy. The sailboats swayed in the water, their ropes and cords ringing out as their bindings banged on the masts. A sweet sound to a sailor.

"Kim, hi."

She laughed. "Canceling on me already?"

The baby was crying.

"Ha, not a chance. Would it be too much trouble if I brought Luigi Cancio along? He said he'd like to see Marco again. I guess they know each other."

"I know Luigi too." Kim fussed with the kid. "He used to be close to Marco's dad, but something happened between them. Let me call Marco. We have reservations, so there'll be room if Marco allows."

Okay, he may have tacked onto the wrong wind here. With the phone pressed to his ear, he edged further from Luigi. "If that's a problem, I can just tell him no."

"Shh, Corey, it's okay. Um, yeah, DR, that might be better. You know how these things can be. Marco is looking forward to meeting you and hearing about your travel plans. You can't imagine how much he wishes he could join you."

"Well, I can't wait to meet him. I'll see you soon." He disconnected and let out a low breath. Man, that kid had a set of lungs on him. Good thing he'd slept through the plane trip.

"Sorry, Luigi. Seems like their table is full already." This may be a special connection with one of the most influential families in Marsala, at least according to many of the harbor merchants.

Luigi's lips pressed into a thin line. Then he huffed, clearly unhappy being left out. "I'll keep calling about the yacht. We'll get this done."

"Who knows, Luigi?" DR kidded, walking out. "He may know of a better vessel. One that costs less too. I'll talk to you soon."

The shops and businesses along the pier were getting crowded. Lunch was only a short walk away, and he made the most of it. Most of the people on the pier were tradesmen, although families with their children lingered, the kids squealing, running up and down the pier. The scents of pizza, cannoli, and seafood began to make him hungry, his Cheerios breakfast long gone. As he leaned against the pier's wood railing, breathing in the scenery, a sense of something stirred him. The clouds came for the sun, whisked by sudden gusts of wind, and a swoosh rushed by.

Minutes later, sun umbrellas shaded pier-side tables as DR approached Harbor House Café. Nice. They served fresh oysters alfresco by the sea. Norman Rockwell couldn't have painted it better.

"DR, over here." Kim waved, and the man beside her appeared a lot older than DR expected. No, that couldn't be Marco. She sprang from her seat and hugged DR like a true Southern belle, long and tight. Wow, she was prettier than he remembered, her curly hair blowing in the wind and her figure scarcely concealed in her white sundress. Marco was a lucky man indeed.

She stepped back and rested a hand on the older man's shoulder. "I'd like to introduce you to my father-in-law, Miguel Ricci."

"Pleased to make your acquaintance." Miguel half rose from his seat to shake DR's hand, his height a good match to DR's. He smoothed graying hair back from a weathered but refined face as he sat down again. "Kim shared your new adventure, and I couldn't wait to hear more. I've loved the sea since I was a boy, and my wife, God rest her soul, also loved to sail. We practically raised Marco on a boat somewhere."

What a perfect connection. DR sank into the faux rattan chair across from his new friend. "I can imagine you've spent eons at sea— you've got a certain sea-ruggedness about you." What had Kim told him about Miguel? "Kim said you were captain of one of the Italian Cup Challenger Series teams back in the day. An accomplished sailor indeed."

Miguel's eyes sparkled, radiating a warm friendliness despite his obvious old money. He rested a hand atop hers. "Ah, it seems you've done some bragging about me, my dear."

"Of course. DR, Marco will be here shortly." Kim tucked curly hair behind her ears, the wind still teasing wisps free. "The mayor needed him to go over some of the changes on the municipal projects he's suggested for the city. And the mayor is always slow keeping his appointment, so Marco will be a bit late. That'll give us just enough time for my favorite, their blackberry sangria." She held her hand up to summon the server.

The young server sauntered over with an eager-to-please smile. Dark hair flowed with a liquid sheen to her shoulders. "I hope everyone here is enjoying this gorgeous day, so how can I make it even better? Might I suggest you start with sangria?"

Miguel rubbed his hands together, smiling like a man eager to dive into a project. "I can most heartily agree with that idea."

Why did the women here all have to look so good? It had been a while since he'd had relations with his wife. Maybe that was it. Must be the salty air. Something had awakened the man in him, but he had to squash those thoughts. Such little distractions could become big ones if left to their own desires. Kim's enticing perfume made it harder to stay focused.

"It's a little early for me." DR waved a hand. "But hey, I'm in Italy. Yes please and thank you—or should I say sì and grazie?"

The server returned with four blackberry sangrias, all topped with a wedge of fresh orange and blackberries tucked below the ice. She took their orders and left. Meanwhile, Miguel delved into DR's itinerary, wanting to know it all, every detail. "As you can tell"—Miguel picked up his drink and saluted DR with it—"this old sailor is eager to get back to the sea and, for the moment, must live vicariously through your dreams."

A glint in his eye suggested the gentleman was thinking of doing more than that, but DR kept the thought to himself.

A younger version of Miguel strolled toward them, lean, muscular, and very much as DR had pictured Marco, well almost. It wasn't hard to see why Kim left Houston.

He extended his hand to DR, then hugged him too.

Whoa. DR almost stiffened. These Italians were friendly.

Marco drew back and laughed. He leaned over and kissed Kim and patted her hand. "Please, everyone, forgive my tardiness. Why the mayor even bothers to schedule appointments some days is beyond me." He claimed the seat beside his wife, smoothed down his crisp tan slacks, and picked up the drink she'd ordered for him. Then he eyed DR over the rim. "Has Dad told you he'd like to accompany you on this voyage as a working passenger?"

"Ah, that's my Marco, always straight to the point. We haven't gotten that far. But seriously, DR, it's been some time since I've sailed through the canal, and the thought of going back to the Indian Ocean is... enticing. When my wife and I sailed to those places, we found them unlike anywhere else. It would be grand—yes, grand indeed!—to relive some of those trips. With you maybe?"

DR slapped the table, laughing. "Wow. This is an incredibly good fortune." Not only a perfect connection but maybe, just maybe, an experienced paying passenger too. God must be shining down on him —*No! Not God. Simply fate. It's my turn.*

Noon turned to dusk as they visited, eating, talking, laughing, building a friendship that might last for a lifetime of adventures.

"So..." Miguel slid his seat closer to DR. "Tell me about your vessel?"

"Ah, that." DR took a pause, lips pursed, and tried not to look foolish. "I've run into a... snafu."

Miguel clucked his tongue after DR shared what was going on. "I know Luigi. He's—how to say it politely? Not to be trusted. We'll work something out tomorrow to expedite the matter."

"See?" Kim clapped, bouncing in her seat. "I told you—my Marco and Miguel will help you."

"Luigi might have been able to come up with something today. I'd hate to trouble you guys if I don't have to." DR reached for his water glass. "I need to give him a call."

"The *SS* is a fine girl." Miguel leaned closer to the table. "I knew her previous owner. He died well over a year ago, so don't let Luigi pull his oldest trick on you. He'll tell you he can't discount or promise you anything, but if you put down the buyer's premium, they might be able to push it through."

Miguel pushed to his feet. "This has been a wonderful afternoon. But you tell him Miguel is going to go with you. Then we'll get this done."

Arching a brow, DR stood as well. "This is incredible indeed. That's the stunt he's trying. You guys... you're amazing. Can you cook too?"

They laughed, parting ways, not realizing how serious he was. Things were coming together. So why did he still feel like something unquenchable—fate—was hanging over his head?

CHAPTER
SIX

Enjoying the sun's last light, DR strolled back to his hotel. Mediterranean sunsets seemed to have a different glow. Maybe it's attitude, but man, what a beauty. He paused by a coin-operated observation viewer and hit the call icon on his phone, finding Luigi's contact.

"Luigi, it's DR." He broke in when Luigi answered. "I was wondering what you were able to find out?"

"Oh. Hi. Uh, DR, the seller is trying to get information out of his lawyers. The other beneficiaries may not agree with the sale price or disposition of the asset."

"That's okay." DR straightened himself and firmed his resolve. "Miguel was there today."

He smirked as he let that sink in. "He's going to help me get something sooner. In fact, he may be coming on the journey with me. Isn't that great news?"

Silence.

"Luigi... Luigi, are you still there?"

"I'm here."

"Isn't that wonderful news? I worried all day about postponing my sailing date and maybe losing my passengers and credibility. But it was like a gift from—well, you know what I mean."

"Well, that is good news." Luigi dragged his sentence out, probably trying to feel DR out to discover what Miguel had told him, perhaps thinking DR wouldn't be so calm if he'd uncovered the scam. "Um, does he know the owners or their lawyers? How does he think he can help you?"

DR scuffed the leather toe of his fisherman's sandal at a bent nail on the pier's edge, the sun fading over the harbor. "He didn't say. He may know of another yacht or two. I like the *SS*, though. Could you try again? Let them know there's a couple other vessels available, so I'm going to need their best deal."

Luigi let out a breath. "I'll call them first thing in the morning. Maybe they can talk the others into selling. Let's keep our fingers crossed."

After DR hung up, Miguel called.

"Great news." He spoke without preamble. "The *SS* is yours if you still want her. They came down on the price too. Our buddy Luigi was putting his hooks in you to the tune of a hundred grand. He gives the marina a bad smell."

As the sun slipped below the sea's horizon, DR hung up. Leaning forward, he gripped the railing over the water. The *SiCillian Summer* would soon be the *Disillusioned Illusion*. If he hadn't met Kim, this wouldn't be happening. Maybe fate was on his side.

As he pushed away and walked along the wharf, thoughts of Willie intruded, and he winced. Why had he grabbed her by the arm? He'd never been that aggressive. Why now?

He shook away the twinge. *This too will pass.*

Willie slapped her purse onto the corner table at Marcie's Place—the table she and Gail always sat at—and sank into the plush padded-leather booth across from Mike. Pop music played a cheerful drone, but she rubbed at her temples. "Why do they have to play that? I could do with some silence after a morning at WREAL."

Actually, she could do with not having to face this meeting with Mike to repair their strained friendship. Having the guy around made her think of his brother now. She ground her teeth. What was up with her inability to get DR out of her mind? Why had Gail confided in her? Why did she have to paint him as *the* white knight? Crushes at her age weren't practical.

"You okay, Willie? You're not... yourself?"

Great, now Mike thought he could play the good guy? Maybe he was. Maybe it was all her.

Rachael strolled through the tables and stopped to chat with Pauline's crowd.

Double great. Couldn't it be anybody but Rachael? The girl was bad news at Christmas.

"Willie? Did you hear me? Why so much stress?"

"I'm fine."

He arched a brow.

"Okay, fine. Rachael puts me on edge." She leaned over to talk softly. "I can't forget what she did to me in high school. I know I'm supposed to forgive her, and I have. But I can't get it out of my mind lately. She doesn't even remember it—and she stole my life."

"Whoa. That's quite a statement?" Mike pushed tight against the back of his seat and cocked his head. He had that look. The one guys get before asking something stupid like if it was her time of the month.

She looked down at the table and fidgeted with the tablecloth. Tears heated the backs of her eyes. Oh, she wanted a husband so badly, but every time, some other girl or woman used their female gifts to spirit them away. She'd never been like that, saving herself. Had it been worth it? *Did* God love her? Why couldn't she have a mate, someone who would love her the way Gail described her marriage to DR?

DR. There *he* was again. Why couldn't she get him out of her mind? Why?

It's stretched my faith, God, and now, here she is—my dream crusher.

Standing there, smiling at me like nothing ever happened. Surely, she knows how much she hurt me.

With a deep breath, she focused on Mike and patching up their little tiff. Then she grabbed her purse. "Sounds good, Mike. Listen, I've got a headache. I'm gonna head out."

She pushed out of the booth just as Rachael returned, forcing her to step aside.

"Is everything okay?" Rachael's voice trailed Willie. "She seemed upset?"

Mike better not spill on her. Not sticking around to find out, Willie rushed home. She'd been a Christian as long as she could remember. But she'd also always been the bridesmaid.

She stepped into her small rented one-bedroom house. She'd always been thankful but not tonight. She jammed the coat closet door shut.

"Being the bride of Christ is all that matters." She'd repeated that motto to herself for ten years. Once, it had served her well. Once upon a time.

She dropped her keys onto the hall table, letting them clatter and maybe even dent the soft pine. Didn't matter. Nothing mattered. Even being Christ's bride didn't seem to matter. "God, do You even hear me? I want the same kind of man Gail adored and described so romantically—DR."

Okay, so maybe not DR exactly.

Or maybe...

She slumped to her bedroom floor against the end of her bed, a bed that had never known a man. Her shoulders hunching, she pulled her knees to her chest and pressed her face into her hands.

"Why, Jesus? Why can't I have a husband? Why can't I have someone to love? I've done everything I can. Why am I being left out? I want to hold someone—I want to hold DR!"

There, she'd said it.

She swallowed hard, her admission sinking in. "I know he's not a believer, but he can be. Please, Lord, I need him. Please change his heart."

Eventually calming, she got ready for bed, grabbed her journal, and sat on the bed. Her heart flowing through her hand, she began to write and pray for DR, for his salvation, safe passage, and affection. *Please, God, maybe this trip can change his heart—about Jesus, about life, and about... me.*

And, as she prayed, she imagined God using her prayers already, the dreamwalkers moving her mountains.

But her journal had far too many tear-soaked pages, and she'd added another tonight. So what do you do when it's no longer fun being yourself? When you want and need someone to love so badly, but it never happens? The answers must be the same answers she gave everyone else—pray until something happens. PUSH they called it. Well, she was going to PUSH harder than anyone ever did.

After one last thought, sleep came: "Tears may come at night, but joy comes in the morning." At least that's what the Scriptures told her.

DR's alarm began its eight-a.m. dance. Ending its joy, he attended to his morning ritual, then headed to the bistro near his hotel. Before him, a bistro server delivered someone's cappuccino, but DR managed to squeeze between the crowded to-go line and the railing, avoid the stares, and find a stand-up high-topped table on the pier. The delicate pastries and cappuccino scents made eating alfresco especially enticing.

Lost in a daydream about finding his first boat with Gail, the *Dream Maker Express*, he nearly spilled his cappuccino when a voice called out his name. *Oh, great. Luigi. Just in time to ruin my breakfast.* "Hi, Luigi." DR dabbed up the dribble of cappuccino. "What brings you out so early? Pull up a stool." *I hope not.*

"No thanks. I came to give you the bad news—someone has

bought the *SiCillian Summer*. Now what do you want me to do? I can put out feelers, see what else may be coming on the market."

DR held up a hand, stopping him.

"Miguel put the offer in for me. He has amazing connections, don't you think? He even got it for a hundred thousand less." DR couldn't help smiling. "Here, I thought I'd lost her, but if that snafu hadn't happened, it would have cost me a bundle. Isn't that great news?"

The color left Luigi's face. "Why, that *is* amazing. How did he manage it? But of course, I am thrilled, and I'm still here for you. Anything you need—anything at all, please come by and see me." Saying goodbye, Luigi left the café, but the tilt of his head and stiffness of his gait suggested the man would seek his revenge.

After breakfast, DR headed to Marco's office to meet Miguel, taking time to enjoy his midmorning walk. All the small shops had just put their wares out on the sidewalk to lure in shoppers, creating a pleasant hustle and bustle. He smiled at the children and the older men and women visiting on the sidewalk. It all left him thankful Gail had talked him into minoring in language with her. Now, he could enjoy conversations in six languages.

She joined him in all the language classes, French and of course Spanish, even though she was born in Spain. She'd later confessed she took it to be near him before they'd started dating. Amazing how many things they'd done just to share time together. They also studied Italian, Arabic, and Bengali. Their professor always encouraged him, saying he had "plenty of brainpower for the task." He rarely shared the knowledge of his language skills, preferring to eavesdrop when others didn't think he understood them.

He pushed through the ornate textured glass door into Marco's office, and Miguel strode to meet him, clasping DR's right hand in both of his. "My friend, we are going to have a fantastic day. First, we transfer the title. Then you register her under your country's flag and file the name-change papers. Doesn't that all sound fantastic?"

"It does." DR caught his new friend up in a tight thank-you hug. "It's all thanks to you."

Somehow, he sensed these Riccis loved celebrating their friends and family more so than themselves.

And today was a day to celebrate. Today, the *SiCillian Summer* became his *Disillusioned Illusion*. Soon, he'd have freedom from the heartache and do-gooders back home.

Why did he not feel the fulfillment he expected?

CHAPTER
SEVEN

"Thank you for tuning in to WREAL. Today, we have a special treat for you. We're joining Dr. Steven Ray, doctor of archaeology, and setting out on a high-seas-and-foreign-lands adventure. We'll be calling him DR, and among many of his wonderful attributes, he's my older brother."

DR shivered over the feeling from the night before. Why couldn't he shake this thought of something pulling him down, his self-worth sinking, lower and lower? The mirror on the wall shared the feeling of emptiness. The sun shining through the window along with his success should've helped. It sure made his sparsely decorated hotel room look amazing. Sitting at a desk across the room from the bed, he rocked back in his chair. "Best shake this," he muttered to himself, forcing himself to be ready to share this monumental moment. Despite his faked smile, the mirror couldn't lie.

Mike kept speaking. "He also made the largest known discovery in India's archaeological history. He's agreed to share this adventure by describing to us the fascinating details about his journey, the people, the land, and the sea. Hello, DR. How are things going in Marsala, Italy?"

"Hi, Mike. Thanks for having me on. Everything is great." DR leaned into the microphone on his laptop. "I've made some new contacts and friends, and they helped me secure the *Disillusioned Illusion*. She's at a contractor being fitted with her defensive arms and having a good going-over."

"Tell us about your yacht." Though louder than usual, Mike's cheerful voice came across genuine, like they were sitting in one of Marcie's Place's cozy booths. "How big she is? And how many passengers are you planning to carry along with your crew?"

"She is a beauty, a one-hundred-and-forty-foot Veloce-made vessel. With over seven thousand horsepower in her engines, she can reach a cruising speed of twenty-two knots." He pushed the darker thoughts deep down inside, hiding them just like always, and puffed up his chest. His jewel was all that mattered now.

The mirror began looking friendlier as he focused on the *DI*. "She has enough berths to sleep up to twelve passengers and six crew members along with four beautifully designed decks, which the previous owner customized to his excellent taste. She's well-appointed for longer cruises, complete with a gym, swimming pool, and floating beach platform to name a few amenities. I plan to have the maximum passengers—minus one—and two crew members, along with myself. A total of fourteen aboard for our shakedown cruise."

"How do you sail a vessel of that size and take care of your passengers with such a small crew?"

"It's what some call a niche boutique cruise. All the passengers will perform various duties aboard the *DI* to keep down the need for a larger crew, thus reducing costs."

"Oh. That's interesting, just as long as I don't have to wash the dishes. So, what's your itinerary, and what do you expect to see along the way? Will you see a lot of dolphins or whales?"

"Our trip sets out from Marsala, and I've left the timetable open for the possibility of bad weather and slow going through the canal. You never know what that will be like." Thankfully, he had his contacts and Lorenzo's expertise in dealing with the maritime agency.

"Along the way, we can expect to see striped dolphins, whales, and maybe even some sharks. At sea, you just never know." He took a quick sip of water. "Our itinerary includes visits to Jeddah, Saudi Arabia; Kochi, Kerala, India; and the village of Nirapada, near Kolkata to visit Chief Mnortarmillc and the site of my discovery. Our first stop is in Jeddah. There we have two single-day trips planned in the areas of Mecca and Medina." How strange it felt saying it was his discovery.

He twisted the chair sides, stretched back in his seat, kicked out his feet, and laced his hands on his lap while keeping his head positioned to see himself in the mirror. "Miguel Ricci and I dropped the *DI* by my contractor this morning. She's getting fit with a water cannon that'll shoot a powerful stream of twenty liters of water per second up to seventy-three yards. That's nearly three-quarters of a football field, by the way. They are also installing a long-range acoustic device—otherwise known as a LRAD—and an electrified rail system. This will provide for our security needs, along with our handheld devices, which we hope will be unnecessary."

"Sounds like you are preparing to meet a lot of bad guys along the way."

"We don't expect trouble, but in that region, anything can happen quickly and without provocation or warning."

A fly buzzed him, the drone an irritant.

"How does the LRAD help keep pirates off the yacht? And how much electricity is flowing through the railing system?"

The fly landed on his jean-clad knee and sat there, insolent, rubbing its face.

"The LRAD emits a sound capable of causing permanent damage to the hearing of those exposed to it for long. But if you're under attack by pirates, their hearing loss isn't your concern. It was invented to protect military vessels in the US fleet. Some law-enforcement units use them now. The rail system has nine thousand volts, enough to stop any attacker."

He waved a hand over the fly, but the bugger just sat there. Great, all those security devices and he couldn't shoo a fly.

"The three together should secure the vessel so our handheld devices can stay locked up, but you never know."

"Sounds like you got yourself well protected, and I, for one, am grateful to hear that, DR. We've got our next call scheduled for just after you leave Marsala."

"That's the plan, Mike. We'll get underway at nine a.m. my time, but I'll get with you at one p.m., which will put us at seven a.m. your time. Does that work for you? That's when you air, right?"

"Yes, it is. Okay, we'll look forward to it—and we're off the air. Great job, DR." Mike laughed, and something like clapping came through the laptop speakers. "I'd say that one went smoothly."

"Excellent. It was even fun. I'll look forward to the next one too. Say hi to Willie. I hope she is well." And just like that, the call was over.

DR scrubbed a hand over his face. Great. Had he really brought Willie into it? *What was I thinking? Am I going mad?*

He slammed the fly, smearing guts all over his palm and jeans. His nose crinkled as he reached for a tissue. Then he pushed to his feet and headed to the sink. *She's one of those people. This attraction to her is toxic, like playing with fire and holding it to my chest.*

Flabbergasted he'd asked about her, Willie froze like stone. She covered her face with her hands, ignoring her bad hair day. Maybe, just maybe... all this praying until something happened *was* making a difference. She'd never prayed so hard or wanted anything so badly. Well, other than Ashton.

But she wasn't Gail, and this wasn't Dukes School either. So... what were her chances?

Mike cocked a brow. Oops, he must've seen her expression change. Would he guess she had a crush on his older brother? "Ah..." He dragged the word out, toying with it as only a good DJ could. Then he leaned back in his chair and kicked his feet up on his desk. "Things are beginning to make sense, sister. That's why you were so upset the night before."

"Why? What craziness are you thinking, Mike Ray?"

Good thing they'd gotten the all clear and were off the air.

"Looks like someone has a crush on my brother." With his singsong teasing, they might as well be in kindergarten.

"What would make you say that?" she sputtered. A telltale heat seared her neck and crept toward her cheeks. She spun away and fumbled, straightening her desk. "I'm happy the call went well. That's all. It looks like we—well, *you*—might have a good show for a few weeks. DR was great at describing his yacht and trip preparations."

"Yeah, okay." He slapped his feet back onto the battered linoleum tiling. "Just don't get your hopes up. You know how your last conversation ended."

He started his search for their next promotional. Then he paused, looking over at her as if unwilling to change the conversation.

"How did you ever get a crush on DR? You're so different, like night and day different. Oh, sure"—he waved a hand—"he's got the Ray good looks. I get *that*, but your beliefs and lifestyles could never mesh. It would take the hand of God. You get *that*... right? Wait, don't answer."

She didn't reply, simply sashayed out the door, humming. DR had asked about *her*. That was more than she had hoped for, for now. She got *that*.

And You've got this, right, God?

She paused at the door, one hand on the cool prefabricated wall as she peered back into their studio. "You won't say anything, will you?"

"No. No, I won't."

Lorenzo's story checked out. Now, DR had a qualified first mate. With Miguel going along, he only needed one more crew member. He'd conduct one interview for his second mate tomorrow morning. As he strolled toward the Cannoli Café to meet Lorenzo, his shoulders loosened, and late afternoon shadows darkened the street. He breathed deeply, the scent from a bank of wildflowers wafting on the breeze.

Then he stepped into the café's quiet darkness, the place almost empty, dinnertime still an hour or so away. A rubato tempo, playing low, kicked up, its wild freedom beckoning him to the seas and leaving a twitching in his legs to get going.

Empty glasses clattered as Cillia put down her serving tray and hugged him. She held on tight, her hair tickling his neck as she pecked a kiss to his cheek. Not a hugger, he almost pulled away, but a guy could get used to this kind of welcome. Then she drew back, grabbed his hand, and bounced her way to the corner, perhaps her free spirit already lifting in flight with the music. "My brother's waiting for you."

Lorenzo sprang to his feet, the chair clattering across the wooden floor with a hollow sound while his smile stretched wide and his warm hand engulfed DR's in a grip nearly as welcoming as Cillia's. "I cannot tell you how excited I am to be part of your team, DR."

"I'm excited to get this venture underway too." DR extracted his hand and slid out a chair. "Are you hungry?"

"I had an early lunch, and I'm afraid it's long gone. Sis wouldn't sneak me any olives today either."

"So, Cillia..." DR twisted in his seat to face the fetching girl. "What's the special today? Anything different?"

She flicked an errant lock of hair over her shoulder, her eyes alight as if she were about to share a secret. "Can I recommend the she-crab soup or crab cakes and legs, maybe?"

"Sounds good to me. A big bowl of she-crab soup on the side and some delicious rolls and honey butter." Lorenzo drummed his hands on the table. "Well, Sis. Think you can put her there?"

She rolled her eyes and pointed to a sign above their table. Over a red-and-green background scrolled the words: *Though we appreciate every special request, we grant few.* Beneath the banner of words, a large cook, his sleeves rolled up, scowled, wearing a sailor's hat, and smoking a cigar.

DR laughed. "Well, Lorenzo, did you sit us here for a reason?"

Someone beckoned from across the room.

"Okay, boys. That's enough." Cillia slapped the menus onto their table, still snickering. "You'll find the specials in here. I've got other tables to serve. So, what do you boys want to drink?"

They ordered their beverages, and DR opened his menu while sinking back on the cushioned seat. His eyes adjusted to the ambient lighting, and he let the atmosphere absorb the day's tension. "So, I've sent the *DI* over to have it fitted. She'll be ready to sail in three days, right on time. Meanwhile, we've got lots to do." He thumped his hands on the table, ready to get at it. "Tomorrow, I'm going to work on getting the rest of the licenses and meet with the passengers. You're welcome to come along. We're meeting at the bistro beside my hotel in the morning."

"I would love to, but I have a lot to do before we leave." Lorenzo eyed two college-aged girls in short shorts who'd entered the café, then raised his glass, and winked at them.

Giggles carried over the music's heady tempo.

"Okay." DR nodded, beating back his own thoughts about the girls. "Then let's plan on meeting the day after tomorrow and getting everything taken care of."

After dinner, he headed to his room. Along the dock, he breathed in the aroma of sweet success. The salty air and skimpily dressed young ladies all added together, intoxicating his senses.

Then Willie came to mind, and he ground his teeth, quickening his pace. "Why?" He groaned. "Why are thoughts of *her* coming up all the time? I've never been infatuated before. Why now?"

It was almost like… like someone or something was triggering these feelings.

What about that evening he came home and found Willie with Gail out back on the deck, a fire burning in the chiminea? The sun setting just like tonight, only over Wall Lake, cast a stunning glow over them. Willie looked pure, innocent—and amazing.

He shuddered. He didn't want to think about *that.* It made him feel dirty then. He didn't need other girls, not when he was such a lucky man to have landed Gail, but still, she'd caught his eye.

The next morning, the sun shining on his face woke him. Nine thirty, already? He groaned. Since when did he oversleep? Good thing, he'd forgotten to draw the curtains since he needed to be at the restaurant.

Showered and dressed, he headed next door to grab a coffee. After the young man took his order, DR sank down in his seat, the sea swelling and rising before him, repeating itself in an ebb and flow similar to his life. The crest of the tide being all the happy prosperous times. Too bad, the deep plunge down to the trough always followed. At least that's how his life seemed. Was everyone else's like that too?

Sitting on the pier without Gail had a different feel to it. Was he getting in over his head with these cruises? But everything was falling into place almost like...

No, God hadn't been with him since he was nine. If God was real, why did He let those terrible things happen? And why did Dad say those things to Mom? *Am I damaged goods?* Dad sure acted that way.

DR always pushed aside these internal struggles, his secret—but lately, he wondered what Dad's secret was. With Gail gone, it became harder to shake.

A seagull flapped nearby, and DR shifted to attention. He'd go over things with David, his new second mate, and Miguel at noon. They needed to order the supplies, and even though this was supposed to be an interview, DR had already decided David would be a perfect fit after a Zoom call together. Who knows, maybe he was even a good cook.

"Is anyone sitting here?" a woman asked. When he glanced over his shoulder, she smiled. "Would you mind if we sit with you, DR?" Long curly brown hair framed her face, and the breeze carried a delightful perfume.

"Uh, no. I mean sure. I'd love for you to join me." Great. Since when did he stammer like a schoolboy? He sprang to his feet and motioned for her to sit across from him. "My name is Steven, Steven Ray, but I ask people to call me DR."

"I'm Trixie, Trixie Robinson. One of your passengers, remember?" She tipped her head, eyeing him with bright brown eyes. "You asked us to meet you here today to go over our plans. Don't you remember?"

"Oh, please, please—forgive me." Wow. He'd almost missed this meeting, even after telling Lorenzo about it last night. He sat on the edge of the seat. "So much has happened in the last few days, and now, well, apparently, I was daydreaming."

Her husband strolled over with a tray of coffee and donuts, and DR rose again to shake his hand. "You must be Craig, right?"

"It's so good to meet you." Craig braced both hands on the table, leaning over it but making no move to sit, his eyes crinkling up around a deep Mediterranean tan. "Trixie and I are so stoked. The others are inside getting their food. Would you like to move to another table over so we can all sit together?" He motioned to the other passengers now coming out of the bistro.

DR nodded, just a bit dizzy over almost missing this morning's meeting. Only happenstance brought him to this café today. *How could this have slipped my mind?*

Did the Willie thing bump his brain into neutral? Trixie still eyed him. He could only imagine what she must be thinking.

"Absolutely, Craig." DR pushed to his feet. "It's good to meet you and Trixie and everyone. Sorry, I was daydreaming about yesteryear."

They chose a more appropriate table, and the others, all around DR's age, came over with their food and coffee. With this group, he'd almost filled his yacht, minus the one berth, a single cabin down below.

About an hour later, he stood. "Everything's progressing nicely. So we'll be getting underway right on schedule. Assuming the supplies arrive and get loaded by tomorrow evening, which shouldn't be a problem here in Marsala."

"Sounds great, DR." Craig stood as well. "Trixie and I are going to wander off. The little lady says she has some sightseeing and shopping to do, and who am I to argue?"

"We better get going too." Laurie turned toward the walkway and threw her last bite of bagel toward the scavenging gulls, causing not too small a flurry. "We have a few group tours over the next two days, and we'd all better get ready for today's tour."

The others left after saying their goodbyes, except for Dr. Holmes. Dr. Debbie Holmes, the paleontologist from America. She settled back in her chair and gave him a good looking over while sipping her refilled latte. "I have to confess, DR, I've been excited to meet you. I knew of the dig you and Gail discovered—well, most people in our circles know about it. It went kinda viral in the international scientific communities, didn't it?"

"Most people in the so-called digging community keep up with others in the different specialties."

"Yep." She tossed a bagel bottom into the harbor. Then, with one hand, she pinned back the shoulder-length, natural-blonde hair blowing across her cheek. Her brown eyes were ablaze, sparkling in anticipation of the trip. "We're always on the lookout to take advantage of those discoveries and maybe link up to pursue our own science as well."

Nodding, he gave her his own looking over. Five two. Gorgeous. Confident. She knew how to care for herself. Too bad, he had to go meet Miguel and David.

After bidding her goodbye, he strolled to his luncheon. It wasn't easy to meet a nice, down-to-earth, and smart girl like that. Pretty too. Would she be a distraction for the single men or himself? Four, maybe five, weeks at sea could be tough. Nature had a way, especially around salt air, bikinis, and the sea.

Odd that she didn't live too far from Wall Lake, just a two-hour drive down I-94. Kinda a shame he hadn't met her before deciding to leave.

Strange, he didn't feel attracted to her in *that way*. Was it his past or a demon? Maybe because she didn't dress or come across provocatively, or because he was raised that way. It was more like a brotherly feeling, the same way he felt for Gail after their competition ended… at first. Maybe he had built up his defenses—afraid of intimacy—again? No matter. He had rules in play for such things now.

At the café, he found David and Miguel by the front windows, away from the door. Cillia popped around the corner.

"DR, Lorenzo is so excited. I haven't seen him like this since he had to leave the navy." She hugged him, her lips a warm whisper in his ear. "Thank you."

Heat crept up his neck, and he eased out of her grasp. "I'm just as excited."

"Well, I'll get back to work. I can't wait to hear all about your trip when you get back. Katie's serving your area." Then Cillia was off, ponytail bouncing and skirt swishing.

DR averted his gaze.

The café added their fall decorations earlier today, glowing red candles nestled in pumpkin-ring centerpieces to give a wonderful feel. David and Miguel rose to greet him.

"I think you've found a keeper in David." Miguel started the conversation before DR even sat down. "Three years as a yeoman and ten as boatswain in the US Navy—that's a lot of first-class experience. I'm impressed."

"Absolutely. David, we were going to discuss this more today, but after speaking with your naval references, I'm inclined to say you're the perfect fit for my operation. What do you say?"

"Well, that is good news." David rubbed his hands together. "Miguel's been telling me all about your yacht. She sounds like quite a girl. Oh… by the way, you should know Miguel here is an excellent cook. I've had the good fortune of stumbling into one of the many charity cookouts and barbecues he's prepared. His is one of the finest Italian flavors you'll find."

They laughed, planned, and ordered supplies and fuel. In Marsala, the marina vendors were always ready to serve. Most could deliver with a "moment's notice," though prices could reflect the urgency of the need.

"One of the greatest advantages of the computer age is speed. We can order today and load it tomorrow. In the past, it could take as long as a week to do what now takes only a few hours," DR said.

"Just order enough meat, cheese, and produce to last until we reached Jeddah. I love preparing foods from that part of the world." Miguel brought the first three fingers of his right hand to his lips and kissed them. "The spices used in the Middle East are unlike anything elsewhere."

"Sounds good." DR nodded. "Beginning in Jeddah, Saudi Arabia, we'll pick up the fresh foods we need in each port."

David pushed back his chair. "If you don't need me anymore, I'd better go get packed."

Miguel rose as well. "Shall we meet tomorrow morning at ten o'clock? By then, the suppliers and Lorenzo should be at the *DI* also."

DR agreed and followed his companions from the café. Sleep likely wouldn't come easily tonight, not when he felt like before Christmas as a youngster. And tomorrow was bigger than any Christmas he'd experienced.

CHAPTER
EIGHT

Arriving in Malaga, Spain, from Dublin, Sara Kelly clutched a U2 hoodie to her chest—something her daughter, Mekie, left behind thirty years ago. Apparently, the concert started it all, the love affair with a no-good Irish-American boy visiting his dad for the school year, the pregnancy, the flight from home—all of it. If only she'd said Mekie couldn't go that night!

On shaky legs, Sara shuffled toward the airport's luggage carousel. Maybe she shouldn't have come. But if there was a chance she could find the woman who buried Gail Kelly Ray, then how could she not take that flight? Was Gail her granddaughter?

Aileen Hara thought so.

Sara sank into a nearby chair. She just needed to catch her breath and her focus. She'd run into Aileen at the supermarket two weeks earlier. She hadn't seen Aileen since Mekie's graduation, Aileen's daughter, Kayleigh, and Mekie were the best of friends throughout all their school years.

Aileen had stopped her for a hug. "Mekie's still so torn. You must be hurting too. Burying your beautiful granddaughter must be awful. So young, so pretty, and so accomplished." Aileen pulled away then, holding Sara at arm's length. Her forehead scrunched. "You know... I don't remember seeing you at the funeral...?"

Sara had exploded then. "I haven't seen Mekie for thirty years. She ran away after graduation to have her baby. My first grandchild." A child she'd never met, a child dead now? Even sitting here, remembering the agony of that discovery in the supermarket, Sara pressed a trembling hand to her forehead. She'd confessed then that she didn't know which city her daughter was living in now or with whom. Then she'd asked how Aileen knew anything about Mekie all these years later.

"Oh." Aileen had waved as if it were of no consequence, as if it weren't something Sara had spent three decades aching and wondering over. "She lived with my Kayleigh all along. You remember Kayleigh, don't you? My daughter? Well, at least until my Kayleigh passed. They were the best of friends, didn't you know?"

Sara's face had started burning then. All the lost years... If only she'd run into Aileen earlier, if only Sean had listened, who knows, maybe he'd be alive too.

"Kayleigh left her bungalow near the Mediterranean to Mekie. Oh, how my Kayleigh loved those girls—Mekie and Gail. Mekie still lives there. She's such a joy, beautiful, and successful. During the funeral, I stayed with her and Nicolas, her husband. Nicolas must have been a wonderful father. He was crushed—oh my."

Aileen pressed a hand to cheek, her eyes goggling. "My memory's not what it used to be, but suddenly—oh yes, I remember. I know why you weren't at the funeral. And here, all these years, if I'd only known Mekie had run away, I could have pointed you to her. Isn't that something?"

Yes, isn't that something. All these years. All lost to pride. Sean didn't— *wouldn't*—go public with her disappearance. After all, what would the town think? As he'd always said, "People in Dublin like to talk."

Well, if they'd talked, she could have found her baby and grandbaby. Too late now. Sara pushed to her feet and marched herself to the carousel. Not completely too late. Her baby was still alive.

DR slept until eight thirty, showered, and headed down to the bistro. Debbie was already sitting at a table on the pier near the water's edge, watching the passing boats, seabirds, and whitecaps outside the harbor.

He approached with a slight wave. "Someone looks like she's dreaming."

She jolted. The slackness faded from her expression, and her eyes regained their focus. "Indeed, I was. Days like this—the memories take over, you know?"

"That I do, and I've been losing myself in them too much. It's a nice surprise to find you here. Perhaps I'll be able to stay in the present for my entire breakfast. That is if you wouldn't mind my joining you once I get myself something to eat?"

"Sounds great." Her smile wobbled, leaving him curious about what those memories were. Had she lost someone too? "I'd like that."

Her smile wasn't relaxed. She'd straightened in her seat, though. Studying her, trying not to take mental pictures, he couldn't deny she was gorgeous. *Don't stare.* The smells wafting from the pastry shop made him hungry, the scavenger gulls too as the buggers fought for every loose morsel, a daily ritual.

"Is there something I can get for you?"

"I'm good." She held up her coffee cup as if to prove it, but no steam rose from it. "But thank you just the same."

Minutes later, he returned with his coffee and a muffin, seagulls flying above. "This is just about perfect. Every day I've been here, the weather has been like this. I'm getting spoiled."

"It is wonderful. The pier is nice too."

"I'm meeting with my crew this morning." He tore a section of muffin top off. "We're going to begin loading the supplies—maybe take her out for a spin to make sure everything is good. You want to come?" He stuffed part of the section in his mouth.

"Yes, I think..." She closed her eyes as if trying to push back her past. "I'd love that. The others went on a historic tour, and I didn't feel up to it. I'm nostalgic already. Mark and I used to visit all the ancient cities and places, and it's going to be harder than I imagined. This is my first trip since he was taken from me."

He knew her pain. "I'm so sorry." He reached out to touch her arm. "It's my first trip without my wife too. Since my sophomore year in college, she was the best part of my life. Well, maybe not my sophomore year. We had a friendly competition that first year. She detested Americans, and well, I was... shall we say, shy?"

"Shy? *You* were shy?" She cocked her head, her lips quirking, and a light flaring in her brown eyes. "I can't see that for one second."

He waved with the muffin section still in his hand, a raisin falling to his plate. "I didn't mean to ramble on and make light of your loss. But this journey should be good for us."

"I believe you're right. I'm looking forward to doing what I love again. When Mark first passed, I avoided everything we enjoyed together. I'd become so miserable." She let out a short sigh. "I'm here to get on with my life and to find a little adventure."

"And that, we shall."

She slapped the table, jostling the silverware on her plate, her eyes sparkling. "Yes, it's time for a new adventure, and who knows... maybe love." She faced the sea and then him, sipping coffee while leaning toward the railing. Her searching eyes reflected the morning sun. "It's been five years. I'm ready... No, no, I *need* to live again."

"Agreed." He checked his Speedmaster Moonwatch, a special gift from Gail urging him out to sea again. "It's only nine thirty. Time for one more cup. Are you sure you wouldn't like one? You should try their pumpkin and spice. My treat."

"Why not?" She nodded in a teasing way, her blonde hair bouncing around her chin. "Especially if it's your treat, but I warn you—I can be a tough customer."

"We'll see about that. Two pumpkin spice coffees coming right up." He pushed back from the table and strode inside. The sun warmed his shoulders as he walked. Its warmth and her company made this morning so much better.

He returned with the coffee and handed her a cup before sitting down. As she sipped, closing her eyes to taste the nuances, he waited.

"Mmm... this is good. Almost as good as mine." She saluted him with the cup, half giggling.

"I told you. So, you're a barista? Hmm... maybe someday, I'll get to try one of yours, maybe on our cruise?"

"Maybe. Not to change the subject, but can I ask you a question? I hope you don't think it's silly, but how did you come to name your yacht the *Disillusioned Illusion*? I've tried to decipher that, but I keep coming up blank."

He sank back into his seat. The loop-back chair pressed against the top of his spine as he contemplated how to impart his thought as gently as possible.

"When you disillusion someone, you take away a true belief or illusion, like all the rumbling and magic of the wizard, but then the curtain rises to show the wizard was a man all along. It has always been that way for me. I seem to find something grand, only to have it taken away and the illusion of happiness right along with it, every time."

"That's..." With her hands folded around the cup, she tipped her head again and seemed to observe his reaction. "Sad. Don't you think?"

"Maybe, but it's the ebb and flow of life, at least mine." He tested another sip, the pumpkin spice sweetening its acrid flavor just like her company sweetened the day—all bright and cheery in her overall shorts over a yellow tee shirt.

They sat, enjoying their coffee. Then they headed over to the *DI*, and along their five-minute walk, he pointed out the different shops and restaurants he'd enjoyed during his stay. In sight of the yacht, he waved at Miguel.

"Well, well." Miguel strolled over. "With such a beautiful breakfast companion, I'm surprised you showed up for work today at all."

"It's still not too late." DR turned to leave, playful. "We could play hooky. I'll make sure you boys are busy, and we'll kick back and enjoy the day. What do you say, Debbie? Are you in the mood to watch someone else do all the work?"

"Well, if the boys are going to be like that." One hand firmly on a hip, the other tilting her head, she swiveled her hips, Marilyn Monroe style. "It's only fair. We'll sit up on the deck or soak in the swimming pool and supervise. I have a lot of supervisory experience, years of it."

"Ouch—easy does it." Miguel held up his hands. "I see we have two wisenheimers with us today. And here I thought DR would be the only one on the trip."

David reached over to help her aboard. "Debbie, it's so nice to meet you. I'm David, the second mate. Let me show you the *DI*. Lorenzo and I are blown away by the sophistication and attention to detail DR and Miguel have given the additions. Come. Your quarters are down on the second deck, not far from the galley."

"The galley, huh?" She tossed back her hair, flashing white teeth against tanned skin. "I might get fattened up. The perfect berth for the midnight snack attack."

Laughing, he showed her the way with his left hand. "We'll be back. Come on. I'll introduce you to Lorenzo. We just call him Lo."

Miguel smirked. "You know, my friend, you might have been hasty putting 'no romancing the passengers' in all caps."

DR winced. Had he been serious about that?

He hadn't known someone as beautiful as Debbie would be coming on the journey. Well, not when he made the rule. She was close to his age too. "We're not here for romance, Miguel."

Maybe saying it would make him believe it.

Fifteen minutes later, Debbie returned from her tour and slammed her hands on her hips, bunching up her overalls and eyeing him with a new respect. "I must say I'm impressed. You thought of everything. Right down to the midnight snacks I'll soon be sneaking. The swimming pool and bar are spectacular. So, when can I start bringing my things?"

Hunching her shoulders, she gritted her teeth and fake cringed. "I'd like to bring a few this afternoon. Any arguments?"

"Things, uh-oh." Miguel stepped back.

With a look, she cut him off. "Yes, *things*. You know, clothes and beauty potions." She formed air quotes around the word *potions*. "Things a girl needs."

"Well, those must be pretty small bags." David rocked back on his heels and exaggerated giving her a going-over. "From where I'm standing, you're not going to be needing a lot of those secrets."

DR rubbed the back of his neck. David appeared rather taken with her. He'd earlier claimed a steady girlfriend, so was this going to be a problem?

"How sweet of you." Debbie shook a finger at David. "But remember, no romancing the passengers. Right, DR? If I remember correctly, that was in all caps."

"Absolutely." He let out a whoosh of breath and gave David a warning look that was only half mocking. "We don't need to be complicating our journey with love. There will be time for that later for those looking."

The suppliers soon began delivering, seeming to converge all at the same time. But at least, they'd get it wrapped up early, and everyone pitched in, including Debbie.

They took the *Disillusioned Illusion* out as he'd promised, putting her through her paces. She performed flawlessly, sending excitement pulsing through his blood. Now, fully loaded, they could be at the port and entrance of the Suez Canal by Saturday afternoon, if they could maintain the planned twenty-one knots, near her top speed.

Afterward, Miguel invited them all to join him, Kim, and Marco at the Seafarer, their family favorite, for a goodbye dinner. With the restaurant on the other side of the city, Miguel directed Marco's chauffeur to take the scenic route.

"She was built in 1823," Miguel explained, powering down the car's back window as the Seafarer came into view on a scenic point jutting out into the Mediterranean Sea, the city on one side, the sea on the other. "At first, she was a layover for the richer sailors coming into town. After a hundred years, they turned her into the restaurant as the city's port grew."

The car stopped, and they approached the buildings constructed from the old beige-like masonry similar to the historic buildings downtown. Wisteria vines climbed its venerable sides.

"In the spring, their clusters of purple blooms hang down on the patios, handrailing, and window frames." Miguel glowed like a proud papa. Perhaps he had a stake in the property. "The landscape's a spectacular sight to see while driving up with the sea behind."

Sea spray, rising from the pounding waves on the rocky coast, created a mystical aura as the last rays of sunlight shone through to produce a myriad of mini rainbows. DR laughed. "It's a scene where one could imagine a magical white unicorn galloping."

"Indeed." Debbie sighed. "A romantic sight."

Miguel nodded his approval. "It's so special to my family. My great-grandfather married his bride here over seventy-five years ago. Their marriage was the talk of the town. All of this"—he waved a hand around—"making it such a fantastical event. I've often wondered how great it must have been. But come. Marco and Kim are waiting."

He led them out back onto the vine-covered terrace with a view of the same inlet. They passed a towering stone fireplace on their way out. A picture of a bride and her groom hung above it, and a brass nameplate confirmed it was Miguel's great-grandparents, in all the splendor of their special day.

"I'm quite jealous." Kim sank back into her vintage upholstered armchair, both hands folded around a glass of sangria. "I wish Marco and I were going with you all."

"I'm so looking forward to it." Debbie slid into her seat, her graceful movements matching the setting while her overalls seemed somehow incongruent, as if she should be wearing period costume. "We've just come from the *DI*. I'm so impressed."

Kim leaned on her chair's armrest, cozying in by Debbie. "I hope the weather is wonderful. This time of year is beautiful on the Indian coast."

After a fabulous dinner accompanied by the heady sangria and equally pleasing conversation, everyone said their good nights, hugging goodbye with an edge of reluctance to let go of the evening.

At the same time in Malaga, "Coming." Mekie checked her zabaglione showcasing Nicolas's favorite Marsala vintage, a light custardy dessert, once more, then dried her hands on a towel, and strode toward whoever was ringing the doorbell with such persistence. "I said I was coming," she grumbled to herself. Who'd ring it like that? The kids must be pranking her. Few people made it out this far to their bungalow. She swung the door open, ready to scold. Then her mouth slid open as well, and a gasp rushed out. "Mom?"

For sure, the woman could be no other. Smaller now, as if the years had shrunk her and stolen the spunk Mekie remembered.

Mekie coiled her fingers around the doorknob, needing something to keep her balanced as they both stood frozen. Tears seared her eyes and slipped from her mother's. Then something broke in her, and she rushed forward and scooped her mother up in a tight embrace.

"Oh, my baby... my beautiful Irish lass." Mom's hot breath misted Mekie's ear. "I've found you at last."

"What are we doing standing out here?" Mekie tried to laugh and motioned for her mom to come inside, wiping her tears on her sleeve.

"Honey?" From the kitchen, Nicolas called out to her. "Who's at the door? Kids?"

"It's my... *mom!*"

Nicolas rushed to their small sitting room, going to Mom, and scooping her off her feet in such a way Mekie almost feared he'd break the now-delicate woman. Then he let Mom go and motioned for both her and Mekie to sit on the sofa. "Mrs. Kelly, I can't begin to tell you how long I've looked forward to meeting you. Can I get you something to drink, maybe some of Marsala's famous sweet red or a soft drink? Something to snack on?"

"Thank you, Nicolas." She held one hand over her heart, the other over her mouth. "I would love a glass. Please, call me Sara."

"How did you find me?" Mekie grabbed the tissue box, claimed one for herself, and passed the rest to her mother—her mother! Here! "I've wanted to see you and Dad for so long. Where is Dad? Didn't he come too?" Or was he still mad?

Mom wadded up the tissue. "Your dad, God rest his soul, passed five years after you left. His heart was broken when he realized how he'd treated you." Her hands shook. She tore apart the tissue, bits of it sprinkling in her lap. "You were always his sunshine. When you left, so did his light."

Mekie's gasped, covering her mouth with her right hand, and tears rushed to her cheeks.

"He wouldn't set aside his stubborn Irish pride. He did step down from being a deacon though. He said he'd brought home a cold religion, not the love of Jesus. He never found his peace again, not after you left."

Mekie's eyes searched the room, unable to settle. Then she hung her head. "It's my fault, isn't it? He wouldn't be dead?"

"Oh, sweetheart, no!" Mom gathered up the shredded tissue, then reached for Mekie's hand. "How I've missed you. I didn't want to leave this earth without telling my baby girl one more time how much I love you."

Mekie laced her fingers with her mother's. "I'm sorry about Dad, Mom. The way it all took place was terrible, but I wouldn't trade the life I had with Gail, not for all the money in the world. But losing her— I can say I understand now how you must have felt when I left."

"I was wondering... Do you have pictures?"

"Oh my! Oh yes!" Mekie hopped up.

They sat for hours looking at pictures, Gail a carbon copy of her mom and grandmother. Mekie tapped a photo of Gail alongside her husband. "DR was like a son to us—still is. And Gail lived such a wonderful life."

"DR?" Mom cocked her head, her eyes big in her pale face. Like an ice-covered willow, ready to crash or weep any moment. "Tell me about him."

As Mekie spoke, Mom held up her hand. "You remember little Ryan, don't you? He's my sister Margie's boy. You used to pull him around the yard in that red wagon, remember? Well, anyway, he's going on a special cruise to the Indian Ocean with someone named DR. He's on board a boat named the *Disillusioned Illusion*, a funny name that's hard to forget."

"Wow. Nicolas, did you hear that?" Mekie settled into the sofa. "It *is* a small world. It's hard to imagine, almost like it was..." She was going to say divine inspiration, the hand of God. She hadn't thought that way since she left Dublin.

"The hand of God? Is that what you were going to say?" Mom smiled and tilted her head, then pressed her hands on her cheeks. "Well, He does move in mysterious ways. Your brothers will be so happy to hear I've found you. They'll all want to see you, and soon."

Mekie let go of her grief, putting the tissues aside. Dad was gone, and she wanted to hear about her brothers. "How's everyone?"

"The house was never the same after you left, you know. Your brothers always looked after their little sis. They're all married, living close to me in Dublin. You must come see your nieces and nephews. There's thirteen in all. Everyone's doing so well, happy, and going to church. I'm proud of them all."

Proud of them... The words stung. No matter how well life had gone, parts of Mekie still ached to hear those words from her parents. Would Dad ever have been proud of her? Was Mom proud of her? Ducking her head to hide the sudden quiver to her lips and the heat to her eyes, Mekie continued to turn the scrapbook pages and peer over at the photo albums now on Mom's lap. Occasionally, an event jumped out, perking her up to talk about it.

"Things changed for the family when your dad stepped down from the church. We started going to one of those new Reform churches in town. They don't follow the Catholic faith and practices." Mom patted Mekie's hand. "It helped all of us. We just couldn't keep following the things that caused your dad to become so much about show, lacking mercy and forgiveness, even for his little girl."

Mekie bit her lip, remembering having to go to Grandmother's, the train ride to Malaga. Her hidden grief began to bubble once again.

Mom's grip tightened on Mekie's. "The new church was all about Jesus, about forgiveness. I can't wait to tell your brothers."

She leaned over and held Mekie's face in her hands, looking into her eyes. Then she kissed both her cheeks, tears raining again.

Mekie closed her eyes, remembering her mom kissing her the same way when she was younger. Oh, what joy it brought her even now.

When the alarm went off the next morning, DR's feet hit the floor with great expectation. The big day was here. He met the crew at the bistro for coffee and a bagel. Then they made their way to the *DI*. The weather was nearly perfect, again, for an adventure, just a little cloudy. Typical for this time of year. All the passengers came together, save two, Miquel and a friend he'd brought along to fill the last passenger cabin. Boarding was smooth and quick.

Getting ready to make way, everyone went to their quarters. Miguel paid the newcomer's fare and introduced him as a longtime friend, Joshua Nunn, saying he knew the area well and would be a great addition to the cruise.

During the boarding process DR called for a meeting fifteen minutes before their scheduled departure. As they gathered now, he clapped. "Welcome, everyone. Welcome aboard the *Disillusioned Illusion*. If we're all ready to make way, I propose a toast to the *Disillusioned Illusion,* her crew and passengers. I joyfully thank you all for joining me. Hear! Hear! To the *Disillusioned Illusion,* her shakedown cruise, and new friendships."

Everyone raised their glass, shouting, "Hear! Hear!"

"Mr. Moretti, will you please raise the anchor? Mr. Lucas, please set out, bringing our speed to seventeen knots on our eastward heading."

Everyone raised their glasses of bubbly, drinking it down. Miguel kept it coming, pleasing his new friends with his mixing skills while the passengers mostly headed out to the pool or lingered by the nearby bar.

It was 8:59 a.m., right on time. He'd have plenty of time in his cabin later to prepare for his one-p.m. telephone interview with Mike at WREAL.

After exiting the port, DR instructed David to bump their speed up to twenty-one knots. With the current behind them and the sea calm, they could make up for the times when sailing may not be so smooth.

CHAPTER
NINE

Willie slid on her headphones as Mike took the call from his brother. Beyond the glass divider, he settled back in the studio's soundproof booth holding tight to the warm cup of pumpkin spice she'd just brought over from Marcie's Place. Good, they still had one minute before they aired.

"Bro, gotta say I'm jealous of you over there in shorts and sandals while we're prepping for a Michigan winter."

DR's warm laugh came through. "Well, there's no skiing here. That's for sure. How are Mom and Dad getting on?"

She tuned out their family conversation, just savoring DR's voice purring over her. She'd been PUSHing hard. She'd seen God answer prayer before, and she'd read or heard somewhere that praying with tears meant a lot to the Lord. Well, there was only one way to find out —no stopping, no turning back. She wanted the love Gail described. Surely, God wanted her to have someone, didn't He? *Can that someone be DR, God?*

"So, like I said, all's good here," Mike was saying. "Listen, we'll be on air in half a minute. Willie's got her headphones on, listening in, and we're all set so in twenty...."

She jerked upright at her name.

Whether it was an automatic response or not, she didn't know. But DR responded, "Hi, Willie. I hope you're okay. Make sure my little brother plays nice and shares his toys with everybody."

"In ten..."

"Oh. Hi, DR. Yes, uh, yes, Mike is good." Heat seared her skin. How horrible she must have sounded, like a scared schoolgirl or worse. Seriously? She spoke for a living. Her big moment to say something intelligent, and she bombed.

"Five, four, three, two, one—And hello, Delton. We're on the air with Dr. Ray who has just started his cruise. DR, can you tell us how things have fallen into place?"

DR described their prep.

"Wow," Mike broke in. "The way things worked out's a good sign God's looking over your journey."

"I don't know about that." A harsh note cut into DR's voice. But really, what did the guy expect speaking to a Christian radio station? "But it's been nice."

After about twenty-five minutes of discussing the *DI*, her passengers, and crew—all anonymously, of course—they said goodbye and agreed to speak again on Monday, after the *DI* came out of the Suez Canal.

Then Mike stepped from the sound room, holding his now-empty mug from Marcie's Place, and laughed.

"Wow, you do have a crush on my brother." He clattered the mug onto her desk, the pumpkin spice scent far too sweet for her now-queasy stomach. Then he rested a warm hand on her shoulder. "Don't set yourself up to get hurt. This Debbie girl—the one he calls Sally on the air? She seems to have an inside track. Blonde, pretty, and on the boat. Meanwhile, you're here—pretty too, sure, but a Christian and someone he's peeved at. You might want to squash some of those thoughts before it's too late."

He squeezed her shoulder as if it would somehow soften the blow of his words.

Well, she was a logical woman too. She could see all that. But he was forgetting something crucial. "Nothing is too great for God." She raised her chin. "I just hope—well, *pray*—God will let me know something soon. I'd like to have someone too."

Her shoulders hunched up. Great. She'd never before shared that she was lonely.

"I'm sorry, Willie." Mike patted her shoulder, then stepped back, his voice soft. "I don't mean to be that guy. I pray the Lord will bring you someone who deserves your love. I just don't know if my brother could ever fill that bill for you."

In Washington, DC, Congressman Max Rice was trying to compose himself. Jennings had leaned on him hard, his words—*"This show better work out, or else!"*—still rang in Max's ears.

He pulled off his reading glasses and rubbed the pinched spot on his nose, tired of the pressure. Why had he ever run for Congress? What a naïve idiot, thinking he could help his constituents. *This* didn't seem to be helping anyone.

If only he'd known about Jennings before accepting his help, his contributions. Maybe he'd have lost, but he wouldn't be involved in… murder. That's what it was—murder.

He shivered and threw his glasses on the padded desk. How could Senator Carl Brummengarten be so cool? It must come with time in Congress. Now he was making Max run the LMMC, the Lake Michigan Men's Club.

Max pushed from his seat and strode to the window, the city lights glimmering beyond, his reflection dark on the glass. His wife was upset as he spent more and more time away from her and their children, now "wasting" his time home from Congress at the club. Leslie said he wasn't the man he was before winning his seat.

"But you don't get it, Les." He whispered to the darkness, the darkness around him, the darkness claiming him, the darkness creeping inside him. "I want out too, hon, back to private life."

But Senator Brummengarten told him he knew too much to walk away. It never ended well for those who tried. "How do you think your seat became vacant in the first place?"

He shuddered, thinking of the former congressman's late winter swim in Lake Michigan. His bloated body not found for three days.

Time for a drink.

"Why didn't I know Carl was such a self-serving cutthroat?"

Naïve, naïve, naïve… The word mocked him. He'd have to have been naïve to think Carl still had any integrity left and to think a few others in Congress did too.

The mirror was missing in Max's own life now, shattered. Soon, he'd add child trafficking and murder to his résumé, first steps in the slow and deadly course some in DC now came to accept as "necessary." Others simply called it the DC shuffle.

The *Disillusioned Illusion* glided through the Mediterranean toward the canal. The day was wonderful, a dream come true. Freshened up, DR headed back to the helm. From the bridge, he could see Miguel sitting with Craig, who looked like an old rock and roller, but his wife, Trixie, was quick to point out she was the rock and roller, not Craig.

DR went to join them, making no hurry about it. The sea breeze carried Miguel's words about it being too long since he'd visited Jeddah, Saudi Arabia.

"Open-air markets," Craig concurred. "They're the best. The natural light allows you to see the color nuances and brush strokes. The roundabouts give Jeddah a certain charm too. And the food. It's always awesome." Craig went on describing some of the artwork he'd purchased on their journey here. "So, what's the itinerary?"

"After we resupply, we're visiting an old friend and a former teacher of DR's and a few smaller digs." Miguel threw a glance DR's way. "It ought to be interesting. His former professor has connections all around the Middle East. I like to speak with people who are up on all the latest. You might stumble across a new adventure, or who knows what."

DR strode over. "Where is everyone? I figured you'd all be out here having a glass of wine or a pool party."

"Some took a dip or had a drink. Now, they're resting up for dinner." Craig out of habit and manners half stood, then sat back down. "By the way, what is for dinner?"

"Potluck." Miguel laughed.

"Potluck?"

"Yes. If anything's in the pot, you'll be in luck. Right, DR?"

DR smiled. Miguel was in his element. "Tonight's going to be a lighter fare, in case the first day at sea bothers anyone. No matter how many times you come out, sometimes your system may not be up to a heavy meal. So, we're going to have a couple of nice salads, a special light pork filet, green beans, and a great selection of tropical fruit."

"Who's doing the cooking?" Craig looked back and forth between them. "I mean, are you cooking, or is Miguel?"

"I had this meal prepared and brought on board. So all we need to do is warm and serve. That way, we'll all get to enjoy this beautiful evening together. Because starting soon, we'll be dining more casually in the galley area—mostly."

A splash from nearby preceded jumping, clicking, and whistling as dolphins lightened the moment.

DR peered over portside at the commotion. He grinned at the pod of striped dolphins frolicking alongside. What a perfect day. "The weather is so nice. It'll be good to slow down for an hour or so and enjoy ourselves."

"Looks like we're not the only ones enjoying the day." Craig nodded at the pod. "I wish I had a fish to get a reaction."

"Indeed." Miguel moved to the glassed-in railing alongside them.

"We've made excellent time with the current and wind helping us along." DR picked up where he'd left off. "So we'll put down the anchor and relax. Lo will roll out the beach for anyone who wants to go for a swim in the sea or maybe ride Jet Skis. We have two."

"Beach?" Craig gestured to the open seas.

"Yes, beach." DR laughed. "It's a floating platform attached to the lower aft deck. Fifteen by twenty feet, it holds about eight people. You can use it to get to the Jet Skis or just sit on it, feet in the ocean. How's that sound?"

"Just swell." Craig rubbed his hands together. "You're quite the host and planner. I can't wait."

With the sea sparkling blue and the breeze gentle at their backs, a mist blew over the bow breaking through the sea. Lo came to join them. "We've got company alongside. Striped dolphins—you guys don't want to miss them."

"Yeah, we've been watching. Sea life is struggling in some areas." DR's gaze followed the pod. His hands gripped the chrome bar above the glass railing. "Several dolphin and whale species are rarely seen anymore. But these guys—they love to put on a show. It's almost like they're auditioning for an aquarium or something." *Perk up, buddy, and enjoy the here and now.*

Miguel pushed away from the railing. "Enjoy the dolphins, guys. I'm going down below to see Joshua."

Craig mumbled his own goodbye. "I'd better shove off too." He winked. "Gotta make sure the wife's happy."

Everyone left DR alone on the deck. He sank onto one of the padded white benches, the sea splashing by. His eyes closed, his thoughts hushed, his senses coming alive.

Someone knocked on his door. "Joshua," Miguel called out, "are you busy, or might I come in for a minute?"

Joshua didn't answer, but his friend pushed the door open anyway.

Crouched by the single bed in his quarters, Joshua didn't look up from his prayers. Miguel would understand. Indeed, his friend settled in the corner chair to wait. After finishing with his Lord, Joshua moved to the bed. The soft mattress sank beneath him, and the sensation combined with the room, a tasteful composition of white, gray, and blue, left him feeling as if he were floating in the clouds. "Miguel, how are things up top?"

"Fabulous." Miguel clapped his hands together. "Dinner will be ready shortly. Any thoughts on our trip so far? I mean do you sense any trouble ahead?"

Joshua stiffened. "Don't look at me like that—like I have some kind of crystal ball."

"Sorry, my friend." Miguel slapped Joshua's knee. "No offense, but you do sometimes have... insights? Premonitions, shall we call them?"

Joshua shook his head, long dark hair flipping into his eyes. He shoved it away with an impatient gesture. "We'll be okay. With difficulties come opportunities. Are the others out? I'd like to talk with Debbie. She seems uptight."

Miguel's tanned forehead crinkled. "She wasn't, but she could be now. Want to go up and see?"

"You go ahead. I've got something to do first." Something was on his mind, something he wouldn't be sharing with the others. Not yet at least. He wanted and needed help—after the cruise.

After Miguel left his quarters, Joshua headed to the aft top deck and found her there alone. She had her guitar and was singing. Unnoticed, he slid down on a chaise behind her and closed his eyes. Raw emotion sluiced over him as she sang. He wept, freeing his own imprisoned tears, sharing an agony released in her song. He felt it too, even twenty years later, the sting of lost love, lost hope.

Ten minutes later, she stopped and spun toward him.

"You have such a lovely voice and spirit." He tilted his head. "I don't always understand things either, but you must know that God works all things—"

She raised her hand. "How? How can it be for good? Everybody always tells you that, but I'm not seeing it. Yes, I love the Lord, but He let me down. I'm"—she waved as if to show her struggle—"having a hard time. I can't find any good. Can you?"

Pausing, she rubbed her temples. "I'm sorry. I didn't mean to…"

"It's okay." He sprang from his seat and sank onto the edge of hers. "I'm here for you. Come here." He held out his arms and hugged her. He spoke against her hair. "Those songs? They said it all. Your love for Jesus is so clear. He won't let you down. Letting your loved ones go on ahead is never easy, but you're on a journey. Other people need you, need your love."

He drew back, sensing her calm.

"So…" She wiped at her eyes. "Is dinner ready yet? Are the others eating without us?"

"Let's go find out." He slid his arm around her and led her up to the dining area.

When the others saw her guitar, they started requesting songs. But she shrugged. "Maybe after dinner, I might be talked into playing."

"You're all in for a treat. She's one talented lady." Joshua winked at her, the thankfulness in her eyes saying everything.

After the meal, everyone sat back and waited for her to sing. She gripped the guitar's neck, and one finger traced its way along the strings before she eyed him. "I will if you join me. I need a male voice to accompany me after all." When he nodded, she started strumming the chords to a song. "This is 'Spirit in the Sky.' " Though she only had her guitar, she gave a moving rendition.

As Joshua scanned the others, he smiled. Even the nonreligious liked it, most knowing it from many of Hollywood's movies. With the mood jovial now, the others joined in toward the song's end. No one visited the beach.

Across the deck, DR closed his eyes. Joshua shifted, wondering if he was remembering the first time he'd heard the song or the words—about his friend, Jesus.

DR lowered his head and covered his mouth with his hands.

~

In the Southern Indian Ocean, Yemen child traffickers were captured and taken in by authorities. They'd taken children from Aden two days earlier. Having come to the Bay of Bengal peddling the young boys and girls, they'd transferred their cargo to their coconspirators, American sex traffickers, before their capture.

The buyers escaped from the Indian Ocean West authority's recovery operation and put into an area near the Sentinel Islands, on an island where the people weren't keen on visitors. The Indian government long ago instituted a three-mile buffer to protect both the islanders and visitors alike. Most local governments and commercial operators knew of the restrictions.

The American outlaws dropped anchor in a secluded cove, in a space overgrown with trees and seagrass. They'd sleep now, after escaping, and sail once all the patrols left.

The tribe, like most homeowners, sensed someone had come to their island home and found the boat. They boarded quietly and surprised their visitors.

CHAPTER
TEN

An unexpected storm rose off Egypt's northern coast that night, just strong enough to stir the sea up. The high waves slowed their progress and cut the time the *DI* had gained. DR piloted through the midnight watch, enjoying his new toy while David and Lorenzo rested. All the men took on eight-hour shifts, ensuring their helmsman remained alert. Even with state-of-the-art GPS guidance, they always needed fresh eyes at the helm. DR overlapped the shifts by an hour on each end to tie up any loose ends.

The waves began rolling in higher. Sea spray exploded over the *DI*'s decks. Each time it hit a trough, he imagined it was hard for some of the passengers to sleep, especially those near the bow or stern.

Finally, he handed over the helm and returned to his cabin. The waves rocked the *DI*. But the great cabin amidships was not rocking as violently, and to DR, it was like being a baby in a bassinet, rocked by a steady hand. Man, he lived for this.

$\sim$

When Debbie emerged from her cabin Mitch, Stephanie, and Penny were on the main deck by the pool. She nodded at them and moved by the railing. Several white orcas swished back and forth in front of the *DI*, seemingly plowing the way. Despite daybreak long since passing and the day already having reached eighty-two degrees, the skies remained dark as the end of the storm pushed through. More rain was threatening, but that too would soon be behind them.

Listening to Penny and Stephanie chatter about Jeddah, Debbie smiled to herself. The girls were fast becoming friends. Ready for some bonding, she eased over closer to join them.

"Hi, Debbie. I was just telling Penny how they'll give you a better price the second or third time you come by at the open market in Jeddah." Stephanie's voice rang out, too high-pitched. Maybe a caffeine high or adrenaline left over from the magnificent storm. "But you'd better watch them, or they'll hand over your purchase already in a box. Sometimes, they don't even want you to inspect it before you leave."

"Why not?" Penny asked, appearing more of an innocent than Debbie would have pegged her.

"Don't you see?" Stephanie squealed. "Be firm. Sometimes, they'll switch it to a cheaper version, so carry your own cloth shopping bag."

"You girls have fun. I'm going to get a snack." Debbie made her way to the galley dining area. An apple. Yes, an apple would be the perfect snack. Seeing the girls bonding was nice. All the passengers were growing closer. She and Joshua also shared a budding friendship. There was... well, something about him.

She found a Granny Smith apple hiding in the basket of Red Delicious apples, scrubbed it shiny, then sank into a plush chair, the white cushion beneath her giving solid support.

Miguel strolled in wearing his faded Challenger Cup captain's shirt and slid into the seat across from her. "It's been an interesting start to our little adventure, I'd say. Your singing last night with Joshua was a topper." He set his mug with its last swallow of his coffee on the table. "You're quite a musician."

"Oh, I don't know about that." She bit into the apple and savored the crunch as juice dampened her lips.

"What do you think of Joshua? Isn't he great?"

"Have you known him long?"

"Forever." Miguel twisted and tugged at the pull top on the mixed-nut can. "He's one of the good guys. Has a way of healing the hurt in others."

"Forever?" She laughed and wiped her mouth. "That's a long time."

"It's been a long time. We've seen a lot together. He transcends all the petty small talk." He tossed a cashew into the air and caught it in his mouth, biting down. "I remember when my mom passed on... Well, you know. With a big hug, he made me feel so at ease. When he said I'd see her again, it didn't seem like he was trying to comfort me, but that he *knew* I'd see her again."

Oh, how I hope I get there. I just can't. She held her chin up.

He started to reach out, probably to console her, but stopped. "I know that sounds crazy, but that's how I felt, still do."

"How did you know? Did he tell you?" she whispered, looking from side to side and then back at Miguel as if someone might be watching. "He hugged me too, and it was almost like God himself had come down and taken me in His arms. I've never felt more loved. I mean... does that sound crazy?"

"No more than I did." Miguel reached across the cherry-inlaid galley table and placed his hand atop hers, not seeming to notice the apple's sticky residue. "The Lord anoints some to carry on His ministry. They're able to give you their peace."

"Peace..." She tasted the word on her tongue, sweeter than any apple. "That's the word I was looking for, the emotion I was seeking. Peace... I felt so much *peace* after he hugged me, almost like he took my burdens away."

"Not all of us get those gifts, and those who do pay a great price. I've seen Joshua praying for hours, tears streaming down his face, even pooling on the floor. He said he sometimes feels the heavy weights of those he helps comfort."

She slid her hand free and wiped it on a linen napkin. "How does he do it, I mean, give his peace?"

"It's one of God's gifts, I would guess, but few can or will carry the weight. Take Paul the Apostle, who was Saul. Look at the things he faced as he went, especially in the spirit. Yes, Joshua is a good man of God." A certain gleam lit in Miguel's eyes.

"God has him on this journey for a reason, and Joshua knows it. He just doesn't know the whys, not yet." Miguel took his hand back and smoothed his hair down, leaning in. "You should know, Debbie, there isn't anyone any more spiritual than the next. God gives us all a measure. Some push in more, developing a deep relationship and reliance on God, and that's the difference—trusting in God, desiring His presence, and spending time worshipping Him in the spirit."

Debbie took the remaining apple and wrapped it in a tissue. She rubbed her hands together, then washed the sweetness down with water so cool and refreshing she took a second drink.

Miguel slid the tissue from her place and tossed it into the wastebasket. He smiled when it went in. "God has appointed us good friends and helpmates for this adventure called life. Something spectacular is going to happen."

"Thanks." She leaned over to see his shot, then raised her eyebrows. "What do you mean something spectacular is going to happen?" She watched him closely, her thoughts unsettled. Nothing else mattered. She had to know.

"In my spirit, I sense we're going to return to Marsala better people, at least better than we left. Don't ask me what that involves, but while I spoke to Joshua, there was a, um, how can I say this? A pause in his spirit. At least, that's how I perceived it." He swirled up the dregs of his coffee and swigged the last sip, getting ready to rise, but she grabbed his forearm.

"I don't know if I like the sound of that." Her hand fell away from him, and she rubbed between her eyes. "I'm here for a getaway, to sort my life out again. I'm not ready for..."

She stopped. DR was coming into the galley with Tom and Laurie.

Miguel stood. Then, after greeting them, he left, saying he was headed to the portside aft deck sitting area to watch the world pass behind them. She followed.

The next couple of days passed quickly. After the storm, the waves died down, and the *DI* was back up to running at twenty-one knots. Soon, they'd be at the canal entrance.

Everyone appeared to be having a great time, swimming in the pool, working out in the gym, watching movies in the theater, or lying in the sun, all while getting to know each other. Then they arrived at the anchorage area by the Suez. Thanks to DR's and Lorenzo's connections and reservation, they were given almost immediate passage, apparently an uncommon occurrence.

The Felix agent Lorenzo knew had forwarded their information to authorities and lined everything up, and they transitioned into line behind a US aircraft carrier battle group. A pilot came on board and maneuvered them into the convoy heading south. The pilot would sail them through the canal with a crew member's assistance. Miguel commented that it was almost like God had made a way for them. DR said Miguel ought to know better. Debbie kept silent.

After leaving Port Said, they were on their way. Most passengers on board had never seen a US carrier group close up, and some even commented that it felt comforting to be on the good guy's side.

During the wait, a general's secret intelligence marked the *DI*. They'd spotted the perfect target for their payback scheme. She was sailing behind a US carrier group and under an American flag. "Yes, the *Disillusioned Illusion* will do just fine," they reported.

The *DI* was still 680 miles from Jeddah. With good luck, they'd arrive in two days, the canal taking fifteen hours. As they entered the canal with the pilot and Lorenzo on the bridge, heavy traffic slowed their progression. DR stepped away from the bridge, and David followed him with stories about his past journeys through the canal. Apparently, the ship he served on was in a strike force too.

"Being part of such a powerful team was amazing."

"It must be something." DR settled onto the sunken couch before the bridge. Several throw pillows in navy and white tones hinted at memories of Gail's shopping escapade at Hammer Throw. He snagged one and shoved it behind his back. Then with steam rising from the hot tub before him, he crossed his arms and stretched out his legs to rest his heels on the coffee table. Whether he was captain or not, the journey through the canal was the same unless he restricted himself on the bridge with the pilot. This was much better. He could watch the Egyptian military escort and the people gathering to gawk at the carrier in the canal's narrow places. "What made you decide to join up?"

"Adventure, I guess." Arms outstretched, David pointed out the ever-changing landscape. A machine-gun-laden Egyptian military escort now stood a mere fifty yards in front of them on the canal's roadway. "I joined the marines to get away from home. If I'm getting shot at, I'd like to be able to shoot back. At least, then I knew who the enemy was. DC has gotten so bad. When a high school friend was shot, I got so mad. He's okay, but not being able to fight back or even know who is shooting at you... You know?"

Fight back. *That's what I've been doing. But no matter how hard I fight, He puts something else in my way.* DR shifted, facing the US frigate in front of them, its sheer size daunting.

There were different types of fighting back. "I heard a lot about it when I was growing up. How old were you? I mean, I know lately it's much worse." He lowered his voice and checked around them, half whispering. "Don't say anything to Debbie about this, but her husband was killed in Chicago."

"Wow, poor lady." David's countenance became sullen. "I guess I was in the fifth grade when the violence started to affect my family. My dad always drove the long way to avoid the rougher streets. A stray bullet hit his boss's car one day, and Dad kind of freaked out. So, naturally... our world shrank."

David gestured to people carrying baskets, their children picking up rocks and throwing them into the canal. "Sitting here, watching all these people, gives me a pause. I mean what terrorist or punk wouldn't want to take a shot? Their religion is... Well, it rewards them for killing people like us, gentiles."

The reason the Egyptian Army's armored jeeps escorted the carriers on land, protecting the canal traffic, a major income source for their country. A few locals stopped to watch the American carrier group pass by. DR slid over to the next seat. "Though carriers frequently use the canal, they still cut an impressive sight."

Ryan, who mainly kept to himself, except for trying to sit beside Debbie at the pool, plunked himself down by them. "I gotta admit"—he spoke in his lilting Irish accent—"I'm curious about Jeddah, the gateway to the holy cities of Mecca and Medina." He waved in its general direction. "You know we are going to be near the epicenter of this whole religious fuss, right? Just think if Abram hadn't let Sarah talk him into his little fling, this whole thing wouldn't have happened. Makes you think, doesn't it?"

"You into that religious stuff?" Craig asked, overhearing across the deck. "Who cares how the different religions developed or how all the tension has evolved over the years? What does a quarrel between followers of a carpenter two thousand years ago and an Islamic prophet's followers from fifteen hundred years ago mean to folks like us?"

Well said. DR almost saluted the guy with his captain's log. Nice how Craig, Trixie, and Lorenzo weren't religious.

But Ryan, with his sparkling eyes and fiery red hair, had the look of a seanchaí, an Irish storyteller. Soon, DR imagined, they would know the whole truth, as best as Ryan could explain it and believed it to be. DR excused himself before Ryan could launch his speech.

After anchoring at the Great Bitter Lake, the halfway point, for nearly two hours while they waited for the northbound convoy of ships to pass and another pilot to guide them the rest of the way, they were off to navigate the rest of the canal. No one took a shot at the task force. The *DI* arrived in Jeddah near DR's estimated time, Saturday evening.

Dinghies, small boats, cabin cruisers, and yachts pressed in close, creating an exhilarating atmosphere after the mundane canal passage. Young boys and men ran back and forth between the vessels, small and large, and the marina shops, selling and delivering anything to make a meager living, but nevertheless a living.

Before docking at the pier, the *DI* pumped her fuel, as David and Lo set about their tasks and some of the passengers enjoyed the shops and stands. While at dock, they'd be spending a lot of time nearby.

DR was bringing fresh local foods on board for the next two days, then the rest for their days at sea on their morning of departure. After securing the *DI*, he headed to the port authority's office to firm up his arrangements to meet with friends and pay their fees.

Afterward, he called everyone together on the lower aft deck, and the heady smell of food and salty water awakened his senses. His passengers took in the busy sights of vessels coming and going with the dock laborers, some workers smiling, most not, hurrying to and from. Horns blared, and bells rang. DR basked in it, at home in this element, his memory refreshed, his body invigorated.

"Two vans will pick us up at nine each morning. One to take us out to Mecca tomorrow, and the other to the shops here in the city. Then, on Tuesday, one will travel to Medina and the other to the Mall of Arabia. The in-town driver can also take you to other points of interest if you'd like." He waved his captain's log in the air to punctuate his next words. "But please, stay alert."

He then tucked the log under his arm. He'd been keeping meticulous notes on the trip in hopes of gleaning the best practices for his next cruise.

"If everybody's okay with that, let's get ready for dinner in an hour. A van will take us to the Shayi Restaurant nearby. Their Turkish food comes highly recommended while being reasonably priced." He stored his log in an aft-deck lazaret before facing his group again. "If we have time after visiting the Kolkata region, we might take a day to stop in again on our return trip. How does that sound?"

Miguel nodded to the others. "I think I can speak for everyone when I say it sounds like everything is good to go. I don't know about everybody else, but I'm thankful to have such a fine captain looking out for us."

"I second that." Joshua rolled his hands and wrist together and spread them while bowing his head in approval.

When the van showed up on time, everyone piled in, chattering their excitement to try the Turkish food and have their feet on dry land. The driver wove through the narrow and bustling streets, wasting little time and having no qualms about using his horn. After nearly running over a small boy pulling a tribe of goats up a side street on a rope, he leaned out the window and shouted at the boy.

And the passengers who spoke Arabic translated for their companions, then later helped order their food, sharing a house specialty, the family favorites dish—shish kebab, döner kebab, kofta, and baklava. "No one," DR insisted, "ever leaves without trying their baklava."

~

Well-fed and worn out, they returned to the *DI*, most of the passengers retiring to their quarters. Debbie, however, joined Joshua and Miguel on the forward swimming-pool deck to enjoy the moonlight along with the sounds and smells of Jeddah. From this vantage point, the lights of the distant downtown twinkled.

While David took first watch, Miguel offered to pour drinks. "It's been said—and wisely so!—'Borders and walls left unguarded would be attacked.' In Jeddah, that includes yachts. I'm glad DR keeps the watch up."

He passed out the drinks.

"Sangria?" Debbie asked.

"Indeed, though I call it Kim's Favorite." He smiled. "I'm a blessed man to have such a daughter-in-law. You liked her, didn't you, Debbie?"

"Yes. She's so easy to talk to."

"I see you're enjoying yourself, my friend." Joshua held out his hand and offered Miguel a seat beside him. "It's so good to see you back at sea."

"I'll drink to that." Miguel raised his glass. "I was thinking about my Marco. How good God has been to me. I don't ever want to take family for granted or not spend as much time with them as possible. I lost sight of my blessings for a while. I'll see my Martina one day, but life is for the living. And God has many jobs for me to do still."

The mid-fall season made the temperature enjoyable as voices from happy celebrations in the harbor carried over the water, reminders of life's blessings. Gulls scavenged in the light of the pier's lampposts. The yacht swayed in a rhythmic beat.

Swirling his sangria around in his glass, Joshua focused as the dark sweet concoction released its berry smell. "We all have much to do—and much to enjoy. Mmm, I can see why Kim likes this." He raised the glass to his nose and inhaled the sweet alcoholic fragrance as if to find out its secret. "I'm not much on alcohol, but this is refreshing. But I fear it might be potent, so I'd better just sip it."

"Ahh." Miguel slapped his friend's back. "That's the downside of sangria. But in moderation, sipping is good now and again for your heart and your attitude. What do you think, Debbie? How do you like yours?"

She'd been drinking the sangria while the two men talked, having finished half of her glass. Being on the smaller side, she didn't need much alcohol to affect her. "I love it—not just the drink, but the night and company. It's been a long time since I've kicked back and enjoyed a glass of wine."

She sank deeper into her chaise. The sea's lapping against the boats sounded like a heartbeat, the rise and fall under the vessel mesmerizing. A waxing moon lit the ocean and landscape, and the familiar song of ropes and hardware bouncing and clanging off their masts rang in the air.

"So, this is what an Arabian night is like in port." She turned her glass in her hand, dipping her nose to drink in its scent, though nothing more. "It seems suspenseful and enticing. I remember watching those old Arabian movies. You know? The ones with beautiful horses and swashbuckling sailors. But this isn't anything like that."

The sprawling old city of Jeddah was alive. The smells and sounds wove a magical atmosphere for her foreign guests.

Joshua patted her shoulder. "God has us all here for a reason. You both know that, besides Ryan, we are the only believers on board, right? The others aren't born again, so they don't have a clue about the spiritual differences between the culture here compared with ours back home. Yeah, they know about the radicals, but not the demonic elements or even the dreamwalkers that may come into play along these journeys."

"Dreamwalkers?" She sat up straighter, edging her shoulder away from his grip. Was the guy nuts? "What do you mean by born again?"

The men looked at each other.

Miguel stiffened. "Oh, I thought you were saved. You said you believe in God, so I assumed you'd received Jesus."

What on earth? Of course, she knew Jesus. Bristling, she cocked her head and slanted her eyes. "I do believe in God, but what do you mean by 'received Jesus'? No one ever told me I had to *receive* Jesus. I believe and pray every night and... whatever. So I'm a Christian and going to heaven when I die." *Great. Receive Jesus?* Her sangria was finished, and she must be feeling it. Only that would explain such ridiculous things these men were saying.

Joshua reached over and stole her empty glass. "Debbie, the first thing we need to do is make sure you don't have a buzz. What do you say we get together in the morning, after the others leave? We'll sit and talk. Afterward, if you like, you can invite Him into your life."

Invite Him in? Why did he act like she didn't know God? And here, she'd thought they'd become friends. She pressed cold fingers to the sudden throb in her temple. "Whatever."

Joshua changed the subject, and the men talked into the night. She watched them, not hearing a word, just enjoying the atmosphere of the old city's port, the scent of the sea, and the drone of friendly conversation.

Invite Him in? It sounded like some creepy séance, but Joshua was talking about *God* and *Jesus*. Joshua carried a peace she'd never had, so much of it that he gave it away to those around him.

Invite Him in? Had he done that? Was that where his peace came from?

CHAPTER
ELEVEN

The vans arrived early, one for Mecca, the other for shopping in the city. DR winked at Trixie as they loaded up. "Looks like you're the only lady going to Mecca."

Craig draped an arm around his wife's shoulders and jostled her. "And she's okay with that, aren't you, hon?"

"Better than okay." Trixie batted his arm away and climbed into the second row of seats while Stephanie, Penny, and Laurie boarded the other van. "This is right up my alley. Not sure why the girls didn't want to come."

As their van sped toward Mecca, DR took up the loudspeaker and described his former professor, his studies under him, and Itasham's different traits.

"Please remember we are the visitors here. Respect their faith and practices, no matter how different they appear." DR made eye contact with Ryan, the part-time Catholic administrator, the only passenger DR worried about. After Gail's mother's experience with a hard-nosed Catholic family... Well, if Ryan was like Gail's father who knew what he would say or do? "These are their holiest cities, steeped in tradition and sensitive points. This year before the hajj ended two months ago, almost eight million pilgrims journeyed here from all over the world to worship."

DR paused to wipe perspiration from his forehead. The AC was working, but it couldn't compete with the ocean breeze they'd just left. He raised the loudspeaker again. "Itasham is Islamic too, so he'll have good insights to share. We'll have a snack with him before he takes us to a village. He's going to leave at midday for Salat al-zuhr, their prayer time. Any questions?"

No one spoke, most watching as the desert landscape passed by. Occasionally, a group of buildings or a shop broke the desert monotony. A place to stop for gas and supplies, maybe a house or so.

Ryan huffed. "Look at all this. Little wonder how the terrorists hide and blend in."

"Maybe." Trixie waved at the land, heat wavering above its expanse. "But, Ryan, what I'm seeing is how hard desert life looks. I can see why the cities are large population centers."

Browsing the shops, Laurie lingered a step behind Penny and Stephanie, never one to miss the opportunity to people watch and not a bit apologetic about it. People watching was research for an author, and she and her husband hadn't become an international best-selling team without good research.

"Come on, Laurie, before we lose you." Penny flounced over, the cheerleader she was, almost stereotyped. Tom would have a fit if Laurie tried to write in a character like her.

"No one is going to lose me—too much adventure here to miss a minute of it."

"I wish we hadn't agreed not to buy too much today, but to come back for it tomorrow," Penny groused in her intoxicating Alabama twang so different from the harsh London accent Laurie was used to. She flipped brown hair back from her shoulders and pouted. "What if we forget where we see it and can't find it again?"

Laurie thumbed through a stack of wraps in every color imaginable.

"Isn't that the goal?" Stephanie, towering over the two of them six feet tall even in her flat sandals, held up one of the wraps with yellow, orange, and red stripes. "Otherwise, I might fill up half the boat. Besides, I warned you about how to shop here."

"I get it." Laurie smiled at them, feeling a bit more mature even though they both had kids while she and Tom had decided to wait. At forty, she had better not wait much longer, but who had time to raise kids when there were adventures to play out via their books? "You guys don't want to buy a lot of stuff."

"If we see something that is to die for, maybe," Stephanie said.

"Well, *I* have to bring something home," Laurie threatened. "Otherwise, I'll never believe this day was real and not just one of my imaginary adventures. Bane of the writer, you know."

"Come on. Let's go next door. There's so much to see." Penny took Laurie's arm, Southern twang to her words and cheerleader skip to her step all charmingly almost too much as she steered her away from the pile of hideous body wraps.

"See how closely those men are watching everyone?" Laurie asked. Maybe the girls hadn't noticed.

"It's kind of creepy," Penny said, still leading Laurie arm in arm.

So even she had noticed. That meant Laurie's mystery-writer brain wasn't working overtime. She shivered.

Lorenzo was lounging on the aft portside deck, catching a few rays, when Debbie joined Joshua in the galley, Miguel having decided to go with DR to meet Itasham.

Holding her head, she eased onto the padded chair, soft leather cushioning her seat. "Oh..." She winced when the motion still jarred her. "I'd forgotten how wine makes my head pound."

"Yeah, same here."

Joshua was nibbling on a piece of toast and tuna, his favorite. Ugh, how nasty this early in the morning.

He brushed crumbs from his hands, edged his plate aside, and leaned his elbows on the cool cherry inlay between them. "So, have you thought about what we talked about last night, about Jesus?"

"Some." The aspirin had started to kick in before Joshua brought up *the* subject. Now, the pounding in her head increased—or was that in her heart? "But what are dreamwalkers? I heard of them when I was young. Are you one? How do you know whether you are or not?"

"I'm not a dreamwalker. They're spirits, not people."

She nodded, though her questions still weren't answered. "I guess I should know this, shouldn't I? I've never really read the Bible."

"No worries." He raised the cola can to rinse the tuna taste from his mouth, ridding himself of the smell too. "That said, we know the battle for souls is set. So many things in this life affect us and our decisions. Things as simple as a hello, a wanton glance at someone, an empty stomach, or even an angry word—all of it affects us, especially our spirits, and particularly sinful things."

Debbie looked around, sniffing, the tuna smell nearly gone. Good thing too. Far too early for that. She took his plate and slid it further down the table in hopes of clearing the air.

He rolled his eyes at her disgust. "Sorry, but a guy's got to eat something. Anyway, returning to the conversation. How we handle them is what matters."

Her head pounded. A deep conversation wasn't something she wanted. Trying not to be rude, she couldn't help showing disinterest. At least until her head felt better.

"Sometimes, prophets hear from God's dreamwalkers, even pastors occasionally. We all can—if we listen."

"Huh?" Her head jerked up. Wow, that got her attention. Maybe he could see she wasn't engaging and knew he had to say something to get her attention, something she'd asked about the night before, or she might go back to her cabin to lie down.

"But that's where it gets tricky, and the main reason I didn't want to go on the journeys into Mecca and Medina. They can enter your gates without you knowing it."

She'd closed her eyes, inhaling deeply. Then he'd hit a nerve, and her eyes had flown wide open. "Gates, what's a gate?"

Maybe religion was far more interesting and complicated than she could've known. "It sounds like a science-fiction movie. Don't forget— I have a doctorate in paleontology, so my mind begins dissecting and classifying information when it hears something."

"A gate is your senses—your eyes, ears, nose, mouth, and any way that can touch your thoughts or thought process. Think of opening a bad email. The enemy plants something in you or on you. They may whisper something in your thoughts, causing you to think about it, maybe just in your subconsciousness. Something like a computer virus, except your brain and your thoughts are the computer. The science-fiction comparison isn't bad. It's like watching a horror movie and going to bed, only to have a bad dream. The movie somehow planted a seed, and the spirit used it to create your bad dream."

"Whoa." She held up a hand. "You mean my bad dreams come from enemy spirits?" Her hand flopped down. Then she slapped the table. "I always wondered where they came from. That sounds kind of wild."

He closed his eyes, then rubbed at the pinched space between his now-furrowed brows. "I didn't mean it that way. Not all dreams are from spirits. I wouldn't think so anyway."

His forehead ridged in deep thought. "I hope I'm getting this across correctly. This is one of those areas most churches never teach their members because the pastors don't fully understand it either. But prophetic dreams are real, and understanding them takes time, prayer, wisdom, and God's guidance. Some dreams take years to come true while others mere hours. God is in control of the prophetic dreams, not the 'evil' spirits."

"It sounds complicated. I never heard of any of this stuff." She grimaced. "And I guess I'm still that kid in school, wanting to learn it all, even taking courses all summer, but needing some kind of textbook to follow, some kind of proof it's all real."

"Remember, God's spirits are the dreamwalkers, and only God can give prophetic dreams. He alone knows what the future holds—not Satan. The Bible tells us everything."

She remembered the day her grandfather brought her to America, leaving her parents and Japan behind. How confusing it all was, including the argument she overheard from her bedroom. Between the nightmares, the mystifying lessons at the dojo, dreamwalkers, tongue talkers, and all that, it was a bewildering time. And here she was again.

Joshua kept speaking, perhaps missing her downturned eyes and overcast expression. "I was almost twelve when I accepted Christ." He let out a long low breath as if caught up in his own heartrending memories. "I needed Him so badly right after my mom and dad's car accident. I had a visit—it may have been a spiritwalker. Long story short, he brought back my granddad or at least the voice of my granddad."

She wanted memory lane to close.

"I remember it like yesterday. I was so lost. But let's get back to the main thing, Jesus."

"I'm sorry." She flattened her palms on the smooth tabletop, needing something to ground her. "I didn't mean to bring back your bad memories."

"Don't be sorry." He touched her arm. "Those are good memories. One of many memorials I've built to point to my beliefs and my salvation. Everyone needs lots of those. When times get tough, we can look to them for strength."

"Memorials?" She rubbed her forehead. Feeling dizzy, overwhelmed, probably sugar dropping, she gathered herself. Food. "This is far more complicated than just believing. Am I supposed to build a memorial? Where would I even build one? Hold that thought." She sprang from her seat. "I'm going to grab a donut."

He breathed in deeply, his face lifted toward the tiled ceiling overhead.

When she returned, munching on a custard-filled donut, she imagined he was praying. She nudged his shoulder, interrupting. "Want one?"

"No thanks. I'm good." Twisting himself on the seat, he edged closer to the table and tucked his legs under his seat on raised toes. He ran a hand through black hair, full and long, exposing again the graying at its temples. "Debbie, everyone has doubts about God or their faith wavers. If you have that one place or an emergency that God and only God could show up and help or fix—and He did—that's a memorial, *if you remember it*. Then you have those experiences to get you through anything, but you have to remember them. In tough times, recall your memorials to strengthen your faith and regain your courage to fight a good fight."

"What about the dreamwalkers?" She plucked a glazed bite off her donut and brought it to her mouth, the spices rising to her nostrils. But before popping it into her mouth, she asked, "Do they really go into our dreams?"

Maybe God would let Mark come back to say goodbye. Oh, how she would love one more chance to say goodbye. Her love for him wouldn't let go of it. Maybe that's why she was here, on this trip. Maybe a dreamwalker had gotten her to come for that reason. Maybe?

Joshua held up a hand as if he could see where this was going and knew he had to nip it.

"Now, just so you know, God's spirits aren't in our heads every minute of every day just to make people feel better about a bad situation. When He sent my granddad, I knew it was so I would find a purpose for my life. At least, that's how I've come to understand it."

"So how does he do it, I mean—Satan? How do his demons dreamwalk?" She'd seen the worst of things in Chicago. The donut left a greasy coating on her tongue. Queasy, she reached for her water glass to chase the taste away. Had Satan sent dreamwalkers to pull her down? Down into the pit with him?

"Remember, I told you about horror movies. Well, that's one of the ways we open our gates, but there are others." He stretched his right shoulder, his eyes briefly searching hers as he took a sip of cola. "When we miss the mark from time to time and sin, that's the major way. God's commandments aren't just something He made up. They are there to protect us, to protect against the evil spirits."

She pressed her palms against the cool tabletop, enjoying the sensation. Her pulse thrummed through her fingertips. She took slow deep breaths and listened to the low hum of the Sub-Zero.

"Just so you know"—he placed the top on the empty tuna-fish container—"one of the first things God teaches His prophets is to guard their gates. Otherwise, they will be at the behest of the enemy and do Satan's work too, not even knowing until God stops it. As humans, we often submit to the desires of our flesh, whether for money, power, sex, or whatever."

He settled back in his chair, crossing one knee over the other and smoothing his dark shorts, apparently warming to the subject right when she wasn't sure she could handle him continuing. "There's so much to learn and trust God for. The enemy can—and does—use those things often. The Bible talks a lot about the spirits, the demonic ones too. I didn't teach you much, except that prophetic dreams come from God, the vivid dreams. Something tells me you'll know more about them soon."

Her head jerked up. Prophetic dreams? *Her*? "Um, how come you used those things, money, sex, and power? And why do you say I'll know more soon?" She was an educated and accomplished woman, but this area...

"Sorry. I thought it would be easier to explain using those examples. Those things just get through all our gates quicker. But God has other ways He uses dreamwalking. He shows men and women, at least some, prophecy through dreams. But the trick is knowing when it is God and when it's not."

Did she want to know more about it? Did she even believe it? Do educated people? Joshua did. And he was an educated man, speaking Hebrew, Farsi, Italian, Greek, and English. Even understanding some Spanish and French as well. Enough to help him make his way home if it were necessary, he'd claimed. She couldn't help respecting him. But trusting him? Believing what he was saying when he was saying such outlandish things?

She shook her head. "I don't like the sound of that."

"I have questions too, Debbie. Questions haunting me from the past. Somehow, since the day I met you..." He cocked his head, eyeing her as if he thought *she* was the way to his answers. To unlocking his secrets.

What an absurd thought. Surely, she was misreading him.

In Chicago, their store had exhibits and products like tools and weapons of human evolution dated back almost a million years, but nothing pointed to serving or worshipping a god until maybe a couple thousand years ago. "Through my studies, I've seen entire religions start when men became self-appointed in their knowledge of God's ways."

"An excellent example." Joshua shifted, for the first time looking as uncomfortable as he'd made her. "I can't talk about that *here*. There are enemy spirits we don't want to encounter, especially in Jeddah, if you know what I mean. No point lowering our gates." He slapped the table. "That's all for today's lesson on dreamwalking. Now, let's talk about Jesus."

"Well, professor, I wanted to know more about dreamwalking. I know you can't push a teacher—supposedly, when they say lesson's over, lesson's over for the day." She turned in her seat and propped herself up on one leg, trying to get closer, intent on continuing the discussion. "But I'm not sure you'll be able to put me off, you see. I was always the girl lingering after class, pushing for more. So when my love for a good suspense is in high gear, you're not going to be able to walk away from the discussion. And, so far, this is better than the novel I brought to read."

"Better than a novel, eh?" He laughed, one side of his mouth quirking.

"Well, I did pick up the latest Laurie and Tom Hughes mystery. I don't deny that it's good." She shook a finger at him.

The inner corners of her eyebrows rose, and the corners of her lips pulled downward. She wanted to ask him about her childhood, about what had happened when she was young. "When I was six, my grandfather took me to a dojo in Tokyo after the courts took me from my parents. They taught me, the masters, how to defend myself and how to have inner strength—peace, if you will. But I had dreams, bad dreams, and still remember some. Sometimes they still—well, I don't know if I can say *haunt*, but I still have them. They scare me because they are so vivid. And..." She swallowed hard, pushing out the rest. "What's strange is I'm always a child in them. Does that sound like they planted a seed in me?"

I've been with some of the most interesting people, but to be with this woman, here, with the unknown feet away. Talking about God. How did I ever get this lucky? Her perfume tempted Joshua's senses, throwing off his thoughts. The flowery fragrance seemed to have a mind of its own. A calling card for more.

"I didn't realize... Wow. What happened to your parents?" He propped up on his elbows, intent to hear it all. "I don't mean to pry, but why did the courts give you to your grandfather? Do you ever see your parents?" Had he just opened one of her gates?

"They said my parents were heavy into psychedelic drugs and something that sounds kind of like what you are talking about. But Pawpaw never said why. I never knew there was such a thing. I thought—no, it was my grandfather who thought—it was drugs that had stolen their minds. They kept calling it tongue talking, but Pawpaw claimed they were tripping on drugs. So, he went to court and took me away."

The calling card was shouting now. His heart raced—from her story—and her femininity. Here, secluded in the galley while most were away, he had to shut these thoughts down. Trying to focus on her words and not her lips, he had to know everything.

"I was six." She shrugged. "So I don't remember. But the dreams... The final step at the dojo was supposed to—and I wasn't allowed to say it at the time—train me in the art of spiritual or mind warfare. But we moved to Chicago before I could start that phase. Pawpaw said he had to get me away from that demonic stuff. Now the master's no longer teaching. He says the skills we were taught aren't practical or useful in today's life. I spent eight years learning, and now I'm—"

"That may explain some of your dreams." He folded his arms on the table between them. Now interested in talking about dreamwalking too, he forgot Jesus was the reason they were talking.

Maybe she could shed some light on it without even knowing. Many things even he didn't understand, but he'd better guard his gates. There was a place in time he had to get back to, correcting his own wrongs. Maybe this beautiful woman could help him get there?

"Are your parents still alive? How long has it been since you've last seen them?"

Tears formed in her eyes. Debbie sniffled, reliving that terrible day once again. "We saw them right before we moved to Chicago. All I remember is how mad Pawpaw was, real mad. He argued with Me-Maw for weeks before we moved away. Right before we left for America, my mom and dad came over and brought me some things. That's the last time I saw them."

Joshua got up and came over and held her in silence as she shook, tears flowing. He whispered something, perhaps a prayer, so low she probably wasn't supposed to hear: "The dreamwalkers are busy, Lord, emotions on board the *DI* raw. Could this be one of those 'all things' moments?"

She let the silence sink in, the tears seep away.

Then he released her. "You're American? How did your family come to live in Japan?"

Good. She needed that. Facts. She could always focus on facts, put her emotions away. "Pawpaw was a naval specialist during World War II, then stationed in Kanagawa. Dad grew up there and met my mom. Her family was stationed there too." She wiped tears from her face. "I never saw them much though. Mom's parents disowned her when she married Dad. Pawpaw always told me how much I looked like my mom, how pretty she was. I wanted her to come and hold me, but she never came, not until the day we left Japan. Then she held me so tight! I still remember how nice she smelled. Isn't that crazy?" She snuffled and reached for a linen napkin. "The thing I remember the most was how she smelled and sounded, and how it felt to be in her arms."

"Not crazy at all."

"Dad kept saying Pawpaw didn't have the right to steal me—'She's my baby girl, you ass.' I'm sorry, Joshua. I had to say it. He just kept saying it. That and 'dreams aren't enough.' " She balled up the soggy napkin and started whimpering again. "What did he mean?"

Joshua held her by her shoulders. This wasn't how he foresaw the day going. He'd prayed he'd lead Debbie to the Lord. Now, that didn't seem likely, not this morning. That would have to come later. There was so much to learn, and she needed to experience truth and forgiveness while accepting Jesus as her Lord.

CHAPTER
TWELVE

In Jeddah, Laurie had managed to free herself from Penny's cheerfulness. Now, with her companions jostling through the chaotic market, her mind spun all the mystery that could arise during an outing in a city of three and a half million. And her master's in history helped her imagine the place hundreds of years ago. "Guess this crowding is what happens when the suburbs are nothing but miles and miles of sand."

"It's wild, isn't it?"

Uh-oh, Penny was back at her side. Laurie pressed her arm tight to her body before her newfound friend could grab it again. Funny how Penny managed to make it feel like the three of them had grown up together. Perhaps there was something to that "Southern hospitality" after all.

"What do you say we try some of the local Saudi food for lunch? I'm starved." On cue, Penny's stomach started to growl.

"Do you see a place you want to try?" Laurie tucked wisps of red hair back from her face behind the abaya she'd donned with the other girls. "If so, I'm game. I wasn't too crazy about dinner last night. Did either of you like the shish kabob, or whatever those things were?"

"It was all right." Stephanie turned a circle while walking. Even with the abaya covering her six-foot frame, she attracted stares from the local men. "But I'd prefer trying the local Saudi foods myself. We don't have a lot of Turkish restaurants back in Paris. Now I know why."

As they entered the small café along the street side, the scents made Laurie hungrier.

"Really, in all of Paris, there's not many Turkish restaurants, Steph? You don't mind me calling you Steph, do you?" Penny flounced into her chair, displaying too much energy for Laurie to keep up. "We've got several in Birmingham, and I didn't care for it there either." She leaned to the young man who was their host. "What is that delicious smell?"

When he just stared at her with a blank expression, Stephanie asked him in Arabic.

He answered in kind, his words as heavy and exotic as the scent. Then Stephanie translated. "It's matazeez. He claims it's a deliciously —yes, he said deliciously—prepared dough ball with lamb and vegetables served in a special spiced tomato-based sauce." Full of herself and light in spirit, Stephanie laughed and added, "I'll bet it won't be *baaaad*. Steph is fine, by the way. It has an endearing sound to it. Some of my friends from school call me Steph."

Bending down toward the table not to be seen, Laurie, also laughing, whispered. "Do you think something's weird here, or is it just me and my overactive imagination?"

Some of the conversations they overheard caused a sensation that something was wrong, or was it the dim lighting and drab tables with their utilitarian feel? There weren't any pictures of the normal things of life, at least not that seemed normal to her, just patterns and designs, no flowers, trees, or even people. And of the other twenty or so guests having lunch at the handful of tables, a few seemed as distracted as she was becoming.

The waiter came back over, took their orders, then hurried away. Although there were other women in the café, she squirmed, feeling strangely out of place.

Penny whispered back. "I think the other ladies here feel the same way we do. Look at their faces. It's almost as if…" She stopped, her gaze falling on several men sitting in the rear corner dressed in black thobes and keffiyeh head coverings, only a portion of their faces visible. "Now, that's a scary sight. You can't see anything above their eyes or below their lips."

Stephanie turned to see, then faced Penny and Laurie. "Just don't stare, and it'll be okay. They're having lunch just like us, and nothing else—although, unlike us, they seem to be enjoying themselves. I'm going to go have them wrap our lunch to go. Penny, call for the van?"

Stephanie pushed to her feet and strode away.

Penny sat wide-eyed for a moment, not moving, then fished out her phone.

Laurie leaned across the table and whispered. "I thought she said there was no need to worry. Why are we leaving?"

Penny just shrugged, already making the call, then disconnected. "They'll be here in five."

A moment later, Stephanie was back. "Lunch will be ready in a few minutes. I went ahead and paid. One of you can get it tomorrow. Any word on our van yet?"

"It's on the way," Laurie whispered.

"I may not particularly like shish kebab." Penny's cheerful face remained taut. "But what do you say? Next time, let's get meat on a stick or something from a street vendor."

So they felt threatened too. Laurie suppressed a shiver. The sight caused her overactive imagination to conjure up thoughts. Even though nothing was said or done. But for the other girls to get jittery… then it was more than *her* imagination, wasn't it?

"Are you okay, Steph? You looked like you just saw a ghost?" Laurie asked, seeing tight lines around Steph's eyes.

"I'll tell you later. After we get back to the boat," Stephanie replied.

And that sent Laurie's heart racing as she fought to control her thoughts.

This wasn't like the Stephanie they'd come to know. The van arrived after their food was ready. Her heart still thudding, Laurie followed the others from the café and scrambled into the van after looking back over her shoulder. They headed back to the *DI*, today's adventure over.

As the van navigated the busy backstreets with horns blowing and people shouting and waving their arms, Stephanie puffed out her pent-up breath, then reached for both of their hands. "Um, let's go to the mall tomorrow. It would be safer, with less drama."

"Deal." Laurie exhaled as well. "I mean I *love* drama, but I'd prefer to experience it between the pages of my books, thank you very much."

Penny laughed, then freed her hand, and waved her finger between the others. "Spoken like dour European ladies—but yes, I agree. Now, when do we get into this food you got us?"

Less drama sounded good because no way would she tell Tom she fled from a restaurant. Laurie rubbed between her eyes, hoping Stephanie was right about tomorrow.

Meanwhile, in Mecca, DR led the group through an interesting but so-far-uneventful day with the professor. Though they should all come away more enlightened, he could sense disappointment. Itasham had left for almost two hours, abandoning them in a small home. When he returned, he apologized profusely, saying it was unavoidable, then began their intended tour. While the others were occupied, at last, he took DR aside.

"My friend, I'm sorry about today, but there is going to be trouble tonight at the port. You might want to consider leaving. Some bad people are in Jeddah right now. From what I could detect, I daresay they are from a terrorist group." Itasham's constant looking around aroused DR. "My friend in Mecca said they have been recruiting during the holy times and are planning a 'special initiation' for the authorities who have been hunting them."

DR rubbed his forehead. Itasham knew the people, and DR should heed his wise professor's advice. The village was just a spot on the road. Nothing of any significance. Although disappointed, they made the most of it.

After about two hours, he asked everyone to board the van for their return back to the *DI*.

"It was good to see you, DR." Itasham clasped his hands as they were leaving. "I hope we'll see each other again soon. Give my best to Clyde McMillen. Remember, keep an eye on him."

"Thanks. I'll call you when we get back. I appreciate the tip. We'll leave this afternoon." Would they, though? Stepping into the van, he counted everyone. This wasn't only disappointing. How could he explain the reason they were leaving early?

The van sped toward Jeddah, but his spirit remained heavy. Itasham wasn't easily scared or excited. An Egyptian native, he knew what to take seriously. They had to leave, and soon.

DR called ahead for their food and supplies, having their orders delivered as early as possible this afternoon. Unwilling to take any chances with their lives or the *DI*, he paid premium delivery prices to expedite his orders. He'd tell the others as soon as they reached the *DI*. No need to ruin the wonderful drive for them, especially Trixie, who sat peering out the window gleaning everything possible, knowing she might never be back this way, taking it all in.

He turned to his window as well, considering the landscape and the roadside shows of life. The locals all going about their daily routines. He shook his head. It was the same worldwide, wasn't it? Everyone pushed by the same desires. Only now, the hard desert living was on display through the windows.

After the girls reached the *DI*, Laurie followed her friends to a table under the shade of an umbrella on the upper aft portside deck to eat. Still jittery, she'd just sample the food and sip water as she regained her nerve.

"Ah, I thought I heard chatter." Joshua came out wearing his red-

and-green Italian flag trunks with a white polo, looking all patriotic. "Mmm, something smells good. Do you have any extra? Maybe just a bite for a hungry vagabond?"

He dropped into a seat at the stylish round teak table between Penny and Laurie. "I was just too lazy to fix anything or walk over to the corner bistro. Say, why didn't you girls eat it while it was hot in town?"

Penny unwrapped her meal and gave him half of her matazeez. "Something was strange in the café where we stopped. It weirded us out, so we got the food to go. So... Steph, what were you going to tell us when we got back?"

Joshua pointed at Penny's lunch. "Are you sure that's all you're going to eat? I don't actually want to take all your lunch."

She waved at him as if to say don't worry about it. Maybe she wasn't sure she could eat any more than Laurie thought she could. Laurie frowned at her meal, the blood-red spiced tomato-based sauce more than her mystery-writer brain could handle right now.

Stephanie stuffed her matazeez into her mouth, licked her fingers, then raised her hand to pause the conversation. "Those guys in the black thingamajigs? They looked like the terrorists I saw on television the other night. What did they call them? El kabob or something like that. Anyway, they were here a couple of months ago during the hajj, their five-day holy thing. Some were recruiting. They had a shootout near where DR and the guys went. I had forgotten all about that." She bit into a dough ball, and her hand covered her mouth as she finished chewing. "I hope the boys are all right."

Laurie nibbled at a piece of lamb, the flavor just too much right now. She also slid some of her matazeez over to Joshua, keeping some of the veggies for herself. "I guess I'll donate to our favorite vagabond. Look at the bright side—Joshua got a free meal out of it."

A few hours later, Tom came aboard with the others. Finding her now under the cover of an umbrella poolside writing an email to her mom, he bent to kiss her forehead. "How's my little firebrand today? I hope your day was more interesting than ours—nothing out there to see but sand."

"It was... interesting." No need to say more. Or to add that, in real life, she didn't feel like much of a firebrand. At least not today. She'd stick to stirring things up with her words on paper. "I'm sending Mom an email, checking up on her."

Tom eyed her, perhaps sensing her discomfort. Like her, he loved to people watch. Little cues never escaped him. But he didn't push it. "DR called a meeting. He wants everyone together on deck. Something's up."

"I wondered." She pushed herself up from the padded seat. "Over the last while, there's a lot of activity loading supplies." Sliding her hand into her husband's, she followed him through the sleek outer passageway, squeezing by a vendor delivery, going from the forward sun and pool deck to the main aft deck.

"Everyone, please..." DR was speaking as they stepped onto the aft deck. "I have some troubling news. Itasham informed me that one of the terrorist groups may have a surprise for the port tonight. He advised us to depart this evening... before any conflicts arise. I've ordered our supplies. Lorenzo is settling our account. Then we're sailing out. I know it's disappointing."

Laurie squeezed Tom's hand, needing extra support. Impossible to think such things could have anything to do with the men today. And yet, hard not to feel she'd been too close to danger.

Beside her and Tom, Miguel's shoulder slumped. Then he rallied the passengers. "Again, our captain has made a wise decision. I say we second it and get busy, readying to make way. Can I get an amen?"

They all murmured their amens.

After Lorenzo settled their affairs, DR asked his capable crew and best helper to meet in the galley to work out a new schedule for piloting the *DI* overnight.

Then Laurie joined Tom by the prow as Lorenzo and DR piloted the *DI* out and around the barrier guarding the port. Tom slipped an arm around her shoulders. "Nightfall's coming soon, and I, for one, am ready for a little sangria and hors d'oeuvres before we retire. What say you, Dr. Watson?"

She slapped at his chest. "Agreed."

He pressed his face to the top of her head, breathing in deeply the shampoo scent he often claimed to love.

"It's been a crazy kind of day, but just another day, as always in this part of the world, wasn't it?" She turned back to the port, thinking about its history. "Here, it's best to expect the unexpected. The people have been at war with one another since Cain and Abel, all over religion, power, and sex."

While putting out to sea, no one noticed the men in black thobes had followed the girls from the café. They watched the *DI* sailing out, disdain tautening their faces behind the swaddling. Their plan for payback against the US president would have to wait. Jennings wouldn't be happy. The *DI* left too quickly.

The leader's headpiece was no longer on as he spoke to someone on his phone. "Tell the senator his American friend will have to wait. They just left the port. Somebody must've tipped them off. It's too late to stop the other plans though."

Joshua rose to his feet, putting down his cup and welcoming his new friend as Stephanie joined him and Miguel.

As they sailed out to sea, she hugged her arms around herself and shared how it felt in the café. "There was an eeriness about the way they stared at everyone. There was a no-one's-home kind of feeling. Just a blank, cold—almost demonic presence. I don't know. I've never been around men that wear those type of khamis, the black dressy thobe ones. The café workers were chattering about the men. My knowing what they were saying added to it all. They were all nervous and felt fearful too—like they expect something to happen."

"DR is going to take good care of us." Miguel raised his chin. "And so is the Lord. Something tells me he's a special man to God." Nodding several times, he watched the yacht's wake rise and its swells dissipate.

"Sure… yes, he will." She gave that weak smile people give. The one that says they're being polite, but they aren't a believer and don't want to discuss it. At least not tonight.

Lord… Joshua closed his eyes. *Show me how I can help her open her heart to You.*

Greg, Mitch, and Ryan joined them.

Mitch turned his glass in his hand. "The drive to Mecca showed how vast the desert is, its sparse population so ideal for terrorists."

"I hear you." Mitch downed the last of his tonic water. "There's practically no police, only the military, and lots more important matters, like making money. Radicalism often flies right under the radar because those empowered to stop it are radicalized too."

"It's normal here. Didn't the terrorists who attacked America come from Saudi Arabia?" Ryan asked, then winked. "Yes, the news in Dublin carried that part of the story—perhaps even more than the major networks in America."

"Come on. Dinner's being served in the galley. We can take it to the sundeck and watch some dolphins." Mitch reached for Stephanie's hand, half pulling her out of her seat.

The calamari, delicious as always, was crisp and fresh. Served along with DR's special dipping sauce, it complemented the sangria well—almost too well as the sangria flowed. Along with the shrimp skewers, fruits, and cheeses, Joshua had his fill. The sundeck was filled also—with laughter and high hopes once again.

"I'll put on a few pounds on this trip." Joshua patted his middle. "But why not. It's not often I get to travel with such adventurers. How was the ride into Mecca?" He leaned to Trixie. "Were the roads good? I haven't been here for years, but I'm sure it hasn't changed much."

"Oh, you've been to Mecca?" Her brown ponytail swung to one side as she cocked her head, her eyes alight, the last rays of sunlight shining in her face. "How long ago was that?"

"I've been here many, many times. So much so that I still have dreams about it. Bad dreams mostly. The people here are so repressed. Fear is a terrible thing, and to fear your own family... that takes it to a new dimension. You have that here in the radicals. Another dimension, but it's not always visible."

"Yeah... okay." Her eyes rolled, sharing she wasn't wanting any part of *that conversation*, and she got up.

CHAPTER
THIRTEEN

The *DI* had traveled well over a hundred miles by midnight. Now, an hour later, the news about terrorists attacking the port reached them. Miguel turned up the volume on the ship's monitor, the satellite feed sharing an international news agency's report.

Tonight, beginning at 11:53, three speedboats firing shoulder-launched projectiles and small arms attacked the port of Jeddah, Saudi Arabia. Whistling rockets and mortars erupted in the night air, at first sounding like fireworks, until they hit their unsuspecting targets. The explosions that rocked the port resounded for miles. These were military-grade weapons used on civilian targets and government facilities, most likely of Iranian origin. The attack lasted only minutes but destroyed untold lives and facilities. Please stay tuned for further news reports as we receive official updates from port authorities and rescue teams.

Miguel shuddered, his gaze meeting Lorenzo's on the bridge.

"Can you believe this?" Miguel pointed as the screen flashed scenes of the dead and injured people being laid on the dock. An American international news agency took over on a different frequency. Images of the night rolled by:

Terrorists laughing, shouting "die, you infidels," whooping it up.

Rescue workers struggling to save victims.

Flames frolicking.

Fuel tanks exploding, ripping apart ships, buildings, and the marina.

"God's looking out for us... and someone must be praying hard too. Look at all those bodies. How could anyone be so..." He closed his eyes, his neck heated, and his face scrunched up. "Ugh... wicked?"

The news camera continued panning the area. The slip on the pier where the *DI* once was moored was gone. Simply gone, destroyed. Another boat had taken their place. Now a total loss, sunken. Fuel burned on the water above it. "With at least twenty-six people confirmed dead so far," the news agency droned on, "hundreds of injured have been rushed to local hospitals, many with life-threatening injuries. The death toll is expected to climb."

Miguel shut off the monitor. Now, only the *DI*'s humming engines and the ocean's slapping waves broke the dark silence. His heart was heavy. Still, he couldn't stem his tremendous thankfulness.

He sank onto the end of the padded bench under the chart plot wall, his voice soft as he thanked God for their safe escape and prayed for those left behind. With his back to his friend, Miguel slumped over. Tears burned at the back of his eyes. It would be a long night.

By six thirty, the news reached Delton, now one thirty a.m. in Saudi Arabia. They didn't know the *DI* had barely escaped the attack and explosions. Since it happened over six thousand miles away, it wasn't something of a local news priority. But it was a newsmaker for the larger agencies, and a major agency in America was broadcasting live from Jeddah's port a half hour after the attack. Perfect timing, prime time, another story to bash the POTUS and his foreign policies. Network executives ate it up.

One of Willie's friends, a WREAL listener, called. "Have you heard about Jeddah? Wasn't that the *DI*'s first port of call for three days?"

Willie turned on the television in her kitchen and stared, leaning on the cold Formica counter. Her heart thudding, she lowered the phone to the counter, then picked it back up. "Um, Jenn, I call you back?" She hit End Call, not waiting for her friend's response, already fumbling to bring up Mike's contact.

Mike's wife answered, then interrupted when Willie started rambling. "Hold up. Calm down. Willie, are you okay?"

"Yes, yes, well... *I don't know.*" She shook her body up and down impatiently. "Is Mike busy? He might want to see something on the world news."

"Let me get him for you. I'm on my way to our den now. What's going on?"

"Just... turn the television on to the news channel."

"I'm handing Mike the phone and grabbing the remote, hon." A rushed drone confirmed the television coming alive.

In Willie's kitchen, the same footage showed the camera panning the wharf and marina while flames from the fuel shot high in the sky from the water. "Mike, do you know where the *DI* was docked? Which pier?"

Mike's grip tightened on the phone Alyssa handed him. "Willie—this is bad. Fuel has exploded in the tanks of the yacht moored there. I don't think it's the *DI*, though. I gotta go. I'm gonna try to reach him via their satellite phone. I'll call you as soon as I know what's going on."

He dropped her call and set up the other. Someone answered in

Italian. Had he gotten through? Were they all right? His heart thudded. "Is this the *DI*?"

"Who are you calling for?" the speaker switched to English.

"I must have dialed the wrong number. I'm trying to reach my brother's boat in the Red Sea."

"And you may have." The speaker laughed, warm and friendly in a cultured tone. "Are you Mike Ray, DR's brother?"

"Yes." His legs gave out, and he dropped onto the nearby couch, Alyssa muting the TV and coming to squeeze his hand. "Are you guys okay? We're watching the world news—the port in Jeddah is on fire!"

"Calm down, my friend. Everyone here's okay. God warned us, and we sailed before the attack. He's been with us every step of the way. I don't expect Him to leave us now either."

Who was this man? This man giving God praise and thanks on his brother's yacht? Did he know how much DR disliked the mention of God or anything associated with Him?

Tears built in the corners of Mike's eyes. He tightened his grip on his wife's hand, her soft "praise the Lord" whispering as their gazes met.

"Who am I talking with? Do you know DR?"

"Yes, yes." The speaker laughed again, the sound such a comfort amidst the chaos playing out on the silent TV. "My name is Miguel, and let's just say I live my beliefs—I do not preach them. Actions speak long before words are ever heard, yes? DR said you were broadcasting our journey over your Christian radio show. Maybe that's why God has arranged these events?"

"Uh, that's right. Is DR around?" Mike sank back into the couch's plush corduroy cushions, flabbergasted, but thankful for Miguel. Maybe a person of this man's stature, someone DR had spoken so highly of, might sow a seed in his heart. No one else had been able to.

"He's sleeping now. We've had to change our shifts around to get out of the port early. Would you like me to wake him? Or would it be better if he just calls you in the morning—well, when he gets up?"

"Morning is good. I just wanted to make sure everyone was okay."

Alyssa slid beside him, her arm warm as she wrapped it around his waist and snuggled her head against his chest.

"I'll let DR know. It was good talking with you, Mike. Thanks for your prayers."

After pressing a kiss to his wife's head and whispering a prayer to the heavens, he called Willie.

"Oh, praise the Lord!" Willie shouted out, the words ending on a whimper, and Alyssa's head came up, her forehead scrunching as she eyed him. "God heard. Oh, He really heard! He's keeping DR safe, isn't He?"

"Indeed." Mike held a finger to his wife's lips, soon hanging up.

"What's up with her?" Alyssa gathered her black hair away from her face. "Willie's the most compassionate girl I know, but still. A bit heavy reaction for the brother of a friend?"

"Our Willie's got a crush. Well, I think it's gone beyond that. I think she actually loves DR, Alyssa, and I don't know what to do about it—or what God's gonna do about it. She keeps saying things, things about PUSHing God."

"Well, you never know what God's gonna do. We'd better pray for both of them."

He drew his wife back into his arms, savoring her presence and aching for both his brother who'd lost the love of his life and his friend who'd set her heart on a man God may not have intended for her.

A dream awakened DR, the same vivid dream now two nights in a row. He sat up and rubbed his forehead. Just a weird coincidence. But he couldn't help thinking about what Itasham said, something about dreamwalkers. He'd heard that word somewhere before.

The dreams were taking him someplace taboo, vile, and off-limits. He'd seen three men taken from a boat and killed. Not just killed—but each of them burned alive in a pit of fire, some sort of ritual. One at a time. Their killers danced around the fire as one burned and the remaining captives—first two, then the one—watched their own fate.

That was only the beginning. Suddenly, Stevie was in a lockup, on the boat the men were taken from. A boat tied to some tree branches or something on a shore somewhere, maybe under brush and trees hanging out over the water. The men had hidden their boat there, on this out-of-the-way island, for some reason.

How did he get from the village where the men were killed to the boat? And why did he feel he was supposed to go there now?

Eerie. As if something was drawing him, like a hook, even calling him.

It ended with the boat bouncing up and down on the waves at the end of a rope. Then he woke... covered in sweat, heart pounding, feeling like he'd run a marathon.

But it was just a dream. No biggie. It'd go away.

After sliding on his beige running pants and a white tee shirt, he headed up to the bridge, having pushed the reason they'd left the port early far to the back of his mind. He checked his watch. Hmm, one forty-five a.m. Saudi time. He climbed to the top stair. Then stilled.

Miguel and Lo were drinking beer on the bridge. Something wasn't right.

Miguel, noticing him, walked over and put his arm around DR, then pointed to the monitor and turned it back on. "We just had to have one after seeing this. I hope you don't mind."

Woozy, DR braced a hand on the console, the scene playing out on the screen assaulting him. More red bags covered the pier. His legs wobbling, he braced on a mate's seat near the console.

Miguel patted him on the shoulder. "I'll get you one."

The night had become even more horrific now, knowing what happened in Jeddah. The moon and sea added other elements to the mystery. Somehow, when tragedy strikes, the senses shift into hyperdrive. On board the *DI*, there were no exceptions. She was sailing at twenty-one knots, the bow's rise and fall causing DR to rock back and forth where he sat, his thoughts mixed, both sorrowful and thankful. His friend's warning saved their lives, but what had Itasham meant by dreamwalkers?

Miguel returned with DR's beer and Debbie. "Look who I found hiding out in the galley."

Seeing her, Lo straightened his hair and sat up. "Debbie, nice 'corns." He nodded to her pink unicorn pajamas.

"Thanks. They're my favorites. So magical and mysterious—kinda like, well, the dreams I've been having. I may have even dreamed last week about having this conversation... with you. Anyway, what's going on?"

Miguel handed DR a beer as he stood and gestured to the images DR was watching on the monitor, almost unaware she had come up on the bridge.

She put her hands over her face, then peeked between her fingers at the screen.

The marina security footage, fed to the marina's main server safe off premises, was broadcasting worldwide. It showed the three boats buzzing the port, firing shoulder-launched grenades and the rockets hitting vessels tied along the piers, along with the facility's buildings and fueling stations. The pier had been full, every spot taken.

As the weapons hit their targets, people jumped off the boats, and some began running... on fire. And the cameras caught all the carnage. The footage dashed all hopes the Meyers family—a nice couple with five small children—and others had left before the attack. DR shook his head, muttering. "I should have warned them."

With daylight still hours away, the fires raged, some flames shooting a hundred feet into the air. The lost lives were adding up.

Debbie hugged her arms around herself and moved into DR's peripheral vision. "I'm running out of tears. This was supposed to be a joyful getaway."

A deafening silence hugged the bridge, lasting eons before DR tried to compose himself. "I'm so thankful Itasham was in Mecca, or this would have been our fate too."

Debbie plucked at her sleeve. "I can't help but think about those who didn't leave when we did, like the Meyers with those precious children." She covered her face with her hands as if she could hide herself again.

Poor kid. DR wrapped his arms around her, holding her tight, allowing her to cry on his shoulder.

He could've told the Meyers and the others. He should've told them. How could he have been so blind? He shook his head, the sweet mango scent of her shampoo incongruent with the sour flavor on his tongue.

"I wasn't sure the warning was real. I didn't want to upset others." He patted Debbie's shoulder and stepped away from her. "I guess it's my turn to relieve the helm."

The others started leaving the bridge. As Lo passed to leave, he stopped in front of DR, rubbing the back of his neck and not making eye contact. "I hope you didn't mind my drinking a beer on duty. Miguel thought it might take the edge off. It won't happen again."

"No worries. I needed one too." Somehow, DR managed to smile. "Go get yourself some sleep—it's been a long night. By the way, anything else I need to know about?"

"No, she's running like a dream. See you in the morning."

Dream. Yes, indeed. A dream.

After the passengers began stirring the next morning, DR stifled a yawn. More than manning the helm had taken its toll on him. Forty-six dead. Hundreds hospitalized. Not knowing them would have made it easier somehow. Still...

Steps sounded in the corridor. While coming up, Joshua told David. "Itasham's warning had to be a message sent from God. Without it, all of us, along with the Meyers and all the others, would most likely be dead. God is looking out for us. I think the dreamwalkers are with us too."

DR sprang from the captain's seat at the word *dreamwalkers*.

"What do you mean the dreamwalkers are with us?" DR growled, looming over them in the helm entryway, several steps higher, tired of all the dreamwalker nonsense. And trying to remember where he first heard it.

CHAPTER

FOURTEEN

Right. Joshua remembered. DR didn't like anything of God, and this morning wasn't the time to go *there*. Yet, apparently, the dreamwalkers were bothering or helping him.

"Oh." Joshua waved it off. "Just a figure of speech."

"A figure of speech for what?" DR jammed his hands on his hips.

"Just something my friends talk about occasionally, spiritual stuff. You know."

DR raked a hand through his hair, then, looking somewhat calmer, let Joshua leave it at that. Stepping aside, DR motioned to the monitor. "I'm sure the others told you about the attack last night. I just hope some of the others got out too. We should've warned them or something."

The news channels were now broadcasting a loop of the earliest video of the attack, just hours after they left.

"We did. We told them all," the two men said in harmony.

DR wobbled where he stood. "What? Oh, thank God!"

Then he seemed to wince as if stunned he'd said that.

Joshua fought a smile, not wanting to pour salt on a bleeding soul.

Funny, how even nonbelievers' first reaction in these situations was often to say "thank God." A human reflex maybe?

Watching the monitor, Joshua tried to see if he recognized anyone on the pier.

"How long until we reach Aden?" David asked.

Aden, Yemen, was their next port of call. DR had said he wouldn't stop there because of the danger, but Miguel had asked him kindly. Miguel wanted to see the Saint Francis of Assisi Catholic Cathedral and his friend's church too, two of only four Christian churches remaining in Aden.

Miguel had traveled there some twenty years earlier. He had a special interest in the children's school and orphanage. Houthis and others fighting a civil war were destroying the city and country, and Miguel fretted about not being able to contact them for several weeks.

A few days ago, he'd confided he was prepared to offer the school a location in Italy if the headmaster wanted it. Joshua didn't need to tell his friend the answer would be no. The children in Aden needed the headmaster, and he wouldn't let danger influence him now.

"We should arrive about this time tomorrow. We've made good time, and the weather is fantastic." DR yawned, evidencing his long night.

"I'll take the helm." David stepped forward. "Miguel can just come up at one."

As DR went to leave, he thanked David for the early relief, then patted the gauge console. "She's running great. If you need anything, Lo or Miguel should be awake in a little while." He glanced at the monitor once again and went down to his cabin.

Joshua could only imagine how the gentle rocking on the waves would usher their captain into a deep sleep. But would the dreamwalkers be there waiting for him?

~

Debbie had only managed a few hard-fought naps. She felt tired all over as she slid out of the pink unicorn PJs and into a pair of baggy cutoff jean shorts and a white tee shirt. Time to join everyone else, to see what was happening in Jeddah, to uncover the fate of the other families. She peeped up at the bridge, expecting DR to be there still. Seeing David, she climbed the steps and hugged him. David was safe. He had a girlfriend. Well, fiancée.

She scooted back, his five-o'clock shadow snagging strands of her hair before she smoothed them into place. "Did they say anything about the Meyers and the others, the Morrises? Did they make it? I mean, you didn't see their boats or anything, did you?"

David smiled. "They're fine. Joshua and I gave them the warning. As far as I can tell, they all left right after we did."

"Oh!" She patted her chest and held her hand there. "Thank God. I was so worried. See, I've been having this bad dream for days and thought that it was an omen or something."

"You need to talk to Joshua. He was talking about dreamwalkers this morning. DR was curious when he overheard Joshua. Actually... more like pissed."

David confirmed their coordinates, making sure the yacht's sophisticated autopilot was tracking properly, then flashed a thumbs-up. "No worries. She's fine. So... what is your dream about? I'm pretty adept at spiritual things."

"Really, what sort of training or perceptions do you have about dreams... Doctor David?" She snorted, trying to keep from laughing or crying. Either could've served her well after the news about the families. But this dreamwalker thing was getting out of control. And Joshua knew more than he was letting on. She had to find him.

David, laughing, waved her off. "You'd better talk to Joshua."

"Okay, Doc. I'll see you later. Do you need me to bring you anything up to eat or drink?"

"I'm good, but thanks."

She found Joshua enjoying a pod of bottlenose dolphins playing alongside the *DI*. She handed him one of the two Cokes she brought out and a bag of pretzels.

"Oh, you dear. You know my weakness for pretzels."

"Especially liked the pretzel rods, you said." She popped open her cola. It spewed, so she quickly covered it with her lips.

"Right. They're harder than the rest. So, what's the bribe for? Let me guess—you're here about the dreamwalkers again, right? You need to give that a rest, you and DR both."

"I'd love to, but rest isn't something I'm getting much of. The dreams keep coming back every night." She sipped her fizzy drink, but it tasted more acid than sweet today. Maybe if she understood what dreamwalkers were, she could stop them, get some sleep, enjoy a Coke. "I don't want to keep dreaming this same dream." She leaned over the railing, but now, even the dolphins seemed a distraction to their conversation.

Argh! She needed peace. He'd given it to her before. Then he started all this dreamwalker stuff, and she'd lost every shred she'd had before she met him.

"I'll try to help, okay?" He tore open the pretzel bag. "Here goes. You've probably heard someone say you were on their mind or came into their thoughts. Well, that's the spiritual world influencing their prayers or thoughts, either for you as an aid or to use you. But not all the time."

Why the riddles? Couldn't he just say something and stick with it? She touched his arm. "That sounds bizarre. Are you sure about all this? Spirits as in ghosts or something?"

Her touch tingled on his skin, and a pretzel slipped from his hand. He picked it off the deck and threw it overboard into the sea. Still, he couldn't help noticing how beautiful she was wiping the sea spray off her face, her blonde hair pulled back into a ponytail, her deep-brown eyes curious. Gorgeous. His type of woman—gorgeous and classy.

Focus, Joshua! That's not what she wants from you. Or you from her.

"Yes…" He drew the word out, taking a moment to find his place again. "It's hard to grasp. That's why I told you about the need to be born again first. Then spiritual things are easier to believe and see. If you are born in Spain, you most likely speak Spanish, but when you are born in Italy, you will speak Italian first, most likely. See? If you aren't born again, in Christ, you can't see the things of God or speak in the spiritual language either."

"So…" She cocked her head, one hand rising to pin wisps of hair back from her eyes. "How do I become 'born again'?" She made air quotes.

"Give me a minute?" He breathed in deeply, exhaled slowly.

"Sure."

The dolphins began jumping in the air as if dancing and singing. Their chattery clicking and whistling overcame the lapping waves and thrumming engines. So loud and joyful, they could almost be serenading the *DI*.

He'd been at sea many times, dolphins often entertaining along the way. But never had he seen or heard of this type of performance in the wild. His blood quickened as if he were being led to seize the moment and help her come to Jesus. Who was he to second-guess the wisdom of dolphins?

"Do you believe Jesus is the Son of God, that He came to earth, born of a virgin, and lived? Then He was beaten and scourged for us, taking the sins of all time from all people, and died on the cross for our cleansing and righteous standing?" Heart thudding, he rushed on. "That He was raised three days later, and now, through your belief, acceptance, and repentance, you can have eternal life through Jesus in heaven with God the Father? That no one can come to the Father in sin, but only through the blood and forgiveness of Jesus?"

"Yes."

"Do you repent and ask for forgiveness?"

"I do." She closed her eyes, precious tears to God beginning to glisten on her cheeks.

And he smiled. She must be feeling it—the warmth coming over her.

The dolphins backflipped, whistling a quick goodbye. They were on their own now, but his heart was soaring, out there racing the waves before the bow. He'd never thought this was part of the plan for his trip, but that's the amazing thing, isn't it? No one can know the mind of the almighty God in heaven. Or His ways.

The boat rocked back and forth as Stevie struggled with the hatch. It wouldn't budge. It was dark and damp. Something smelled terrible, like dirty towels, socks, or maybe rotten potatoes. Stevie pushed harder. Still, it wouldn't open. He screamed for help, and someone put a hand over his mouth, shushing him. He struggled, getting free, then began screaming even louder. Someone else covered his mouth from the other side and spoke in Arabic. "Be quiet, or they'll kill us too."

Us. Yes, the hold was full of other kids. Kids just like him.

Then the dream was over, ending with the clang of the alarm clock. Every time, he woke covered in sweat and scared. Why did he keep having these dreams?

He wouldn't tell anyone else he was scared, not because of a dream. He couldn't. He was the brave captain.

He'd heard wise tales growing up, tales of recurring dreams, of dreamers feeling like they'd been somewhere before. Just tall tales, though. Nothing to be taking literally. He hadn't taken the dreamwalkers seriously either, but now, he just wanted relief. Even enduring the senseless never-ending pining about Christianity may be worth it—*if* it gave him a better perspective and ended the dreams.

Dreams? Was that what they were? Hard to believe when they were so vivid, like he was there.

He'd have a talk with Joshua. Coming up from his cabin, he approached Joshua sitting with Debbie on the aft deck. She was smiling and crying. Probably a private moment.

He diverted to the pool. The others were out having fun, the trip still a success. Their presence in Jeddah saved lives—a good feeling.

Miguel, a hat covering his eyes, relaxed listening to the sweet sounds of the sea and laughter, living at its finest. In his black Speedos, he appeared in tune with nature. The other men don't seem to notice, only DR. His humble upbringing kicked in. But Miguel was Italian, and it was the style in Marsala, sort of like the statues and artwork there.

The girls—Trixie, Penny, Laurie, and Stephanie—huddled together. Ryan was with them as they compared notes about the men in black thobes, the ones they saw in the restaurant wearing their keffiyeh head garments, lowered to eat, covering everything but their faces.

"Oh, hi, DR. You might have heard us." Stephanie waved him over. "I was saying how I thought for sure the men in the restaurant were part of the attack on the port."

Miguel sat up, taking the hat off. "DR, I was wondering when you'd come above deck." He motioned him over. "Please come have a seat. I'm curious about something and have a question."

"I'll be over as soon as I get a sandwich." DR waved. "Does anyone else need anything?" After no one responded, he started over to the stairs to the galley.

But Laurie intercepted, tugging on his sleeve as he passed by. "Do you think I could ask you something? In private?"

She ducked from the water Tom was trying to splash her with from the pool.

"Sure." DR sidestepped the water too, laughing. "Why don't you come to the galley with me before your husband drowns us. We can talk while I fix my sandwich. Who knows, maybe you'll change your mind. The turkey's fabulous."

"Well, I don't know about that, but I might have a beer. I'm so glad you stocked some London Porter for Tom and me." She took hold of his arm, then turned back to Tom, and winked.

DR eyed her, then Miguel. What did they both want? In the galley, he rummaged through the stainless steel Sub-Zero refrigerator, laying out his ingredients on the quartz counter, then constructed a mountain-sized turkey sandwich, the kind he called a Dagwood. He wrapped up by grabbing some chips.

Laurie motioned for him to sit with her at the table on the dining area's portside. "From here, we'll have a good view of the steps so no one can sneak up on us."

"Well, I'm game. You've got me curious." He handed her a chilled London Porter after opening it for her. Then he opened his own Italian Birra Moretti, brought on especially for Miguel, the satisfying hiss almost as good as the first sip.

"Ryan's birthday is on the fifteenth, and we'd like to sneak a cake on board in Aden, along with a few other things, and maybe put them in the refrigerator in the cargo hold. What do you think? And maybe we could have some hamburgers too? Slow down for an hour or so and have a party? Tom and I will spring for it."

The beer soothed his parched throat even as her words soothed his worries. "That's all? Sure, we could all use some celebrating. We'll turn down the engines and put out the beach. Super thoughtful of you. Ryan is kind of a quiet guy. How'd you find out his birthday?" He munched on his sandwich. Oh, this was good.

"He was telling Steph how he flew into Malaga from Dublin with his aunt, on his way to Marsala. She was visiting a daughter she hadn't seen in years and wanted his company. He hates to fly, but she had given him the ticket for his upcoming birthday. Well, long story made short, Mitch asked him when that was—and voila!"

"Well, aren't you the sneaky ones?" He raised his beer to salute. The light shining through the large galley window lit up her red hair, reminding him of Gail. "I mean that in a good way. Do any of the others know about this?"

"Not yet. Tom and I wanted to get with you first to see what you thought."

"We'll work out the details. Why don't you come down to my cabin with Tom after dinner?"

"Sounds like a plan to me." She rose and high-fived him. Then they went back up top. By now, his sandwich and chips were gone, only their beer remained.

Sliding down on the chaise beside Miguel, DR relaxed. "So, what's on your mind?"

"Who do you think told Itasham about the attack? I mean, terrorists are a secretive lot. They don't have any friends except their comrades."

DR stretched out his legs and laced his hands in his lap, the beer gathering condensation on the table beside them. Itasham had told him the source of the warning. It labored him to answer accordingly, but the truth would haunt him if he passed it off as something else.

"A few Christians practice their faith in an underground church right outside the city. Since Itasham began studying the effects of Islamic radicalism in the area, one of his many hobbies, he's come to know some who profess the faith. With the promise of his identity being kept anonymous, a man who claims to experience *prophetic dreams* made himself known to Itasham."

He huffed and told the whole story as Itasham had told him, for better or worse, at least most of it.

"He claims to be a prophet of Jehovah God. Itasham ran into him Sunday afternoon on his way back from his midday prayer. That's why he was gone so long. He said the man seemed distraught and told him of a dream he had the night before and how he was shown to find 'Itasham' and tell him."

Miguel rose on his right elbow as his jaw dropped. A smile streaked across his lips. He sat the rest of the way up, beaming.

Miguel's reaction brought a sickening feeling. If only DR could say something else. He scowled at the almost empty beer bottle. Perhaps he shouldn't continue? He moved to the edge of his seat before finishing his beer, ready to leap to his feet before fifty questions began. "In the dream, he saw terrorists attacking the port on the civilian side. They came in fast and hit the boats and marina and left, killing and injuring many. He told Itasham there were bags and bags of bodies laying out on the dock. I didn't want to believe the man's dream, but

Itasham insisted most of the *dreams* he'd heard about came true, sooner or later. I couldn't take a chance on it being true or not. Now could I?"

"Or we would be the ones dead." Miguel reached over and slapped DR's shoulder. "Wow. That's some story. Aren't you going to share it with the others?"

"Not if I can help it." Too bad, he couldn't have told Miguel something else.

"Some of them might think God saved our lives. I know I do." Miguel arched a brow. "Why not give credit where credit is due?"

"As far as I'm concerned, it's in the past." DR grabbed his beer bottle, hoping to find one last sip. Nothing. He pushed to his feet, out of sorts. "Excuse me, Miguel. I need to speak with Joshua."

As he rounded the vessel's side rail to the aft deck, he stopped once out of sight of the others. He leaned against the rail, his eyes searching the vast sea, seeing nothing. If only he could've lied to Miguel.

But you don't lie to your friends or anyone else, for that matter. He had been raised differently. Liars, he was told, have their own special place.

CHAPTER
FIFTEEN

Collecting himself, DR rounded the vessel to the aft deck where Debbie and Joshua were still talking. He joined them anyway. He needed to know about these dreamwalkers—or whatever he was experiencing. Debbie's tears remained fresh on her face. She was smiling though, so he wouldn't be imposing now.

In a one-piece blue bathing suit, she looked incredible. Yep, that no-romancing-the passengers rule was gonna be hard.

Joshua stood and gave him a hug. "Please, join us." He slapped DR's back before moving away. "We're talking about dreamwalkers."

Dreamwalkers? DR's head snapped up. "Have you been reading my mind?"

"Well, not your mind, just your body language." Joshua guffawed. "I saw how you perked up earlier at the subject. Sooner or later, I knew we'd end up talking about them, so why not the three of us since Debbie is having some reoccurring dreams too? You don't mind do you, Debbie?"

Startled by this new revelation about his dreams, she looked at DR. Her eyes grew bigger, and her smile widened.

"Too?" She pinned hair back from blowing in her face so she could see him better. "Of course, I don't mind. Maybe we can discover something new together. Maybe uncover a mystery like our sleuthing writer friends."

DR folded his arms against his chest, even his thin red tank top suddenly too hot. "So tell us, Joshua, what are dreamwalkers and what do they have to do with my"—he waved a finger between him and Debbie—"ahem, *our* dreams? If you don't already know, I don't believe in Christianity."

"But Debbie does, so you'll have a different perspective from her." Joshua rolled his eyes knowingly between the pair. "Some things require the Holy Spirit to show you their full meaning, but I'll share the things I know."

DR, standing across the teak wood table from Joshua and on the same side as Debbie, now pulled up a cushioned chair to maintain a safe distance for his eyes and thoughts.

Joshua's back was to the water, leaving him nothing to focus on but his new friends. Reaching forward across the table as far as he could, he patted the tabletop. Perhaps puzzled about where to start, yet confident in where he was taking them. He smiled directly into DR's eyes, bobbed his head, then captured Debbie's gaze with his. "Let's use a true story I heard on television one night." He sat back in his seat now, tilting his head between them for a reaction. "There was a man carrying a wooden cross around the globe—Arthur Blessitt was his name, I think. He was in trouble in one of the Middle Eastern Muslim nations. Some men had guns on him, possibly to kill him. Halfway around the world, a lady—the founder of a Christian network's wife, Jan—was awoken and led by the Holy Spirit to pray for him at the exact same time. The men dropped their guns and ran or something like that."

"Really?" Pushing back in her seat, Debbie lowered her chin, focusing on Joshua. She grabbed the blowing hair out of her eyes and gestured with her other hand. "What are the odds of that? I mean, well, that would clearly be supernatural."

"That's what Jan said on TV, and I believe it. I don't have a reason not, do you? I consider this one form of dreamwalking. God doesn't intervene in our situations—no matter how dire—until someone prays and opens that door." He paused, making eye contact. "So what do you think, DR? Ever heard of someone on their deathbed make a dramatic recovery?"

The guy was nuts, but DR managed to keep his face expressionless. At least, he *tried* to. "I don't see what us having these dreams has to do with that. After all, we're the ones with the dreams, and we don't know who to pray for, even if we were praying people—and I'm not, not by any stretch of the imagination. So why, if there were a god, would He send the dreams to *me*?"

"I don't know." Joshua rubbed at his forehead. "I didn't say I was a prophet. I only know what I've seen and heard from either God or man. Maybe someone is praying for someone else and... I don't know, maybe you two, by the power of God, hold the answer to their prayers. I know this, though—if it's from God, we'll know soon enough." Lacing his hands behind his head, he looked first at Debbie and then DR. "Maybe you should share your dreams with each other. Maybe there's something in common. It's like working on a mystery. And the Hughes aren't the only ones who love a good mystery. Debbie and I do too."

"But what about the thing you told me yesterday?" Debbie breathed deeply behind her folded hands. "You know the seed-sowing thing? How's this like that? Does God do it or not? You said there are good and bad ones? I'm more confused now than ever."

Joshua opened a bottle of sunscreen and dolloped some into his palm before passing it along. "I also told you it's complicated, and I don't have all the answers. But if it's from God Almighty, we'll know soon enough." His tan had been growing darker by the day, but he rubbed on sunscreen. "He's not going to give you both reoccurring dreams that don't mean anything."

DR passed the sunscreen to Debbie. With her natural blonde hair, she picked up the sun fast. As she smeared lotion onto her pinked shoulders, he leaned forward, letting his laced hands hang loose between his knees. "But I'm not a follower of God, so just for kicks and giggles, why would He give me these dreams? Are you saying it's demons in my dreams since I'm not a follower?" He bit into his tongue to hold back a burst of laughter. After all, he didn't want to hurt Joshua's or Debbie's feelings.

When Joshua didn't immediately answer, DR held up a hand. "Here goes with my dream—and don't laugh." He hadn't laughed at them. They owed him the same courtesy. "When the dream starts, I can sense I'm young again, a kid, and I'm locked in a boat's cargo hold. I feel the boat rising and falling on the water. It's tied up to some trees, bushes I think, like it's in hiding. Someone or something has taken the men from the boat—I don't know who the men are or who took them, but it sounded like three of them. It was with great force they were taken, and I don't think it went well for them."

His heart thudded, his palms sweating now. He swallowed hard as bile rose in his throat. "Then I start pushing against the hold door, but it won't budge. Something smells, maybe spoiled potatoes or body odor. When I can't get the door to open, I shout for help. Someone, a kid, shushes me and clamps his hand over my mouth. I break loose and scream for help again—only this time louder. A hand from the other side covers my mouth. In Arabic, someone says, 'Be quiet, or they'll kill us too.' Then I wake up."

DR shrugged at Debbie as he finished. This one was going to be hard to top—he hoped.

"Wow, that is stressful." Joshua pushed his chair back and crossed his legs. "I can see why you want it to end. Is your dream like really vivid, or is it just like any other dream you have?"

"It's vivid, extremely vivid. Just like being there. I don't normally remember much about my dreams. How'd you know? Anyway, it's your turn De—" DR stopped. Tears were streaming down her face. Something wasn't right. "Are you okay?"

"I'm fine," she murmured.

Fine? That's an understatement. Man, she looked sexy in her blue bathing suit. He'd better not release his eyes to their own desires.

"I think I know what happened to the three men in your dream." She locked her gaze with his. "In my dream, I see myself first, and it's strange. It seems like I'm stroking the hair of someone who looks just like me—maybe it's a mirror or something. Anyway, suddenly, like you, I'm on an island somewhere, hiding in the bushes, or so it seems."

DR leaned back, ready to take notice. His hands grabbed the chair's sleek arms, their hard high polished corners cutting into his fingers.

She swallowed visibly, and her voice shook. "Then I see what looks like backwoodsmen or something, savages maybe, and some kind of tribal thing going on. They've captured three men, men who look like Americans, and they burn them alive! One at a time, making their buddies watch their own fate."

She was shaking now. Joshua rose to sit beside her, one hand resting on her back, though DR doubted she even felt his comforting touch.

"I can hear their screams and smell their flesh burning. It's horrible, like a ritual or something. I can't take my eyes off them either. The savages were dancing and shouting songs or chants. Then I don't know? Maybe they hear someone or something. Most of them leave to go look, as if there were more people to burn." She hugged her arms around herself, rocking back and forth. "The whole village seems crazed."

DR didn't say anything. But it was like his other dream. Could it be? How?

She let out a whimpered breath. "Then someone comes twisting up out of the fire—they just rise from the ashes. That's when I see it, a boat tied to a tree. That's how my dream ends. See why I want it to stop?"

Teary-eyed, she exhaled and sank back into her chair. "I can't take it much more. I just need the dreams to end. Maybe I should've just stayed in Chicago with my patronizing friends."

Joshua sat silently, perhaps thanking God he wasn't experiencing their dreams. Then he spread his hands apart. "Okay, what are the odds you are both dreaming of the same boat and men? If so, the kids in the boat are going to have a hard time either way. I hope this is a dream, not a premonition. But if God is using dreamwalkers, it may not be all bad. That someone rising out of the ashes? It kind of sounds like a hero or something. Of course, that's assuming it's not an evil spirit conjured up by a burning ritual."

DR pushed to his feet. He'd had enough of this. "I hate to break up our little dream-weaving session, but there are more important chores at hand. I've got war-game simulations preparing us to defend the *DI*." He strode away, leaving them to whatever it was they wanted to conjure from their discovery. Joshua could comfort Debbie. DR couldn't. He couldn't even comfort himself.

The plan was to prepare for attacks, testing them—crew and passengers—on how to defend themselves. With Marco and Miguel's help before sailing, DR had put together a comprehensive plan to thwart any boarding attempts. In case of a real attack, the exercise should teach everyone their role and its importance.

David summoned everyone to the aft portside deck. David or the person piloting the *DI* at the time, *if* they were attacked, would set out the alert, a horn installed for this purpose alone. In their written boarding instructions, DR had established the procedures and exercises each would need to play.

DR grabbed a coffee and joined them. Then, as everyone came out on the deck, he handed out copies of their assignments. Since Iran attacked the Saudi Arabia oil fields recently, the need for a vessel to be prepared was an understatement. Now, the attack on Jeddah boosted everyone's attention to detail.

"Okay, everybody. It's fun time." He held his hand up for everyone to get serious. "Our success depends on everyone doing their part. When I call your name, tell me your duty assignment and how you will perform it, ask me or the crew any questions you have now or think of later. I want everyone comfortable and knowledgeable about their roles."

"Yes, Captain," everyone answered.

"Now, if we do get attacked, we're not taking prisoners. So you know what that means. We're going to use deadly force to defend ourselves and each other."

DR paired them as couples, ensuring those married stayed by their mates. The only exception being Tom and Laurie since Tom was an expert marksman and possessed competition-level sniper skills. Something DR planned to utilize if they were attacked. So he paired Debbie with Ryan and Joshua with Miguel—one of the crew, either David or Lo, would join them in their important position.

"Okay, let's see—Craig and Trixie?"

"Our job," Trixie spoke out, "is to go down to the engine room below the galley and unlock the locker to retrieve the communication and protective gear, then bring it to this deck. Then we head down to the gymnasium and strap ourselves in where our job will then be to monitor the stairway down."

"Very good." Sipping his coffee, DR skimmed his list of crew and passengers. "Tom and Laurie?"

Tom rubbed his hands together. "I go to the bridge and get the key from the helmsman to the firearms safe in the maintenance room, here just below the helm, where I meet Laurie, and we bring all the gun cases here."

"Every firearm is in its own lockbox with ammunition for each person's job." Laurie reached inside her vee-necked tee shirt and pulled out a key on a chain. "We all have a key to our assigned box. It's on the neck chain you gave each of us at the castoff party."

"I go up to the bridge"—Tom picked up where she left off—"and give the helmsman his firearm and stay on the bridge, preparing to defend the vessel from its high vantage point. Laurie goes down with Greg and Penny."

Feeling like the captain of a military operation instead of a yacht, DR rocked back on his heels. All that aside, this was necessary, though he hoped it wouldn't be needed. His earlier ventures to the area he and Gail explored were more about evading attackers than confronting them. Although they were never attacked, they fled to avoid the possibility several times.

Identifying a possible attacker remained a fine line. While he didn't like to stereotype people, certain groups required more scrutiny than others. Life and death hung on those decisions.

DR brought the mug up for a sip, the scent teasing him long before the rim reached his mouth. Then he nodded to Greg and Penny.

Penny, dressed in a silky black bikini in her own sexy, playfully tartish way, swiveled her hips, pulled her finger pistol, and pointed toward the sky, then winked. "My honey and I come to the aft portside deck and receive our communication gear and hearing protection, along with our firearms. We then run down to the galley and join Laurie, locking the doors, and protect the sangria Miguel so loves."

She pretended to blow smoke off her finger pistol, grinned, swiveled her hips again, and holstered the pistol. Greg just stood by, shaking his head and laughing. Then he spread his hands out. "What can I say? She nailed it."

Everyone clapped approval for her performance, but this was serious. And everyone knew it, even Penny. Their galley position was crucial. The kitchen accessed a downward staircase to the engine room where Mitch and Stephanie would be stationed with their guns and gear. If attackers reached the engine room, they could disable and control the *DI*.

Setting aside his coffee mug, DR was smiling too. "Thanks, Penny. You're a hoot and managed to bring it all back down to earth." Then he held his hand out to Mitch and Stephanie.

Mitch, a fellow archaeologist, was still half laughing. "We come up and get our gear and equipment. Then, through the galley, we go down to the engine room. Once there, we lock the forward doors, barring them shut along with the aft entrance. Then we sit waiting and listening for orders to disable the engines or drop the security anchors remotely, from you only, DR."

"If anyone attempts to come into the engine room without our password, we shoot them dead." Stephanie kept her chin high.

Being from Paris, she'd seen her share of terrorism, so DR was counting on her being able to shoot to kill. "Excellent." Fist balled up, he jabbed the air. "And what is the password?"

"Marsala," she said.

"It seems everyone has read and studied our plans well, and we're on our way to being fully prepared. Debbie, you and Ryan ready for your job?"

"We are. We'll come up to the aft deck and retrieve our gear, then go to the forward poolside deck where we'll take cover under the bridge overhang and prepare to defend it, if necessary."

Good. No playing around here, not on her watch.

After she finished, everyone turned to Joshua and Miguel. The guys would take up position on the aft lower deck below, along with a crew member, that being the easiest point to board at sea.

"First, we remove eight bulletproof protective vests from deck storage and pass them out to David, Lorenzo, Tom, DR, Debbie, Ryan, and ourselves. Then we get our communication gear, firearms, and munitions and go below to set up on both sides of the lower aft deck, strapping ourselves in, waiting for instructions to engage."

"Outstanding." DR clapped his hands together once. "Everyone seems to know their jobs. I'll be floating wherever I'm needed most, but my basic position is on the bridge. From there, I'll be able to oversee what is happening, fire the water cannon, and do what needs to be done. Remember—turn on your headphones and put them on as soon as you get them. David, could you go over that for the group again?"

David held one up. "They're pretty self-explanatory. Press the test button to ensure they are working immediately. That's how we'll be communicating, using the Bluetooth system. Each headphone is equipped with a mike. Simply push the button in the middle of the right earmuff to talk. See? Simple."

DR paused to sip his coffee, surveying the group for questions.

"Okay." He swirled the dregs and downed the last of his drink. "We've put blanks in your firearms. Double-check to make sure it's loaded with the blanks for this exercise. The blanks are colored with a blue dye for identification purposes. As soon as you come up and get your gear, return to your posts, and check your weapon, making sure it is loaded with the blanks."

Unlike the weather DR experienced in Marsala, the weather had changed once they got past the first day, now becoming sketchy at times. The rainy season was coming to an end, but clouds overhead threatened most of the time. Storms in the distance disturbed the atmosphere as the wind at times exceeded twenty knots, accompanied by occasional rough seas.

"We will err on the side of being aggressive. If we feel threatened, we will work to assess the situation and react. We'll begin that process at three-quarters of a mile out."

"I'm sure you're about to cover this, DR," Miguel broke in. "But I just wanted to insert that most attacks are by a minimum of two speedy boats."

"Precisely, Miguel, and they will split up and continue toward us if they are pirates. If not, they'll attempt to communicate by radio. At the half-mile point, we begin taking our defensive positioning. When we blow the whistle, we only have thirty seconds to get to our positions."

DR waved his index finger in the air to be sure David saw him. "David, turn on the water cannon, please."

A powerful stream of water shot from the cannon mounted over the helm, David, standing on the bridge, directed the water in a circle around the *DI* to show its 360-degree capability. He laughed as the spray's mist soaked Lorenzo just outside the helm listening and watching while their anchor was in the water. The powerful jet caused friction in the nozzle, which resulted in a fine mist at the release point.

DR smiled after Lo's soaking. "To test the would-be attackers, we'll begin firing the water canon when the suspected attackers come within seventy-five yards. At that distance, it will only take them about twenty seconds to reach the *DI,* depending on ocean conditions. Once the water canon starts hitting them, Tom will fire armor-piercing rounds at the boat the water canon is not hitting, first to hit the attacking vessel's bow. If the boat—or boats—continue to approach, we will turn on the electrical barrier to protect against boarders."

"Wow, that's incredible." Ryan shaded his eyes to view the powerful spray. "Yeah—that ought to help."

Miguel held up a hand. "Getting back to the electric barrier—remember, don't accidentally touch them yourselves."

"Right." DR shot Miguel a thumbs-up, sharing a grateful glance. "That's also when we'll turn on the LRAD sound system. It's especially crucial at this point that we have our headphones on for communication and, just as importantly, for our ear protection."

David turned the water cannon off, coming from the helm to where Lo stood soaked and smiling. He slapped Lo on the back. "Guess we'll know about that next time."

"Please, everyone." Miguel stepped forward again. "This will all happen fast. That's how they are successful. It's crucial that we follow DR's instructions and prepare ourselves mentally."

DR looked at his watch. They needed to start planning dinner soon. "David, click your timer, please. Speed is their key to getting on board. That's why we're taking a hyperaggressive stance. Once Tom fires his first shot, we will be in full repel mode. After we determine they aren't friendly, fire first and ask questions later. Shoot for the kill once we turn on the LRAD. Dead people don't get to ask questions, so—"

Miguel nodded at DR and strolled over to talk, privately. "What time do you want to do dinner?"

"Let everyone do their own thing if they want?"

"Sounds good. I'll go down in a minute."

"Mark," David called out.

"That was thirty seconds," DR explained. "Now that you've seen how quickly thirty seconds passes, any questions?"

Everyone talked between themselves. Then Tom spoke for them. "It's a good plan. We're willing to be ready before attackers reach us."

"Miguel and Joshua come up to the back deck to get your

bulletproof vests on. Laurie, bring the weapons assigned to them back here to optimize our time. Then return to your cabin with your firearm and lock the door. On the bridge, we'll take turns watching and piloting the *DI*, so we all can stay alert and focused. After our practice, we'll see how long it all takes, always keeping in mind—speed is essential."

The whistle blew to signal their start. Everyone began performing their duties and going to their battle station. When David called out "Mark," the practice had taken thirty-one seconds.

DR called out over the headphones, "That was awesome, folks. Now remove the blanks and load your live ammunition into your weapons, then return them to their case before locking them up again. Ready for use, if needed, and bring them back up so we can put them away."

The trial run behind them. They all settled in for a fun day at sea, enjoying dinner on their own schedule. They heartily consumed shrimp rings, oysters on the half shell, steamed broccoli, and grilled asparagus, along with Kim's Favorite and Birra Moretti.

With the swimming pool refreshing his passengers' spirits, DR absorbed the party-like atmosphere along with everyone else, watching Ryan and the games being played.

Ryan kept trying to get a chaise closer to Debbie, her being the only single female aboard. But the group took all the chaises to try him. As everyone watched and laughed, he seemed unaware of the show his struggles were giving them. Poor Debbie, though, appeared to look on in dismay as the others had fun at his expense.

After the couples started playing a game of That's What She Said, a card game with adult situations and innuendo, the singles went about their business soaking in the pool, reading, or talking well into the night. Ryan, DR noted, finally got the chaise beside Debbie, but by then, she had a covering over herself, having finished tanning.

Nightfall came with David at the helm, another uneventful night ahead with a sense of satisfaction in DR's heart. Everyone could sleep safely in their cabins, resting up for their next adventure. The weather cleared, nearly perfect, and salty spray blew over the *DI*'s decks as he reclined on the lower aft deck, watching the sun's magic act once again, a scene he never grew tired of. Yemen became closer by the minute, everyone excited.

Hopefully, it wouldn't be as bad as he thought.

CHAPTER
SIXTEEN

I n Delton, Willie met Mike at Marcie's Place to relax and discuss tomorrow's show with DR. She arrived first and claimed their usual table by the front corner window. The checkered tablecloths were gone, replaced with pumpkins and scarecrows. Fall had come, and over by the front entrance, Marcie had built a scarecrow and turkey display. Willie smirked. Marcie loved celebrating the seasons, and her flare helped promote the shop's specialty flavors.

Beyond the window, a foggy, drizzly October day bogged the world down, the kind when taking a nap was so sweet. Marcie had the fireplace burning this afternoon, the smell of pumpkin spice and cinnamon rolls heavy in the air.

Looking out the window, Willie watched those passing by. Mike better hurry so she wouldn't have to face Rachael alone today.

A shadowed reflection blurred past the window, and Willie stiffened, not daring to turn, just knowing it was too late. Rachael saw her come in. Easy enough, the shop being almost empty. Willie slid toward the window as far as possible to escape. But Rachael was already there.

"Hi, Tonya."

Ouch, no one called her by her given name anymore. Willie flinched at memories of high school flooding in.

"Can I talk with you for a minute?" Rachael fidgeted with the necklace she'd bragged that her husband had given her for courage before he was deployed. "I need to ask you something... about high school."

About high school? Willie squirmed. Surely, Mike hadn't ratted —*Had* he? "Sure, Rachael, Mike's going to be a couple minutes late. What's on your mind?" Willie eyed her, unable to see what Ashton saw in her. *It's no contest. I'm much prettier... and smarter.*

At Willie's once-over, Rachael wiped down her red uniform blouse, perhaps to wipe something off or smooth it down and then down the sides of her pants too. Then the girl firmed up her chin as if she'd decided she'd started this and wasn't turning back.

"Well, I'm just going to come out with it. Your friend at WREAL told me why you always ignore me, even though we went to school together all our lives. So who was it? Who was your boyfriend that I, well, you know... slept with?" With her head ducked, Rachael scraped at red nail polish that was now showing the wear from days at work.

She looked tired, her black hair dull, and her brown eyes missing the hope they had in high school. Willie always thought she was pretty, but now, Willie could almost feel sorry for her. She'd aged a lot. Well, just a little sorry. After all, the girl stole her life, her dreams. But Willie had forgiven her many years ago because that's what Christians do.

"Ashton. His name was Ashton Dupree. I saw the two of you leaving the hotel down by the lake right before graduation." Blood rushed to Willie's face. She flattened her hands against the vinyl tabletop, trying hard to stay composed. Still, her voice began rising with each word. "I saw it. I thought Ashton loved me. Oh, he denied it, of course, even called me for days. But I know what I saw. It took me years to come to grips with it, and you never even knew?"

Rachael's mouth dropped open. Then life returned to her eyes, like a fire being stoked, and her countenance seemed to lift. She reached over the table to console Willie by placing her hand on her arm, but Willie jerked away.

"Didn't you know? Ashton Dupree is my cousin. His sister worked at the hotel. I sometimes gave him a ride to pick her up. They only lived a block from my house, and we were always together. Martha was older than Ashton. Her butthead of a husband left her for another woman. She was working to get back on her feet."

Willie sat stunned, blood that once rushed to her face now in full retreat. What was Rachael saying?

"Miss Holier Than Thou." Rachael braced both hands on the table, leaning into Willie's space. "So you're the one who broke Ashton's heart. He sulked for days. Ha! I've been feeling icky since Mike told me, and now? Now, I'm not the bad guy—*you* are!"

Willie winced as Rachael jabbed a finger at her.

Rachael tossed back her hair, her lips curving into a smirk. "Didn't you know he was a Christian and not the type to sleep around? You listened to Kelsey Briggs, didn't you? Didn't you know she wanted him for herself? Almost worked too. I think, but I'm not sure, that's why he moved to Texas to work on the oil rig in the Gulf. I haven't heard from him since. I guess he's gotten caught up in life like everyone else. Wow, after all these years, only to find out that's why you've always treated me like trash. How sad."

Willie opened, then closed her mouth. At first, she tried to deny it, cupping her hands over her mouth.

Yes, she knew Ashton was a Christian. They sat in services together twice a week. That was one of the many reasons she loved him. How could she not believe him? She lifted shaky hands and pressed a cold finger to her throbbing temples. Why didn't she ask Rachael or anyone else for that matter, someone besides Kelsey? Kelsey was supposed to be her best friend. It was her idea to go catch him.

She didn't even tell Ashton what he'd done with whom or where she'd seen him. How could she have been deceived so? *No, you didn't even give him a chance. You simply told him you knew he was sleeping with a little tramp, and you didn't want any part of him.*

Cammie, the other server came over and whispered to Rachael that she needed her help. Rachael pushed away from the table and sauntered off. Then she paused, stepped back, and patted Willie's arm. "Look, I'm sorry, Tonya. I wish I'd known this was what you were mad about and why Ashton left town."

Through her teary eyes, Willie saw Rachael reach her station. Now, she didn't have anyone to blame but herself, not even God. A little blonde-headed girl came rushing out of a side room and reached up to Rachael. She bent down and scooped her up, twirling her around and around, big smiles on their faces. She looked relieved. Maybe she was, just to know she hadn't hurt Willie.

Willie pressed her palms to her eyes. She'd questioned God, sometimes angrily, for ten years, and this was her fault all along?

She put her head down on folded arms and cried. Thoughts of that horrible time flooded her memory as if Satan were punishing her. "Lord..." she moaned. "Did a spirit or something come over me when I saw Ashton with Rachael? Deceiving me?"

Mom was right. Ashton wasn't the type of young man to do such a despicable thing. He was the catch of the county, and theirs was going to be a special union. God had brought them together, and she'd ruined it. Thinking back, she could see the torment fresh in his eyes, this-morning fresh. Funny how things can change the way they look once you know the truth. Now, she knew why he was so mad. Her reasoning blinded her. She hadn't cared.

"Hey, kid?" Mike stood over their table. He cuffed her shoulder. "What's up? This sure doesn't look like the strong, brave Willie I've known for five years."

When she didn't respond, instead of sliding into the open side, he sat beside her and hugged her. She twisted toward him on the bench seat and buried her head into his shoulder. Tears, so many tears her eyes had cried unnecessarily. They sat that way until Rachael came over.

Willie sat up and faced the window as she used napkins to dry her eyes and cheeks. She scrunched them up, feeling so foolish. But how do you fix something like this—or even explain it? Her religion was based on faith, and she didn't have any, not in God or in Ashton, not then.

Had her whole life been a lie? It suddenly seemed so, so different from what she'd been telling herself, praying, and living.

Mike looked at Rachael, who shrugged, their images clear in reflection on their window.

"You had better bring us something strong. Maybe with that potent pumpkin spice flavoring and two cinnamon rolls, okay? Thanks, honey."

"You got it." Rachael snapped her fingers.

Mike got up and sat on the booth's other side. "You ready to talk, kid?"

"Kid?" Willie sniffled. "Like I'm any younger than you are. And I'm a lot older this afternoon than I was this morning, by the way." Mondays were one of her regular days off. But, lately, she'd been a ball of nerves. He must have wondered what had gotten into her, where his verbal sparring partner went.

Somewhere, Ashton told her Rachael was his cousin, but somehow, it didn't click the evening she saw them. She grabbed a wad of napkins and slammed them over her eyes, another rush of tears coming. "I–I made a mistake. Rachael's Ashton's cousin. She didn't sleep with him."

"Oh man. That's harsh." He got up and came over to her side again.

She slumped against him, their shoulders bumping. "I screwed up my life and Ashton's, Mike. All these years of thinking God and Ashton let me down. Rachael's right. I'm the bad guy. How do you fix something like that? I wanted Ashton's babies so...."

Rachael returned with two double espressos and their delicious homemade pumpkin spice. It smelled like she'd put an extra squirt of topping on each of them. She plunked down two plump cinnamon rolls, heaped with extra frosting. The goop clumped off their sides, pooling on the plates as she straightened and jammed her hands on her hips. "Guess you thought I was the little tramp. Now I know why you were upset with me."

Willie snuffled. "He told you about that? That I accused him of sleeping with a..."

"A little tramp. Yes, he said his girl said that. 'Course I didn't know you were his girl or I was the supposed tramp. He wouldn't have married you after that anyway. He was crushed. I hope you both enjoy your drinks, toodle-oo." She waved a flash of red nails, then sauntered away, the spring back in her step.

And yeah, she deserved it. Willie winced. A little payback was justified after years of mistreatment.

While she loosened her grip on the fistful of napkins, then spread them out on the table as if she could save them from the damage she'd done, Mike returned to his side of the booth. He sipped his espresso until she spoke.

"I'm going to take some time off from work. I–I need to understand how to come to grips with what I've been believing wrongly for so long." She shoved aside the napkins and picked up her espresso, holding on with both hands, elbows planted on the table to steady herself. A blank in her heart where she'd once felt strong.

"Willie, all that's in the past. You'd already forgiven him. Why go there? Just let it go."

But she wouldn't be swayed. It was too late to let go. She smoothed at the napkins again. But it was too late to fix it all. Once such damage was done, it was done.

With their coffee and rolls finished, she pushed to her feet. Mike rose as well and hugged her, saying his goodbyes. "I'll handle the call tomorrow. Take a week off. See how you feel then, okay? I'll tell Giggles."

"Yeah." Willie tried on a smile. It didn't fit well. "See if she can laugh this one off for me."

Mike winced. "I *meant* I'd tell her you wouldn't be coming in. I'm not going to be blabbing your business to anyone again."

~

In Washington, DC, the deal was done. The senator had expected to call a news conference, once again bashing the president over his foreign policies. But he had to tell Mr. Jennings he was sorry instead. The show would have to take place a couple of days later.

His staffer was sorting through the day's mail. Ordering it, pulling out the junk like always. Just another day in the Senate. The man paused and eyed him, watching as he paced behind his antique desk. His face was probably twisted, his ears red. The staffer poured him a glass of water and unfolded one of the many local newspapers, then retreated to the other side of the office when the phone rang.

Senator Brummengarten picked up the phone, keeping his voice low as he responded to the outburst. "They must've been warned somehow. But we're on top of this. They've got some of their best men on this. They want the sanctions lifted, so they'll do just about anything we ask."

"Do you have any idea, Senator—*any* idea—how much this has cost me? And my reputation with Circle? They'd better be on top of it. I'm not going to stand for four more years of this clown in the White House. He'll reverse everything we've accomplished. You had better get this done, or your state will have to replace you. Oh, and that presidential run of yours? You can just forget about that." Jennings slammed the phone down on the senator.

Senator Brummengarten stood, trying to maintain a calm exterior so the staffer behind the other desk wouldn't see him shaken.

Halfway around the world, Stevie was back on the boat. Whoever took the men was coming back for them. They'd heard Stevie's screams. Now the other children helped hold him so tight he couldn't scream or move again.

The smell was much worse, a mixture of burnt flesh and human waste. One odor, the burnt-flesh smell, was coming from outside the boat, through a crack in the hatch door's insulation. It smelled like someone had a cookout, but the odor wasn't pleasant. He was going to gag. The heat in the cramped compartment was also becoming unbearable in the late morning sun. He couldn't imagine a worse wretchedness.

The kids were pressed in so tight. Most were girls, except for him and the ones on each side of him, best he could tell. He winced as a bright light shined down. His heart quickened. Someone was opening the cargo door. Only the door wasn't opening—so where was the light coming from? Wherever it was, it was warm and bright, and for a moment, there seemed to be relief from the wretchedness, a sweet fragrance replacing the horrible smell for just a flash. Then a familiar voice spoke in English. "Hold on tight, Stevie. Hold on. Don't open the door."

The tribe was running toward the boat, chanting something. He'd never heard their language before, but the voice that warned him sounded like one he'd heard years before. He was sure of it. Maybe... he remembered. That same voice always warned him when Uncle Bill came to the house, warning him to hide his brothers.

That voice always said, "Stevie, run. Run now, Stevie."

DR bolted up in bed, covered in sweat, heart pounding. He slammed a shaky hand over his eyes and sucked in a shallow breath. He could almost smell the burnt flesh, even now. But the ending had changed. Why? What did it all mean? Maybe Debbie had another dream. If so, there might be something more to these.

That voice in his dream... that voice from so many years earlier... He knew its purpose, but *who* was it?

He grabbed his watch from the bedside table, the crocodile leather grounding him as he tipped its face to the light. Only three a.m., but no way would he risk going back to sleep. He rubbed his achy eyes, the burning sensation behind them reminding him he hadn't slept well since they'd left Marsala. He ground his teeth. "This isn't fair!" The words burst from deep in his chest. "I counted on this trip—*needed* it to recover my sanity and restart my life again. Debbie did too."

Why he spoke aloud, he didn't know. No one was listening.

He glared at the picture hanging behind his bed. Gail, stunning as ever, was dressed in her pink formal. Her red hair had become darker, and her eyes sparkled. She'd been his. He was so lucky to have had her those eight years—and he knew it.

His gaze shifted to where he'd stored her journal. Why did he bring it, to punish himself? She was gone, their time together now etched forever in his soul. He didn't need this.

He crossed the room and opened the cabinet. He stood there, just holding her journal, remembering all the times he'd seen *her* holding it, writing in it. Sometimes smiling, her pen flying as she scribbled. Sometimes frowning, her motion pensive with each loop and line she added.

Was Willie telling the truth? Could Gail's outlook on faith have changed? He didn't want to know... but his gate swung open. What would it hurt, just a peek? It wasn't like Gail was going to catch him or something.

He opened the journal. The first page crackled, their picture with Chief Mnortarmillc pinned beneath the heading Our New Adventure. He swallowed hard, absorbing the pleasant surprise. Then he lifted a finger to trace the dirt still on their faces, their Kool-Aid smiles. Everything looked and felt so wonderful, the intention of the book's author.

If only he could go back to those times. Even when times were hard and money short, the joy he felt just being near her, knowing she felt the same way, was more than enough, always would have been enough.

With a deep breath, he turned the page. A picture fell onto the floor, facedown. He bent to retrieve it and frowned at the handwritten note on its back—"To my dearest and best friend ever. I love you so much, Willie."

The picture slipped out of his hand and fell to the floor, in a slow-motion, seesaw kind of way. Horrible thoughts tumbled into his mind. Maybe Willie wasn't lying? Why did he have to look?

He sunk into his captain's chair by the cabinet. What happened?

Did Willie brainwash her? Why would she need to dig up a two-thousand-year-old carpenter to lift her spirits?

Bending down, he picked up the picture. Willie was sexy without trying, dressed in yellow shorts and a white polo, so preppy. He shut the journal, her picture inside, then hurried up to the middle aft deck to get some air, leaving the journal on the bed. Thankfully, no one was in the gym.

Cool and crisp, the night should bring him back to his senses. The *DI* glided through a calm sea at twenty-one knots. He lay back on a chaise and watched the stars pass by. Why had he invaded her journal? Had evil spirits come over her? Maybe when they were digging in the graves of old? He'd heard of that. Old timers often said funerals were dangerous, that evil spirits had to come out and go somewhere. Could it happen? After all, India is an epicenter of almost all major religions.

Of course, the only way to ease his mind and find the truth was to read her journals. Tonight, he'd only seen a couple of pictures, no hard facts. Maybe he'd look again—after the cruise. Would it change the way he saw Gail? Would it diminish his love for her? No, nothing could. Not now.

After reaching into a storage compartment and taking out a light blanket, he stretched back onto the chaise. Then, watching the sea disappearing behind them, he fell asleep.

CHAPTER
SEVENTEEN

When DR woke again, the port of Aden was coming into view. He relieved Lorenzo so he could rest before everyone went ashore. With its prominent location, Aden once was an important Roman trading port. Now, with its proximity to the Suez Canal, those things combined to make it a large and special city.

But it could be dangerous, especially for foreigners. Terrorists inflicted their damage, and rebels battled Yemen authorities with help from Iran, meanwhile a Saudi-led coalition supported the Yemen government in the civil war.

In October of 2000, seventeen sailors were killed, and thirty-nine were injured by two suicide bombers in a boat attack on the USS *Cole*. If a US Naval ship could have problems, so could a private vessel. DR would make their stay short. Especially now with the Quds funding all sorts of terrorist activities.

He found a suitable spot to tie off the *DI* close to the port office and under good observation. Since the US embassy closed in Aden back in 1969, Americans traveling in the area did so at their own risk.

The weather was nearly perfect, a cool breeze blowing in from the

Gulf of Aden. After breakfast, DR stood and addressed his group. "We'll head out just before ten. I'm going to ask everyone to dress low-key. No jewelry or anything to make you stand out." He tucked his watch up under his sleeve. "Ladies, I'm also going to ask you to don thobes over your clothes while traveling."

Miguel, already dressed fashionably in khaki pants and a silk Hawaiian shirt, raised his glass of black tea. "A good plan, my friend, though I must say it probably won't help. Their beauty and charm will shine through. After all, all of our ladies are educated, beautiful women living a blessed life. That's hard to hide in a place of such desperation."

The ladies tittered and teased him for being a charmer. Then everyone headed below to their quarters to comply. DR hesitated before leaving his watch behind. Few on the street would know its value, and he did need to know the time. But who would he be if he broke his own rules?

When he rejoined the others, they loaded up in the van for the short journey, leaving David to watch over the *DI*. DR hung out a window watching the few busy streets. So many buildings appeared deserted, war-torn with windows broken or boarded up on this side of the grand city.

Miguel had informed the monsignor of their projected arrival. As they exited the van, he emerged from the cathedral, strode over, and embraced Miguel. Then he stepped back and bowed slightly to the others. His slender appearance threw DR. The monsignor wore no jewelry, so his ecclesiastical ring must be in safekeeping, but the purple cassock stood as a reminder that this is a man of God. Phooey.

"Welcome, everyone."

As the monsignor spoke in Arabic and some broken English, Miguel acted as translator when necessary for those of their group who, unlike DR, didn't speak it. Still dressed in a pair of khaki pants and a blue-silk Hawaiian shirt, he looked sophisticated and important, not at all the look DR was going for.

"The building looks like it's seen a bit of... excitement lately, Monsignor?" Ryan motioned to the damaged windows and building.

"They came to break out our stained glass window of Jesus last night. The outer glass covering it was too thick for their rocks, but it has a small hole in it now. But still, the rock didn't hit the stained glass, for that I thank God."

"Rocks?" Miguel cocked his head after translating.

"Ah. Most of this was done by younger boys. They're in training, being radicalized. It's all still a game to them. The older men won't attack us. They retain a little respect. But not those young ones. They throw firebombs and whatever they can get their hands on. One day soon though, they'll come back with more and finish the job. Even so... Jesus is still in the cathedral and unharmed." The monsignor's shoulders sloped now, Miguel keeping up with the translation. "But the cool air last night caused it to get some condensation. We'll have to do something to protect it, to keep it from rusting or corroding—and soon. The window is a beacon and symbol of faith and hope for our worshippers."

On the smallish side, the white cathedral was built in 1892. The stained glass portrait was donated and installed the same year. Now the exterior was showing its age, especially after the recent attacks mostly went unrepaired.

The monsignor slapped his hands together. "But like everything else, we'll have to hide it too. Which is one of their goals, making us go underground." He stepped closer and clapped a hand on Miguel's shoulder. "Hopefully, we can stay here. Miguel, it's worse than any other time I've seen. A week ago, ten children were taken from the children's home next door. The home's taken in girls since the government's gotten involved, and now, it's a target for sex traffickers. Well, I believe that's who took them. It's so sad. The priests are beside themselves."

"What about the authorities?" Miguel responded without translating this time, Stephanie's voice filling in for the others. "Do they know who took the children? Are they looking for them or do they have any leads?"

"The authorities… huh! What a joke. They aren't concerned. Can you believe that? I tell you, Miguel, I don't know how much longer we can stay here. People are scared. So many have been persecuted that it's causing many of them to worship at home or somewhere in hiding." His dark eyes glistened. He shook his head and turned with his arm outstretched, palm open, showing them the area. "Who can blame them?"

As the others entered the building, they stopped just inside the entrance to survey the sanctuary. "This is just sad." Ryan's Irish lilt broke the solemn silence. "She is a beautiful church, ornate and colorful, but such years of neglect…"

"Wouldn't have happened on your watch, eh?" Trixie teased their Catholic caretaker.

His ears reddened to match his hair. "If I had the money to stop it. Clearly, finances are to blame, not the heart of the people."

DR tipped his head back. The condensation on the stained glass window of Jesus took on a reddish hue, likely a combination of dust and the metals holding the glass together. The hole in the thick protective glass was just behind the warm glass near Jesus's eyes. Already, the moisture became too heavy, dripping down like tears on DR's shoulder.

"I'm so sorry, friend." The monsignor put his hands over his mouth, eyes widened. "See? Even now, Jesus is crying on your shoulder. That was what I was afraid of… condensation. It will ruin the glass. Let me get something to wipe that off." He strode away, his steps echoing in the hollow chamber. Coming back with a bottle of water and a clean cloth, he handed them to DR.

"What are the odds that it would have dripped on me?" DR peered at the window, at the reddish water coming from the eyes of Jesus. It was the only place with condensation. Indeed.

"See, even now, Jesus is weeping over you," Miguel repeated and smiled.

The room went quiet, everyone taking in what had happened. DR wasn't a hard man, but everyone knew his take on Christianity, on religion. Everyone knew what Miguel was implying... so did DR. He pretended he hadn't heard the comment, looking up at the beautiful, centuries-old stained glass picture of Jesus crucified, from where it had wept only on him.

After a light snack and heavy conversation, everyone said their goodbyes, thanking and blessing the monsignor for his time and hospitality. DR still occasionally wiped at the reddish stains holding onto his white blend sport pullover.

When everyone walked to the children's home next door, Miguel stayed behind.

DR saw a side to Miguel he hadn't expected. While he didn't push his faith on anyone, he didn't shy away from it either. How would this affect their friendship? He and his childhood friends had to go their separate ways. Was he beyond all that now?

The children's home priests met them at the chained gate.

"Hello, friends." The taller man extended his hands, speaking in English with a heavy Middle East accent. He clasped DR's hand in both of his, then moved on to greet the others similarly. "I'm Father O'Reilly. Welcome to Saint John's Children's Home. Monsignor Ricci called us. We're happy to have you. I'm sure the children will be too."

"The children need a distraction, but they may not be too welcoming to strangers." The shorter balding man who'd introduced himself as Father Walters folded his arms across his chest and clucked his tongue, the perfect Saint Nicholas if only he had hair. "You've heard about the trouble we had a week ago? Some of our children were taken. We pray they will be found and returned soon."

"Pardon me." Laurie stepped up. "But did you say Monsignor Ricci?"

"Yes?"

"Hmm... our Miguel's a Ricci, isn't he?" Her green eyes twinkled as if she were on the verge of uncovering some mystery. "I wonder?"

"Don't mind my nosy wife." Tom patted her shoulder. "Could just be a coincidence, hon."

DR pushed past them, despite one part of his mind wondering what Miguel's true reason for visiting Aden was. He had more important things to ask. He couldn't stand people messing with children. He'd been there and knew the damage it could do to a person's soul.

Heavy black iron doors hung broken off to one side, doors that once protected the entrance, now riddled with bullet holes. Like the cathedral next door, the once stately facility showed its age and wear from both the attacks and years of neglect.

He spun back to the priests. "How many children did they take?"

"Ten in all, two boys and eight girls." O'Reilly sank backward. "They tied the rest of us up and locked some of the children out in the fenced yard. That's how we were able to get free. The children shouted over the wall to Monsignor Ricci as he was leaving for the night."

"What did they look like?"

The other's questions fired off alongside DR's.

"Were they Muslims?"

"How long were you tied up?"

"Yes, Muslim, but not from around here." O'Reilly shook his head and waved his left hand. "They sounded like Pakistanis, maybe? We don't know, but we fear they'll be back."

DR gritted his teeth and smacked his hands together, his face hot.

Their soft steps muffled the conversation as they moved into an ancient hall.

Walters hunched his shoulders, and his lips turned down at the corners. "We were tied up for several hours."

"What makes you think they'll come back?" Debbie asked.

Walters rubbed at his bald spot, then spread out his hands. "The fox always returns to the henhouse—if he isn't caught."

O'Reilly's thin shoulders slumped as he wiped a hand over a damaged hall table. "This is the first time kids have ever been taken from the home."

"It's true." Walters edged closer to his friend and patted his back. "In all our years—I've served here for a quarter of a century, and O'Reilly began living here when he was six—we've never feared for the children's safety, much less our own."

"Until now."

"My friends"—Walters spread his hands again, perhaps a habitual gesture formed from years of ushering children—"things are spiraling out of control. Lawless terrorism is overcoming this once prosperous city. The jihadist regime of Iran is giving weapons to every terrorist group and street punk. Every day, their ranks explode with newly radicalized members."

"Yes." Ryan stepped in. "I've been reading how the computer age is helping the jihadists get their message out."

"What are the authorities saying?" Debbie asked. The sun poured through the ancient windows, giving her an angelic glow. The ancient glass with all its imperfections transformed the rays into different colors and hues that refracted off her.

"Nothing." O'Reilly blocked the same rays from his eyes. "They don't care. They've already cut our funding for the missing children."

"So... how can you protect the children and yourselves?" Miguel spoke up. DR hadn't noticed him rejoining them. "Have you installed any new security? Have the authorities helped you address those issues, so it won't be so easy the next time?"

"That's a joke, right?" O'Reilly rolled his eyes. "They look at it as ten fewer kids to feed and clothe. The government only took over the home to negate the effect of Christianity. Soon, sharia will be the rule of law here. The Americans deserted the area and the fight, and terrorists and their friendlies are taking full advantage, filling the gap. You saw the iron doors when you came in? Well, they were rock solid, until..."

"So, what would you have the Americans do? We've spent so much money here in the past twenty years. So many lives have been lost— and for what?" DR raked a hand through his hair. Wasn't the US already doing too much? "We haven't made any gains."

"The pallets of money your country sent to Iran wiped out all of our gains. We'd spent years making that progress with America. Now, we're feeling the effects. Here and all around the area, the attack on Jeddah, it's all connected one way or another. Their dirty hands are on it all."

Walters shuffled his feet, opening and wringing his hands. "The news organizations aren't reporting the truth, just their agenda. If you were here, you'd know the opposition isn't letting up."

"So that's it then?" Penny hugged her arms around herself, making her voice a little sharp, even in her Southern drawl, her usual lighthearted manner put aside. "All hope is lost for the abducted boys and girls? How old were the children, and where were they from... what country?"

O'Reilly held up his hands as if to surrender. "The children are nine to fourteen years old. The girls were the youngest. Most were from the Syrian fiasco caused by ISIS and the war. Several were from Aden, including the youngest, a nine-year-old girl who was taken along with her two sisters, twelve and ten. We pray and fast, but it's up to God."

"We're worried about all the children," Walters spoke up. "But especially Habiba, the oldest sister. It's bad enough they're being sold, but she has cystic fibrosis." His jaw set as he closed his eyes, age lines blurring amidst the heat of his rage. "When they grabbed the kids, they just took them. She doesn't have her inhaler or enzymes, and her condition can be rather acute. As the oldest, she's protective of her sisters, Amal and Derifa. She's already had to grow up far too early. Now, her dear sweet soul..."

The red stains on DR's white shirt were still fresh in his mind. He clenched and unclenched his hand, then worked on taking in slow deep breaths as if he were psyching up for an exam. Watching, listening, absorbing, but trying not to feel anything.

"I can't imagine how those kids are handling all this. How scared and alone they must feel. I hope somehow..." No need to go on. They'd already discussed the odds of the kidnappers being caught.

When DR raised his gaze, Debbie was looking back at him, her lips pinched tight, and her eyes scrunched together. Could their dreams be connected? Were they both dreamwalking? What did that even mean? Once they returned to the *DI* and he completed his interview, he'd speak with her.

Tom and Laurie stood with Craig and Trixie, whispering back and forth.

"It's a great idea. We should ask everyone else too," Trixie said aloud now.

DR followed the others down a clean inside hallway. The comfortable home offered a decent space to learn, play, and run. They slept four in a room on bunk beds. Every two rooms shared a bathroom, a luxury indeed. Some in Aden were using outhouses or porta johns, thanks to the neighborhood skirmishes.

The priests fed the children hot and nutritious food, and though their books were tattered and worn, they were up to date. The hour went fast. Then everyone agreed to help the home financially.

In the community room, toys and home products made from wood were in various stages of completion. The children worked on crafts, which the priests sold to the community, bringing in finances to support the extra needs. DR picked up a small half-finished hobby horse, then nodded to Walters. "How much do you sell these for?"

"That is a toy for one of the kids here. They have to make their toys since money is tight." His eyes seem to droop as DR's heart broke.

"These are some special kids. We want to help. Send me a list of what you need." Hot liquid burned DR's eyes. When he turned to wipe them with his hand, Debbie saw him.

They prayed together before leaving, being respectful. DR handled all the "religious" activity, giving it due respect. Then everyone said their best wishes and goodbyes, and DR gave Walters his card. "Call me."

After a visit to Saint Francis of Assisi, they returned to the *DI*, saddened by the day's events. Hopefully, there wouldn't be any more surprises along the way. Somehow, they'd managed to land in the middle of a terrorist attack and now... kidnappers.

DR strode to his quarters to prep for his talk with Mike and his listeners. Most of the others went into the market near the marina, staying close to the *DI*, some picking up supplies for Ryan's party.

Going into a shop near the pier in Aden, Laurie let out the breath she'd been holding. "This feels weird. Like we're an enemy or something. Maybe because of all the things we've seen on this trip. I don't know."

Tom took her hand to guide her around the damaged shop door. Then, looking over his shoulder, he held the door for Penny before finishing Laurie's thought for her. "It feels like every eye in the harbor is on us. We'd better get what we need and get out of here."

Little wonder they worked so well as a writing team. They so often saw and felt the same thing.

"Have you been here before?" Penny asked Stephanie before sliding her arm back through Greg's, flashing him a woolly eye.

"Yes, several times, but not this particular area. Usually, everyone's friendly." Stephanie frowned at the ravaged shop's nearly empty shelves. She shivered. "But not today."

Leaving the store with their intended purchase, the birthday party supplies, Laurie slowed her steps. The people on the sidewalk seemed to step around them cautiously—plague-like cautious. "There's an air here. I almost wish..." Her gaze tripped over a caricature of a man hanging from a second-story window. "Do they celebrate Halloween here?" Half whispering to Tom, she quickened her pace.

"I don't know. Why?"

"Look up there." She pointed to the window. "It looks so... so, real."

"Looks like somebody's into creepy gore." Penny nudged Greg to look up at the display.

"I almost wish we'd never come on this trip. Everywhere we go, something bad is going on. It was never like this in the past." Stephanie slowed down, speaking over her shoulder to Penny and Greg. "Or maybe for some reason, like Mitch said, we never noticed."

"I know." Penny scooted up to hug Stephanie and Mitch, then Laurie and Tom. "My heart aches for these people. But if we hadn't come, we could've never met y'all. I'm so thankful we did because making friends with people like you is worth several crappy trips."

With the *DI* now in sight, thankful tears formed in Laurie's eyes.

"We better stop this before we all cry." Stephanie wiped at her own eyes. "With this mush and the humidity, my makeup will make me look like a raccoon."

CHAPTER
EIGHTEEN

Down in his cabin, DR sat talking with Mike on the satellite phone, doing another interview on live radio. The painting of Gail loomed behind his bed.

He stretched the satellite phone cord over to his bed. "You wouldn't believe all the craziness we've seen. Jeddah was so nice. Then they blew up the port. Miguel wanted to stop in Aden, making up for the day we didn't spend in Jeddah, and we ran into a children's home where ten of their kids were just taken. I hope that's all the bad we'll see."

He flopped back on the bed to relax, reminding him of his college days. "So... how's your partner. I don't hear her in the background?"

"Willie's taking some time off. Something went down the other day. Why? I'm surprised you'd ask about her."

Rolling his head sideways, DR stared at Gail's portrait. "Curious that's all. I'm not going to carry a grudge." He smoothed the comforter and stared at the dresser where Gail's journal seemed to call out. "What did the pastor always say? Only the person carrying the grudge ever felt hurt, not the other person. I'm over it."

"That's awesome." Mike gave out the type of hoot they'd do at a game rally. "I shouldn't be saying anything, but she was torn up that you were mad at her. She's a kind woman, DR. She just lives by her convictions. That's all. We fight a lot at the station because we're both hardheaded, but she's a good friend, the best kind."

"Yeah... I know." DR checked his watch. How many seconds until they aired? "I could see it the day at the coffeehouse. Anyway, are you about ready to start the show?"

On-air, they talked about the attack on Jeddah and the children taken from the home. They agreed it was time for clear sailing ahead, then set a time to talk Tuesday, next week. After saying goodbye, he went up in search of Debbie. He stopped by the helm first and spoke with David, who was wiping down the electronic gauges, removing the salty film that accumulated at sea.

DR wanted to be far out to sea before darkness fell, so he confirmed their speed and headings. Looking out over the bridge that sparkled from David's extra attention, he sighted Debbie talking with Lo and Ryan on the sun and pool deck.

He enjoyed being near her, not simply because of her beauty and sexuality but also because there seemed to be an aura about her, a loving nature much deeper than the touch of one's flesh. Almost like when he was first with Gail at the Dukes School, he felt an inner peace around her.

He'd begun daydreaming, but David's voice jolted him back.

"David, yes, that sounds fine. We'll eat as soon as we get an hour or two behind us at sea." DR started toward the helm stairwell, then paused. "I've got something to attend to. If you need anything, let Miguel or Lo know."

DR headed down to grab a beer before joining Debbie. When he reached the galley, Joshua and Miguel were enjoying a glass of sangria. Joshua dressed in his patriotic bathing suit once again, with a towel draped over his shoulders, must've been soaking up the sun by the pool.

Moving their way, DR popped the top on his bottle Birra Moretti and saluted Miguel with it. "Cold and delicious. Thanks for introducing me to this brand."

"Pretty decent of a Michigan man to admit he likes European beer." Miguel winked, then beckoned him. "Come—sit with us."

DR slid down beside Joshua and slapped him on his shoulder. "Can we talk to you about our dreams? I had another, and I'm willing to admit it—I need a full night of sleep again."

"Don't mind me." Miguel pushed to his feet and patted at his Hawaiian shirt. "I need to go change anyway so I can prep my special spaghetti recipe. My famous sauce goes well with a lot of things, but not sure it would be good on this nice shirt."

"It'll be a treat for everyone." DR held the beer up. "I still can't get over the fact that you cook too. Finding you was—" He stopped, about to say, "a miracle." He wasn't willing to say "a blessing" either. "Helpful."

"DR," Joshua interrupted, "when you say 'we,' are you talking about with Debbie or just between us?" Joshua eyed Miguel as if Miguel knew something they didn't.

"If you don't mind, I'd like to hear about your dreams too," Miguel said. "My mom once said something about dreamwalkers. I'll change in a bit."

Seemed Miguel and Joshua already discussed it.

"I'll ask Debbie to join us." DR rose to his feet faster than a speeding train, Miguel staying put. "Then the four of us can put our heads together."

"Sure." Joshua peered out the square porthole window and rubbed his left biceps, already showing a little too much sun.

DR half sprinted to the forward deck. He was going to stop these dreams. Lo was playing quarters, a beer pong drinking game with Tom, Mitch, Greg, and Craig, while Debbie and Ryan lay on chaises talking. She was wearing her favorite white bikini. Poor Ryan couldn't take his eyes off her.

DR hated ruining the moment for him, but he needed to talk to her.

"Wow. This sure is one beautiful sight." He stopped by them, pretending to look out over the sea, then winking at her. "I hate to interrupt, but I'd like to talk to you—down in the galley if you don't mind."

"So, you like the view, do you?" she teased, obviously knowing what he meant. "I wondered how long it would take you to come up this afternoon. This morning, I sensed you'd had another dream."

"I did, and I have some help lined up to get us to the bottom of them." DR scrunched his face and held out an apologetic hand. "Ryan, please excuse me for stealing your lovely companion, but we have an important issue to settle."

He extended his hand to help her up as the other girls watched. They didn't miss a thing. But then neither did Ryan. She looked gorgeous, the sun glistening off her bronzed, athletic body, her blonde hair pulled back in a ponytail. She slid on an oversized shirt, the gauze fabric rippling about her.

The women talked together in a hush-hush girly way as he and Debbie passed. When DR glanced back, Ryan had nearly fallen out of his chaise watching her walk away. The poor guy was probably thinking about how she'd make a great birthday present tomorrow. DR could relate.

Ryan shook his right index finger at the women laughing at him, now laughing along. "Now, girls, you shouldn't be having fun at someone else's expense."

Debbie must've suddenly felt self-conscious as she wrapped herself more securely in her shirt.

As DR and Debbie entered the galley, the guys' rousing conversation ricocheted along the sleek corridor from the galley dining area. Eyeing them with their sangria, Debbie crossed her arms, planted herself in the doorway, and blocked DR's approach. "DR? Do you think this is a good time? It looks like they've had a couple glasses too many."

"Oh, they're okay." He leaned into her and placed a hand on her shoulder. "I was just talking to them. They're just cutting up a little."

They welcomed her in unison, Miguel adding with his old-world charm, "Debbie, you're looking especially lovely today."

Hands on her hips, she eyed them like an impatient schoolteacher. "Just how many sangrias have you boys had?"

"Why, Debbie, you know we're not lushes?" Miguel winked.

"Okay." Joshua rubbed his hands together. "So, what are we dreaming about these days?"

"More of the same." DR slid into a free seat, the sun shining into his eyes. He scooted to his right, in front of Debbie, to get it out of his vision. "I keep hearing you all talk about them, and I want to know more, like why we keep having these crazy dreams."

In the humidity and heat, he started sweating.

"Remember what I told you earlier? Believers that can discern His directions through the Holy Ghost. He's been known to wake from sleep to pray for others."

Miguel propped his elbows on the table.

"We can't understand or comprehend the mind of God. Scripture says that He uses all things to work together. We don't know His ways or even what 'all things' are. So, first, we should determine what they mean to both of you."

Penny and Greg came down. Perhaps sensing the conversation's seriousness, they excused themselves to rummage around in the galley. As Joshua continued, Penny sauntered over.

"Can we join you? I remember my dad preaching on that."

"Oh no, hon." Greg tugged at her arm. "We don't want any part of *that* conversation."

DR rubbed his jaw, surprised Penny could be so serious. She came across as flighty. Maybe because of the way she dressed and talked, like someone who loved to be the center of things. Right now, she was wearing a bright-yellow bikini that was more like a one-and-a-quarter piece. Potholders hanging from the stove had more material than the triangles covering her bosom, but that was just Penny. Her cheerleading days helped her figure and her modesty too.

"Well sure, why not?" Debbie patted the chair beside her sarcastically. "The more the merrier."

Penny plunked down beside DR, pushing Greg onto the seat across from her by Debbie. Greg cast a longing glance at the corridor, making it obvious he preferred to be topside. But like most good husbands—DR remembered how that felt—he'd hold his peace. No need getting the wife riled up.

Just like that, the atmosphere changed from a drop-dead seriousness to curiosity.

"What do you know about dreamwalkers, Penny? We didn't know you were a spiritual person?" Joshua tried to maintain eye contact, but color crept up his neck, his gaze slipping now to her barely covered bosom.

In her deep Alabama drawl, she told of her childhood, how her dad was a traveling evangelist and how she'd grown up poor because of it.

"I know more than you may think." She shook a finger between them, and her bosom jiggled with the motion, the lack of clothing doing nothing to support her. "When I was a young girl, my dad had a dream—well, he said it was a dream. He called it dreamwalking. He said the Lord showed him, in his dreams, that we were supposed to move to the city of Birmingham. So... he packed us up and moved us away, just like that. Mom was pissed. We left her family and everything, just because Dad said he had a dream."

Miguel settled back in his chair, bracing a hand on the back of Joshua's chair beside him. "How did that work out for you and your family? Was it a prophetic dream?"

"He passed away a week after we moved. Mom had to take on a job, so she became a secretary for the Church of God in Birmingham. They were praying for someone for over three months and were excited to have Mom. That's how I got the finances to go to college. The congregation got together and gave me most of the money I needed. I earned the rest and worked while going to classes. So here I am." She gestured to herself, seeming innocently naïve about the fact DR and the guys were struggling *not* to look at her. "Without Dad's dream, I wouldn't be here today."

"I'd say that was a divine dream. But I don't know if it was dreamwalking. Unless someone was praying for your family to move or for some other reason? Maybe God heard the prayers of the church." Joshua turned to DR. "So, back to what we're discussing. We just don't know how God is working everything together. Looking around at everyone on this trip, I'd say that the Lord used 'all things.' "

DR held up a hand, impatient with the Christian tail-wagging. "Can we get back to the matter at hand? Debbie, what was your latest dream?"

"The dream I told you about earlier seemed like a man or spirit came out of the fire, right? Well, my latest dream started there. What looked like a man came out of the fire, only to become like a wind, like a spirit or something. The wind became so powerful it pushed the boat on the coast loose from the tree it was moored to, pulling up the tree—roots and all. Trees all over the island were falling over."

A sunbeam reflected off the stainless backsplash behind the stove, hitting Joshua where he sat. He slid over to relieve himself. With him aside, the beam continued until it struck the cut crystal bowl on the white speckled quartz countertop that held the apples Debbie loved to snack on. There, it shattered into colorful prisms of light breaking in every direction and on the overhead tile. The refracted light added an element of openness to the closed-in galley with only one large square porthole on each side.

"The ocean's tide begins going sideways. The wind is so powerful, a downpour follows. A hurricane or tempest strikes the island. I don't know what happens to the tribe. I don't know whether they make it or not. But the wind blows the boat and the smell of burnt flesh away. The boat goes bouncing wildly in the ocean, waves washing it further and further from shore. That's when I woke up."

Nauseous, DR leaned over the table and studied the bowl. "I don't know if our dreams are connected. You know how I feel about spiritual matters, what some people call the divine." He traced a finger across the cherry inlay, smudging a straight line, the way he usually saw things. Then he huffed and squiggled the line out. "But at times, there does seem to be an influence in our lives that commands the authority of the very elements we live in. So I'm trying to be open-minded. I just want these dreams to stop. I'm sure Debbie does too."

As he raised his arms and tipped his head toward Joshua and Miguel to signify his cooperation, Debbie nodded, but didn't speak. He felt that too, the inability to get this across. After nights of vivid dreams, he was tired. She must be too. They were cutting into his peace, not to mention his lost sleep.

The *DI* rocked to the right, jolting them. Suddenly, it was much more real. DR held his breath, waiting for the boat to counterrock. It didn't.

Miguel placed his hands on the tabletop and glanced at the staircase from the deck above. "What are the odds, DR, that the boat you dream about could also be the boat Debbie sees being blown out to sea? Maybe that's where the dreamwalkers are taking you both? It would seem to be the only logical reason for convergent dreams about a boat."

"See... that is what I don't get." DR waved to stress his frustration. "Why do you keep saying dreamwalker? What is that? What does it have to do with us?"

Miguel ducked his head and rubbed the back of his neck. The sheepish posture suited him less than the clothing DR had suggested he don for their trip this morning. "Dreamwalking, in part, is being led by God to pray for a specific person or event anywhere in the world. Thereby, allowing God to interject His authority through whatever means He chooses, to answer the prayer as He alone can, as He determines or sees fit. It's called dreamwalking because often God awakens people from their sleep to pray, but the actual dreamwalker is a spirit that comes to, well, to whoever is awakened or having the dream." Miguel gestured to his friend. "Right, Joshua? Isn't that what you figured out?"

"Yes." Joshua's eyes widened, and he hunched his shoulders and palms up. "First, assume there is a dreamwalker. Then I say to you that, somewhere, someone is in trouble, based on your dreams. Now, you have to let go of your own understanding about the divine and acknowledge this is beyond your understanding. Then, finally, we can start to decipher the problem."

"Okay." Debbie wrapped her shirt tightly around herself, a habit of hers. "Let's say a dreamwalker is giving us a prophetic dream. If so, what is the dreamwalker doing, and who is he... or she?"

"Well..." Miguel took a deep breath and raised his chin. "That's not the question. The dreamwalker is a spirit... who is sent by... God."

DR rolled his eyes.

"You see?" Joshua broke in. "That's where you have to go beyond yourself. It requires you trust in something higher, something you can't see."

DR glared, but Joshua spread his hands.

"You wanted answers, my friend. I am not going to sugarcoat it." Joshua rose to his feet. Hands on the edge of the table, he leaned toward DR to add emphasis to his words. "Now, assuming we are right, the boat with the kids is in trouble. God must have someone praying for the kids somewhere. Then answering the prayer, He sent a storm to save the children. Maybe the men who were killed in the fire were bad guys. This could make sense, yes, since the kids are locked in the boat's storage area?"

Debbie reached over and laid a hand on DR's forearm. "DR, you said you were screaming for help in your first dream and someone in the boat shushed you, telling you the tribe would kill you too, if they heard, right?"

DR's head jerked up, his heartbeat picking up. "A boy sitting on my right side shushed me the first time, and the boy on my left helped him when I screamed again. The next time, a bright light shined down on us. It looked like someone opened the cargo compartment door. But the compartment door never opened, so I couldn't tell where the light came from. I heard a familiar voice say, 'Hold on tight, Stevie. Hold on. Don't open the door.' " His stomach wasn't just nauseous. It hurt now.

He resisted the urge to wrap his arms around himself and rock back and forth like a child in need of comfort, like Stevie. "The voice from the light was telling us all to hold on, but why hold on and not try to escape?"

As the *DI* traveled along, the sun's position had changed, and so had the brilliant sunbeam. The prisms of light disappeared. Maybe the dark dreams might too. Laughter called from the deck above, and he wanted to leave but couldn't. He'd called the meeting.

"Inside the boat, we could hear the killers running toward the boat. I'd never heard their language before. So I don't know who was coming or what they were shouting. But the voice that warned me... Well, I've heard it before." Closing his eyes, he sank into the pain that always followed the voice. "I'm sure of it. Maybe—and this is a real stretch for me—the kids in the boat are the kids taken from the children's home? Didn't the priests say they'd been praying and fasting days for their safe return?"

Could it be that simple? This whole thing was kind of making sense—except he didn't believe in the divine. So how would he reconcile this to his beliefs?

Everyone sat quietly after his comment.

Then Joshua slapped the table. "You could be right. After all, didn't you say the rest of the children were girls?" He looked over at Debbie, who nodded her agreement.

"We should look at weather reports for storms around here," Joshua suggested. "If so, we may have part of our answer."

DR pushed back his chair, then waved everyone back into their seats. "Please stay here. I'll run to my cabin for my tablet."

In his cabin, DR closed his eyes and leaned back against the shut door, knowing he was walking into a trap. "Why me?" He didn't want any part of anything God put His hands on. But God wasn't playing fair, wasn't giving him a choice. What were the odds this was the real reason anyway? Slim to none, and hopefully, slim had already left.

When he returned with his tablet, they'd lost half their number. "Did we bore them stiff?"

"No, Greg wanted to get some sun, and Miguel went to change before starting dinner." Debbie sat snacking on another apple. "He asked that we fill him in later."

DR connected to the *DI*'s Wi-Fi system. Since the *DI* ran the latest technology, the tablet screen sprang to life after mere seconds.

"I'll check NASA's archives. They have detailed weather reports, much better than the other agencies." He plugged in the parameters. A spurt of apple juice struck the screen as Debbie leaned in alongside Joshua to view the screen with all its color maps and footnotes. DR dabbed it away, careful not to change the parameters with his touch. "You really like apples, don't you?"

"Yep."

He couldn't stop his gaze from traveling down her shirt. The perfume and tanning oil were now strong aphrodisiacs calling him. Oops. She must have sensed his gaze, covering herself more securely. Heat stung his neck before his gaze met hers.

"Do you understand this thing?" She gestured to the weather notes. "What are we looking for?"

"We're looking for high volatile winds. See the squiggly lines? They're isobars and indicate high and low pressure. The closer they are, the higher the pressure and maybe the winds. Look for the arrows and feathers to address that more directly. The program is going to run us through a seventy-two-hour cycle for this portion of the Indian Ocean. We can zoom in if we see something of interest."

Feeling like he was caught with his hand in the cookie jar, he braved catching her eye again. She looked a little sheepish too. After all, she was the one half naked. His tight shoulders loosened up as she halfway smiled, letting him know everything was okay. Huh, maybe she even liked his attention?

Joshua pointed at the screen. "What is that, right there?" He touched the screen, enlarging the image. "There, by all those close squiggly lines? What island is that?"

"Trouble." DR frowned. "Real trouble, with a capital *T*. The North Sentinelese Island. You don't want any part of that. No one's visited that island and lived to talk about it. Not for years. It's off-limits. It's even against the law to go there."

He massaged the tension creeping into his neck, his stomach tightening. "I once heard of two fishermen who anchored a short distance offshore, only to have their boat somehow wash ashore while they were sleeping. It proved to be fatal."

"Do you think?" Debbie tucked wisps of sun-kissed blonde hair behind her ears, but her headshake shook them loose again. "No... That would be too easy."

His heart was pounding as their gazes met, and her mouth formed a perfect *O* while they shared their unspoken thoughts. He braved a whisper. "Could it be?"

"Well..." She dragged the word out. "The three guys from our dream boat were burnt alive. Could this be our place, where our dreams are taking us?"

"Whoa, there. My dreams aren't taking me anywhere." DR shoved the tablet away. "This is just a hypothetical hypothesis. We're assuming a god is directing us to rescue ten children bouncing around the ocean three thousand miles away." Hands up, he turned his head from side to side.

Debbie's jaw dropped. She froze, probably collecting her thoughts. "You brought me down here to talk about this. Is that all you want to do—*talk*? I need this to end so I can get some rest." Red mottled her neck and flared across her cheeks as her words grew heated. "It's ruining my entire trip."

Joshua placed his arm around her shoulders, cutting DR a look.

DR locked his hands atop his head and briefly closed his eyes. "I must have been nuts to have considered it. I'd rather keep having the dreams than go bouncing off in hopes of being a knight in shining armor. They might have us all committed after something like that."

Debbie reached toward the screen, her finger hovering just above the dark isobars flashing their high-wind and torrential-rain warnings. Somehow, with that expression, he imagined her caressing a child's face. Then her shoulders slumped. Her eyes dimmed. She drew back.

"You're right. I got caught up in the moment. Yeah, that's a long way to go on a baseless hunch. Don't you think so, Joshua?"

He stood silently. But the look he gave them...

DR shuddered. It was as if he were saying he knew full well that, if this was "a calling," it wouldn't stop until they answered it. Or someone else did.

DR ground his teeth, his gaze drawn with theirs to the screen. It seemed to be screaming out, "We're here. Please help us."

CHAPTER
NINETEEN

Heartache's a terrible thing, especially over a lost love. He'd been her only love, and she'd blamed him all these years for cheating on her, breaking off their relationship. Now, Willie had to reconcile a cruel truth.

She wrote in her journal:

All these years I tried to forget, to forgive. I thought I'd forgiven, but had I? Rachael told me it was her and his sister he was with, an older sister I'd never met. No wonder he got mad, didn't understand. But neither did I. In the nine months we dated, I thought I knew his entire family.

But what do I do now, Journal? It's myself I need to forgive. And I don't know how. Especially with this new infatuation—or is it love? Rachael told me he was on an oil rig in the Gulf near Houston. Do I contact him? Do I leave him alone? My heart says go get him, but my head says forget it. What do I do, Journal? God won't help me.

One day later, she added:

> *I found him, Journal. He's married and has two little girls and a newborn boy. They look just like him. And, man, he looks great with that dark tan and rippling muscles. He could've just stepped off a GQ cover. I remember his gentle eyes. Those should've been my children.*
>
> *Oh, what do I do, Journal? His wife isn't nearly as pretty. Should I go see him? I pray every night until there isn't breath in my lungs, but God doesn't answer. Does He hear me?*

Tonight, she picked up her journal and pen again, her soul pouring itself onto the page.

> *Journal, his wife is short and thin with brown hair and no makeup. She looks homely. Ashton could do so much better with me. Look at her, Journal. She's smiling with their newborn tucked in her arms. Ashton looks like a great dad. You should see how his eyes shine with the two girls cuddled up to his legs, one on each side.*
>
> *He'd planned to grow old in Delton with me, but God had other plans. Or am I the one to blame, Journal? Why did I listen to Kelsey Briggs? Did she want him for herself? Did she set me up so she could have him? Answer me, Journal. I was seventeen. How could I have become so blinded by rage?*

With his social media page open, she touched the picture where the small wooden cross hung around his neck, the same wooden cross he'd worn while they dated. His family all wore similar crosses, now, except the baby.

She bent her head back over the journal.

He wanted a family that glorified the Lord. He even told me so. How could I have forgotten? He was the one I'd wanted, desired—or was that an infatuation too?

She jotted down the email address and closed her computer. Now, she didn't need to see anymore. After years of tears, years of accusations, now she could shut down her private pity party. She shut her journal as well, whispering one more PUSH.

Time to see what God would do now. After all, He was her high tower where she had sought refuge for so many years. Now, she needed His hand to go forward, to embrace her self-made heartache, and to show her how He could use it for *her* good.

"If only Gail were alive," Willie whispered. "She understood me. Oh, wow! Maybe, just maybe, Gail was the divine appointment. After all, well... maybe she was one of those 'all things.'"

Putting your past behind you isn't always easy, but it seemed as if God had touched her heart, renewed her spirit, and removed her anger toward Ashton and her hatred of Rachael—through the truth. Jesus had that effect on her. Sometimes, it took a little longer than other times. Weeping had endured during the night, but now, joy was coming in the morning. Wasn't it?

After the *DI's* visit to Kochi, in the state of Kerala, India, a four-day voyage from Aden, they would sail another three days to Kolkata, their last port of call, their ultimate destination to see Chief Mnortarmillc and the site of the exciting discovery DR made there. In all their time at sea to reach their final destination, with two days spent at Kochi exploring the animal refuge and touring the city to come, a total of nine days remained before they arrived in Kolkata where they'd spend three days visiting.

The state of Kerala promised everyone a glimpse at a rich culture, lush waterfalls, and exotic animals, including elephants, monkeys, and tigers. There the Indian coastal areas were well-known for lush palm trees, plantations of spice, coffees, and teas.

"Okay, David." DR leaned over the console of gauges centered on the control panel. "Let's set our GPS for the port of Kochi, our speed to twenty knots and our hopes for smooth seas. We'll make it there in four days."

"Yes, sir." David pointed at the weather radar. "And it does appear to be clear sailing ahead. At least for now."

After patting David on the back, DR headed to his cabin for a little personal time. Maybe a nap. Maybe, this time, he'd have sweet dreams. His centrally located cabin avoided the wild ups and downs of the bow or stern. Just on the other side of Debbie's, near the galley, he also easily accessed midnight snacks.

Without explanation or notice, several hours later, the ocean's waves began to rise—up to seventeen feet, affected by a tempest nearly three thousand miles away a day earlier. When the bow rose and fell with unexpected violence, DR called David on the helm and slashed their speed to eight knots to ease the overall effect of the waves.

He flopped back on his bed, hands laced behind his head. Gail's portrait smiled at him from its reflection in a mirror. Tomorrow was Ryan's birthday, and everyone was looking forward to showing him their love, love Ryan's big Irish heart well earned. DR appreciated him too. After all, Mekie and Gail were Irish through and through.

Ryan, like so many Irish, loved fried potatoes and onions, so Miguel was going to "try" to surprise him. The smell of frying onions and potatoes may prove too tough to hide, along with the beef kielbasa and fried okra, more of Ryan's favorites, and hamburgers. All served with his favorite Irish beer, Extra Stout, so it should be a special time for him.

~

At midnight, Stevie was back on the boat with the children. The air had grown far more rancid, the smell of vomit encroaching as the boat was tossed about like a twig in the sea. It seemed as if they were flipping, end over end, at times flying through the sea and air. The children screamed, crying and praying that God would come.

The storm that tore the boat away from its mooring was now sucking them further out to sea. A tempest had struck the island. Now, the winds blew even harder. They were caught in a tropical cyclone, bouncing around in the sea, locked away in the hold. Stevie cried and screamed aloud for God too. To anybody. Then gagged, realizing the vomit was his own. He was covered in it, head to toe. They all were.

One of the girls seemed to be having major trouble. Her sisters kept calling her. "Habiba, Habiba! Please wake up. We're scared, Habiba."

But she didn't answer. With them jammed in tight, the hold was barely big enough for them all. Was this going to be their end?

Then, just as quickly as it had come, the wind began to subside as the storm raced away. It had pushed them far offshore and churned up the sea. Some waves reached as high as thirty feet. Even now, hours later, there were waves over ten feet. Yet, by some miracle, the small boat didn't capsize or shatter. Bruised and bleeding, the children were alive. Safe from the tribe.

More hours passed. The battered boat stayed afloat. Did God hear them?

Stevie heard voices—lots of voices. Could they be saved? In hopes, they screamed for help, their voices weak, but they were heard. When the hatch swung open, the bright sunlight blinded him, and Stevie couldn't make out their rescuers at first.

Someone was shaking him, shouting at him. "Wake up, DR. You're dreaming."

DR jolted, screaming, crying out for help, flailing his arms. He sprang from bed, then gulped in air. Yes, dreaming. He'd just been dreaming—again.

As Miguel got him a glass of water, DR slouched on the bed's edge, his eyes burning from a lack of sleep. Soaked in sweat, his king-sized bed looked like there had been a struggle, the comforter and sheets strewn about, half on the floor.

"Are these dreams ever going to end?" He gestured with the cup, splashing half of it. "What's the meaning of it all? I've never experienced anything like this before."

Miguel put his arm around him. They sat on the bed, neither able to say much. Then Miguel stood. "So... are you okay?"

"Yes, and thanks, Miguel." DR rubbed at his burning eyes, his muscles taut. But what could he do?

After Miguel left, DR glared at the cabinet where he'd buried Gail's journal the day before. He thought he knew everything about her, how she felt, and what she believed—or rather, didn't believe.

Yet he didn't, did he?

He had things he'd hidden from her too, though, didn't he? Yes... yes.

He never mentioned the times he took up for his little brothers and hid them. If there was a god, he didn't understand it, not all this.

Was he a bad person? He didn't deserve it... did he? He marched to the cabinet, flung open the drawer, and scooped up the offending journal. Then, right there, standing in the middle of his room, he started reading. And his thoughts moved faster than his eyes could read as Gail shared her delight in the Lord.

He slammed it shut. What did that even mean? Delight in the Lord? What happened to being happy with him? Wasn't he enough?

Heat pulsing from his heart, his rushing blood searing his skin as the words seared his mind, he opened the book again.

A single entry caught his eye:

As much as I love my husband and tried to push the emptiness aside, it called out to me in the night, in the middle of the day, everywhere. I just couldn't conquer it. Thank You for sending Willie to me. Thank You for her helping me get my sanity back. Now that Jesus has replaced the loneliness and emptiness, I can love DR the way he deserves to be loved.

He sank to the floor and slumped against the wall. The love of his life had converted. The woman—no, the *person*—he respected more than anyone became a Christian?

His tears began to build.

A long time ago, Jesus was real to him, but then...

Well, he wouldn't relive that again. Yet something or someone made so many things on this trip come together. Itasham's warning, the stained glass mural "weeping" on him, the perfect connections like the Riccis... Was it all a coincidence, or was there actually a—

No. No, no, *nooo!*

"I need a good stiff drink. That's all. Enough of the past." He pushed to his feet, ready to focus on the present. Gail was gone. No use polluting his struggles with hers. Life was so much easier before Willie told him to read her journal. Now, there'd be no turning back.

With a glance at the clock, he grabbed his robe and headed for the special stuff. Miguel's blackberry sangria—it packed a punch. When he reached the galley, Debbie sat nursing a glass herself. Her PJs sported a litter of puppies tonight.

"Care for company?" He set his glass on the table.

"Sure." She slid the bottle to him. "You know we have to go find them, right?"

"Find who?" He wasn't going to find anybody.

"Whoever is in the boat. You had another dream too, didn't you?" Blonde hair hung limp against her shoulders, and mascara smudged her under eyes—no, not mascara. The same bruising from sleeplessness that haunted his eyes. She lifted her glass to her mouth, but she lowered it without sipping. "Why do you think we're going through this? It has something to do with that island, but I don't know what."

"I don't know anything—except that these dreams have got to stop. It's two a.m., but here we are. It's discombobulating." He raked his fingers through his hair, hair that felt as rumpled as his bed had looked after the dream.

He focused on her blue puppy PJs. One of the puppies seemed to be chasing his own tail. Laughing, he pointed at the critter. "That's how I feel."

Smiling, she reached out for his hand. "These dreams are going to show us what to do. Crazy as it sounds, it's supernatural. You might not agree, but seriously, here we are. So, what happened in your dreams this time?"

He nursed his sangria, stalling. But Debbie wasn't the kind of woman who'd let him divert. "The other kids and me—we're tossed around at sea. My best guess is it's about a fifty-foot boat. I'm covered in vomit, probably my own. We all are. The waves are huge, and the boat feels like it's gonna break up. Once or twice, we seem to flip end over end—you know, like your worst rollercoaster-ride nightmare. Plus, the air is hot, humid, and stinky, filled with cries out of fear to a god that never comes."

She reached for a tissue on the counter, lightly brushing his arm.

DR stopped, the light touch wakening his senses. He sat up straighter. His gaze darted left and right seeing nothing, then settled on her. Was this so important that he was missing this beautiful woman in front of him? Moving the tissue box closer to her, he leaned back. He could hear her breathing, just feet away. Nothing used to excite him more than... Stupid rule, but maybe it was for the best. Still, his choice moved back and forth quicker than the waves could hammer the *DI*.

He shared the rest, then exhaled, a weight lifted. She looked different somehow. "What did you dream about?"

The *DI* slammed into the trough of a wave as if they were riding those same waves.

"It's strange," she began. "I'm not a character in my dream. It's like I'm floating."

Her deep-brown eyes teared. "I saw three boats... like you'd guessed about the boat in your dream, fifty-footers. They're returning from another country—pirates, drug runners, and thieves, maybe terrorists?—heading back toward Burma. They've been at sea for days. Everyone's just lying around, not drinking or partying. But they've celebrated something, and quite heartily. They've got empty booze and beer bottles everywhere."

Brain fog overtook him from the lack of rest. Even earlier thoughts about her and the rule descended in the order of priority. Sleep must come.

She pulled a hair tie from her pajama shirt pocket and began fingering through her hair, gathering it into one of her ponytails. "While heading back, they spot a boat on the radar. The boat is northeast of the smaller islands. It's not moving either. They change their course to intercept the lifeless boat and get a line on it, drawing it to the largest of their boats." She tipped her head upside down and tied off her hair before facing him again. "After securing it, they board."

He nodded, urging her to finish. Where did she get all her energy? "So what else happened?"

"Are you sure you want me to finish? You look like you're going to pass out." Her frown crinkled her eyes.

"Yes, of course, I do." His tongue betrayed him.

"One of them says it seems like a treasure hunt, but after not finding anyone or anything, they became disappointed. They start kicking the chairs around, complaining there wasn't anything to take, just food and water, no alcohol."

Her ponytail bounced with her shudder. "Then one of them accidentally kicks a latch or something. A cover falls off a false bulkhead. Bingo, their luck changes. They found a hidden cargo hold as the door swung open and revealed ten kids squeezed into the smelly hold."

His heart leapt. She'd finally finished. Yes, he wanted to know, but he couldn't keep his eyes open much longer. He leaned back and eyed the passageway to his room. Could he make it down that? The whole twenty-five paces?

She grimaced and spread out her hands. "Then I wake up. Our dreams must be connected somehow. I believe you see it too."

He focused on the overhead. "It's nuts—nuts with a capital *N*. Let's sleep on it. Tomorrow—or, rather, today—is Ryan's birthday. I'm going to my cabin and hope there won't be any more dreams." He pushed back his chair, stood, then paused, and clamped a hand on her shoulder. "Thanks, Debbie."

He held her gaze, those browns somehow so soothing. Was that admiration in them? No, he must be tired. "Thanks for sharing with me. Something tells me we'll be learning more soon. I'll see you in the morning."

She raised her hand and covered his on her shoulder, holding him there. "Can I ask you something first? Do you remember your other dreams like this, or do you forget them after only a minute or so—like I do?"

"I don't usually remember them." He squeezed her shoulder, then slid his hand free, and strode to the galley door.

"That's what I thought." Her soft voice followed him. "Sweet dreams, DR. Sweet dreams."

Was she having a sweet dream herself? A daydream, that is. Yes. It had been a long time in coming, but she was beginning to feel the desire to have a male companion again. When he'd turned to leave, the moonlight seemed like a spotlight shining on him. Even unkempt, he was a hunk.

Despite the whole no-romancing-the-passengers thing, she was becoming attracted to him. It wasn't just his rugged good looks. Now, the dreams were helping to build an emotional bridge, life's circumstances bringing them together, bonding them.

She felt wanted again, as a friend, and earlier when she noticed his glance, as a... Well, that was for a later discussion. She'd felt uneasy, even dirty. But really, it was nature running its course, and she was attracted to him too. She'd wanted his attention.

He was unkempt, having rushed out of his cabin likely not expecting anyone to be in the galley. But so what? She was disheveled herself, so it didn't matter. She liked feeling alive. She'd been on quite a few dates, but the guys were all about the same thing. Maybe, just maybe, she was turning the corner now. He never came across in that way, making it easier to be near him. He put her at ease. She could be herself, no pretending.

Standing, she tucked her chair back in at the table, then moved to tuck his in as well, breathing in a faint hint of Eternity cologne and his manliness still lingering before she headed to her cabin. Were these feelings because of the dreams? Was it raw nerves, or was she ready to move on? Had the dreamwalkers choreographed this? Were there kids locked in a cargo hold somewhere?

She had so many questions, and surely, he had the same ones.

CHAPTER
TWENTY

Later that day, DR went out to the swimming pool and retrieved Ryan against his will, finding that Ryan had the chaise beside Debbie. It was his birthday, and he'd jumped through all their hoops to get beside her. He squawked and fussed all the way to the galley. DR couldn't believe Ryan hadn't somehow smelled the potatoes and onions frying or heard the commotion. Maybe it was because he was lying out with Debbie and the girls, perfect distractions.

At the galley door, DR stepped aside, gesturing Ryan in first.

"Surprise, happy birthday!" everyone shouted, the girls having followed unnoticed.

"Oh, wow!" Ryan clapped, ogling the decorations and wrapped gifts. "Guys, this is just… I had no idea anyone even knew, much less cared, that it was my birthday." His smile was wide, his eyes moist. He lowered his head as everyone sang for his special day.

During the singing and backslapping, Lo stopped the *DI* and sent down the anchor as planned. DR called him, "Don't worry about the beach. The waves are too rough. There will be no beach today."

Watching the girls give Ryan more hugs and a kiss on the cheek while the men patted him on the back, DR saw how their love, kisses, and gifts overwhelmed him, especially the love. They'd made Ryan's cruise. "Our family in Dublin never makes over me like you, my newfound friends, have today. Of course, they don't celebrate each other's birthdays either. Money's scarce."

With the galley hopping, Miguel and David, appointed masters of the ceremony, served fried potatoes, burgers, and brats and pointed everybody to the open bar, stocked with Guinness Extra Stout beer straight from Ireland. A sparkle lit Ryan's eyes while he drank his favorite. It appeared everyone had a wonderful day.

"I'm thankful for all of you, my new friends, my new shams." Raising a bottle of Stout, Ryan shouted out a traditional Irish toast. "Sláinte is táinte."

DR smiled. "Yes, indeed. Here's to health and wealth." Gail loved that toast.

And the party was on.

The rough seas were taking more time than DR planned or wanted, but it helped everyone bond friendships that might last for many years and more adventures. They played games, with and without booze, and spent hours talking about their lives and dreams, their hopes and beliefs. The pool seldom rested. Penny was right—good friends were worth crappy trips.

Ryan, probably having seen how Debbie was cozying up to DR's stories, now whispered "it's now or never" to himself, but DR overheard as Ryan fought even harder to get close to her.

Ryan didn't hide how he liked her and often catered to her by bringing her a drink or a snack, but she mostly ignored it all. The others watched to see just how far he would go. Often playing pranks, putting obstacles in his way to see what he would do. It was too funny, but not to Ryan, though whenever he realized what some of the others were doing, he laughed too.

〜

DR was in his own little world, reconciling the present with his past, trying to move on. He began going out on the aft deck just before sunset rolled around, alone, to watch the sun set behind the *DI*. Sunset being a treat he'd especially enjoyed all his life, the most beautiful and magical sight in all of nature. It helped him feel safe, grounded.

It wasn't long before Debbie began joining him.

"When I was young"—he rolled over on his side to better see her—"my parents took me and my brothers to church two or three times a week. I remember some of the things the pastor spoke on. But I have a hard time reconciling how a god—one who created everything—would allow all this evil to happen to those He supposedly loves so much... children, like the ones in our dreams."

She nodded. "I know. When Pawpaw took me from my parents, he said they were nuts, tongue talkers, spiritwalkers, even crackheads, but I never saw anything but love." Her glowy brown eyes moistened. "So, yeah... I guess. I believe in God, but I just don't know what all I'm supposed to believe Him for. It's confusing sometimes." She placed a hand on her hip, watching him closely as if seeking a signal to how he felt. "Maybe if I'd gone to church, but who knows?"

"Well, I don't want any part of someone who could stop all this madness and doesn't. How can they explain all that? Like the Catholic priests, how can anyone justify it? What do you say we change the conversation?" He didn't want to take the conversation any further about a god never there for him. At least not that he'd seen. He'd had to earn everything, and there were much better things to consider, to talk about.

She reached out to touch his arm, studying his eyes, probably trying to figure him out. "I've lived a good life. I've traveled and owned my own business. Like yours, part of it ended. I may seem strong and independent, and I am to a point. But sometimes—*now*—I want someone to love, to be with me."

Her face seemed angelic while she shared her deepest thoughts. With a red-white-and-blue wrap over her white bikini, she looked amazing. The pain of his losing Gail was becoming different each time they were together. He no longer felt like he was betraying Gail's memory, maybe the journal had eased his guilt. He needed—wanted—that special someone again, and especially passionate love. He could only deny his manhood for so long, particularly with a beautiful woman around scantily clothed and available.

He waved to the horizon, the sun now hovering over the edge of the glistening sea about to slide down to hide behind the water. "I've always loved this. To me, it's nature's most spectacular show. The only bad thing is it happens too quickly."

The next morning, Ryan knocked on DR's cabin door. DR welcomed him inside and offered him a seat on the sofa by the window.

Before sitting, Ryan shook DR's hand, getting stuck halfway between a handshake and a hug. "DR, that was one of the nicest things anyone's ever done for my birthday. I knew something was special about this trip from the moment I heard about what you'd planned. I'm so glad I..." He stopped mid-hug, then pointed at the wall behind the bed, at Gail's portrait, the only picture of her on the *DI*.

DR frowned at Ryan. "Is everything all right?"

Ryan waved at the portrait. "Who is...? Where did you get that picture? Did it come with the boat?"

DR laughed. "No, it didn't come with the boat. She's my late wife. Do you know Gail?"

"Uh..." Ryan stood and walked over to get a closer look. "Well, no, but she looks like my cousin and aunt. She used to pull me around in my red wagon. I remember her well. Then Mekenzie disappeared. I never knew why."

"Did you say Mekenzie?" DR, leaning against the cabin wall beside the window, jolted upright. "Surely not Mekenzie Kelly of Dublin, Ireland?"

"Yes, Mekenzie Kelly. Well, isn't that something? You know her?"

DR dropped onto the edge of his bed. Were all those years of running just to save her family's face now ending? If so, he'd be happy for Mekie.

"She's my mother—well, mother-in-law. Did you say cousin, to Mekie? I knew there was something different about you." He sprang from his seat, walked over to Ryan, and hugged him. "It is a small world."

~

Willie looked out the window. She shivered. It was getting cold in Delton, and fall was coming to an end. This was a busy time at WREAL, but she needed to get her head on straight. After learning of her mistake, she'd begun to understand how all the pieces fit together, finally, in this new reality, the true reality.

She'd spent so much time praying, speaking to God. "Lord, thank You for showing me why Ashton's parents wouldn't even look at me. I don't blame them for changing churches. I know—now—why they blame me for Ashton leaving Delton, and rightfully so." Her eyes burned, exhausted from the tears. "Do you hear me, Lord? I need a sign —something. One moment I feel like I'm getting a breakthrough and the next as if my whole world is crashing, just a lie."

Searching for solid ground to start again, she'd pored through the Scriptures, then dug through letters Gail had written to her. "Why did You bring her into my life only to take her away again? Was she a divine appointment? A chance for me to do a little good?" Her voice quivered. Did He even hear her?

Across the room, a picture of her with Mike beckoned. She did have friends at WREAL. They had their differences, but he was always there for her. Maybe, just maybe, she needed to get back to work.

Preparing for bed, she thought about Gail's description of DR. Willie prayed again that God found a way to bring her and DR together. She wanted the kind of love Gail spoke of... with kids. Oh yes, lots of kids. Her time was running out. But what about Sarah of the Bible, Abraham's Sarah? Indeed, God could do all things, and hopefully, He would for her.

"Lord, I ask You to keep DR and his passengers safe. Lead them on an awesome adventure. Give him revelation and enlightenment on how the Holy Spirit can guide him in all circumstances. Lord, I pray that my man is on the *DI* and he will come to me soon... that I'll be in his next adventure in this life. Guide him to a new understanding of how You move in him and all Your people."

She hugged her arms around her chest, her chest rising with a deep breath. "I know they've been traveling in areas filled with enemies. Please hold back the destroyer with Your strong right arm, letting no weapon prosper against them. Help them overcome all their obstacles."

She loosened her hold on herself, giving herself over to the Spirit in prayer. "Jesus came to set the captives free to follow You. You amaze me. Even in my mistakes and sin, You lead me and watch over me. Please watch over the *DI*. I ask that everyone enjoy the trip and be amazed by Your glorious works along the way. As I lay down, let me rest in the sweetness of Your peace and Your vision of a wonderful future for me and for DR. In Jesus's name, amen."

Peace, even when one's experiencing the best of times, could be elusive. Like something wedged just so in our spirit, we don't understand it or can't shake it. Sometimes, it's unforgiveness for ourselves or someone else. Years can pass, unforgiveness becoming like a grain of sand in an oyster's shell. We coat it—over and over—for relief, but relief never comes without forgiveness. Many have lived entire lifetimes without finding peace. Had she found hers, and the pearl that finally comes with it?

DR followed Ryan to the pool where most of the others were lounging in the sun, playing cards, and watching the waves. DR got everyone's attention by having David on the helm call out to them on the PA.

Ryan turned to him, holding his shoulders proud. "Do you mind if I share the news? I'll go grab some glasses and sangria so we can toast. This is a big moment for me."

"Sure, coz. You go right ahead. I'd be privileged to have you introduce us to everyone as family." He patted Ryan's shoulder and waited for him to return, asking everyone to come together. "Ryan has an announcement. He'll be right back."

After passing out the glasses and bottles of sangria, Ryan gave them time to fill their glasses, then called out. "Hear, hear." His accent teased. "I want to toast to our captain, our new friend, and now my newly discovered second cousin, by marriage." He raised his glass in salute. "Here's to family."

After the clinking of glasses ceased, the questions began.

"So, Ryan"—Greg grabbed him into a man hug—"does this mean you're going to get a discount on your trip?"

"Well, let's not go that far." DR shook his finger at Greg. "Miguel has dinner in the galley. Don't forget to grab you something."

Greg mockingly saluted.

DR headed up to the helm after dinner. He watched the waves as he went up the stairs. They had smoothed out somewhat. Beyond the stairs, Lo stood munching on a banana and eyeing the bow and the passengers.

"Lorenzo, how's she running?" DR glanced over the gauges, noting their fuel and engine temperature.

"She's running smooth. I was getting ready to summon you. Do you think we should pick up our speed?" Lo pointed to the smaller waves now rolling in from the south.

"Excellent idea. We can make up the time we stopped yesterday for Ryan's birthday party." DR rubbed the cherry finish around the console. "You heard the news earlier, right?"

"Yes, sir. A small world indeed." Lo wiped his lips with his sleeve, then tossed the banana peel in the wastebasket.

"Yes, it is." DR rubbed his hand over the brass-edged gauges, still feeling the need to pinch himself. "If you need me, I'll be in my quarters."

Satisfied and at peace, he took fifteen minutes to fill in today's captain log, thankful for another uneventful day at sea.

October 16: Today was uneventful. We passed two cargo ships sailing under the Egyptian flag, one tanker sailing under the Italian flag, and up to a dozen personal or corporate vessels. All sailing on a westerly course within a nautical mile of our easterly course. Approximately at three p.m., yesterday's twenty-foot waves had reduced to under eight feet, I estimate. The time of this entry is 5:55 p.m.

He added some of the finer minutiae and put the journal away, his lost sleep now piling up like cordwood. Even so, he wouldn't miss the big show if he could help it. He claimed his usual seat on the lower aft deck, the lowest deck. It allowed for a better view of watching the *DI*'s wake and the seabirds far off to the north closer to shore. The *DI*'s propulsion splashed at top cruising speed, also good to cover any conversations that need to be kept private.

The sun was hiding this evening, peeking out from time to time, a special timing promised to make this evening's sunset different from the previous. In quiet, he sat alone with his eyes closed and his thoughts returning to the day's big surprise, amazed by all the good Gail had brought into his life.

When someone's bare feet slapped the wet deck, he sat up to see the intruder.

"Hi, DR." Debbie sauntered over, not wearing a wrap over her red bikini. She slid down seductively on the nearby chaise. "I hope you don't mind if I join you again tonight. These sunsets have been amazing—even better than Miguel's meals."

"Ha. That's saying something. David was right. Miguel's *is* the best Italian flavor. And yes, please, I'd love for you to join me." His gaze slid to the red bikini and her beauty, and his voice dipped with a catch in his throat. "These moments have been the highlight of my trip. Tonight, there's supposed to be something special, a blue moon. Well, this moon's not going to look blue. I've watched them before, but I want to see it over the sea. Why am I explaining this to you? You already know."

"I'm sure this evening will be special, blue moon or no blue moon." The sun's last rays lit her face.

After seeing her in the bikini, he couldn't keep his thoughts on the setting sun or his gaze on the horizon. He ground his teeth. If only he hadn't made that stupid rule. What was he thinking? He'd seen her picture. No romancing the passengers. Silly rule. Her perfume must have been an aphrodisiac. All he could think of was—

No. He better not go *there*.

Unless...

Could she be thinking the same? Why hadn't she worn a wrap? She always grabbed a wrap. Had she left it behind on purpose—to please him?

After the sun set, she stood and slid her chaise closer. Now, they were touching. Tantalizingly, she lay back down only a foot or so away.

"So, I was thinking... I sure wish you hadn't made that rule. You know, the one about not romancing the passengers. I would like a little"—she let her gaze roam over him, the appreciating in her eyes quickening his blood—"romancing. How about you?"

So she had left her cover-up off for him.

"Yes..." His throat closed over the admission. His gaze also roamed her, admiring her beauty. "That wasn't one of my more brilliant plans, but at least, it's kept Ryan at bay." His desires awakening, his body leaned into her space of its own accord. Oh man. He had to squash this and now.

"Are you kidding?" She giggled. "His Irish blood is boiling over. Haven't you noticed the little games being played out on the deck? He tries to get the chaise as close to me as possible. Once the others noticed, they started putting all kinds of things, obstacles, in his way, wanting to see just how far he'd go to sit beside me." She tucked the wisps of hair blown by the breeze out of her eyes. "I'm flattered. But it's gotten comical, some of the things they did... Well, until he caught on."

"Did he get mad?" Good. That had broken their intensity. DR settled back in his seat, taking slow breaths to regain his control.

This is the place—that place where you know what you want so badly, but the rules or something gets in the way. The physical and emotional thoughts about a relationship become tangled. He wanted to reach out and take her into his arms and, well, honor his manly feelings for her. Then there was that stupid rule.

"Just so you know. I understand how Ryan feels. You're smart, fun to be with, and gorgeous. I would love to spend time... time getting to know you much better." His gaze drifted down her figure, allowing her to know his intended thoughts, and back up to her eyes, which were ablaze in the twilight.

"Maybe"—he twisted on his lounge and propped up on one arm— "after the cruise, we could see each other. What do you think?"

She reached out and took his face in both of her hands. Then, bringing her body close to his, she pressed herself against him.

The passion in her kiss riling him, he kissed back. Eyes closed, bodies straining... Just like that, "NO ROMANCING THE PASSENGERS" was thrown overboard, caps and all, with a big splash, and he didn't even care.

After the kiss, she relaxed her embrace. Her body still drew him closer as he sensed she wanted him as much as he wanted her. But rules were rules. He tipped his forehead against hers, breathing in her perfume, still tasting her breath. At least he knew her intention—and she knew his desires. He could live with the rule for a while. No one had to know.

"I would love that. Oh my." She wiggled backward, half panting. "I think you're the most complete man. Your confidence is, well..." Now, she took a turn to ogle him ever so slowly. Her gaze moved down him, along his shoulders, his chest, and lower, as palpable as a touch. "Sexy!"

When she looked back into his eyes, an invite shone in hers. He reached over and yanked her into his arms, kissing her as he flattened her against himself. Her heartbeat thudded against him, and a whimper escaped her while her passion built, his too. He could live here forever, but he had to stop.

"Dumb rules!" He growled, and she laughed.

He slid back, his hands moving from her warmth to tangle in her hair. "Any more of this, and no will become too hard."

She held his gaze.

Yes, they both knew the moment had to end, or...

He would've preferred or.

But prudence wouldn't allow it.

He brushed her blonde hair back with his hand, working to overcome his decision-making. They wouldn't share this with the others—at least not on the voyage.

They stayed out on the lower aft deck for another hour or so, talking about their feelings, dreams, and hopes, watching their wake break behind them, speculating how this could work. She lived in Chicago, and he lived—where? His home was up for sale.

After she left, he stopped by the helm before going down to his cabin. His turn was at six, and he wanted to check on Miguel before retiring. They were coming into Kochi in the morning. Lying in bed, hands laced behind his head, he retraced the evening. Then, still smiling, he fell into a deep sleep.

He awoke only an hour later—horrified.

He rolled to the edge of the bed, head in hands, then banged his fist down on the bed. "Every night, not one time, not one time..." It was always something. "What do You want from me?" He glowered at the overhead. No one was listening. Of that, he was sure.

Staring at the moon's reflection on the sea through his portside window, he kicked the nightstand beside the side chair, banged his foot hard, reached down, and rubbed it. "That was smart."

Why was this happening? Was it his conscience, or had a dream awakened him? Was this a rebound? Had he given his grieving the time it needed? It'd been sixteen months since Gail passed. Would people talk?

They would. Was he being sleazy?

He raked a hand through his hair and tugged at the roots as if he could slow his thoughts. Then he spun to face Gail's portrait over his bed. "What's the big deal? We'll take it slow."

No way, conscience chided. He dropped to the bed's edge and rubbed his foot.

She felt so good and looked so gorgeous. There'd be no taking it slow. She was too... And he groaned. Yeah, not the way he felt tonight.

He played the scene over and over. Struggled to bring it into perspective with his upbringing, Michigan Strong, then surrendered. What's wrong with letting nature run its course?

Finally, he went to sleep. Five hours later, he shoved his feet to the floor and paced to his bathroom. After a shower and shave, he'd be ready for his turn on the bridge. At least, last night helped him look forward to the new day, his perspective and energy toward life seemingly beginning to evolve.

First, he stopped off to get a coffee in the galley. Just steps from Debbie's room, he paused. Electricity shot through his body, and he didn't know what to think. *Better get that coffee.*

Coffee in hand, he headed to the helm. After they went over the previous shift's charts and discussed it, he relieved David.

Moments after David left, Debbie called out, "Good morning, lover boy." She sauntered over, first sticking one leg seductively around the corner of the stairwell, then slinking around to reveal herself. "Did you sleep well?"

In the captain's chair, he spun to see her fully. Wow. Dressed in a pair of cutoff jeans and a black tank top, she looked fresh—and gorgeous. She mustn't have had the same restless night he'd suffered.

When he stood to greet her, she almost pressed up against him. "I was up almost all night, tossing and turning... thinking about you."

Man, she didn't look it. He swallowed hard. *Michigan Strong, Michigan Strong... you can do this.* "Me too—well, not about me. There's so much I wanted to tell you, but—"

She held a finger to his lips, then rested her hand on his shoulder, warmth seeping through his polo. "It'll wait. That's fair. It'll give us both time—time to get to know each other. But, for now, I must say I liked kissing you." Her hand slid down his chest, her gaze exploring him. She breathed in, then exhaled, obviously embracing the moment.

He backed up a step to ease the intimacy.

"I was thinking last night...." He let out a low breath, the words coming fast now. "Maybe the rule isn't so bad. I want to know you before, well, before anything else happens."

Whoa. Why was he saying that? Had he gone nuts or something?

"I guess I let the moment get too big. I wanted you." She slid a step toward him, her actions not matching her words. They couldn't. "I still do."

DR closed his eyes tight, fighting his own thoughts, needs. He found himself against the helm's back wall with nowhere to go. Not that he wanted to anyway. "Let's continue as if nothing is going on between us around the others."

And just how was *that* supposed to work out?

She slid her hand from his chest and shook a finger at him. "Okay, I'll behave myself, but it might not be easy." Relaxing and breathing deep, she stepped back, caught her breath, and changed her tone. "When do we reach Kochi? Have you been here before?"

"We'll be there before you know it. I've only stopped there once, and then one other time, I barely put down anchor enough to refuel. Maybe we could ride together? We'll just have to behave."

She jammed her hands on her hips and thrust out her chest. "Little ole me misbehave?"

He laughed, then led her to the staircase down, resisting the urge to place his hand on the small of her back, the smooth tan skin exposed below her black tank. "Sounds like a plan. We're taking several rickshaws into town so I can leave early since I have a phone interview this afternoon. I'll rejoin the group at the restaurant for dinner. Unless I let Lo go into town for dinner and take on the watch for the *DI*?" He raised his brows at her. "Maybe you could come back with me, and they could bring us something back?"

"So, sneaky." She wagged that finger at him again. "How do you expect me to pull that off with no one, namely Ryan, suspecting?"

With her smiling like that, she must like his plan. He winked. "We'll figure it out."

"How many days are we here for—two? After all, I don't know if I want to miss the elephants just to guard a boat?" She stopped walking and pushed closer to him again. "That is what we'll be doing, right?" Her eyebrows hiked up, and her eyes searched his in an unspoken communication. "Guarding the boat?"

He poked at her stomach, his finger sliding down to find her naval through the thin tank material. "Something tells me I'll be running."

He found her naval. His breath came short. If anyone was running, it wouldn't be him.

"Something tells me you'll run just slow enough to get caught." She swatted at his hand and scooted back a step. The knowing glint in her eye called him out.

There'd be no running, just hard self-restraint.

Miguel turned the corner. With one look at their closeness, he cleared his throat.

"Hi, Miguel." She glanced over her shoulder, her blonde hair swishing. "We've been discussing Kochi. I'm so excited."

She gave DR a look and winked with her right eye where Miguel couldn't see her as she made sure he caught her double entendre. "I can't wait to see the elephants and cats. I'll leave you two alone to discuss the day."

Miguel crossed his arms as he watched her saunter away with a schoolgirlish skip to her walk. Then he eyed DR with a knowing glint. "Somehow, I don't think elephants and cats were on her mind."

Heat crept up DR's neck, and Miguel slapped him on the back. "I'm glad to see you're figuring out what everyone else has known since we boarded the boat. That woman is smitten. You'd better open up those baby blues because you like her too. Poor Ryan has done everything besides backflips—although, come to think of it, I think I saw him try one of those into the pool—to get her attention."

DR clicked the monitor on, then clicked it off just as fast. He might as well get this out of the way.

"It's been entertaining, watching the great lengths he goes to. And if I were a younger man, I would too."

DR raked a hand through his hair. Would Miguel stop smiling like that? "Please don't say anything to the others. You know, the no-romancing-the-passengers thing."

"Well, sometimes, we have to strike down the rules—the unnecessary or inconvenient ones. After all, we're only human... with human needs." Miguel put his hand on DR's shoulder and winked, obviously knowing how badly DR wanted to know her. "I'll keep the secret—for now, but don't let this good thing pass you by."

"Is it that easy to see? It's only been sixteen months since Gail passed. Isn't that too... soon?" DR turned away, pretending to tweak something on the instrument panel, uncomfortable looking to others for validation, but these were uncharted waters. This was where Michigan Strong tore at his very soul.

The port came into focus, the sun hiding, rain clouds threatening, the monsoon season nearing its end. Miguel put his arm around DR. "I've found that living my life the way I feel led, by God—or my inner spirit—I can be free of the burdens my mind wants to place on me."

DR stiffened and pulled away. "You know how I feel about the being-led-by-God thing."

He pointed toward the horizon. They were closing in on the shore, lush vegetation coming into view, and seabirds more plentiful. The air seemed to have a different smell, maybe it was excitement or adventure.

"I'm sure you heard it said that your first thought is usually the correct one. It comes from your spirit to your mind. What's your spirit telling you about Debbie? She's a wonderful woman. Her spirit and love are so sweet."

DR relaxed, knowing he could trust Miguel's wisdom, a good friend who was becoming the most influential person in his life, Jesus or no Jesus. He put his arm over Miguel's shoulder.

"I do trust your wisdom. In matters concerning the heart, I seem to fall short." Holding his face to the overhead, he took in a deep breath and exhaled. "I've allowed some things from many years ago to dominate that part of my life. It's time I get over it."

"My friend"—Miguel nodded his understanding—"leaving loose old dead bags lying around always trips us up. I used to be the world's worst, especially when my Martina was alive. I let the smallest offenses fret me. I couldn't see all the good in my life for focusing on the bad."

"I have let 'loose baggage' sit around." DR slid his arm away from Miguel and crossed to the console again. "And now, I must put it away."

"We hold onto things. It's what our flesh and enemies want, taking away the joy of living, replacing it with or without religion or religious actions. Either for or against God." Miguel spread his hands. "But if you can leave all that aside, get back to living according to your conscience.... You're a good man, one of the best I've had the pleasure to know. I'm sure you still live by your conscience, right?"

"Thanks for saying I'm a good man, Miguel." DR let out his pent-up breath. "You're a good friend, and I respect you—not just for your wisdom but also for your heart, your kindness." Yeah, Michigan Strong was still messing with his mind.

Miguel nodded. "Thanks to you and this trip, I feel alive again. You are my godsend. But now, the port of Kochi and indeed the whole state of Kerala, India, is looming large. The other passengers and Lo and David should be down in the galley waiting for breakfast." Miguel patted DR's shoulder. "I'd better head down to help Joshua before there is a mutiny."

Alone on the bridge, DR radioed the port to confirm his reserved spot on the pier and get directions. Afterward, he placed a call to his real estate agent in Delton and asked him to pull his home off the market. Now, he could move on. He loved Malaga and living with Mekie and Nicolas, but he wanted more. He wanted a partner.

This seemed to be how he would find his way forward. Maybe memories should be cherished, not packed away. His time with Gail on the lake was magical. He wanted some new magic now—for the future. Who knew what tomorrow held? But he knew what Gail would have wanted for him. Or did he?

CHAPTER
TWENTY-ONE

DR had arranged for personal guides to go see the lions and tigers tomorrow and explore some of the countryside today, but the threatening rain could cause major problems. "I'm sorry." He spread his hands toward his passengers now gathered on the poolside deck. "Rain this time of year can be deadly in India's hillsides. That type of flooding was what uncovered thousands of years of living to help us find our Kolkata site."

"So?" Penny bounced from foot to foot, obviously eager to do something with her boundless energy. "What does that mean? Just city tours today?"

"I'm afraid so." The breeze carried the scent of today's bountiful catch, fishermen working hard to get their prize to market and pulling laden nets on board their boats. "The waterfalls are especially to be avoided. Getting too close to streams feeding the beautiful falls in the downpours can be fatal. But we still might see a few surprises along the way. The port itself was cut out by monsoon rains over six hundred and eighty years ago." He winked at Mitch, his fellow archaeologist, then the Hughes, their mystery writers. "So, I'm going to trust there will be something diggers and lovers of adventure might find interesting here too."

"Sounds good by me, cousin." Ryan checked his reflection in a porthole window, then sidled closer to Debbie. "I guess we'll have to be city dwellers and plan to catch the lions and tigers tomorrow."

"Okay, then." DR clapped. "Let's all get prepped for the excursion."

As everyone left, his thoughts wandered. Later, before the interview, he'd ask Mike and Willie for help directing the movers where to put his things when they brought them back to his home. Since he met Debbie, he hadn't thought about Willie, at least not in the same way, proving it was just hormones.

Debbie had heard Miguel claim his breakfast normally consisted of different types of bread with butter and jam or biscuits and cereals, but for his foreign friends, he prepared eggs, sausage, and bacon. Now, the scent filled the galley and wafted to the deck above, lassoing most of the passengers, including her as she headed for a seat next to Joshua in the galley.

Joshua began describing his travels, how being Jewish came with blessings and curses. "I've seen hatred and prejudices no one should ever know, as well as kindness and love that most never experience, all due to my bloodline." He munched on a piece of jelly toast. "I understand why the apostle Paul said he learned to be thankful, whether abounding in abundance or in lack, depending on where I am. Here, in Kochi, there's a large population of Christians and Jews, so I'll be accepted with open arms, but not back in Jeddah or Aden."

He spread crumbs as he waved the hand holding a quartered piece of toast.

Debbie brushed them away before they could land on her clothes. But at least he wasn't eating tuna. "But isn't that so for all of us?" She planted her left elbow on the table and propped her chin in her hand. "Especially in Saudi Arabia and Yemen? They don't like anyone who isn't Muslim. Well, maybe not all of them, just the radicals."

"You two better get some of that bacon before it's all gone," Tom said in passing.

"It's a spiritual thing." Joshua nodded to Tom but let it pass. "But getting back to what started this—talking about the tours. We'll see the Paradest Synagogue and Santa Cruz Cathedral Basilica, along with a couple other churches. They've arranged a half-day tour too, so you don't have to go along all day."

"I want to see the wildlife refuge—you know me, I like exotic animals and ancient fossils. Things you can't see in Chicago. I'm not into checking out historical churches." She wrapped her arms around herself, not letting the true reason out. "Now, if we were going to a museum of natural history, that would be different. I love fossils." Truth was she couldn't wait to feel DR's arms around her again. She needed it, wanted it, and yearned for his touch.

The guides arrived at ten a.m., and everyone, except Lo, disembarked. Everyone opted for the full tour, except her and DR. Although Ryan appeared suspicious, he still chose the full tour.

Debbie settled alongside David in their tuk tuk, a motorized two-seat autorickshaw. While it shaded them, it also included a covered area for the driver, and the contraption was quite warm. Miguel rode with DR, at DR's request. While Ryan and Joshua shared a tuk tuk, all the couples stayed together. At noon, she rode in DR's tuk tuk back to the *DI*, the driver exchanging them for Lo.

"Join me on the lower aft deck?" DR held out his hand for hers. "My phone call's still an hour away. With so much on my mind, I'll wing it."

"No." Playfully taking his hand, she pulled him toward the galley. "I'm going to the galley to get me a snack first. *You* come with *me*."

Just like that, DR followed, her beauty and aura captivating him. And he loved it! At the bottom step to the galley, she pivoted, peered into his eyes, and shoved him against the wall. Pressing hard against him, she kissed him.

The encounter seemed like only moments... but was much longer. He groaned. They had to stop, or it would get out of control—especially so close to their cabins. Pulling his mouth from hers, he pinned her against his body, her passion now electric. The moment overpowering his senses, he leaned back to regain composure and breath.

Debbie, nine inches shorter than him, lifted onto tiptoes to meet his gaze better, her breaths hot and lusty against his neck. "Is everything okay? I didn't mean to come on so strong, but I've been waiting all day to kiss you."

"Okay"—collecting himself, he reached for her hand—"is an understatement. I've been thinking about you too. I love holding you, kissing you. I'm talking way too much, aren't I? Let's get the snacks and go to the lower aft deck. My brother's going to call in a few minutes." He leaned down, kissed her again, and savored the moment. Oh, how he had missed these moments.

"This is something I want to get used to." She squeezed him, breathing in, her arms still locked around his waist as if she were trying to hold on to the feeling of his body pressed to hers.

"Sure. Let's get those snacks." She eased away, took his hand, and sighed. "Those rules of yours, DR... They're still standing in the way."

He started back to the aft deck, Debbie in hand. "I've got my call. Then I'll be right back, unless you want to lounge by the pool? Either way, I'll come find you." After another kiss—a quick one this time—he ran up to the bridge to take the call and be on the watch.

Before the interview, he needed five minutes with Mike. Once Mike answered, DR broke in. "I need a favor?"

"That depends—it's not a loan, is it?"

"Be serious, bro, can ya? And no, nothing *that* serious. But I'd appreciate your help and maybe Willie's too. I've taken my house off the market. I've decided not to run from my memories but embrace them. Being at sea with people of different backgrounds can help you see things from a fresh perspective. I need to address things back home. Especially with Mom and Dad."

"Um, hold on?" Mike then spoke louder. "You hear that, Willie? Okay, I'm back, bro. I can't speak for her, but I'll be glad to help."

"Sure... count me in, DR," Willie piped up. "Wow. I'm glad you're coming back to Delton!"

What? Her enthusiasm unnerved him. Seriously, what would she have to be so happy about? It wasn't like they'd gotten along the last time they'd been in the same room.

After eyeing the satellite phone for a second, DR settled in for the interview and described the whole Jeddah thing again, then their visit to Aden.

"Miguel knew the monsignor, so our time there was well spent. The church is under constant threat and often attacked by teenage thugs. We were able to help them financially." Discussing the kids, he didn't mention the dreams, his or Debbie's.

In the pilot seat, he felt like a kid with a big prize. He rocked back and watched life out the tinted and slanted windows. Man, what a day. Did he ever need to pinch himself! The leather settee beside the plot chart wall behind him looked inviting. With it calling his name, he moved there, stretched out, and admired the cherry instrument panel.

"Now, finally, things are looking up again. We've docked in Kerala, India. With the monsoon's last-minute effort to threaten the countryside, we stayed in the city. One of our passengers, the one I'm calling Sally, wants to see the animal refuges. So, we're going tomorrow. At least if the rain doesn't wash it out. According to radar, the monsoon season is supposed to be over."

The bridge was quiet. Only the slight rock of the boat reminded him he was on water, and the space had become like home. Shiny and new, but nevertheless home. He couldn't hear or see Debbie on the lower aft deck, but his heart raced knowing she awaited him.

"The most amazing thing—I met Gail's second cousin. He's here— on the *DI*. What are the odds? My mother-in-law hadn't seen her mom for over thirty years, right? Her mom flew to Malaga with Ryan, to see Mekie. It's a miracle."

Sitting up, he nearly gasped. Miracle. Had he said that? Did he mean it? What else could he use to explain it?

But he had listeners, so he glossed over. "It seems Kayleigh's mom, Mekie's friend who took her in when she was pregnant, ran into Mekie's mom in Dublin. Then one thing led to another. Gail always wanted to meet her grandmother." He exhaled low and deep, shaking his head. "It's too bad all this happened too late for that."

"So… don't leave us in suspense. What's the other thing?" Mike pressed.

"Let's just say a lot has happened. I'm not going to go into anything right now. We'll see how everything works out. But the best part of the trip is getting close to the passengers. We've all become good friends." He twisted his watch face into view. "I know your time is up. Thanks for helping me and thank you, Willie, for helping the movers get my things moved back to the right rooms. I'll treat you both to a nice meal when I'm back in town. Take care, and I'll talk to you in a week. Tell Mom and Dad hi."

"Will do, DR. Be safe and have fun." The line went dead.

DR left the bridge. He found Debbie on the lower aft deck, sangrias in hand, her black-and-white polka-dot bikini especially enticing. She'd covered up with an oversized pink shirt this time, and her matching pink retro sunglasses gave her a nostalgic look as she lay there listening to the oldies of the seventies. Apparently, she loved beach music.

Coming to the deck from the descending stairway and admiring her beauty, he let out a low whistle, then whispered. "Man, what have I done to be so lucky?"

He never had to pursue the girls he'd been with, yet they were the prettiest, smartest, sweetest girls of all. Of course, he could count them on two fingers. He swiped sweaty palms across his polo shirt. He wanted to know Debbie, *really* know her.

The wolf whistle announced what he thought of her appearance as he sprinted down the last stairs.

"Now, now..." She winked. "We don't want to get ahead of our skis, do we?"

In the sky, dark clouds moved quickly through. The wind seemed to be around ten knots and steady. Rain threatened any minute. Still, it was warm. If not for the breeze, the humidity would have been extreme.

Breathing deeply, he tried to find the correct words. "Exactly. I don't know how to say this, so I'm just going to say it. You are incredible—beautiful, intelligent, sexy...." He let his words fall away, permitting himself to enjoy some of her beauty. "A marvelously wonderful woman. Holding you in my arms and kissing you is like being in... um. It's all I can do to control myself, and I don't want to."

"Then don't." She sat up and flicked a hand through her hair, shaking it into place and letting her loose cover-up open. "We've both opened the cookie jar."

He sat on the chaise beside her, trying to maintain a safe distance. "I was taught to respect and cherish the special woman in my life. Not letting sex confuse my mind without a commitment—no matter how difficult. I may not be pure, so to speak, but I want to treat you right." His heart thudded. *Thanks, Michigan Strong, for nothing.* He was bungling this, wasn't he? Might as well stop rambling and just say it. "I enjoy you and want your love."

He took a long lustful glance as if to reassure her of his needs and desires. He was raised in church and baptized when he was ten. He'd heard all the sermons on relationships. Although he'd rejected the whole thing a year after being baptized, he heard the right way to live. Whether from the preacher, his granddad, or his mother, he understood the reasons for abstinence.

When he met Gail, even though neither followed Christ, they waited until they were married before having a sexual relationship. Gail's mom had gotten pregnant before marriage, and it altered her entire life. Debbie was worth waiting for. Maybe his next good thing.

She puckered her lips in a fetching pout. "Seems to me that, once the cookie jar's been open, it's okay to have a cookie or enjoy the love of a lover, if it's with the one you love or might want a future with."

She shifted to peer out over the sea beyond the port, the offshore breeze teasing her hair across her shoulders. "Are you sure?" She spoke with her back partially to him. "I don't want to come across as desperate or something, but that could be a while, if ever. Holding you has brought back desires, awakened something I haven't felt for five years. I don't know how long I can wait."

After she stood, still peering out over the back of the *DI* with her hands clenched at her sides, he almost reached to comfort her. But no. That could lead to places he wasn't ready to go. Because he *was* sure.

A silence passed, filled with the regular port noises and an occasional shout in a foreign language.

Then she raised her chin and faced him, her smile wobbly. "I'll settle for your kisses, for now." Her smile firmed, and her brown eyes flashed as she held up a hand. "Don't take too long getting to know me, though."

He laughed. "My sentiments exactly."

They shared a moment, a moment like coming into port after a wild storm.

"Sooo…" She dragged the word out. "How do we do this without driving ourselves bonkers? All I wanted was for you to carry me to your cabin."

He winked. "I almost did scoop you up and carry you off. Don't think I'm a saint."

"Wait!" She slapped his arm. "Wait. How will I see you after the cruise? Do you even have a home in the States?"

"May I have a glass"—he pointed to the wine—"before we get into details about the future?"

As she leaned over to pour the wine, he wrapped his arms around her, pulled her to himself, and kissed her, holding her, breathing in her breath mixed with her lotion and perfume. He shuddered.

"I wouldn't want to miss a single moment kissing you," he teased.

"If you want your wine, you'd better stop." She breathed seductively, rolling her head and eyes, apparently confident in her abilities to lead him on. "Because there's plenty more where that came from."

He hoped.

With the ground rules established, he enjoyed the rest of their afternoon. Shortly after three, the downpour began, moving them to the media center to watch old movies. Careful not to be sitting too close, they chose separate seats in case Ryan and the others came back early.

Debbie fell asleep in the leather recliner while DR stretched out on the floor at her feet, unable to fathom a better place or moment in time. He loved lying on the floor watching TV or movies like he and his brothers did growing up. And today, he needed that space while maintaining a certain intimacy. Her delicate bare foot poking off the recliner just above him drew his focus from the screen to tanned skin and slim limbs. Well, this abstinence thing might be way too overrated —and difficult.

It rained nearly two inches in an hour and a half. Then the clouds vanished, dissipating with the fog and leaving the hillsides lush and the vegetation dewy. The monsoon season ended with the fast-moving clouds. DR confirmed the roads weren't washed out. So tomorrow would be lions, tigers, and waterfalls. Debbie would be ecstatic, and so would Ryan.

The rainstorm stirred local tributaries and the ocean. With runoff from city streets pouring into the harbor, the *DI* rocked more noticeably. The cleats and bindings on the sailboats tied up played a chorus in the breeze. Seagulls were back out, beginning their search once again for the ever-elusive last morsel and squawking out their skirmishes when they found said morsel. Life had resumed.

Nightfall found DR lying on a chaise watching his favorite channel. Only tonight, Debbie didn't join him. Who could blame her? He raked a hand through his hair, trying not to think of going below and knocking on her cabin door. Just to make sure she was all right, of course. After all, it wasn't like her to miss a sunset or to retire without saying good night to anyone.

The sun slid behind the horizon with no fanfare. He kept his hands laced behind his head, his thoughts elsewhere.

"Where's Debbie? I didn't see her inside." Miguel came out on the deck. "Is everything okay?"

"Yeah, we talked after my interview—or rather, I talked." DR grimaced and settled his glass of lemonade on the table beside him.

"Oh?" Miguel sat on Debbie's favorite chaise. "And what'd you do?"

"I told her we needed to go slow, not having a… a physical relationship yet. I hope I came across well—at least I know I came across clearly. She's probably tired, or this is just part of her slowing down the process, letting me know abstinence isn't what it's cracked up to be."

Laughter rang out from the deck above.

And DR shifted, sat up, and jammed his hands into his short pockets. He dragged the toe of his fisherman's sandal across the polished hardwood deck. "I had to show her I respect her and even though she's so pretty and… well, you know. It's gotta be special if and when we get together."

Miguel leaned back, eyeing DR long and hard. Then he turned sideways in his chaise to sit on the edge facing DR. "You're a hard one to figure out. I mean, for someone who hates God, you live more by His precepts than most of my Christian friends." Miguel reached over and slapped DR's knee, then jostled him. "What gives with you?"

"I never said I *hate* God." DR bristled and jerked his knee away from his friend's grip. "I just don't follow all that religious stuff. I was raised to respect women, to think of others more than myself. I guess it stuck. Do you know what I dislike about Christianity? It's what you said… about your Christian friends. They don't live the part but expect everyone else to."

The vessel next to the *DI* began to set out to sea, horn blowing to notify any other vessels of similar mind its intentions.

Apparently, taken by surprise Miguel jolted, nearly tipping over the chaise.

DR laughed.

"Well, don't think I didn't see through that a long time ago too." Miguel repositioned himself on the chaise. "I like people who are sincere and walk the talk. Everybody talks a good game—until it costs them something. Then you see their *faith* and their commitment to it."

"That's the part I don't like." DR cut in. "People get hurt—*I got hurt!*" His body jerked, his shoulders inching up. He didn't mean to let that slip.

"Which is it?" Miguel's dark gaze pinned him. "Do you hate God or His followers?"

DR rubbed the back of his neck, working his shoulders loose. No need to get so tense. This was just a conversation between friends. Just because God snuck into it and something he'd never exposed as an adult slipped out didn't change that. "What do you mean?"

"Your beef sounds like it's with the followers of God, not God."

The question lingered. They sat as the last sliver of sun disappeared behind the horizon. DR sipped his lemonade awaiting Miguel's next move, not responding to his comment. Maybe, hopefully, he didn't catch that slipup.

"All that aside"—Miguel raised his glass—"what did you think of the guides this morning? They showed us a good time and seemed to enjoy their time with us too. Makes you wonder how people in Europe and America become so hard. These people have about a third of the things we have, and yet so many seem like they haven't a care in the world. Ready to share what they do have."

Good. Another reason DR respected Miguel—the guy knew when to stop. The tension left DR as he drained his glass. "They came highly recommended. Some of the guides here do quite well. Look where they work—with rich foreigners tipping them well and showing off the most beautiful forests and refuges in the world. If you can get over the heat and the radicals, it's a good life."

"Well, tomorrow's going to be great." Miguel patted DR's shoulder.

"The girls are looking forward to the wildlife refuges, especially Debbie."

The horizon had cleaned up after one of the greatest disappearing acts. DR pushed to his feet, stifling a yawn. "Time to turn in—at least for me."

Miguel stood as well. "A bit early for me, but a big day tomorrow. So I may follow your lead."

CHAPTER
TWENTY-TWO

At breakfast on the sundeck near the swimming pool and bar, DR informed both David and Lo they could go on the tour. "I've been there before, so I'm okay staying behind. I'd rather you guys enjoy this place."

Debbie shot him an annoyed look.

But Miguel saluted him with his coffee mug. "That's thoughtful of you."

"Thoughtful. Huh, well, two can play at this," Debbie muttered, sitting close enough only he could hear her, though maybe she didn't think he could. Then she raised her voice and flashed a dazzling smile. "Excuse me, please, everyone. I'm going to go change into something more comfortable and less confining for such a long, warm day."

Clearly signaling that somebody wanted attention, she returned in a well-worn pair of daisy dukes and a red halter top barely halting anything. DR shook his head. In her haste, she must've forgotten their Indian hosts' requested code of dress.

And she'd miscalculated his reason for staying on board. He wasn't just avoiding her. He needed to talk to Mike and apologize for being such a jerk for so many years. He, too, had been a hypocrite as these last days pointed out. He'd meant what he said about treating Debbie like a queen though, and his commitment to his queen was always absolute.

The driver honked his horn, letting them know he'd arrived. With it too late to remind Debbie of the dress code, DR finished cleaning up after breakfast, then ran out to the van where everyone waited. One crumb left would summon every seagull on the pier, something he wanted no part of. He waved goodbye and wished them all a pleasant trip. Seeing Debbie in that outfit gave him a slight rise, but he didn't have a claim on her. She was still her own woman and always would be. It was her decision, not his, to ignore local dress recommendations. Odd, though, for her to be disrespectful of others.

Unnoticed, a few hundred yards off the pier, two men dressed in black thobes, like those in Jeddah, stood by with a scuba diver. They'd tracked down the *DI*, and they wouldn't lose her again, not with the GPS device they placed on her hull, along with a charge on her bow, just below the waterline.

The *DI* would pay for the sanctions against the regime. She was going to be a spectacular show for the world to see—live. The regime demanded it. The senator ordered it. Mr. Jennings paid for it—and he would be satisfied.

The man in charge spoke on his cell phone. "Tell the senator it is done. Just have the news media there. I'll give you their coordinates before the time comes."

Debbie arched her back and shook her hair loose as DR checked with the shuttle bus driver, his words drifting her way.

"Make sure you get to the Periyar National Park and Refuge around eleven a.m.—no matter what you have to cut back on. Our ladies are looking forward to the park." Perhaps unconsciously, he rubbed the shuttle's mirror bracket.

"Yes, sir, and we'll only briefly visit the waterfalls, depending on how well the roads have recovered."

As their group boarded, DR smacked the bus hood and caught her eye. But she didn't even wave. Her glare probably wasn't something he'd expected.

She tossed her hair over her shoulder, turned her back to him, and boarded the bus. Huh. It had an older style of bench seating where two rows faced each other, each able to hold two passengers. Great. She slid into a seat beside the window as Ryan hunkered down across from her, all smiles. She ground her teeth and let her hair slide forward as a partial covering while she looked out the window, heart heavy, feeling like a mackerel on full display.

Ryan leaned back. "Hi, Debbie. Isn't this great?"

"Absolutely." Her mind was on fire. All this to make DR jealous, and he didn't say a word. *What is the driver staring at? Me. Oh no.* She searched the other passengers' faces. Only Penny was looking at them, and she winked, shaking her head up and down.

After they pulled onto the road, horns blew, and drivers shouted. With their driver watching her more than the road, several vehicles had to swerve to miss their bus.

Ryan's gaze was affixed to her too. "Looks like today is going to be perfect. Don't you think?"

"Ryan, I'm sorry, but I'm not in the mood to talk." She turned toward the window to watch the road, the driver still all eyes. Shortly later, they stopped at a small tourist spot with shops.

Penny came toward her, smiling, took her by the arm, and led her inside a shop. "Girl, let's get you some clothes."

"Oh, thank you so much. How did you know?" Debbie gripped Penny's embrace as a lifeline.

"Honey, I've seen that look from my cheer friends a hundred times." She jostled Debbie with a sisterly hug. "Nothing like sitting in a

Dairy Queen with every guy trying to look up your cheer skirt to gawk at your half-naked butt."

Penny's friends worried about what someone saw? I guess you never know. "Well, thank you. You're a lifesaver." Debbie picked out a long skirt and top that younger Indian women wear. Now maybe the driver would just drive.

Then she sat across from Ryan so she could look into his eyes. His Irish good looks, red hair and all, made him easy to look at and talk to.

"Ryan…" She spread out her hands. "I owe you an apology. I may have been leading you on a bit today. I'm sorry, but well, I…"

"You like DR, don't you? I'm too late, aren't I?" He slumped against the back of the seat, that red hair falling into his eyes. "Well, at least, he's family."

He released his eyes once again, checking her out, causing her to wrap her arms around herself to shelter from his prying eyes. The rest of the ride, another twenty minutes, they spent discussing their trip.

After enjoying a wonderful day and the evening meal outside Kochi, they reached the *DI* around eight o'clock.

Good thing he'd allowed his crew to go on the excursion. DR had needed a little "me" time to clean house and get things straight in his mind. The wait until four thirty to call his brother allowed him to sneak time to wonder, time to reflect as he polished the galley appliances. Unknowingly before he caught himself, he started whistling "Spirit in the Sky," the song Debbie had performed.

Funny he'd never seen that as a spiritual song. He stopped whistling at the line about where the singer was going when they died. Seeing his reflection in the now sparkling Sub-Zero, he stared. He'd been steadfast in his denial of faith since he was eleven. Why was that becoming harder and harder? Michigan Strong. For just a moment, he saw the small boy again, looking back at himself, the one in his dreams. He shook his head. *I need a drink.*

He grabbed a Birra Moretti and went out to the lower aft deck, his favorite spot on the yacht. The lowness of the deck afforded more privacy while allowing him to watch the sea pass behind when they were at sea, along with his problems, usually.

Did Gail get it right? He closed his eyes and turned his face to the sky. *Is there a place to go to when I die?* Was Miguel right? *Was it Mom and Dad I've been running from, not God?*

He needed Debbie to get back. She'd help him forget all these thoughts.

Four thirty couldn't come fast enough. He shuffled off to his quarters to get comfortable and to change afterward. He felt sticky from the extreme humidity in the port.

They were close growing up. DR always looked out for his kid brothers. Sounded like Mike would like that closeness again. DR swallowed hard and dialed his brother. He'd like that too.

After an awkward start to the conversation, he shifted his phone.

"Not much going on here." Mike sounded muffled. "Except Uncle Bill's in the hospital. His liver's shutting down from all the years of booze. You remember Uncle Bill, don't you? He had that old reddish-pink car. What was it?"

"A Chevy Caprice."

"Anyway… it's sad. The alcohol has destroyed him. I don't think he's saved either. Dad's struggling."

Why aren't I happy? I should be relieved.

DR stood. As Mike continued about their uncle, DR walked over to the large square porthole window. Beyond the window and port, the vast ocean was a blur. The feeling of a weight came upon him. *Why do I feel guilty?*

Mike droned on. "Mom said he hasn't talked to Bill since I was a kid. I hope the guy gets his life right with the Lord. What was that?"

"Just several people out for a little fun in the water." DR raked a hand through his hair, smiling now. "Looks like they're playing some form of chicken. Girls riding on their fellows' shoulders while they're trying to swim, albeit not too successfully."

"DR"—Mike's voice dropped—"Dad's not looking too good these days either. Something's been eating him since you went back to Europe. Mom knows what it is, but she won't say."

DR rubbed at the tension in his neck. Something burned his throat. He swallowed it down. "Ooh... I'm sorry to hear that. I'll have everyone over as soon as I get home and settled in. I'm sure Dad will be back to normal by then. He's a rock." *Nice to be able to talk about something more pleasant.* "I appreciate your help putting my house back in order. I'll make it up to you and Willie."

Okay, enough small talk. DR walked away from the porthole and leaned over his desk, staring in a mirror at himself, unsure. Time to get this over with.

"About Willie, DR..." Mike spoke slowly.

"What?" DR sat in a chair. "She's okay, right?" Knowing how Gail felt about her, he couldn't hold his grudge.

"I want to tell you something, but you can't tell anyone, okay?"

"Well, that's like asking me how's the pie before I get to taste it. But sure, why not?"

"Ha! When we were young, the pie thing was one of your favorite lines. I kinda miss that kid, you know the kid you were? You grew up and got all serious on us too fast. Anyway, about Willie. She's gone and got a crush on you... a bad one. She's always been a fireball, but now, she's a ball of emotions. Can you, please, in a nice sort of way, let her know it's not going to happen, without telling her I told you? She's even praying for you."

"You're kidding me, right?" DR jumped back to his feet. *Why is Mike saying this? She'd kill him if she knew.* He paced to the other side of his cabin, then back again. His mind replayed her reaction to him grabbing her arm. How could she ever have a crush on...? "I mean... wow! She is quite the looker. I could do a whole lot worse, ya know."

"Really, DR? You're going there?"

A strange sensation caused him to shiver. He stood at the porthole once again. Beyond it, things suddenly looked a lot different. "I can't lie to you. After our dispute in the café, she ran through my thoughts, if you know what I mean." He smiled thinking about her. "She's probably the top catch in all the Great Lakes."

"Anyway..." Mike drawled. "You don't want anything to do with Christians, and she's one of the best. So will you help me out here?"

"No worries."

"Why'd you call, anyway?"

"It can wait." Straightening his hair, DR rubbed an index finger over his front teeth and relaxed his thoughts. "I'll let you get on your way. But we'll talk before the next broadcast. Have a good one, Mike. Give Mom and Dad and the gang my love."

Sliding down in the seat again, he hoped—almost prayed—Bill wouldn't die before he could see him. He had to get something off his chest.

The news about Willie brought a smile. He pushed to his feet and walked over to his dresser. There, inside Gail's journal was the picture of Willie, and she looked... sweet.

Few women he'd seen, except his Gail, could compare to her, even in her modest dress. Her long black hair in a ponytail, her more-than-ample athletic figure, and her brown eyes had enticed him even while Gail was alive. Yes, he'd snuck that peek. Had he known she was interested in him would he have dropped his hook in a different lake? Was there a future with Debbie? She sure was acting strangely today.

It was seven o'clock when DR went out to his favorite spot, taking with him a mile-high turkey club sandwich and a glass of Laurie's fresh-squeezed lemonade. After enjoying his meal and the sounds and sights of the port, he drifted off to sleep. No dreams.

He almost missed the show. A photograph regrettably still on his lap.

Debbie went straight to her cabin, not coming out again the rest of the evening. But Miguel journeyed out on the aft deck. He bent to pick the picture up for a closer look, waking DR.

Miguel sat, studying the picture, then cocked a brow at his friend.

"Her name's Willie. She led my wife to Jesus. I found out the other day. I read one of Gail's journals. I wish I hadn't. Willie made me so mad, but she brought joy to Gail's life." Lifting himself up in the chaise, DR reached for the picture. "Miguel, I feel like I can tell you anything and there's no judgment, no condemnation. I've never had the pleasure of knowing anyone like you."

The sun began its journey to other parts of the world, sliding under the horizon. The lights from Kochi shone more brightly in its absence, and the excited voices of other visitors on the pier reached the *DI* and beyond. It was dinnertime for lots of them, and smells wafted across the harbor. DR breathed in deeply, enjoying the aroma of traditional Indian food before clearing his throat. "I need someone who will just listen... hearing me and not judging. I trusted Gail with my life but held things back from her. This trip has made me realize I have to let them out of their dark prison, so to speak, before they shackle me to their ugliness forever."

"Sure..." Miguel cast a glance toward the steps down to the galley, then rubbed his hands together. "Do you mind if I get us a drink first?"

"Absolutely, but none for me." DR lifted the lemonade from the nearby teak table. "It might not be icy cold now, but I'll just finish this." He sipped his drink, the lemon stinging his throat—or maybe it was the confession he'd planned to make. Miguel headed down to the galley. *He may need that drink, better to be prepared.*

Then, hearing someone behind him, DR half rose while twisting around. Nodding to the Nicholses, DR settled back into the chaise. "Hi, Penny, Greg. How's the pool?"

Penny pranced around to the left side of his chaise, then waved to the still color-streaked sky. "DR, you do realize we had one of those up front, right?" She jammed her hands on her slim hips, her hot-pink bikini shouting, "Look at me!"

"Where's Debbie?" Greg scanned the deck for more stowaways. "We thought she was out here with you. Don't tell me she's a party pooper?"

"Maybe she's in her cabin. A terrible waste of a good sunset." He wished she'd been with him, of course. "I haven't seen her since you all returned from the waterfalls and game reserve." It must've been something he did or said last evening.

"She isn't mad, is she?" Penny's face scrunched up. "She was all about you earlier, if you know what I mean." Making big eyes, twisting her hips, she smiled to get her message across.

"I don't know what she'd be mad about," he lied. "You two go on. Have some fun with the others. I'll be up in a while."

"Okay, Captain. Get your quiet time, then come out and play." Greg put his arm around his wife's bare waist to escort her back to the pool. "Ahh, that food smells good. Wanna get a snack?"

They disappear down toward the galley, and Miguel returned, eyeing Penny in her hot-pink bikini. He raised the two beers in his hands and winked. "One for now and one for later. Just in case, you know."

Deep in thought, DR didn't laugh. How would he begin? At the beginning, of course. After the hard discussion, his mind was more at ease. After over twenty years, someone else knew. He understood how girls felt when their innocence was taken, afraid to talk, accusing themselves at times. Lost innocence and lost respect for Dad.

Miguel exhaled. "I doubt that was an easy thing to say. It's not an easy thing to hear. Not to diminish what happened to you, but only to say I understand your pain... Well, you see, our families apparently have something very dark in common. Maybe that's why we connect so well. Maybe, somehow, your spirit sensed our common bond."

DR's brows rose and his jaw dropped. He leaned back.

"What you are talking about"—Miguel set aside the beer he'd opened, but never drank—"sometimes becomes a generational curse if it is passed down from one generation to the next. Your uncle's situation was different, maybe the start of a curse, but the Riccis... they were a depraved people two hundred years ago. By sharing it, you're putting it to rest. My seven-times-removed great-granddad was molested by his dad... and his dad by his dad... and so on down through the generations. It led Grandpa Ricci to move to Marsala. Where I'm happy to say, he—along with God's help—broke the curse."

"Come on, honey." A drunken man's voice drifted from the dock. "Just one kiss, just one."

Miguel smiled at the man's request, then sobered, refocusing. "He told his son to tell their story to his son and so on. So each generation would understand we were no better than anybody else. Grandpa Ricci received the baptism of the Holy Spirit and left the church. He went to that new reformation church, and it helped him break free." Miguel stopped, held up his hand, and whispered, "Listen."

"Get your drunken hands off me. Every time you have a night out, you come home like this. When's it going to stop? I'm tired of this, Carl."

DR rose from his seat and faced the voices. All he could see was a man struggling to stay on his feet. Surely, whoever Carl was talking to could defend themselves. DR sat back down.

"Is everything okay?"

"Yeah, just some drunk getting ready to pass out." He waved it off with his hand.

"Okay." Miguel shook his head. "Well, continuing on. As for the monsignor's side of the family"—he reached for his beer again and took a sip—"I don't pry, I pray. I can't imagine what you've been through, but you're on the right track. Forgiveness, it's the only key to unlock our self-imprisonment, where we confine, then define ourselves. I know your mom and dad will be happy to have their burden lifted."

Miguel paused, wiped condensation from his beer bottle, and flicked it to the boat decking. It left spots that lingered in the humid evening. "But what about Willie? Such a beautiful woman... I can't imagine how she stayed single and pure all these years."

DR shrugged, casting his head to the side. "If I'd known she liked me before the cruise, I would've told her to buzz off. We're not equally yoked, at least by her standards. I'd never ask anyone to put aside their ideals for my love. As for Debbie..." He closed his eyes, searching for words that were up to the task. "Something is pushing or pulling me to her. But I need to know it's not just physical. That wouldn't be fair to her."

Miguel rolled his eyes.

What was that about? "I hope I haven't run her away. She didn't come out the last two nights or talk to me this morning." DR sat up, slammed his feet to the decking, and reached for his now-warm lemonade. Huh, the sourness was gone, but maybe it wasn't just the drink. Everything seemed sweeter after his disclosure. "I'm ready for some sleep. How about you?"

Peering out over the aft rail where the loud drunk had just stumbled off into the darkness, Miguel finished his beer.

DR stood and clamped a hand on his friend's shoulder. "Thanks for being a good friend, one I need."

Miguel sprang to his feet, and they embraced.

The next morning, DR joined his passengers to enjoy a full assortment of Indian treats fresh from a market on the pier. He planned to set out at ten thirty, sailing to Kolkata. Lo began bringing on the food products for the three-day leg of the cruise. David started checking the vessel to ensure she was ready to get underway. The engine and props all passed inspection. Now, David only needed to sweep the vessel's hull for any aquatic life, barnacles, and the like.

"DR." David came up alongside him, his face ashen, his voice low. "I need you and Lo to join me on the bridge. Call Miguel too."

"What—" But DR silenced the question. David never looked like that. DR smiled at his companions and tapped Miguel on the shoulder when he arrived too, leading him to the helm.

The spacious helm easily accommodated all five of them as they stood waiting, watching David. "What's up?"

"Yeah, um." David raked a hand through his disheveled black hair. "Okay. So I finished the onboard inspection, then did my usual sweep of the hull. I almost missed it. It's hard to see in the daylight, you know."

"What?" DR furrowed his brow. "You're not making any sense. Has the *DI* sustained damage from the storm?"

"Impossible," Miguel inserted. "She's a strong vessel. She..." His voice fell away as David's expression twisted, and he shook his head no.

"DR." David faced him fully and stepped into attention as if before a commanding officer again. "When I looked over the edge, I saw this... this faint red light flash. Someone else might have ignored it, but my naval training told me something was wrong. What I'm saying is—someone attached an explosive device to the *DI*."

DR sucked in a breath, bowed his head, and gripped his forehead. Silence held.

Then he realized everyone was looking at him. But he wasn't military. "What now? How do we—get it off?"

"Without it going off," Miguel added as if that needed to be said.

And they both looked at David.

"You have explosives training from the navy—don't you?"

With a grimace, David gave a solemn nod.

"So... what happens now?"

David let out a deep breath and took over. "Miguel—*discreetly* practice evacuation of all the passengers. Don't alarm them or alert anyone who may be watching them. Just take them shopping nearby, not arousing suspicions. Okay?"

"Got it." Despite looking paler than usual, Miguel gave a jaunty salute and left.

David continued without missing a beat. "DR, Lo—survey the area around the vessel, check for anyone who may have planted it. Try to avoid being spotted so they won't trigger the explosives before the ordinance is taken off the hull."

"And that, my friend," DR interrupted. "I am most interested in—particularly removing it without triggering it."

"I can do it—I think." David straightened his frame, expanding his chest. "That and defusing the device. Fortunately, from what I could see without closer inspection, it appears to be a remote-only detonation device. I doubt whoever put it there was aware the *DI* had ex-navy men on board trained for this. If they left after planting the devices, not leaving a scout to monitor the *DI*, we should be good."

"Okay, guys." DR regained his calm and control. "We have our assignments. David, good luck. We'll meet back here when you've disarmed it."

Twenty minutes later, David returned with *two* devices. He flipped the second over in his hands. "They also tagged us with a GPS locator."

"And the other?" DR asked. "Can it still be detonated?"

"No. I've disabled it. But that's not what's worrying me."

"Right," Lo spoke for all of them. "We know now that we're being hunted by someone."

DR exhaled and pointed to the other device. "Place the GPS transmitter on the pier's sideboards. It won't be long until it's noticed, but we should be able to get out of port untagged. I'll catch up with Miguel and get him to bring the passengers back aboard just as discreetly as they disembarked."

Within ten minutes, DR and David had the *DI* out of the port and headed toward Kolkata.

"David, keep her at twenty-two knots. We need to get as far away as possible before they miss us."

Miguel and Lo returned to the helm, bringing a sense of urgency to the passengers watching and pointing from the forward pool area. Lo stood against the helm's bulkhead. "They know something is up, DR. When are we going to tell them?"

"I'll tell them in a minute. I want to explain to you all what I'm thinking. In a while, I'm going to call the US embassy and try to arrange for the navy to get involved." DR leaned against the gauge console. "But I don't want to call too soon, or it may alert whoever this is, giving them the opportunity to do whatever they will do."

A fuel tanker passed going west at a hundred yards starboard. They sounded their horn. David returned the favor.

"Once we get contacted by the navy, whether a message or a call, we'll know more about our choices. For now, we have to be on high alert. Lo, call our passengers to the aft deck."

"Are you sure this is the way you want to do this? It seems like a big risk." Miguel rubbed his brow. He looked tired.

"How can you know?" DR crossed his arms. "We don't know who marked us or why. I would rather have the element of surprise and fight than sit in a port ready to be attacked. We've got a good defense plan, let's trust it, and hope it's over and done with."

Lo summoned the passengers, and DR pushed off the console and saluted him for a job well done.

After the passengers all assembled, DR waved his arms and let out a shrill whistle to get their undivided attention. "I'm sorry to interrupt everyone's fun, but it seems someone—terrorists or pirates—are targeting us. I suspect the Iranians planned the attack—and yes, you heard correctly. We have removed an explosive device from our bow. David also found a GPS transmitter. He deactivated the bomb and planted the transmitter on the pier. We don't think they've noticed we've left the port yet."

"Have we called the embassy or the navy yet?" Greg asked out over the others.

DR held his hand up to stop further questions or comments. "Please hold your questions until the end. There's a lot to cover."

Taking a moment, he surveyed the concerned faces. "I don't think we're dealing with amateurs. Which is why we practiced battle stations and war games earlier. They're probably monitoring radio communications, so I've initiated radio silence until we reach Kolkata. We have an active situation, so be ready to respond to our signals. I'll answer your questions now."

"If you're not going to radio until Kolkata, how will you get help from the navy or the American embassy?" Penny looked around for seconds on her question.

"That's a great question. Terrorists can monitor open radio waves, so I'm going to use our satellite phone. They can't monitor that. I'll call the emergency hotline in Kochi and have them forward our situation to the naval command in the area." Sounded good so far. He gripped the back of a chaise, leaning over it. "Once the navy gets involved, things will accelerate. With any luck, we'll breeze right into Kolkata ready for a little adventure."

Tom was frowning. "What are the odds they're trailing us now?"

"Tom, before I came down, there wasn't any traffic within a half mile of us. But things can change."

Laurie crinkled her forehead, the mystery writer's brain at work. "Did they plant the devices on us in Kochi, Aden, or Jeddah? How can we know?"

"We don't know." DR tightened his grip on the chaise, grinding his fingers in. "Although we have been checking our hull every time we leave a port, David said he almost missed it in Kochi, so maybe that happened earlier. Where we picked up the devices is all a guess. After all, Jeddah did get attacked, and Iranian-backed terrorists were involved. We can only speculate on that one."

As he looked for more questions, his gaze caught Debbie's. She looked tired, sad, and downcast. Not her normal upbeat self, daisy dukes and red halter exchanged for knee-length khakis and a loose-fitting green tee shirt. His heart skipped a beat. Yes, he wanted her love.

"I wanted to inform you all before we departed but realized that could put everyone at risk if they were monitoring us and most of you departed. I'm sorry, but it was a calculated risk. If anyone feels the need to make other accommodations, please get with me, and we'll make a way, maybe find a port as we sail to Kolkata to make that happen."

Watching and listening to the passengers speak amongst themselves, DR shuddered.

They announced all together they were ready to do whatever was necessary to stay on course for Kolkata.

"Keep in mind that, the attackers, if there are any, will most likely be just like those we practiced for." He nodded at Miguel and Lo, catching their eyes. DR stood there, legs spread, trying to project cool confidence to comfort everyone. "There won't be any Iranian warships. Our plans, if we implement them, should afford us all the protection we need."

"Do we have any idea what this is about?" Ryan braced an arm on the side of his chair, having twisted to face DR while drinking his Stout.

DR rolled his eyes. They'd already covered that. "No, not yet. I don't think these are a couple of terrorist thugs, so they're probably monitoring the airwaves. We'll make contact in a little while, once we are far enough away to make a difference." He let out his breath, holding in his questions, still having as many as his passengers.

CHAPTER
TWENTY-THREE

Miguel caught up to Debbie after the meeting broke up. He placed a hand on her left biceps stopping her. "Are you all right? You don't look to be your normal self."

"I'm okay." She started to pull her arm away, then frowned when he held fast. "I'm just ready for this trip to be over."

Poor kid. She'd let the stress from this incident and her bad choices yesterday scuttle her joy. "Come on." Holding her arm, he guided her to the staircase down to the galley. "Let's sit and talk. I could use a little company."

"I made such a butt out of myself yesterday, Miguel. What a fiasco." She shuddered. "I don't want to talk. I just want to go away, maybe find a port to catch a flight back to Chicago."

"Okay." He winked, ready to charm her back to herself. "I'll talk, you listen. Let's go somewhere private before you make a big mistake. How about your cabin?"

"My cabin's a mess. Thanks, but I—"

"Shh." He pressed an index finger close to her lips. "You're going to want to hear this. You can't fix one wrong by making another."

"Just for a minute." Her shoulders sloped as she eased away from him. "I feel a headache coming on."

Minutes later, she closed her cabin door behind them and offered him the seat by the ornate dresser, moving a few things around to neaten up.

"I love shipboard cabins. Really nothing like them, is there?" He crossed to the seat, scooped up the daisy dukes and halter top crumpled there, and relaxed into the pleasant atmosphere of a small, but well-appointed cabin arranged for maximization of space and comfort.

She took the discarded apparel, tossed them onto her unmade bed, then sat on it, and pressed a hand to her forehead as if to comfort a headache or shelter herself from inner turmoil. "So... what do you want to talk about?"

"I have these two friends, and they both like each other a lot." Dipping his head, he peered up at her. "But they can't seem to get out of their own way. It seems that they have everything going for them except..."

She waved him off. "I hope your friends are better at this love thing than I am. Look at me yesterday! Dressing to make one man jealous—a man who wasn't even aware I existed—offending an entire culture, and teasing another poor soul who's been drooling over me since we set sail."

She hung her head and rubbed at her eyes. Then her voice dipped to a mere whisper, forcing him to lean closer. "Add to that the dreams and... Well, this hasn't been a happy getaway."

When her voice cracked, he came and sat beside her, holding and comforting her. "Shh." He rocked her, pressing his cheek against her soft hair and imagining what it would have been like to have a daughter. He'd have wanted her to be like Debbie. "You've let your imagination run away with you. That's all. That man you said doesn't know you exist knows you exist and wants you too."

She snuffled. "He hasn't even talked to me today or last night. That's a funny way of showing me. I'm too old for games."

He returned to the chair so he could see her. "He waited for you on deck last night where you've been sitting together. When you didn't show, he thought you were offended."

"He told you that?" She half rose from her perch.

"Not everything. But he told me other things he wants to tell you. I can't tell you them, but I can say something's happening on this trip. Like Joshua said, I sense the hand of God upon us."

Now Miguel was teary-eyed, the Holy Spirit stirred inside him. "Just give me a moment." He took out a handkerchief, wiped his face, and blew his nose. Composed, he started again. "When we returned yesterday, you took off. Maybe I overestimated you, but that's not the way I'd have handled it. Anyway, a young woman who works with his brother at the radio station has become infatuated with our DR. She knew his wife and led her to Christ, which you can imagine pissed DR off."

Debbie held both her hands out. "What's this all got to do with me? That's supposed to make me feel better? A young beauty queen is head over heels for the man I like?"

"All I'm saying is he wants to get to know you and no one else. DR is a different animal, but God rest his soul, his mom and dad got it right. He has more sincerity than most of my friends. Now that's the kind of man a wonderful woman like you should be with. Don't quit."

"Look what two days has driven me to do?" She grabbed the daisy dukes and shook them in the air. A packet of gum slipped from a pocket. "I wear those, sure, but not out with strangers, not against a cultural dress code. That's not like me. I'm not some love-starved nut job! Well, I wasn't before this cruise." She flung the short shorts into the corner of the room, just missing the trash. "I felt so sleazy yesterday, not by what I wore, but by my intentions. I shouldn't have to go to that length to get his attention."

"Why did you do it?" Miguel picked up her gum and handed it to her. "Did you think, if he saw you, it would cause him to change his value system? Or did you think it would push him into a corner, changing things? Honey, your conscience bothered you because of your recent acceptance of Jesus as your Lord. That's why you felt sleazy and why you're pushing things in ways you've never done before." No need to go too deep, but she must know faith came with the bonus of the Holy Spirit chastising and helping her grow. Even allowing her to be pushed by the enemy to grow.

"Things you once thought acceptable may change with time. In many ways, it's like taking the training wheels off. You exercise your faith and keep pedaling—that's Christianity. God has big plans for you and for DR, so take your time. You'll have your answer before the cruise is over."

Debbie pulled the covers over her bed, straightening it and likely her thoughts. When he picked her pillows up and placed them at the headboard, she patted them both with a serious thumping.

He raised an eye as she let out her frustration on the innocent pillows. "Where you are doesn't determine your worth, but what you've overcome. Think about it, then go out there with him. You know where he'll be. Okay, sweetheart?"

He got up, hugged her, then left. Outside her door, he stopped and leaned against the hallway, thanking God for the courage to speak. Not only was DR becoming like a son, but she was fast becoming like a daughter. *Ha! God, You move in so many mysterious ways.*

Debbie picked up her shorts and looked at them. How had she come to this point? "Maybe he's right? I've worn these shorts and this top so many times... never feeling sleazy. Was it the Holy Spirit thing?"

She showered and dressed in a longer pair of jean shorts and a yellow tee shirt, feeling radiant and confident—ready to face DR. She passed through the galley. Ryan was at the table eating grapes and listening to his music. Stopping beside him, she put her right hand on his shoulder and waited for him to remove an earbud.

"Ryan... I'm so sorry for the way I behaved yesterday. Please forgive me."

"What's to forgive?" He popped another grape in his mouth and winked. "I enjoyed spending the day with you. If you ever decide DR's not the one, remember me. Okay, good looking?"

Already her spirits lifted. Maybe she was the only one who knew of her disastrous plot. Well almost. As she climbed the steps, Penny came bouncing down.

Penny stopped with an equally jaunty wave and a quick pep talk. "Honey, girl, it's something we girls have all done—no biggie."

Confidence building, anticipation growing, and heart pounding—Debbie felt it all. She wanted this to go right—*needed* it. Especially since terrorists planted explosives on the *DI*. She might just get what she'd wished for, a shortened trip. As she climbed the last step to the helm, she could see DR's hair, then his lean muscular body. He was standing by the captain's chair beside David, pointing at the horizon. She stopped at the top and took a deep calming breath. No more acting like a fifth grader trying to read minds.

As if sensing someone watching, he turned. How'd he do that?

She climbed the rest of the way. Everything was calm, no terrorists in sight.

DR patted David's shoulder, put down the binoculars he'd used to scan the horizon, then nodded toward her. "Excuse me for a moment, David." He started to the door, then paused.

"On second thought, let's get Miguel up here. It's a lot easier with four eyes and ears. And I might be a bit." He winked at Debbie, then called Miguel.

Once Miguel reached the bridge, DR took her by the hand, surprising her since he'd never held her hand in plain sight. He led her down the steps to the lower aft deck and back to the chaises where they'd spent many evenings.

"I missed you," he whispered, turning her way and tucking wisps of windblown hair away from her cheeks. "I hope I didn't say anything that upset you."

"Everything's fine." A rushed laugh escaped for everything truly was fine. "I just, well, you caught me off guard. I'd become so used to guys who—you know. And you... you really want to care about me. I didn't process that rightly."

Sitting on the edge of their chaises, he took both her hands. "I want to see where this can go. I want to know your dreams, your desires, your fears, and I want to tell everyone on board."

Whoo-hoo! Miguel was right. Laughing, maybe even crying, she squeezed his hands, more than ready to explore the possibility of love with this incredible man. She leaned closer, giving him all the opening he needed.

Raucous, joyful whistling and clapping interrupted their kiss. Debbie jolted, her gaze meeting Miguel's as the older gentleman winked. Yep, he'd summoned everyone. There would be no more sneaking around.

"Thank you, everyone." DR bowed, pretending to take off a hat and dip it. "That was quite a surprise. I've broken my own rule—it wasn't my intention. As you all know, Debbie is quite the woman, and we enjoy each other's company."

"Is that what they call that... *company*?" Clapping and kicking up her heels, Penny teased. "Well then, that's *my* kind of company."

She danced an old cheer move until her husband snagged her by the waist and pulled her in for a showy kiss, even tipping her back like at the end of some romantic ballroom dance. "How's that, hon?"

Laughing, Penny fanned herself. "That'll do!"

"Anyway, I hope I haven't offended anyone." DR reached down and took Debbie's hand, now free to explore their love openly.

"We'll discuss your punishment later, cousin." Ryan harrumphed, arms folded across his chest and green eyes twinkling. "The proper Irish way... over a beer."

Debbie joined DR in laughter.

Miguel was at the helm at three thirty p.m. when an unusual message came over the ship's radio. He reached down and turned on the voice recorder. Then he bolted to the staircase. "DR, you're going to want to hear this. Now." As he returned to the captain's seat, he thought he heard the *DI* mentioned along with American.

DR hustled up to the bridge, taking two steps at a time. "What is it?"

Leaning on a seat near the monitor, Miguel pointed at the radio where the conversation wound down.

"How long did they talk?" DR asked.

Miguel reached for the voice recorder replay button.

"It's not how long they talked—it's what they said. I couldn't understand much. Here, you listen." He flipped on the replay and flopped back down in the captain's chair not making a noise.

DR sat, elbows on the wooden console, fingers on a gauge, then stopped fiddling. "They're talking about a payment, fifty thousand American. Sink the *Disill*... Better not screw this up... The general's not happy." His face white by the time the recording ended, DR peered over the slanted front windows, eyes searching the horizon.

"And what else did they say? I heard *Disillusioned Illusion*, didn't I?" Miguel held his breath, hoping above all else he was wrong.

"Yes, you did." DR tapped his foot while Miguel simply sat still.

"What are we going to do?" Miguel didn't move a muscle beyond his lips, every bit of him stiff. "We can turn around, maybe use the radio now. Now that we know what's happening."

"No." DR put his hand over the VHF radio. "We have surprise and preparation on our side. It sounds like our attackers aren't fully prepared to take on a team like ours."

"You got that all out of that little bit?" Antsy now, Miguel reached for a water bottle and squeezed its sides like a stress ball.

DR scowled at the bottle. "They weren't in the loop, so to speak. It sounded more like a commission or something. Not like a part of the original plan. They said Mekaastic—I think it's an Arab name."

Miguel put the empty water bottle in the trash, his release valve. "Why don't we just go back? Maybe we can make it."

"Nothing's changed." DR snapped around. "We knew something

was up. We stick to our plan. Call David and Lo. We need to set a plan for our turns on the helm for the next couple of days, a new rotation. Then we'll inform the passengers."

Then, using the satellite phone, not their radio, just in case, DR called the US consulate in India seeking help. When he finished, he stood. "Come on. Let's go break the news."

Nightfall found DR with Debbie on the lower aft deck, watching nature's greatest, not worrying for tomorrow. He sat there, carrying on as if no explosives had ever been found, no port attacked, no children taken, and no dreams drawing them into a conflict.

They sat closer, holding hands, more intimate. Nature's show far more brilliant tonight against the backdrop of romance, the sun's glow and descent eclipsed this evening by the promise of love.

After a wonderful evening, they said good night with a kiss, both hoping sleep—sweet peaceful sleep—would come. But it wouldn't—not tonight. Stevie was back, back on the boat where the pirates discovered their prison/hiding place. The pirates shouted, laughing about finding a gold mine. On the underground market, the children would bring forty-thousand dollars, the younger girls especially valuable, demand being high on the American market.

Stevie could see the others now, the sunshine lighting up the hold —two boys and eight girls. One girl, the oldest, didn't look so good. She was sleeping, unresponsive to her sisters' cries.

The stench overwhelmed their captors. They fanned the air, faces contorting. Their newfound cargo was valuable, though, so they would protect their prize. They dragged Stevie and his companions out for a dip in the ocean, nude, rinsing off vomit, urine, and feces and cleaning their clothes too.

Soon, they smelled much better. The men gawked at the girls, but the leader shut that down. Stevie's plight wasn't good, but after almost three weeks, he and the others were out of the dark, stinky hold. He hadn't eaten anything or drunk any water for three days. The pirates gave them water and food from the lost boat.

Habiba lay unresponsive, but alive, for now. One of the pirates nudged her with his boot. "No reason to keep this one. Just throw her overboard. My sister is a nurse. I've seen this before. She's not going to make it, anyway."

Her sisters ran and threw themselves over her, protecting their Habiba, their protector. It was their turn to protect her now.

At the girls' pleas, their leader put his hand up, rubbing at a long scar on the left side of his face partially hidden by his well-kept beard.

He radioed someone to inform them. They tied the lost boat to one of their own, bringing Stevie and the others onto their boat. When the time came to collect the "payment" for the Iranians, they'd drop anchor on the damaged craft, put the kids back on it, and return for it later.

Stevie heard all the plans. When the time came, they'd be left.

DR woke, dripping in sweat. Somehow, this time, it was different. He felt like he'd seen the trailer of a new thriller, not a random dream, but a real plot, and he was a leading character.

In the next room, Debbie was having a dream too. Her dream was different. She was floating, somehow like an angel hovering above the ocean. The cyclone gone, only the massive expanse of water and four boats visible.

One boat had a red cross on her top. She did a double take. Yes, from straight above, it was a cross.

"My child, be careful." The voice sounded like her mom's. But how could that be? Was she being haunted? No, the voice didn't sound ghostly.

A fragrance from years before surrounded her. "They're coming for you. Don't harm the boat with the cross. You'll need it."

The boats split up, two turned north while two continued east before shortly turning north also. They were attempting to trap someone.

As she woke, the voice said, "Tell Stevie."

Debbie sat up, clutching the tangled bedding, her heart thudding.

This was getting creepier.

Was this prophecy? Was that her mom's voice... but how? Was Mom dead? She didn't know, but she needed to tell DR.

A storm had passed a hundred miles to the south during the night, its clouds still hiding the sun. Around seven, she ambled into the galley to see what Miguel was cooking up. Putting her arm around her friend, she whispered. "Thank you for caring enough to help me. I almost made a big mistake."

She rose onto tiptoes and kissed his cheek, then fiddled with a gas burner knob. "I had another dream last night. These can't be coincidence. I heard my mom's voice. Does that sound nuts?"

"Maybe DR knows what to make of it." Miguel pointed toward the bridge with his head. "He had another dream too."

While he flipped pancakes, she went up to the bridge and caught DR in the middle of another call with the consulate, phone on speaker mode.

"The US military has been advised of your position and the explosives found on your vessel," the person responded. "The military will determine your need based on the information given. If there's nothing else I can do, have a good day."

She shivered. "He said it so matter of fact—like a recording, not a living, breathing person?"

"Yeah." DR switched the satellite phone off, placed the receiver back on the SatPaq, and kept his back to her. "I imagine it's not an easy job, responding to need." His grip lingered on the phone as he composed himself. They were on their own. At least, for now. The sanctions making many of the Iranian connections desperate. Since September, terrorists had attacked Saudi Arabia twice, the oil fields once, and now Jeddah's port. They were ramping up the attacks, planning them bigger and bolder.

The man on the other end sent word to a certain senator. "They're asking for help. I gave them the runaround."

"Good. The next time I hear about this better be on the news."

His supporter, Mr. Jennings, wasn't relenting. The FBI was running cover once again, along with his other friends.

"I've got to call my connection in Tehran. If they want the sanctions lifted, they'd better stop this president. He's dangerous to our plans."

Debbie wrapped her arms around his waist. He relaxed in her embrace. They stood still, not saying a word, simply enjoying the intimacy.

"Now, this is the way I like to hear good morning." He lifted one of her hands and kissed it, then turned, taking her in his arms, getting a good-morning kiss.

"I hear you had another dream." She drew back and cupped his face between her palms. "Is this getting crazier, or is it me?"

"It's intense."

"Last night, I heard my mom's voice."

"What did she say?"

"She warned me not to harm the boat with the red cross on it—we would need it." She related her dream. "The whole time, I was looking down and seeing things that wouldn't be visible from the sea."

Man, it was like a script out of Hollywood, but this wasn't Hollywood. Were they in the middle of someone's payback scheme? He took both her now-cold hands in his and squeezed them. He didn't want to raise her fears, but...

"Is that all you saw or heard? Was there anything else?"

She pulled away, sat on the captain's seat, and stretched as she "relived" the dream.

After she shared it all, she added, "Her voice... it told me to tell

Stevie they were coming for us. How am I supposed to do that? Who is Stevie?"

His pulse quickened, his old name causing him to stiffen. "I'm Stevie, at least in the dreams. I'm around ten—the boy I was back then." He raked a shaky hand through his hair, frightened but hiding it. Then he reached out, grasped her hand, and patted it to reassure her. "My dream is out of the same script."

Taking this seriously now, he shared his dream as his earlier doubts gave way to commonsense preparation. Something, call it fate, seemed to be drawing the *DI*. Could he hope they'd escape unharmed once again?

"The oldest sister taken from the home"—he almost held his breath—"wasn't her name Habiba?"

At Debbie's nod, he shuddered. Hopefully, the dreams predicting a violent attack were just that—dreams.

The waves rolled higher, making it harder to keep up their speed. As the *DI* rose and fell, they reduced her speed, and everyone came up from the galley. Having breakfast was becoming an adventure, and the violent waves queried an early look-see by a few passengers. The sun hid in the clouds amidst the high hopes it would make an appearance.

When DR called Lo to the bridge, their speed now six knots, Miguel came with him. He nodded to Debbie and DR before his friend faced their first mate.

"Lo," DR began, "you may not have heard about our dreams. Joshua and Miguel—and now Debbie and I—are considering that they might be more than bad dreams. So I'm asking you guys to work with me and begin setting a strategy in motion. Please tell everyone to get their equipment in their rooms and positions today—no, this morning!"

"Sounds wise, DR, dreams or no." Lo palmed the back of his neck.

"Time saved could make the difference between success or failure. Life or death."

After Debbie and DR headed down to the galley, Lo moved to the captain's chair, speaking with his back to Miguel. "I gotta say I'm impressed you and the rest of the passengers didn't book other passage home after that explosive debacle."

"And miss the adventure of a lifetime?" Quirking his lips, Miguel spread out his hands. "Though I will admit if my Martina were here, I'd be making arrangements for her. I heard Mitch begging Stephanie to consider it, but our girls aren't going anywhere. But don't tell DR that. He might take it personally."

Joshua came up the staircase and stopped on the last step. "Um, can I say something?"

"Of course, my friend." Miguel pushed away from the console where he'd parked himself.

Joshua rubbed his eyes. "I'm getting this nudge.... Miguel, the best thing you can do is call the monsignor. Tell him what's up. Get him, O'Reilly, and Walters praying."

"Done." Miguel snapped his fingers and winked. "Nothing like calling out the cavalry. Should have thought of that myself."

"Indeed."

CHAPTER
TWENTY-FOUR

Later the next morning at Marcie's Place, Willie and Mike began discussing the day. Mike mentioned DR's call. How he sensed things changing in his attitude toward God and, just maybe, her.

"When he called this morning, I thought he was going to ask me for prayer. I noticed a change I don't know how or why. Last night, the Holy Spirit woke me to pray for him and his passengers, and I—"

"Get out of town," Willie blurted out, reached over, and pushed him lightly. "Me too."

She then shared how she'd been led to pray. "What are the odds? What time was your prayer? Mine was around two this morning. Do you think...? Could it have been? Wow."

"I think so," he agreed. "Man, this isn't good. It confirms our concerns were legit. That's when I woke... two a.m. I heard about this once, but it was on television... so who knows?"

"Isn't that like saying I heard it on the radio? Hopefully, people believe what we're telling them." Yep, television and radio had the same obstacles, especially in this era of fake news. "You said he's changing his mind about me or something else. What do you mean? Do you mean about me or about Christianity?"

That night in their own homes, they each prayed for DR and those on the *DI* again.

The meal plan on the *DI* for the next day was sandwiches, peanut butter crackers, cheeses, and fruits so they could eat quickly. They were prepared and stored, ready for quick consumption. Weapons were checked and double-checked. The defensive elements on the *DI* were activated and run through again. Everyone was focused. Now they waited, and those who prayed... prayed.

After spending the morning with Debbie and then going over their schedule with the crew, DR went to his cabin and called his brother. It was seven thirty a.m. in Delton. Mike would have time before going back on air to finish the morning drive. Kerala nine and a half hours ahead.

"This is a surprise. What's up?"

"We may be in the middle of some trouble. We've been targeted. We're ready to protect ourselves, but tell Mom and Dad, well, you know, if things go sideways. Say hi to Willie for me." Taking off his brave captain's persona, he fixed his gaze on the view out his large porthole window. The rhythm of the *DI*'s ups and downs felt like an omen. "I'll be home in a month or so—hopefully."

He rubbed sweaty palms together. How do you—or, rather, why would you—ask someone to pray for you after denying to them the existence of God?

"We'll pray for you all. God's got this." Mike must've sensed his apprehension, if not the fear in his voice, a side DR never let his little brother see.

Mike's confidence buoyed him. DR almost said thank you, but something held him back. "Sounds good. I'll talk when I can."

"Um, bro? You won't want to hear this, but last night... the Spirit led me to pray for you and your friends on the *DI*. Willie said the same thing happened to her last night—something woke her up and said 'pray.' So yeah, we're praying."

DR didn't answer, just kept peering out the porthole as he ended the call. Afternoon on the Indian Ocean in late October was a beautiful scene. The sun had played hide-and-seek with the clouds most of the day, but now, it declared its full glory, readying itself for another journey around the globe. The waves were rising even more, sunlight reflecting its last light off the water.

Until now, the dangers had seemed make believe, surreal. But that had changed.

Further southeast, now the terrorists had firsthand knowledge of their payment's location. Excitement built, the thrill of killing now as much a part of their nature as breathing. If the weather and ocean cooperated, they'd reach the payment just before six tomorrow evening, allowing their two-pronged assault to merge with the target.

Battling the same waves as their target, they planned their course to take advantage of them. The leader followed in the rear vessel so he could better direct their actions. Telling his men that after this operation they'd be off to collect their money, including a hefty bonus for the children.

"You had better not miss this time. America can't afford another four years of this president, and neither can you. Do it right." Senator Brummengarten told the general.

Irritated by the bullying tone, the Iranian would deal with that later. But with the man's words, he could agree. This whole thing needed to show how "reckless and dangerous" the president's policies were, an opposition talking point, political rhetoric.

"You just make sure the news outlet's there," he replied.

"For your sake, I hope so." Brummengarten hung up.

DR's protective nature had him wishing Debbie would've been positioned with him and not Ryan, but Ryan would do everything possible to keep her safe.

David and Lo took the helm beginning at midnight. They'd do 2 two-man teams, DR and Miguel taking over in the morning. They monitored their radar, radio, and sea more diligently now. Having two at the helm lengthened their hours, but within a day or two, they'd return to normal protocols.

DR radioed the navy's emergency channel earlier seeking nearby unidentified traffic or terrorist activities. The response, a recorded message, asked for their longitude and latitude to access exact reports. DR gave them the coordinates of Chennai, India—thirteen degrees 4' 2.7804N and eighty degrees 14' 15.4212E—a location one hundred miles due west, not revealing his exact location. The news came back good, but 844 nautical miles separated them from Kolkata.

At this slower speed, they'd need almost four days. Perhaps he'd investigate other ports along the way. If the waves subsided, they could speed up, but they wouldn't make port if someone tried to intercept them. The weather had ensured that.

"Why can't we dock in a nearby port?" Miguel rubbed the cherry inlay, pushing firmly and smudging circles with his index finger. "Maybe they'll stop their pursuit? *If* we're even being targeted…"

"Puri would be our best chance until Kolkata, but there's no guarantee the water would be deep enough to allow for the *DI*'s draft. The harbor entrance is restricted due to low-tide depth, which is why the port of Puri isn't busy. Just between us… David spotted terrorists watching us at Kochi. Likely, they've invested too much to turn back now. If the storm hadn't popped up, we would've made a good port, maybe even the inlet at Kolkata. But we're better off now defending ourselves at sea. At least, here, we have the element of knowledge and surprise on our side."

Indeed, knowledge played a crucial role. David seeing someone in

Kochi surveilling them caused DR to elect to escape to Kolkata. Then the ocean became choppy. Now they'd stand their ground, hoping the US Navy would charge to their rescue first.

If attacked, he planned with his crew to increase their speed to twenty-two knots, regardless of the ocean's volatility, switching to a zigzag pattern to avoid boarding.

Everyone had agreed—pushing forward toward Kolkata was best along with their maximum-force policy. Despite the now-electric atmosphere, the women donned their bikinis, enjoying what could be their last fun in the sun. Good. His salesmanship had persuaded them to relax and enjoy the day. Tomorrow would worry for itself. And no one wondered what inspired that saying.

A voice awakened Debbie, her mom's voice. Shivering, she headed to the aft deck in search of fresh air and peace, but the darkness seemed eerie, mysterious, and even dangerous. The *DI* rose and fell, waves pounding her, adding even more suspense. The ocean's spray hung heavy. She hugged her arms around herself but couldn't stop shivering. Then she spun around and altered course to DR's cabin, one she'd never even seen.

She knocked on his cabin door, her heart pounding.

The door edged inward, exposing DR peeking through the gap, half awake... with only boxers on.

"Um." Her teeth started chattering. "I hope I didn't wake you. Can I come in?"

"Sure—let me get a shirt on."

When he turned, she followed him, reached out, and grabbed his right arm. She wrapped her arms around him and pressed into him, then looked away to hide her fear and whispered. "I had another message this morning, from my mom—at least, it sounded like her. This is starting to scare me. I want to be brave. But... I've lost one man I loved, and I don't want to lose you." Holding on ever so tight, she finally looked up into his understanding eyes.

He loosened her grip enough to see her better, then grasped her upper arms. "No one—you hear me, sweetheart?—no one is going to lose anybody on my watch."

She let her shoulders relax, then trailed her fingers along the wainscoting, admiring his cabin's finishes. Then she saw *the* picture, and her breath gave a strange catch.

"She is beautiful, your wife." She nodded to *it*. "Ryan does favor her."

DR exhaled, the sound heavy. "I guess. After all, they're cousins. But he has green eyes, not blue. Anyway, he's agreed to come to America to give me a hand. I may be having a problem with my helper working in my Delton lab. He'll work with Clyde to check things out. My friend, the chief who we're on our way to see, Chief Mnortarmillc, is concerned about how Clyde is handling the documentation of size and weight of the artifacts, along with their valuation."

His hands trailed up and down her arms as he soothed her. It was working.

He leaned in and pressed his words right by her ear. "That should give us the opportunity to get to know each other much better, if you'd like or want that."

"I'd love it." She brought her hands to his face, drew him further away from her, and tipped it to make eye contact. "I think about you all the time, especially at night when it's so quiet. I want to know you in every way. But I came down just now because of a message. The voice told me to shoot him. Can you believe that? Shoot him—that's all."

"Wow. I guess, if the moment comes, you'll know. But it sounds like good advice if we are attacked." He stepped back from her and rubbed his neck, exhaling. "The dreams do seem to have a divine element, somehow. Something won't allow us to escape this appointment. The warnings, the kidnapping, the explosives, and the storm... It all seems to be leading to a rendezvous with something."

She hugged him close, not saying anything. For DR to admit such a thing was a stretch, even with his upbringing in faith.

Then she slipped away from him. "You and Miguel begin your turn at the helm at seven, right?"

When he nodded, she tugged at his hand and led him from his cabin to the galley next door. While she made coffee, he claimed a seat at one of the dining tables as Miguel entered. "That smell will call a man from bed, my dear."

Miguel nodded at DR while pouring his coffee. DR was smiling, almost laughing. "Is something amusing?"

"I was thinking about my need for control, especially now. My tenth-grade teacher used to beat into the debate team that control was an illusion trusted in by men who think too highly of themselves. Alluding to the fact that, one day, we all face the reality that, without God, there is no such thing as control in a cosmos where the elements are forever changing. The only hard question remains, who do you trust?"

Miguel added sugar to his coffee and joined him. "She must've been one tough old girl."

"She was only like twenty-nine or so. An absolute doll. That's why the club was the school's most sought-after extracurricular activity. This was back when the miniskirt was the fashion. Do I need to say more?"

"Really?" Debbie passed over a mug and slid into the seat beside him. "So how many years did *you* debate?"

"No, not really. She was as old as the cosmos itself, but it did add something to the story. Don't you think?" Laughing, he ducked away from the towel Debbie threw at him, which made him and Miguel laugh even harder.

Trixie came over to get coffee for her table. "What are you boys up to now—mischief?"

"Mischief, me?" Miguel pointed at DR. "He's the one you have to watch out for."

"Oh, I bet you're right about that." She hugged DR around his waist, then winked at Debbie where she sat enjoying some fruit. "But he's still pretty handsome. No wonder Debbie can't take her eyes or hands off him. I can't say that I blame her either. But on a serious note, I'm glad to have you guys on board planning for our safety. Your teacher was right. There's no control, and who knows what today will bring? But at least we're trying to face it with a semblance of control."

CHAPTER
TWENTY-FIVE

The morning passed with nothing eventful to report, but after lunch, a message came from the US Naval command, Indian Ocean task force, along with specific details in respect to their appeal for information and backup. They reported four boats of equal size approaching their vicinity. Two came from the south and two from the east, and the satellite pictures came with a strong warning:

Given the conditions of the ocean, please be advised... Intelligence indicates these are suspected pirates, human traffickers, and known Iranian proxies. The US fleet task force is four hundred nautical miles from your location. Be advised— Currently in range time, nineteen hundred hours Indian Standard Time (IST). Task force radar is monitoring your situation ongoing. Take evasive action if possible.

Handing the message to Miguel, DR stood looking at the picture provided by the communication. One of the boats appeared to have a cross on it, a red cross. It would intercept on the bow, from the east, if this was an attack.

At 1320 IST, the *DI*'s radar began picking up two blips off the aft deck... forty-one nautical miles south of their position, and then two blips in the east at 1350 IST. Based on their current speed, the radar system calculated the contacts would both be within the *DI*'s defenses around five thirty-five p.m. DR had four hours and forty minutes.

Shore wasn't an option. The navy wouldn't be any help, at least not for an hour, maybe an hour and a half after contact. Still, there wasn't any confirmation this was an attack.

"I need to ask Debbie something." He rested his hand against the chart plotting wall. "Would you call her on the PA, please?"

Miguel frowned. "Do you really think this is a time for romance?"

"This isn't about romance. She mentioned something about a marking on one of the boats, a cross."

He held up the satellite photo. "See this here?" He pointed at one. It appeared to be a red cross on the roof of the helm. "Does it look like this boat's being towed?"

As they examined the photo, Debbie reached the bridge. "What's up?" She snagged the paper from Miguel, then fumbled to turn it over and reveal the picture.

"Oh, wow. Where did you get this?" Her face lost its color as her voice rose. "It's the boat from my dream!"

DR braced his right hand on his hip. "Are you sure it couldn't be something else?"

"Doesn't that look like a red cross to you?" Holding the paper close so he could see it, she stabbed a shaky finger at the roof. "Didn't I say a red cross, one that wouldn't be visible from the sea? Look where that cross is. This is *the* boat."

She shivered.

DR turned away, his neck becoming red. *Wow... I wondered, but now... oh man. Confirmation of an encounter with God? Miguel and Joshua insisted God gave me the dreams, but a prophetic dream, for me, unlike so many fakes running around speaking of doom and gloom that never comes. This was—now. How will I explain this?*

He started pacing from the radar screen to the wall plot chart behind the captain's seat and back to the radar. He touched the gauge console briefly, his steps echoing hollow on the golden teak flooring. "Here's what we're going to do. Miguel—just you, me, and Debbie, okay? No one else needs to know this. We'll proceed as if the dreams are for guidance. Debbie, what else did you say about the boat in your dream yesterday?"

"The voice said not to harm the boat with the cross. We'll need it for survival. Whatever that means." She held her hands to her face as if to hide any show of fear.

"Okay, well..." He frowned at her body language. He'd better go easy. "We'll hold our fire on the boat. Somehow, we'll have to mark it or know where it is. Let's get everyone together. Miguel, would you please call everyone to the aft deck for a short meeting at 1600 hours and reduce our speed to five knots so you can listen over the radio too?"

DR took her by the hand and led her down to the deck, ready to deploy every team to their positions. "Let's relax for a while to give Lo and David more time to rest before joining the others." He raised an eyebrow. "Our usual spot?"

And her smile melted the tension from her expression. "Sounds good."

At 1600 hours, DR held his hand up to calm the passengers and get everyone's attention while he waited for Lo and David to come up from their cabins since they'd worked the night shift.

"We received bad news from the navy, and now, our radar confirms we may be being tracked by terrorists. Contact will be in about an hour and forty minutes. We'll all make it through this. But remember—if this is real, if you get a clean shot at any of the perpetrators—take it. They will. We can and will defend ourselves successfully if we follow the plan. Any questions?"

Joshua slumped against the bulkhead. "Do we take the first shot or wait on them?"

"We take the first shot. We begin defending ourselves before they can get on board as discussed." DR tried to keep his voice even. Seriously? They'd gone over and over this. Did Joshua need it spelled out again? Did he expect DR's response to be any different?

Everyone nodded their agreement. If anyone boarded the *DI*, they'd first pay a heavy price.

"Okay, everybody. Be safe and don't take any unnecessary risks. Let's relax and clear our minds. Maybe get some dinner before going to our positions. Remember, put on your gear so we can communicate. I'll run a com check five minutes before we make contact with the intruders to ensure everyone's gear is working."

"David, Lo, why don't you go down and get yourselves something to eat. We'll meet on the bridge at 1645 hours. That will give us around forty-five minutes to gear up and line up our navigation. I don't want to be rushed."

"Yes, sir." Lo nodded, then faced David, eyes widening.

After they left in a rush, DR hugged Debbie, kissed her, then drew back to her contented sigh.

Heart thudding, he tucked a wisp of hair behind her ears, then framed her tanned face with his hands. "I'll be watching over you and Ryan from the bridge. It's going to be okay. I promise."

As she pulled away to go to the galley with their friends, she winked. "Everything's going to be fine. Ryan and I have it covered."

Watching her walk away, he let out a low whistle and whispered. "There's nothing like a confident woman."

Time passed quickly. Lo and David secured all the loose furniture and galley supplies. The passengers took care of their rooms. The *DI* would accelerate if attacked, even in rough seas.

"We'll do the fighting if need be." DR rested a hand on Lo's shoulder. "You take care of the ship. Lo, you know these waters. I know you got this."

"We've got this." Lo patted the console. "The *DI*'s a trustworthy mistress."

DR's voice came over their noise-canceling headphones.

"Showtime, everyone. Radar estimates contact in five minutes on the aft and six on the bow. Strap yourselves in with the harnesses installed at your stations. You'll need them as we push through the larger waves. Good luck, everybody. We'll see everyone on the other side. Four minutes until we turn on our LRAD."

From his overview, both via his vision and the strategic cameras placed about, DR surveyed his crew at work:

Tom was busy securing his ammunition and firearms for quick access. Miguel joined Joshua on the lower aft deck. Most of the action would likely take place there. Good, he strapped in, gear on, weapon ready. DR was about to move to another view when Miguel pushed his talk button and began. "Dear God, Father of our Lord Jesus Christ, by Your divine hand, we're here today. We ask for Your protection and deliverance from all our enemies that You may be glorified. In Jesus's name, we pray, amen."

Everyone said amen.

David joined them on the lower aft deck with his Barrett M82IA and three cans of Raufoss 50 ammo, each containing ten rounds. Navy Special Ops used the firearm to kill aircraft and radar units. DR smiled. David had brought this one, one he claimed he'd relieved the navy of, "just in case." The high-power ammunition could penetrate bricks and concrete to deliver the kill. But David admitted this would be his first live situation using the rifle.

With Tom on the bridge, DR now had two positions in full sniper mode with high-caliber weapons. The vessel was fully prepared to defend itself.

DR activated his microphone. "Don't fire on the Number 2 boat from the east. It looks like she's stopping. I repeat—do not fire on the second boat from the east. She has a red cross on her hardtop."

"Western contact—one thousand twelve yards aft." The programmable calculator started the countdown at one-half nautical mile. It continued, then announced: "Contact now in range. Contact now in range."

DR ground his teeth, loathing the warning, but ready to respond.

It repeated the process with the eastern contact, making him glad he ordered radar with this special feature.

The terrorists from the west were battling the *DI*'s wake and the waves, now four times their normal size. DR fired the water cannon at the east contact. Their evasive action practically capsized their boat, slamming down into a wave trough, almost sideways. The powerful jet of water nearly washed a terrorist off the boat.

Tom fired. His first shot struck the helmsman of the first boat from the west. The man dropped and gripped his left shoulder, but the *DI*'s zigzag and the extreme waves affected Tom's shot, saving the terrorist's life.

The smaller boat swerved hard to the right as another man dived over to take the helm.

Regaining control, they continued their push. David's first three rounds struck the first boat just above its waterline, punching fist-sized holes in the bow. As it began taking on water, his next shots attempted to deadline the boat.

Seeming shocked by their target's sudden aggressiveness, their apparent leader took the helm of the second boat and screamed something over the radio, maybe for everyone to stay down.

DR activated the sound cannon, the LRAD system. The terrorists, appearing in agony, covered their ears, which made it hard not only to navigate but also to fire at the *DI*. Still, they pushed on. But the *DI*'s evasive maneuvers caused their smaller boats to bounce off the yacht and punch down to the bottom of the deep troughs.

Until now, the sea protected the terrorists from the *DI*'s snipers, but now, shots fired struck their targets with a higher frequency. One of the pirates from the east stood to grab hold of the *DI*.

Tom's kill shot struck the man in his face. He toppled into the ocean.

The terrorist's weapon flipped in the air and slammed into the electric fencing protecting the *DI*. The weapon bridged the current between strands—shorting it out.

The second of the four men stayed low, grabbed the bow, and dangled over the sea as his boat sped off. The fencing down, he tried to board. The LRAD adding agony to his attack only seemed to drive his zeal.

The *DI* smacked violently into a twenty-foot wave and slammed down the trough, DR and Lo tumbled to the flooring. Even before DR regained his feet, he kept his focus on the cameras. David had bounced up into the air, and a bullet struck his left leg. He'd loosened his straps to gain a better vantage point and now scrambled to avoid falling into the sea. His initial shots three minutes earlier worked to sink his target. The first boat from the west now listed dangerously to starboard.

The terrorists kept coming, even with one boat beginning to sink, one dead, and one injured. Three men in the sinking boat sprang into the second.

The boat from the east tried circling to the *DI*'s rear, but a fifteen-foot wave struck its side, banged it against the *DI*'s portside, and smashed its bow. It careened hard. But two more terrorists grabbed the *DI*'s fencing before their boat toppled, rolled, and flipped upside down, engulfed by a wave. The very thing that hindered their getaway now defended the *DI*.

Lo and DR struggled back to their feet. Lo resumed zigzagging the *DI*. Their size advantage negated the smaller boats' speed.

Three terrorists now clung to the *DI*, one on the bow and two on the portside.

The *DI* swerved into the last boat as another enormous wave pushed them higher. The terrorist who hung on the front bow was bounced high into the air and tumbled down in the fencing. He screamed. Then he hung motionless, his blood mixing with the ocean's water, creating a sea of red on the deck.

The *DI*'s bow rose before slamming into the trough of another massive wave. The terrorist worked to untangle himself from the electric fencing.

Miguel fired four shots at the apparent leader as the guy fired a shoulder-launched grenade. One shot plowed through the terrorist right wrist, nearly severing his hand, but the grenade struck the bridge. The leader screamed and clutched his now-gushing wrist. He wouldn't last long if left bleeding unrestricted.

An eerie silence claimed the *DI*. The grenade struck her electronics, shutting down her propulsion, LRAD, and Bluetooth communications —but at least the cameras DR was counting on for his overview ran on a separate surveillance system. She stilled, lifeless in the water, bouncing on the waves. Only a backup engine remained—*if* they could bring it online.

Tom finally regained his footing on the bridge stairway and fired two more kill shots on the leader's boat. A scream came from the foredeck. The terrorist once stuck in the fencing now crawled back to where Ryan and Debbie lay strapped down!

DR grabbed another clip for his pistol, rushed toward the situation, and loaded the clip, leaving Lo on the bridge with Tom. Then, as he was in a blind spot, four shots rang out.

Heart pounding, he rounded the corner.

The terrorist fell, firing his pistol, then bounced as another wave broadsided the *DI*. He slid on the deck, his blood again coloring the deck dark red before another wave tossed him and he flopped into the ocean. Ryan was cowering in the corner. Debbie's gun steamed in the ocean's spray.

DR gasped, struggling for breath, holding on to a rail to keep from being flung off as well.

"Not on my shift." She flashed him a thumbs-up.

After grinning at her, he rushed back to the bridge, holding on tightly, to help Lo fight the fire the grenade started. Now with the LRAD gone, the terrorists could communicate again. The leader's hand appeared to be hanging on only by his shirt and several tendons. As he passed the launcher to a man beside him, Joshua rose and fired three shots. One hit the other man in his face, slammed him into the boat's deck, and slung the launcher with his momentum.

Three men remained on the boat, one already wounded from the first shot fired.

Two terrorists still clung vicariously to the *DI*, trying to climb on board without being noticed before being thrown into the sea. Each wave and trough tested their strength, but something—hate? adrenaline? fear?—drove them on.

At least DR's passengers below were staying put. They must be worried, no communications, no engine sounds, and heavy smoke in the air. But he'd warned them not to leave their stations until they had to swim. So far, everyone had heeded him.

Five terrorists still fought on, the *DI* sustaining one wound, David's leg wound, but the monitor showed him strapped in again and holding his position. Miguel fired at the leader and missed. A shot struck Miguel's right arm, and his firearm skittered across the deck. As DR came down from the helm, he caught a clear shot at the helmsman on the remaining boat and killed him. The boat raced by as flames consumed the *DI*'s bridge. DR retreated to the galley staircase for another extinguisher, the waves dissipating somewhat.

Now only having his Glock, David took another shot and struck the man Tom had shot in the shoulder, finishing the job. Only the leader remained alive on the last boat. Now, he shouted, "Die you, satanic pigs—die!"

Blood gushed from the almost severed hand while he steered, one-handed. He struck the *DI*'s bow as they descended together to the trough of another wave. His smaller boat rolled onto its starboard, rocked, and struggled with the pull to capsize. His good hand lost its grip, and the impact tossed him into the ocean.

The flames on the *DI* still burned hot. DR sent Tom to check on David and Miguel. Joshua began applying first aid to David while Lo went below to get help to fight the fire and treat the injured men, the lifeless vessel still being tossed about, making standing difficult, much less movement.

DR headed to the bow for Debbie, getting ready to hold and comfort her. But the first terrorist finally was able to clear the electrical barrier and stood to fire at her. Ryan, only feet from the would-be shooter, wasn't paying attention. The terrorist didn't see DR as he fired. DR jumped in front of Debbie, knocked her down, and fell on top of her.

Three shots rang out, two striking him. One bullet on his right inner thigh left a nasty exit hole. Another found the side gap in his body armor. The third glanced off his bulletproof vest.

He lay motionless, the terrorist now standing over her ready to kill, smiling, pointing his weapon at her head.

A shot thundered. Then another, jolting Debbie. She eased DR's weight off her and craned her neck. Ryan had risen to the occasion, shooting the terrorist twice in the chest.

She searched DR. "How bad is it?"

Through her teary eyes, she caught something move. Then her mother's voice said, "Shoot him." Just like in her dream, it repeated, "Shoot him."

Fire flashed from the nozzle of another intruder's gun, but his shot narrowly missed Ryan when a wave sent the *DI* listing and knocked the shooter off his feet. He righted himself.

She scrambled for her gun, fired once, and nicked his leg, the yacht rocking. She fired again and again, not giving the terrorist another chance. Two of the shots entered his upper body. Still, she continued to squeeze the trigger even as it clicked on empty chambers.

He toppled backward into the fencing system.

"Somebody... help us!" Heart pounding, she was screaming now. "Where is the navy? I can't lose you too!"

DR opened his eyes. Somehow, he managed to smile at her. "It'll be okay, honey—I promise." His last words drifted away as the *DI* twisted on the waves—lifeless.

She rocked back and forth holding him, crying. Ryan went for help and returned with Penny, Stephanie, and a first aid kit. While Penny created a tourniquet to keep his thigh from bleeding, Debbie removed his body armor and shirt, but her hands shook so, thoughts of Mark dying from his wounds rushing in. She had to step back and let Stephanie pack the wound to staunch the blood loss.

They were all alive, only three injured, but DR was bleeding. Dying? No, she wouldn't think that.

"Guys." Miguel, holding his arm, came up behind them. "Lo sent me to tell everyone—the *DI*'s in serious trouble. Without her engines, we might capsize in these waves."

As if in confirmation, a scraping sound came from the starboard side as the *DI* brushed against the hull of the boat the terrorists left anchored. The smaller boat somehow didn't capsize in the massive waves. The *DI* had traveled almost two nautical miles during the fight. What kind of freak thing brought them right where the other boat now anchored?

Leaning on the forward bow deck, Debbie saw the cross, then a desperate David, crawling, dragging his injured leg, toward the hull, aiming his weapon to fire at the smaller boat. She gawked as Joshua rushed over, grabbed the barrel at the last second, and pushed it up in the air as the shot rang out. He fell and clutched his ears.

"Look!" Stephanie shouted. "There's a red cross on top just like DR said. Don't shoot." She pushed away from DR, leaving Debbie to hold his wound, and ran to Joshua, now kneeling, holding his ears.

David lowered his gun and held out a hand to Joshua.

"Are you, okay? I didn't see the cross."

As Joshua nodded, Debbie stared at the random boat. Was it the boat in her dreams? Why would they need another broken-down boat?

CHAPTER
TWENTY-SIX

"I t can't end this way, not again." Her eyes were cried out. This wasn't the trip she needed or wanted, finding the start of love, only to lose it again. "When's the navy supposed to get here?"

Miguel now patched up, thanks to Penny, had come to the bow. Now, he hugged her. "They'll be here soon, but, sweetheart, we need to get off the *DI*. Lo and Joshua are going to tie us off to the other boat and then fight the electrical fire here on the *DI*. Tom, Craig, Mitch, and Greg will help get everyone off." He stepped back and placed his hand around her waist as Tom and Greg came to the bow. "They'll take DR down to the aft deck of the other boat for the time being, until the navy arrives."

Debbie, Miguel's arm still supporting her, followed the guys with DR to the lower aft deck where Lo and Joshua tied off to the smaller boat. The women took stock of their injuries as they wrapped and finished administering first aid to David. Joshua knelt and prayed for them and for DR. All while the out-of-control fire burned hot in the *DI*'s electronics. They needed to put it out and get off her soon.

"Oh, sweet God, help us," Miguel whispered aloud while the others grabbed water, food, and first aid kits or helped the injured.

Everyone followed Joshua and Lo to the smaller boat now bouncing behind the lower aft deck. Lo and Tom lowered DR and David onto the boat. Then Lo and Craig went back to fight the electrical fire on the *DI*.

"We know what the dreams were now." Joshua watched as he nursed his own arm. "They saved us. God heard someone's prayers and saved us."

Miguel smiled, concurring by nodding.

After safely boarding the smaller vessel and settling in with the girls by DR, Debbie stilled. She almost heard… noises? Almost like shouts for help, coming from belowdecks. Her heartbeat quickened. DR's dreams… the children locked? Could it be? "Guys!" She sprang to her feet, her words shooting out. "We have to search the boat."

Stephanie, still holding DR's wound, cocked her head. "Why?"

"Don't you hear it?" With her heart racing so fast now, she could scarcely breathe. "It's… it's…" Dare she say children's voices? Or was she being hopeful? She met Joshua's gaze, seeking confirmation.

"The children," Miguel whispered for her, and her pent-up breath whooshed free. So he heard it too—or did he just believe more than she did?

She sprinted ahead of him to the lower decks, the sound stronger now, a definite cry for help.

"Maybe it's a recording?" Penny asked. "There's no one here."

"They're here all right," Debbie insisted. "DR said the compartment's just hidden."

Penny cocked her head at her but didn't ask how DR could know that or when he could have said such a thing. She must remember their dreamwalker discussion.

"Over here," Miguel called. "The wooden boards here don't match up. It could be a secret hatch…."

He jerked backward as the hatch moved.

Stephanie and Laurie crowded in, but Debbie hung back, nerves swirling in her stomach. Could this be happening?

"It's children," Penny gasped. "Ten children are hidden inside."

Tears burned Debbie's eyes, and she slumped against the nearest wall as her knees gave out. Neither the bonus nor the payment was cashed, not today.

The children came up one by one, all blinking wide, fearful eyes against the light and strangers. But they thirstily drank all the water they were given, then tore into the ham and turkey sandwiches brought from the *DI*'s galley.

Debbie clapped her hands to her mouth in horror, witnessing DR's dream come true too.

When three little girls remained in the hold, refusing to budge, Stephanie went inside and dragged two of them out. "I think they're sisters," she called over her shoulder. "But they're so scared or something. C'mon, sweeties. You need to come out. You need to eat and get water. No one is going to hurt you now."

Still, they fussed and fought all the way.

"Come on, y'all." Penny beckoned like she was beginning a cheer rally. "You so want to be out of that ugly ole space."

The third girl lay lifeless. Her sisters struggled against Penny now, trying to go back to her, screaming in Arabic, but Debbie only understood the name, Habiba.

Laurie ran over to join in, consoling and comforting them while keeping them from going back into the hold. Tears streamed from her eyes as if she too sensed something terrible was playing out. They hugged the girls, holding them tight, but the girls continued struggling.

Finally, Tom went into the hold to help Stephanie. Being gentle, he scooped up Habiba and handed her motionless body from the secret hold to Greg who took her topside and laid her down beside DR. There, they both lay unconscious, breathing shallow, time critical.

He saw her coming, running across the meadow, her smile as bright as the sun. He stretched out his arms. "Habiba! I'm so happy to meet you." DR laughed. "You're just as beautiful as I dreamed."

They danced in the meadow, the light ever so warm and bright. The weight of loss and heartache gone, only complete joy and contentment remained, and laughter—lots of laughter and love.

"Hi, Daddy!" She giggled.

"Hi, sweetheart."

Life would be happy now. Just rejoicing and singing in the meadow, butterflies, daisies, hummingbirds, and rainbows abounding. "Abba has made everything better, just like He said He would!"

When it was time to leave, a voice asked, "Are you ready, Habiba? Ready to go home, with your new dad?"

"I'm ready for my new daddy," she responded, looking to the sky to see where the voice came from, but knowing a joy such as this she'd never imagined.

Showers had started falling, a cool treat. Debbie held DR. She was all cried out, exhausted, drained, defeated. A helicopter hovered in the distance. In a moment, it was two and then three. Then they fought to extinguish the flames on the *DI*. She wouldn't be sunk, not today.

Debbie steadied the basket taking DR up. As the SEAL team secured them, she gazed at the boat they'd seen in their dreams. Wait. She squinted. Something was scratched in the wooden hatch door—*Stevie was here.* As a sob burst from her throat, she snapped a picture with her phone. Still, no one would believe this. She climbed into the basket, leaving the boat named *Providence*, and whispered, "Thank You, Jesus."

With everyone loaded, the chopper banked and whirred to the hospital, over an hour away in nearby Sri Lanka. Lo and Joshua stayed with the *DI* and *Providence* until the US Navy got a vessel to tow them to port.

At nine a.m., a call interrupted Mike's break during the Delton rush-hour show. He pinned the phone between his shoulder and ear while cutting into the cinnamon roll Willie had brought him. "Hello. This is Mike. Who am I speaking with?"

"It's Miguel. We had trouble today near India. Terrorists attacked us, and well, DR's been hurt. They don't know if he's going to make it. But I believe God's going to heal him and little Habiba."

"Wait—hurt? Not going to make it?" His fork clattered to the floor, and Mike fumbled to grab the phone. "What happened to him?"

It couldn't end like this. DR wasn't ready.

In a monotone, Miguel related a battle with terrorists the way a newsman would, not like someone involved. Then his voice picked up the passion Mike had sensed in the Italian during their previous conversation. "I believe Habiba is the reason for the whole thing. Had we not been there—she'd be in heaven now. That's what the doctors said. Her little body was in rapid decline from hunger and cystic fibrosis."

Mike jumped to his feet, walked to a window, and stood there, staring into space.

"Please pray for us all. DR is in surgery and needs prayers. Perhaps you can enlist your listeners? WREAL's a Christian station, yes? And they know him, yes? He was shot twice. The one in the right thigh is three inches below his groin—a nasty wound, but we packed it right away. The second wound, though, may have damaged his liver. He lost a lot of blood. But God didn't bring DR to this moment for it to end like this."

There was something he should be asking. Something Miguel hadn't covered. But in shock, Mike fought to find it. "Where are you, Miguel? Are you and the others okay?"

"Sri Lanka. They have some of the best medicine in the world here. David was shot in the left leg. He'll be good as new in a couple of months. My wound's on my right arm, but wound is romanticizing it.

It's more like a grazing shot. Everyone else is banged up and bruised, but otherwise fine."

Returning to his desk, Mike gulped his coffee, needing the sugar rush before he could pass out.

"I'll text you our location, so you can come if you want. I'll call again when the surgery is over. Oh, I almost forgot. Let your mom and dad know before they see it on television or the internet. You see, your president just made a speech about the attack and the US military response. There's talk of a retaliatory strike. It's all over the news here. They have satellite video showing the *DI* on fire. One American news channel is showing the attack live."

"Live?" Mike burst in. "How is that even possible?"

"I don't know, but something smells. The news was airing even before the US Navy reached us. Your brother is being hailed a hero, but you and me, we know God's the real hero." Miguel chuckled. "I've got to get back to the others. I'll call later."

"Thanks, Miguel. Take care of yourself too." Mike managed to mumble. Before he could think, the phone rang again. Mom was crying, saying God woke her to pray for Steven and his friends.

"When I raised my hands to pray for Steven, the Lord—I think it was the Lord—showed me a vision or something. Steven and some little girl were walking down the road from the meadow up by his lake house. They were smiling, and she looked into his eyes and said, 'I love you, Daddy.' Then he said, 'I love you too, Habiba.' Mike, I don't know what to think!"

Oh man! Wow. He slammed down in his chair, peered at the ceiling, and sucked in a sharp breath before tears began spilling. "Mom, are you sitting down?" He let out a low whistle. "Oh, Mom... I've got some news. Bad news. DR's been shot. He needs prayer, Mom. I don't know where that vision came from, but he helped save a little girl named Habiba today."

Mom screamed.

The phone clattered on the floor.

Footsteps shuffled.

"Tammy Ray?" Dad's voice called out. "Tammy Ray, honey, wake up. Hello, Mike? Are you on the phone? What did you do? Your mom fainted."

As Dad checked on her, Mike repeated their conversation. Then Dad hung up to minister to her.

"Mike. Mike!" Willie ran into the studio. "It's DR. Look at this."

She turned on their news monitor. The headlines scrolled across the screen—*American yacht attacked by terrorists! Daring fight for life at sea!* The feed showed the attack in a loop. The show's hosts and ex-military officials talked as the video rolled. They lauded the *DI*'s captain and passengers who'd fought off ten terrorists in a coordinated three-pronged attack.

The feed showed everything—the attackers' boats sinking, DR diving in front of Debbie to save her life, terrorists being repelled, killed. Everything, including the rescue of the ten young children taken from Aden, Yemen. The news spread around the world. The Iranian regime was soon blamed for the attack.

Willie cried watching Debbie holding DR, crying over him. Mike rubbed a hand over his face as Ryan shot the terrorist and saved Debbie, then Debbie shot a terrorist too. All of it was on the screen, uncensored in eight action-packed minutes that forever would alter countless lives around the world.

Washington, DC, was hopping. Senator Brummengarten was mad—and in trouble, to say the least. And mad about that too. His supporter, Mr. Jennings, was on the line. Not happy... not at all.

"How do you think we'll ever get him out of office? You people in Congress keep making him look like a freaking hero. Tell the inept general his protection is off and good luck. Now it's time for damage control. So, you'd better come up with something fast, Senator."

The senator's phone went dead. He leaned against the hallway of the Capitol building—powerless.

Debbie couldn't sit still. She crossed her legs, then slammed both feet to the waiting room's linoleum floor, and thrust her hands under her thighs. The cracked vinyl seat pinched her palms. In her hand, she clenched DR's fancy nautical watch. Someone—she didn't even remember who—had given it to her before they wheeled him into surgery. Almost nine hours earlier.

"You sure you don't want to try to sleep?" Miguel handed her another coffee.

"Thanks." She curled her fingers around the warm mug. "Even without all the caffeine, no way could I sleep. Not until I know how they're doing."

But at least the dreams would be over now, wouldn't they?

"I just spoke with a nurse. She doesn't think it will be much longer." Miguel sank into the chair he'd claimed beside her.

Across the room, Trixie leaned on Craig, Penny cuddled against Greg, both Laurie and Tom slept in their own chairs, and Steph— Stephanie had Mitch's head in her lap. Funny, Debbie initially pegged her as his trophy wife, but their relationship was much deeper than that.

The waiting room door opened, and a surgeon stepped in. Everyone sat to attention, except the Hughes. "Mr. Ray is resting, and his internal injuries, while significant, aren't life threatening any longer."

Aren't life threatening. Aren't life threatening. Aren't life threatening. As the words ricocheted in her head, Debbie sucked in a gulp of air, then another. No, not just air, she was sobbing. Miguel wrapped his arm around her as the surgeon continued.

"Going in, we feared his liver may have sustained catastrophic injury. That was not the case. We stopped the bleeding, and with lots of rest, he should have a full recovery. We'll go into the details later. He's sleeping but should be awake in the morning. We'll let you know when you can see him."

"Shh... sweetheart," Miguel whispered against her hair, his arm warm around her shoulders. "Shh... our prayers are answered."

Moments after the surgeon left, another doctor came in, and Debbie's heartbeat jittered as she went stiff in Miguel's arms. Surely, this woman wasn't about to take it all back, to say there'd been some mistake, DR wasn't going to be all right. *God, please no.*

"The little girl is in recovery, and after receiving several IVs, she's come out of her coma. Habiba is one tough kid, a real fighter."

"Fighter?" Miguel laughed, his joyous voice ringing out all over the room. "Yes! There are many fighters among us. God made sure of it."

"Where are the other children?" Trixie asked.

"The US embassy has them." The doctor smiled, her eyes aglow behind her mask. "They're awaiting court directions. Then they'll go back to the home from where they were taken. Habiba will be with us another day or so."

"What about her sisters?" Laurie sat up, apparently awake now. "They're so little and scared of losing their big sister. I can't imagine how scared they must be. They should be here too."

Remembering their frightened faces and having experienced some of their ordeal through her dreams, Debbie covered her face with her hands, overcome by emotion once again.

"They're at the embassy. I'm sorry." With an apologetic shrug, the doctor turned and left them.

"This is all too hard," Laurie told Tom.

"I know what you're all thinking." Miguel spread out his hands. "Most of you are wondering, if there is a God, why did all this have to happen. But God has a plan. He's not through yet."

DR jolted from sleep, sweating again, sore and hurting, but alive. Light streamed through an unfamiliar window. Groggy, he fought the fog to remember. No! This time, it hadn't all been a dream. Terrorists were still on the *DI*. They were coming toward Debbie! He had to—no!

"Shh." She soothed beside him. "It's over. You're all right."

Now why was she saying that? She'd been the one he'd been racing to save....

Oh, now it was coming back, the pain in his side confirmation.

She nodded. "You were shot." Her voice cracked. "For me."

Ah, so she was okay. It was all good now. He sank back against the pillows, and she hugged and held him tight. "I've been here all night. Everyone else will come later this morning, wanting to see and thank their friend. Yes, now, we're all going to be okay."

He drifted asleep again, content in her arms. Later, he'd ask how everyone was. But she'd said everyone, hadn't she? So everyone was all right.

Hours later, he looked at them smiling. But one important friend was missing. He pushed up on his elbow—or rather tried to before Debbie stepped in.

"Where's Miguel?" he asked.

Their heads shook and faces scrunched. "We're not sure," Laurie spoke up. "But he's fine, DR."

Penny rolled her eyes. "Probably on the hunt for sangria."

DR smiled and sank back against the pillows, but there was something, something he wanted to tell Miguel. "While I was unconscious, I dreamt about that girl taken from the home again, the one named Habiba. She ran to me. Then we ran, danced, and laughed together in an exquisite grassy meadow near my home on Wall Lake. Then she called me Daddy. Can you believe that? She had the most beautiful face and voice I could ever imagine. Were our dreams for real or just dreams, Debbie?"

"Real, sweetheart. Real!"

He closed his eyes, having some thinking to do. How could he and Debbie have dreams... dreams that saved his passengers on the *Disillusioned Illusion* and the children? Was Miguel right? Was it the followers with whom he was angry? Stevie had never read the Bible. He didn't understand that with a great life came great challenges. Attacks aside, by all rights, his had been a great life—look what he'd accomplished.

He fell into a deep sleep, the loss of blood, the surgery, and the excitement overtaxing his body. Now a peaceful rest could come, making up for all the lost sleep.

Debbie sat at his side where she had stayed all night and would stay as long as they allowed. Around her, the passengers talked about what he said, speculating if it would come true too. It had been a wild ride, so why not? Then a nurse called behind them, they parted, and the doctors rolled *her* into his room.

Habiba looked at DR and spoke in Arabic. "He looks just like my daddy in the dream." She gripped her wheelchair arms, half rising in her seat as Stephanie translated her words into English. "Where's Amal and Derifa?"

"Right here, Habiba." Miguel called out from the hallway. "Right here, sweetheart."

Her sisters shrieked, ran to her, AND wrapped their arms around her.

She edged them back, then pointed to DR, her Arabic lilting. "This is going to be our new daddy. Abba said so."

The light rain stopped when her sisters reached her, holding her ever so tight. A rainbow splashed across the sky, and butterflies landed on the outer windowsill, avoiding the fast-flying hummingbirds.

Habiba was released the next day and returned to Aden with the other children.

She cried, "Abba said we were going home with the man in the hospital. Abba promised he would be my new daddy. We ran together and danced in the meadow. A pretty lady led my sisters by their hands. I know. I saw. *Abba* promised."

US authorities in Sri Lanka gathered all the information about the boat the children were held captive on, *Providence*, tracking its owner to a town on Lake Michigan near Chicago. Senator Brummengarten had notified Chicago authorities only two days earlier that his boat had been stolen.

$$\sim$$

That afternoon in Washington, DC, during a presidential news conference concerning the attacks on an American vessel, among many things, the president said, "*If you attack...*"

The *Disillusioned Illusion* had survived. Thanks to its defenses, brave passengers, and crew. Newspaper headlines simply read, "American Vessel Fights off Terrorist Attack, Rescues Children."

From his US capitol office, the senator with Representative Max Rice scowled at the unbelievable newspapers. "All the planning and time that went into the 'big show' to shake up the presidential election was for nothing!" Brummengarten shouted over the phone, then slapped the desk, causing Max to flinch. "My friends will not be happy. If you want the sanctions lifted, you know what you have to do!"

The next time, the caller vowed he wouldn't miss. "No one embarrasses me."

"By the way, General, my supporter said to tell you the protection is off, whatever that means."

$$\sim$$

Debbie remained in Sri Lanka with DR until he was given the okay to fly to Detroit by charter, traveling by medical transport to Wall Lake and his waiting home. Willie hadn't given up her hopes for love either. After all, God had heard her prayers... for DR.

Debbie would take care of DR in his home, and they were well on their way to another great love story. But how could Willie give up?

With their love affair on track, would DR remain "Michigan Strong?"

The *DI* was towed back to Marsala for repairs, with Lo and David given charge, and back to Luigi Cancio's brother, Raymond. Miguel said that was a mistake. The *Disillusioned Illusion*'s shakedown cruise now complete, everyone exchanged hugs and kisses and returned home thankful while promising to meet in Alabama at the Nicholses' home in the spring.

And Jennings? He was already planning ahead. "No one—not even the great Dr. Ray—makes a member of Circle look bad," he told himself. "No one."

To be continued in Obsessed Intentions—No Forgetting Providence

Find Lee's other books at:
https://www.amazon.com/author/leewimmer

DISCUSSION GUIDE

1. DR and Mekie grew up in religious families where faith in God was of the highest value. How did they both end up running from religion? Do you see any parallels in their circumstances in society today?
2. Why does DR go away to college in Spain? Is this a part of the "all things working for good"?
3. Throughout the story, the other characters think and say that DR hates God, but he never says that. He does say that he doesn't like Christianity and wants no part of a god that would let bad things happen to children. Is there a difference?
4. Did Willie do the right thing in telling DR about Gail and her journals? If you were in his place, would you want to know?
5. Willie was deceived by Satan or tricked by her friend, Kelsey Briggs, into believing Ashton had cheated on her. Could she become so mad that she couldn't ask Ashton?
6. DR packed up his home on Wall Lake and put a For Sale sign on it when he left. Can you understand why he wanted to leave? Was it all about memories, or could something else have contributed to his departure? In his place, what would you do?

7. When DR was young, his uncle sexually assaulted him. If you were his mother or father, would you have notified the police?

8. DR often sees his difficulties while missing the fact that he is living a blessed life. Can you see a path forming as God uses him while blessing him too?

9. The story title is *No Romancing the Passengers*, can you see why DR would have made that a rule? Was his shortsightedness a part of his grieving process?

10. Often, some think that when you're born again you automatically start living differently. In the story, DR and Debbie have two different opinions on "opening the cookie jar." Shouldn't she have lost her worldview directly after her conversion? Is that possible without the knowledge of God's Word or the Holy Spirit?

11. Throughout the story, DR is torn between his upbringing, Michigan strong, and the choices before him. (More about Michigan strong in the next book.) What do you think Michigan strong is?

12. Ryan, DR's second cousin by marriage, is a part-time church administrator. How do you think he came up with the money for the cruise?

13. Two generations ago, most Christians wouldn't think of having a drink, especially in public. Here, sangria is flowing, even with the believers. Is that something you feel comfortable with?

14. Did DR make the right decision in leaving the port of Kochi after removing the devices on the *DI*? Especially after spotting the terrorists watching them?

15. Why would Jennings send all the way to Yemen to traffic the children?

16. Did you sense a spirit rising up in Debbie when she was talking to Joshua about the differences he felt in different places because he was Jewish? Was she right?

17. Can you feel the plot forming as the story unfolds? Is God's hand on DR and using his heartaches to propel his successes?

VISIT LEE

Visit Lee:
https://www.leewimmer.net

You'll find the free bonus chapter, Disgraced,
and inspiring printable bookmark PDF files free to download, plus free
short stories, novel news, and Lee's blog.

Find Lee's published books at:
https://www.amazon.com/author/leewimmer